Praise for Lexi Blake and Masters and Mercenaries...

"I can always trust Lexi Blake's Dominants to leave me breathless...and in love. If you want sensual, exciting BDSM wrapped in an awesome love story, then look for a Lexi Blake book."

~Cherise Sinclair USA Today Bestselling author

"Lexi Blake's MASTERS AND MERCENARIES series is beautifully written and deliciously hot. She's got a real way with both action and sex. I also love the way Blake writes her gorgeous Dom heroes--they make me want to do bad, bad things. Her heroines are intelligent and gutsy ladies whose taste for submission definitely does not make them dish rags. Can't wait for the next book!"

~Angela Knight, New York Times Bestselling author

"A Dom is Forever is action packed, both in the bedroom and out. Expect agents, spies, guns, killing and lots of kink as Liam goes after the mysterious Mr. Black and finds his past and his future… The action and espionage keep this story moving along quickly while the sex and kink provides a totally different type of interest. Everything is very well balanced and flows together wonderfully."

~A Night Owl "Top Pick", Terri, Night Owl Erotica

"A Dom Is Forever is everything that is good in erotic romance. The story was fast-paced and suspenseful, the characters were flawed but made me root for them every step of the way, and the hotness factor was off the charts mostly due to a bad boy Dom with a penchant for dirty talk."

~Rho, The Romance Reviews

"A good read that kept me on my toes, guessing until the big reveal, and thinking survival skills should be a must for all men."

~Chris, Night Owl Reviews

"I can't get enough of the Masters and Mercenaries Series! Love and Let Die is Lexi Blake at her best! She writes erotic romantic suspense like no other, and I am always extremely excited when she has something new for us! Intense, heart pounding, and erotically fulfilling, I could not put this book down."

~ Shayna Renee, Shayna Renee's Spicy Reads

"Certain authors and series are on my auto-buy list. Lexi Blake and her Masters & Mercenaries series is at the top of that list... this book offered everything I love about a Masters & Mercenaries book – alpha men, hot sex and sweet loving… As long as Ms. Blake continues to offer such high quality books, I'll be right there, ready to read."

~ Robin, Sizzling Hot Books

"I have absolutely fallen in love with this series. Spies, espionage, and intrigue all packaged up in a hot dominant male package. All the men at McKay-Taggart are smoking hot and the women are amazingly strong sexy submissives."

~Kelley, Smut Book Junkie Book Reviews

Lost in You

Other Books By Lexi Blake

ROMANTIC SUSPENSE

Masters and Mercenaries
The Dom Who Loved Me
The Men With The Golden Cuffs
A Dom is Forever
On Her Master's Secret Service
Sanctum: A Masters and Mercenaries Novella
Love and Let Die
Unconditional: A Masters and Mercenaries Novella
Dungeon Royale
Dungeon Games: A Masters and Mercenaries Novella
A View to a Thrill
Cherished: A Masters and Mercenaries Novella
You Only Love Twice
Luscious: Masters and Mercenaries~Topped
Adored: A Masters and Mercenaries Novella
Master No
Just One Taste: Masters and Mercenaries~Topped 2
From Sanctum with Love
Devoted: A Masters and Mercenaries Novella
Dominance Never Dies
Submission is Not Enough
Master Bits and Mercenary Bites~The Secret Recipes of Topped
Perfectly Paired: Masters and Mercenaries~Topped 3
For His Eyes Only
Arranged: A Masters and Mercenaries Novella
Love Another Day
At Your Service: Masters and Mercenaries~Topped 4
Master Bits and Mercenary Bites~Girls Night
Nobody Does It Better
Close Cover
Protected: A Masters and Mercenaries Novella
Enchanted: A Masters and Mercenaries Novella
Charmed: A Masters and Mercenaries Novella
Treasured: A Masters and Mercenaries Novella, Coming June 29, 2021

Masters and Mercenaries: The Forgotten
Lost Hearts (Memento Mori)
Lost and Found
Lost in You
Long Lost
No Love Lost

Masters and Mercenaries: Reloaded
Submission Impossible
The Dom Identity, Coming September 14, 2021

Butterfly Bayou
Butterfly Bayou
Bayou Baby
Bayou Dreaming
Bayou Beauty, Coming July 27, 2021

Lawless
Ruthless
Satisfaction
Revenge

Courting Justice
Order of Protection
Evidence of Desire

Masters Of Ménage (by Shayla Black and Lexi Blake)
Their Virgin Captive
Their Virgin's Secret
Their Virgin Concubine
Their Virgin Princess
Their Virgin Hostage
Their Virgin Secretary
Their Virgin Mistress

The Perfect Gentlemen (by Shayla Black and Lexi Blake)
Scandal Never Sleeps
Seduction in Session
Big Easy Temptation

Smoke and Sin
At the Pleasure of the President

URBAN FANTASY

Thieves
Steal the Light
Steal the Day
Steal the Moon
Steal the Sun
Steal the Night
Ripper
Addict
Sleeper
Outcast
Stealing Summer

LEXI BLAKE WRITING AS SOPHIE OAK

Texas Sirens
Small Town Siren
Siren in the City
Siren Enslaved
Siren Beloved
Siren in Waiting
Siren in Bloom
Siren Unleashed
Siren Reborn

Nights in Bliss, Colorado
Three to Ride
Two to Love
One to Keep
Lost in Bliss
Found in Bliss
Pure Bliss
Chasing Bliss
Once Upon a Time in Bliss
Back in Bliss
Sirens in Bliss
Happily Ever After in Bliss

Far From Bliss, Coming 2021

A Faery Story
Bound
Beast
Beauty

Standalone
Away From Me
Snowed In

Lost in You

Masters and Mercenaries: The Forgotten, Book 3

Lexi Blake

Lost in You
Masters and Mercenaries: The Forgotten, Book 3
Lexi Blake

Published by DLZ Entertainment LLC

Edited by Chloe Vale
ISBN: 978-1-942297-12-3

Sign up for Lexi Blake's newsletter
and be entered to win a $25 gift certificate
to the bookseller of your choice.

Join us for news, fun, and exclusive content
including free Thieves short stories.

There's a new contest every month!

Go to www.LexiBlake.net to subscribe.

Acknowledgments

The last year has been one of change and I want to thank everyone who helped me get through it. If you even spoke to me in the last year, wrote or emailed me, waved at me on social media, thank you for being part of this transition. I'm in a different place than I was at this time last year and continue to grow and change—hopefully for the better. Thanks to my whole team who helped get this book ready. Thanks to Kim Guidroz, Maria Monroy, Margarita Coale, my son, and my husband who round out the team who has to work with me on a daily basis. Thanks to Jillian Stein who heroically tries to teach me how to work social media and Liz Berry who always lets me bounce ideas off her. Thanks to my beta team who worked their butts off to make sure I got this right – Kori Smith, Sara Buell, Stormy Pate, and Jennifer Zeffer. Thanks to Jennifer Watson and Social Butterfly for all the PR help and to all the book bloggers who work tirelessly to lift our genre up. A special thank you to my amazing audiobook narrator, the superlative Ryan West. He's been the voice of McKay-Taggart since the beginning and I now hear his voice when I write. And thanks to the readers. The ride is at the top of the roller coaster. It's time to see what's on the other side…

This book is dedicated to Lila Dubois without whom it wouldn't have gotten done on time. Thank you for your friendship, your counsel, your never-ending dirty mind. I was down and you lifted me up. I couldn't find words and you showed me the way. I love you, my friend.

Prologue

Paris, France
One Year before

Ariel Adisa looked down over the Place Vendôme and sighed. This job was taking longer than she'd thought and she absolutely had to make it back to London by tomorrow. She'd told her boss that she would be back in two days, and she wasn't about to push his patience. It had been pushed enough lately. And there was the fact that she was supposed to meet with Robert to discuss the progress of a few of his teammates.

Robert. Even his name sent a thrill through her, and that was dangerous as hell because he was a patient. She was supposed to think about how she could help him, not how good it would feel to have his big, strong hands on her body.

It wasn't professional but she couldn't get him out of her head.

"Okay, who are you thinking about? You've got your 'should I sleep with him or shouldn't I' face on."

She glanced to her left, back toward the bed where the reason she'd taken the train from her home in London to Paris currently lay on her side, her head propped up in her hand. Kimberly Solomon was dressed in jeans and a T-shirt she managed to make look chic with black Louboutin flats and a simple Chanel necklace she'd probably bought at the store across the circle from the hotel. If anyone looked at her, they would see another pretty tourist enjoying the glorious Paris day in one of the most expensive parts of the city.

They wouldn't see the CIA operative at work, and that was one of the reasons Kim was good at her job. She didn't look like a lady who regularly got blood on her hands.

"I have that face? I was completely unaware," Ariel replied. She had met the woman most people called Solo many years ago, in a life far, far away. It was good to see her again, but Kim's reappearance and the favor she'd asked her to perform were reminders of why she'd gotten out of the spy game in the first place.

Not that she'd gotten far. When she'd realized she couldn't go out in the field again, she'd found herself on Damon Knight's doorstep. He was the former MI6 legend who now ran a security and investigative firm called McKay-Taggart and Knight. She was finally using her ridiculously expensive education for what it had been meant for—to help people. Oh, she was sure many of her fellow operatives would say taking down terrorists had certainly helped, but there was so much gray in that world. Gray that often bled to black and blood red.

Kim sat up, shifting her body with the ease of an athlete. "You definitely have that face. Remember when you weren't sure if you should sleep with that incredibly hot guy in Shanghai? The one at the club we spent time in."

She winced. Kim had often been her Agency contact when Britain and the States decided to work together. She rather thought the higher-ups enjoyed putting two younger women together and seeing what they could do—and who would underestimate them. "I was smart to not sleep with him since he turned out to be working for the North Koreans and nearly gutted me with a sword. Who uses swords these days? That was utterly ridiculous."

Kim simply smiled. "Yeah, I saved you with a frying pan. Good times. Are you sure you're out? Like totally out?"

Well she would be if Kim didn't stop pulling her back in. "I'm absolutely out, and this has to be the last favor I do."

The smile on Kim's face turned upside down and she seemed a bit lost. "It's all different now. I hate change. The chick who took your place at MI6 is boring. 'No, Solo, we can't get mani-pedis while we're stalking a traitor. No, Solo, you can't assassinate that Ukranian mobster just because he's offensive and has BO.' She doesn't even do GNOs. She's all about the job. Boring. She doesn't even gossip. I have no idea what happened between Velma the analyst and Dick Face John."

Kim always made her laugh. Often when they worked together they spent long hours watching and reporting on their targets. She'd wiled away the hours by sharing some good gossip. "Velma and John married two weeks ago, and I'm fairly certain he's already cheating on her. But I can't be sure. I'm getting everything secondhand since I left."

She looked back to the plaza. It was quieter during the week than it would be this weekend, but it was never empty. The Vendôme Column rose from the center of the thoroughfare, the oxidized bronze making a brilliant contrast to the bright blue of the sky. It was a gorgeous Paris day, and she wondered how it would feel to walk around the parks with Robert's hand in hers. They could stroll through the Tuileries Garden and enjoy the day. Maybe if they were away from London, they could be normal. Maybe they could pretend he hadn't had his memory ripped away by a mad woman and she could pretend she'd never…

A Mercedes circled into the lane in front of the hotel. Not the one she was looking for. She forced a deep, calming breath.

"I miss getting to spend time with you," Kim said wistfully. "Like I said, it's all changing just as I'd started to find a rhythm again."

Ariel knew what she was talking about. She'd met Kim right before she'd gotten a divorce from her fellow CIA agent husband. The divorce hadn't been Kim's idea.

Should she say something about the man who'd shown up at The Garden? The truth was Kim probably already knew. "I met your ex-husband."

She wasn't sure what to call the CIA operative since he wasn't going by his legal name. Damon had introduced the man as Ezra Fain, but she knew that wasn't what Kim called him.

Kim nodded. "Yes, I heard Beck was going to interview a few of the men Taggart picked up when he was rescuing his brother. How is that going? I assume you're the one working with them. Do they really call themselves the Lost Boys?"

Ian Taggart was an American and sort of her boss, though she worked directly for Damon. She rather liked the big man. He'd been a Green Beret and a CIA operative, but he'd gotten out for many of the reasons Ariel had. Now he ran his company a bit like the Army, though he was an indulgent general. And he never left a man behind, not even ones who didn't belong to him. When his youngest brother had been taken, he'd gone after him. When he'd found a whole group of men who'd been treated the same way Theo Taggart had, he'd freed them and set them up in London under Damon's watchful eye.

That was how she'd met Robert.

They weren't really boys, but they were definitely lost. "The nickname is something Kay came up with. You know she's quite cheeky, that one."

Kim stared at her with intelligent eyes. "What are they like? Has Tag made any progress on finding out who they used to be?"

This was the fine line she always walked when she was with Kim Solomon. She liked the woman, truly cared about her, but it wouldn't do to forget that she was still a working spy. "Are you asking because you're curious or as an operative wanting to gain intelligence?"

"Can't I be a curious operative?" Kim asked before sighing. "All right, I'm asking because I don't think Beck knows what he's getting involved in. He offered to be the liaison because of his relationship with McKay-Taggart. I know him. He thinks he's doing good."

She kept her eyes on the plaza, watching for the right car. "I don't see a problem with that. He was good with them. The lads can be difficult, but Ezra handled them well. He made them comfortable."

"Beck," Kim insisted. "His name is Beckett. I know he's good at his job and he'll actually give a damn about them, but there's far more on the line than figuring out the identities of a small group of men."

Perhaps there was something to be learned here. Though she'd left the business, she still knew how to play the game. "You're talking about McDonald's research."

Hope McDonald, the wicked witch of the pharmaceutical industry. She'd developed a drug that helped her build a small army of soldiers who were completely enslaved by her. She'd wiped their memories and tortured them into compliance.

She'd done all of that to Robert. He still bore the scars of his time in her company.

It should have been over when Taggart had liberated the men and taken down McDonald, but now the race was on to see who could get her research first.

"Yes," Kim agreed. "You should know that I believe there's a faction in the Agency who will try to gain that intelligence and use it to quietly restart some research a lot of us think is better off left buried."

Kim wasn't telling her anything her team didn't already know. "What makes you believe that?"

"Levi is slowly maneuvering himself into a position where he can potentially take over the case."

Kim had a long history with the CIA operative known as Levi Green, and it all played into her relationship with her ex-husband. Ariel had met Levi briefly, and Beckett Kent not at all before he'd walked through the doors of The Garden and presented himself as Ezra Fain.

It was all confusing and made her happy for her staid and not at all messy love life.

"And that worries you? I know you have history with the man, but I haven't heard that he's dirty."

Kim stood and started to pace. "He's never been dirty before, but Levi can be…opportunistic. And he hates Beck for some reason. I'm worried, but naturally I can't contact him. He wouldn't pick up the phone for me."

Because that divorce hadn't been an amicable one. That was precisely why she couldn't take Kim's worries too seriously. She would take them to Damon, of course, but Kim couldn't think rationally when it came to her ex. "The Lost Boys aren't a group you should worry about. The outside factions might be dangerous but the men themselves seem solid. They're just trying to feel their way through all of this. They're actually quite likable, most of them. Given the trauma they've gone through, they're surprisingly well adjusted."

If one excused the fact that a couple of them were walking time bombs.

"You like them." Kim's blue eyes turned shrewd.

"They're my patients, but you know it's completely impossible to keep all emotion out it when you're working this closely. Of course I've come to have opinions of them." Some of them more strongly than others. She glanced down at her watch. "He's more than an hour late."

Kim waved that off. "I told you I thought he would go off schedule. He's got a mistress here in Paris. He'll return sometime this afternoon. I promise. Now back to the real stuff. It's one of them, isn't it? The man you're thinking about sleeping with, but it's not just sleeping, is it? You like him. You like like him."

She hated the fact that she felt a blush go through her system. It was Robert McClellan's fault. He made her feel like a schoolgirl with her first crush. It was ridiculous. She was a trained operative with a doctorate in psychology. She didn't go gooey over a boy. Still, it wasn't like she could talk about this with anyone else. She certainly wasn't going to her boss to tell him she had some nasty sexual thoughts about one of the "lads," as he called them. "They're all lovely men and it's been a long time for me."

She hadn't had a regular man in her life for years. She'd had a couple of flings, but nothing serious. Now even though one of the perks of her job was a membership to a BDSM club called The Garden, she still hadn't dated or even found a casual partner to sleep with. It should have been an excellent way to burn off her stress. She should have found a hot Dominant partner and indulged. But no. She'd met Robert and couldn't do much more than play a bit. No sex. No affection. None because they couldn't come from the man she wanted.

Kim stared at her with wide eyes. "Whoa. This is a serious thing."

"I told you it wasn't."

"Which is precisely how I know it is. Who is he? Come on, Ari, you know you need to talk about things. Do you have someone you can talk to? Kayla Summers?" Kim asked.

She couldn't talk to Kay because Kay was far too close to the lads and she was a horrible gossip. Though apparently everyone knew there was something between her and Robert. "His name is Robert and I'm attracted to him."

"Robert." She seemed to go through her memory. "He's the one who was found with Theo Taggart. He's been out for longer than the rest of them. So you're sweet on him."

Ariel sighed. "I suppose I am. I don't know why, but he moves me in a way no one has for a long time. Maybe ever. It can't happen though."

"Why?"

"Because we work together."

Kim shrugged. "Who do you see outside of work that you might be able to date? You live in the building where you work. You spend all your time with your coworkers, so unless you're planning on living the celibate life, I'm not sure where you're going to find a partner."

She wasn't wrong. "I've met several lovely men through the club attached to my office."

"And yet you haven't dated any of them."

Because she couldn't get Robert out of her brain. "I've certainly played with a few."

"Have you slept with anyone?" Kim kept up the questions.

There was only one answer to that question. "No."

"Is he kind, Ari? Is he a good man?"

She felt the beginnings of tears pulse behind her eyes and tried to banish them. "He's a good man."

He made her feel. He made her feel so much and it scared her.

"Is Damon opposed to you seeing him?" Kim wouldn't give up.

She'd thought about this a lot as she lay awake at night, wondering how Robert was doing. He had trouble sleeping at times. Nightmares. He was plagued with nightmares he didn't understand because he had no idea what he'd been through in his life. "I haven't talked to Damon about how I feel. He's never had a problem with it before. After all, he worked with Penny before they got married." And now they were happy and settled and had a lovely son. They were thinking about getting a place in the country. They were going to have a life.

She was only a few years younger than Penny and she wasn't

even close to having a family. By this time in her life, her mother had already immigrated to England from Nigeria with her father. At Ariel's age, her mother had been pregnant with her. Ariel spent her nights playing with Doms she knew she wasn't going to sleep with, and it was all starting to feel empty.

Who was she fooling? It wasn't her age that made her feel empty. It had started the day she'd met Robert and he'd looked at her like she was the sun in the sky. For a moment, she'd felt that way, like she was the center of the world and not some supporting player in another person's story.

"Ari, if you care about this guy you have to go for it. Can you move him to another therapist? Is it an ethical thing to date patients, even if they are no longer your patient?"

She'd already moved him off personal sessions. He was talking to another therapist, one in Dallas. They had sessions over the computer. But she still regularly worked with him.

There was far too much sexual chemistry between them for either to ignore. She was getting sick of pretending like it wasn't there between them, that mystical tug that whispered to her this time would be different, this time would be good. "Robert is in a transitional phase of his life."

Kim nodded. "He's transitioning from a mindless zombie soldier to a dude who doesn't know what he did before he was a mindless zombie soldier. I think that was a pretty quick transition. One minute he was getting his mind erased and the next he's got a nice place in The Garden and likely takes a lot of shit from Taggart. I haven't met the man personally, but he's got a reputation."

Robert had actually figured out how to handle Taggart quickly. He let all that sarcasm flow right off his back. He didn't let Tag bug him at all. He was cool and composed and had slid into a leadership position. All the men looked to Robert. He was the big brother of the group and he didn't seem to mind the responsibility. "He wasn't a zombie soldier and he was never mindless. He was forced to commit crimes and he has to deal with that. He still has nightmares."

"You don't want to date him because he has nightmares?"

"It's not that I don't want to date him," Ari explained. "I think it could be a bad idea. What if it doesn't work out? We live in the same building."

"So you think he could be an evil ex? You know Beck and I lived together and worked together. It was apparently easy to stop doing that. We untangled hard and fast. Do you think Robert would give you trouble?"

"Never." Robert was one of the most honorable men she'd ever met. It was one of the things that attracted her to him. Somehow, even through all that pain he'd experienced, even with his memories being erased again and again, he'd kept a core of goodness in his soul. The doctor had forced him to rob banks, but she'd never been able to warp his soul. "Robert would never hurt me. I know I would tell anyone else that she was being naïve, that anyone can hurt another person if they're pushed too hard, but I believe that of Robert. I don't think he could ever willingly hurt me."

"He sounds amazing and you should go for it." Kim leaned over and put a hand on her shoulder. "You can't let these moments pass you by. You have to be brave. I wish I'd been braver. I wish I'd fought harder for Beck."

But guilt had weighed her friend down. "He should never have blamed you for his brother's death. You couldn't have known what was going to happen."

She shook her head. "That's ancient history and we need to talk about the now. Beck had his reasons and I suppose I had mine for walking away. But if a man you might be able to love is standing in front of you, don't push him away because it doesn't feel like the right time. Time is a funny thing. We always think we have time, and then we open our eyes and wonder where it all went. You deserve to find happiness. I can't think of anyone who deserves it more. You've helped so many people find their way out of darkness, you need some light for yourself."

She couldn't help the tears that pooled in her eyes now. Robert *was* a light in the world. He was a man who'd looked into the heart of darkness and still been able to turn away.

What would it hurt to try? The only thing she was truly risking would be her heart, and she knew very well that a heart wasn't worth much if a person never risked it.

She sniffled. "I don't even know how to date anymore."

Kim's face lit up. "We should game-plan. Over drinks. I used to be a super-good wingman. I know I can't go with you, and you'll pretend like I don't exist at all to your friends at The Garden, but I can help prep you."

She held her friend's hand. "Damon knows what I used to do and who I worked with. He also knows I'm here with you today. I don't keep secrets from him. I keep quiet about it because it might make the others uncomfortable to know their friendly shrink used to be MI6's go-to assassin." She glanced out the window and her heart rate ticked up slightly. Ah, sweet adrenaline. It helped her focus. "There he is."

Kim picked up the sniper rifle she'd brought along for the assignment. "Thank god. These people will be back at some point in time and then we'll have a lot of explaining to do. Although I'd like to ask a couple of questions about their choice of lube. This is a ridiculously expensive hotel. They could upgrade the lube. Poor woman. Can you ID him?"

She didn't have time to think about the people whose room they'd broken into. She could only hope they were out enjoying the Parisian day for at least another twenty minutes or so.

She was on this particular mission because the Agency needed a positive ID before they assassinated someone. It wouldn't do to get it wrong, and she was the only one who'd seen this notorious bomb maker in person. She watched as the hotel employees opened the car door and helped the man out. They were solicitous to the man responsible for at least a thousand deaths. He made bombs and weapons for jihadists around the world.

"Give it to me. I'm a better shot. You get ready to go," Ari said. A little more blood wouldn't hurt, and she really hated this guy. He made his money off the suffering of others. "I've got a positive ID and I'm going to finish this job."

Kim turned over the rifle and Ari did what came naturally. She'd done it so many times her muscle memory took over and she was in position in seconds. Thank god the windows opened in hotels in France. If she was in the States it would have been much harder. Here, she lined up her shot and took it. She didn't even spray the valet.

Now it was time to take her own shot. With Robert.

She handed the rifle over to Kim as the shouting started. "Time to go."

Kim had the rifle in pieces in seconds and stashed in her massive bag. "Meet you at that little café by the Louvre for drinks?"

"Sure." She could go back tomorrow morning. It would be good to have some girl time. The truth was she could use some advice and she wasn't ready to get it from anyone on her team. "I'll head out the south entrance. See you there."

She stepped out of their borrowed room and walked toward the stairs, a bounce in her step.

Robert should watch out because she was coming for him.

* * * *

Robert watched from the fourth floor as Ariel strode through the doors of The Garden, wheeling her overnight bag behind her. She'd only been gone two days, taking off to see some friends in Paris, but it had felt like forever to him. Somehow she'd become necessary to his everyday sanity. Seeing Ariel—even when he didn't get a chance to talk to her—was the best part of his day, so he'd felt every one of those forty-eight hours.

"You know the word stalker comes to mind when I think of you," a sarcastic voice said. Jax. Though honestly it could have been any of them. They were all sarcastic bastards.

"I was standing here and she walked in."

On the floor below them, Penny walked out with her son on her hip. Ariel immediately opened her arms.

"Sure you were. You didn't remember that we were told when to expect her back. It's mere coincidence. Nothing more." Jax leaned on the railing, looking down where the women were talking and laughing.

"I wanted to make sure she's okay."

"Hah, I win," another voice said. Tucker moved to his other side.

Jax frowned Tucker's way. "You don't win because no one was willing to bet that he wouldn't be here. He's probably been here since the morning meeting because we didn't know exactly when she was coming back. I don't know what he was worried about. She went to

Paris. According to Kay, it's a magical place where shopping is a sport and nothing bad ever happens."

"Tell that to Marie Antoinette." It was odd how easy it could be to remember facts about other people's lives. History came quite easily to him, but he couldn't remember if he had any family. He couldn't remember his own damn name. He was Robert. What she'd named him. Some of the others had taken new names, but he'd kept his. His name—even though it had been given to him by the very woman who'd taken his personal history—was the only thing of any permanency he'd had in his short life.

That and pain. Fear. Desolation.

"I don't like Paris." Tucker turned away from the scene playing out below. He grimaced and put a hand to his head.

Robert knew that look well. "You're trying to catch a thought, aren't you? Let it go or you'll end up getting a migraine. We've got work to do."

Jax crossed his arms over his chest and a stubborn glint hit his eyes. "So we're supposed to accept it? We're supposed to be okay with the fact that we're never getting our memories back?"

He turned away from Ariel. He seemed to be doing that a lot. His men needed him, and it was a bad idea to get involved with someone as lovely and gentle as Ariel Adisa. If he ever exploded the way he knew he could, she would be caught in his aftershock, and he didn't want that for her.

He'd never told her that he dreamed of killing at night. He dreamed of wrapping his hands around a delicate throat and squeezing.

It wasn't an unpleasant dream.

There was something damaged inside him, and he wasn't sure any amount of therapy could fix it. It didn't help that he was forced to hide inside The Garden since the minute he stepped outside there was the possibility that some rogue intelligence operative would kidnap him. They would hand him over for experimentation in an attempt to figure out what Hope McDonald had done.

Ariel would be collateral damage.

"No, but we've already gone over this," he pointed out. "Trying to force a memory doesn't work. You have to let it flow over you.

Write down everything you remember and we'll start rebuilding our pasts from there. I know it's a long process, but Rome wasn't built in a day."

"Yeah, well my life was ruined in a second," Jax replied. "I'm going to hit the gym and then I've got some work to do. Damon put me on a corporate espionage case. I wish I could go onsite, but I'll be going through about half a million lines of code instead. Movie tonight?"

He nodded. It was good to stay busy. It would keep his mind off the fact that The Garden would be open for play and Ariel would be down there. Well, it wouldn't make him forget, but it would give him something to do beyond creeping on her. "I'll see you there."

Tucker sighed and seemed to relax a bit. "I'll stay away from Paris. That won't be hard since I don't go anywhere."

That could be changing. "Damon and Big Tag have been talking about loosening the leash a bit. They think it might be safe for us to go to Dallas if we're with a senior agent."

Tucker's eyes went wide. "Seriously?"

"Don't get your hopes up. We're not entirely sure yet, but we've been cooperating with the Agency and MI6. We've shared intelligence and been open in interviews with them." It was odd but he didn't want to be the one to go. He had friends in Dallas. Some of his only good memories were of his time in Dallas.

The doors to the elevator opened and the reason he wanted to stay right where he was walked out.

God, she was beautiful. Ariel was the single most beautiful woman he'd ever seen, with her halo of dark hair and doe-like brown eyes. Her skin seemed to be made of velvety night, and when the light hit it, he could see jewel tones in her sweet flesh. He dreamed about what her skin would look like pressed to his.

If only he didn't dream of other things…

"Hey, Ari." Tucker had perked up, the way he always did around a woman. Tucker didn't discriminate. He would flirt with any female. Young, old. Perfectly attractive or gorgeous in her own way. Tucker seemed to need female attention. "How was your shopping trip?"

Robert had been like that when he'd first been rescued. He'd viewed females as comfort objects. Now he only wanted one, and she was the one he couldn't have.

Ariel smiled Tucker's way. "It was excellent. I got some great deals." She turned to Robert. "Can I see you in my office for a moment? I know we're supposed to meet in an hour, but you're the only person I'm meeting with this afternoon. Do you have time now?"

Did he have time? Maybe that was the only thing he had to give her.

"Of course." They were supposed to talk about who might be ready to go visit Dallas. Big Tag wanted some time with the men.

"I'll go find Owen," Tucker offered. "And not think about Paris so my head doesn't explode. See you tonight. Maybe we can get pizza. We've only gone through fifty of the one-thousand, three-hundred-and-one combos."

His gut clenched at the thought because Tucker tended to get stuck on things. When they'd started the great pizza experiment, he'd thought they would work their way through a couple, deciding what they did or didn't like. Pepperoni? Sausage? Tucker was on a quest to try them all in every combination possible. He couldn't seem to make Tucker understand that adding mushrooms to anchovies didn't make them less gross. Still, he had an odd soft spot for Tucker. "Of course."

Tucker jogged down the hallway that would take him to the offices they were using while they worked. Damon gave them investigative tasks, and a couple of the boys had taken to it quite well.

He followed Ariel to the other side of the building. The Garden had a huge atrium in the center of the building, and every floor looked down on it. Ariel's lush offices were on the opposite side of theirs. Their offices were decorated mostly in white boards someone always drew dicks on, but Ariel's was a work of art. It was a temple to peace and serenity, much like the woman herself.

He stepped inside as she turned the lights on and rolled her suitcase next to the door.

"Why is Tucker avoiding Paris?" Ariel asked, turning to him.

Normally she would sit behind her desk and he would take the big chair in front of it. There was a space with couches that allowed for a more intimate setting, but he'd always chosen to keep the desk between them. "I mentioned you'd spent the last couple of days there and he said he didn't like Paris. Then he did what so often happens to us."

She pursed her sensual lips and nodded. "He tried to figure out why he didn't like Paris and started to get a headache. You must have caught him quite early. A few months ago he would have been retching even at the thought."

They'd been in bad shape the days after they'd been rescued. Ariel had helped them all through. She'd been by Robert's side, taking care of each of the men. She'd worked closely with him because he'd been through all of it. He'd been rescued long before they'd found there was a secondary site.

Seeing her kindness, how she'd handled his men with care and empathy, had sparked something deep within him, and he hadn't been able to douse that flame.

If only she were another agent. If she'd been an Erin Taggart or hell, Charlotte Taggart, he would have been all over her. He would have pretty much fallen at her feet and begged her to take him, but she wasn't a warrior. She had no real defenses against the kind of violence he could bring into her life.

"Everything went all right in Paris?"

"Of course. I met with an old friend and did some shopping and had some lovely meals." She frowned his way. "I did not need a bodyguard. I heard you went to Damon and requested one be sent. The last thing I needed was Brody or Nick being forced to follow me around while I shopped for handbags."

"They could use you to get to us," he argued. "I don't think Damon is taking this threat seriously."

"Did Ezra bring new information to light? Because if he hasn't then I doubt anyone would kidnap me in an insane attempt to get McKay-Taggart and Knight to exchange me for the lads. Anyone sane would understand that would end poorly for them."

He hated that she wouldn't take her safety seriously. He'd spent two whole days worried about her. "And how about all the insane assholes? Because they're out there, Ari."

"I can handle myself. I'm quite good at self-defense and I'm not exactly unarmed."

He knew she carried, but that didn't mean she was good with a gun. "Let's go to the range and you can prove to me you know how to use it."

"I don't have to prove anything to you. And I don't need a bodyguard." She shook her head. "I didn't intend to fight with you."

"Then don't. The next time you want a girls' weekend, take a guard with you."

"As long as that guard is you, maybe I will."

When had he backed her against the wall? They hadn't made it far into her office. Now he realized he'd been stalking her, getting into her space without even realizing he was doing it. Ariel's back was to the wall but she wasn't pushing at him. She wasn't trying to take back her space.

Her eyes had dilated and her chest moved with her breath. Toward him. Not away.

All those months of training, first at Sanctum in Dallas and then here at The Garden, had taught him to watch a woman's body. Everything about Ariel told him she wasn't afraid. She was aroused.

That made him afraid, though not so much that he moved away from her. "You know why I can't do that."

"I want you to tell me."

Where the hell was this coming from? "We've talked about this."

His hand was moving toward her like she was magnetized.

"A long time ago and we resolved nothing," she replied. She brought her hand up to rest on his chest. "We agreed to shelve the discussion for another time and go on as we had been. It can't last, Rob. I know you feel the electricity between us. And you don't ignore it. You act like my boyfriend all the time. You take rights over me that aren't yours."

"I'm trying to protect you." He'd inched closer. He could smell her. Ariel's unique scent washed over him. It was more than enough to get his cock going.

"From all the evil agents out there who want to kidnap me?"

That was where she was wrong. "I need to protect you from me."

"I don't want to be protected from you. That's the last thing I want or need." She went up on her toes and her lips were mere centimeters from his. "I can take care of myself. Play with me tonight. If you can't handle a relationship outside the dungeon, I understand, but give us that much."

Because he'd been playing her Dom for months. Whenever he could he ensured her comfort, watched over her, acted like a bossy asshole at times.

Before he could reply, his lips were touching hers and he couldn't think straight. His every sense was attuned to her. Something primal threatened to take over, and damn if that didn't feel good.

Her arms wound around him and the minute he felt her tongue trace the seam of his lips, he was gone. He dragged her body to his. There was nothing sweet in the kiss. There was hunger so long denied. He'd needed her arms around him from the moment he'd awoken in that fucking lab, blinking into the white light and finding only pain.

She could be his prize, his reward. She could make all that torture worth it because she would submit to him. She would sit at his feet and he would feel like the king of the world. Beyond that, she would let him have his way with her. Any way he wanted. Any time he wanted. She would be his.

He held her tight and took control of the kiss. She followed his lead beautifully, moving with him like they'd kissed a thousand times, like she'd been made for him.

He let his hand trail down until he found her breast. His cock strained against his jeans.

Just a moment. He would let go for a moment. It was only a kiss and honestly, what was really stopping them from becoming lovers? They were adults and consenting. They could play in the dungeon because no one would let him hurt her down there.

He could indulge his dark impulses, and someone would be there if he lost control. Someone would save her.

No one would let him wrap his hands around her throat because he lost sight of who she was in the moment.

A sudden vision of Hope McDonald blazed across his brain.

He stumbled away, backing up as fast as he could. "I'm sorry I did that."

Ariel took a deep breath. He'd managed to pull at her dress enough to drag it over her shoulder. He'd been halfway to ripping it off her and shoving his cock deep, with no thought at all to her.

"Did what? Kissed me? Rob, I'm not sorry about that. I'm only sorry you stopped. I know this is difficult for you, but you can't let that woman take everything. Please. Sit down with me. Let's talk about it. I spent the entire time I was away thinking about you." Her gorgeous eyes beseeched him.

His hands were shaking. She was right. Hope fucking McDonald was always there. She was the monster under his bed, and he was still a damn child who couldn't get up and turn on the light.

He needed. He needed to hurt someone, to break something.

It wasn't going to be her.

"I can't." He had to get out of here. All the nastiness that resided inside him was bubbling up, threatening to boil over. It needed an outlet. He'd kept it under the lid for too long, pretending he was better than the rest of them. Like he was above it all.

"Talk to me. Don't leave it like this." She stepped in front of him.

He pushed her out of the way. Harder than he'd intended. She stumbled but managed to stay on her feet.

"It's okay. Something triggered you, love. Let's figure it out and work through it." There were tears in her eyes.

Fuck it all. He'd hurt her.

Without another word, he strode out the door.

Sasha was there, walking off the elevator with a bunch of files in his hands. Sasha. He didn't understand the man half the time, but he had to hope he would understand what was going on now.

Ariel came out of her office. "Don't leave it like this. Come back."

If he went back, he would take it out on her. He knew himself well enough to know when he couldn't pretend to be the nice guy anymore.

"Let him be," Sasha said, stepping between them. "He needs a minute."

The beast inside Rob didn't like Sasha coming between him and Ariel. Logic meant nothing when he was in this state.

Sasha put his hands up as though showing him he wasn't going to try anything. "Let's go to the gym."

Rob stared at her, indecision wracking through him. Sex would be the more pleasurable way to go, wouldn't it? She was here. She was asking for it.

Fuck, he hated himself when he got like this.

Sasha slapped him lightly, enough to drag his attention back. "No. We go to the gym now. You would not allow me to do this. Look at me, Robert. You do not want to do this."

He growled Sasha's way, but now there was a hint of fear in Ariel's eyes.

When Sasha gripped his arm, Robert let him.

She was too vulnerable to ever handle him. He walked away from Ariel and knew he'd made the right choice.

Chapter One

Present day

Robert stared at the monitor and listened to the big boss drone on about what was a simple op. He'd thought they would have time while they were in the air to relax a bit before they got to Munich. He'd planned on sitting next to Ariel and having some time to talk to her, but no. The private jet they were on came fully equipped with a conference room and Internet, so he got to listen to Big Tag instead of sharing a glass of wine with Ariel and talking about where they would have dinner this evening.

He had it all planned out. He'd found a nice Italian restaurant since he wasn't sure how Ariel felt about sausages made from all kinds of weird meat. They were staying in a lovely hotel in downtown Munich—two rooms, of course, because even if the night ended up going the way he hoped, he wouldn't sleep beside her. He would go back to his own room to sleep.

They would talk about that, too. Even though she'd been his therapist for a while, there were things he'd never told her.

He was more in control now. He could handle a relationship.

"Do you think there's something wrong with the signal?" A deep voice cut through his thoughts. "He's been still for a long time. If it was Tucker, I would say he's fucking with me. But Robert's always been solid."

He held himself still a moment more. Maybe if Big Tag thought the system was down, he could get out of this. The flight from London to Munich wasn't a long one, then a car would pick them up and they would spend the afternoon prepping. If Big Tag took up all his time on the plane, it would be hours before he got to be alone with Ariel.

"He's been blinking," the man beside Big Tag said. "How are you in charge of everything? I think old age is hitting you hard."

Adam Miles. He and Big Tag were sitting next to each other and bickering like an old married couple.

"So he's not listening to me?" Big Tag put a hand on his chest. He wore a dress shirt and tie that let Robert know he was probably meeting with clients at some point in time today. There would be a suitcoat hanging off the back of his chair. "I'm deeply offended. What do you think has his attention if it's not our very important mission?"

Miles's lips quirked up. "I think I can guess."

The only thing worse than Miles and Big Tag arguing was when they teamed up. There was only one thing to do now. He was the "reliable" one, after all.

"I'm to facilitate Rebecca and Ariel's meetings with several employees of Kronberg Pharmaceuticals, the company that formerly funded Dr. Hope McDonald's research. You're sending me files on each of them. Rebecca knew them each personally and our cover is that she's in town and wanted to get back in touch. We're trying to discover if Kronberg has any data left from Dr. McDonald's research that might help us decode the files we found in Toronto. Additionally, we're to try to find a woman named Veronica Croft and attempt to interview her."

Veronica Croft might be the most important part of the mission since they had real intelligence placing her in the right place and the right time to have worked on McDonald's experiments.

"We have reason to think she's still in Europe." Adam seemed to get serious, opening a folder in front of him. "But she doesn't want to be found. She didn't finish out her internship. From what I've been able to find out, she didn't even pick up her last paycheck. The last time we can trace her, she was coming back into Germany from France. Might have been a vacation. I don't know because I can't find records of her in any hotel or use of any of her credit cards with the exception of her buying a train ticket from Paris to Munich. From there I've got her at the train station and then she disappears for the next two years. Her passport has expired. She has no status with any European country. I have to think she's hiding."

"Wouldn't you, after the rest of the team you worked with died mysteriously? All of them with the singular exception of Rebecca Walsh." Soon to be Shaw. Rebecca was a doctor specializing in neurological diseases. At one point she'd worked at the very building they were going to check out. She'd worked with Hope McDonald, though she'd had zero idea what the doctor had actually been experimenting with.

Him. She'd been experimenting with him. And Tucker and Jax. Dante and Sasha. Theo. Victor. He'd hated Victor, but not even that psychopath had deserved what she'd done to him.

"Are we sure she's not dead?" Big Tag asked. "With the exception of our Dr. Walsh, everyone else seems to be dead or out of his mind."

"Tucker is not crazy."

"We'll have to agree to disagree on that." If Big Tag had heard the warning in his tone, he didn't show it. "You should know that I have reservations about taking Tucker on this op. I believe he needs to be carefully watched."

"Because of what happened in Toronto, or do you have other reasons?"

What had happened in Toronto was Tucker had discovered who he'd been before McDonald had erased his memories. He'd been positively identified by Rebecca as Dr. Steven Reasor, McDonald's right-hand man.

Tucker had not taken the news well.

"He's the only one of us who worked in that building, and you know he often remembers things he shouldn't." The door behind him opened and his whole world brightened. She was also his partner for this mission. "Dr. Adisa, thank you for joining us."

Ariel smiled his way and took the seat next to him. "Sorry I'm late. I had some trouble with my laptop but it's working now. Hello, Ian. Adam. What did I miss?"

He could feel Ian's disbelief from a thousand miles away. "Seriously? Dr. Adisa?"

Adam elbowed him. "Don't. I want to see how far they'll take it."

Ariel chuckled and proved she was far better natured than he was. "I worked hard for that title, Adam. It doesn't hurt to remind you how smart I am."

"Is he going to call you doc when you're cuddling?" Ian asked.

"Hey," Robert began, his shoulders tensing. Maybe he wasn't as settled as he thought he was.

Ariel put a hand on his arm. "It was Canada, Ian. Our cuddle on the couch was strictly to share body heat. It's good to know the gossip flows steadily between the teams. How is your brother? The last time I saw him he was trying to track some mysterious intelligence. Care to share since he obviously did?"

Theo and his wife, Erin, had shown up during the recent mission to Toronto that resulted in Dr. Walsh joining the team. Theo was the youngest of the Taggart brothers, but he was apparently as gossipy as the rest.

"Nothing I can talk about yet." Tag sat back and his expression seemed to shutter. "This is something I won't let out until we're absolutely certain it's true."

Robert felt his gut tighten, and it took all his willpower to not reach for Ariel's hand.

He was not going to use her like a freaking teddy bear. He was going to be strong and in control. "So it's about the traitor."

"We don't know there's a traitor," Ariel replied quickly.

"I've got the bullet wound that proves otherwise." They'd been careful when they'd fled Toronto. They'd gone to a safe house, and no one beyond the team had known where they were, and yet Levi Green had been waiting for them. Green had flushed them all out and nearly cost he and Ariel their lives. Owen and Rebecca as well, but Robert had been the only one that asshole had shot. "According to Owen, Green told him he has a plant in our group."

"Levi Green has been known to lie," she pointed out.

Tag sighed, a weary sound. "Yeah, well, the devil knows when the truth is far more harmful than a lie. I can't talk about that now, but if this lead pans out, you'll be getting someone else to interview."

Somehow that felt more like a threat than a promise.

"Dr. Adisa, did you get the files I sent on the employees I think we should target?" Adam's tone had lost its playfulness.

Because this was serious, and someone in their group had sold them all out to Levi Green and his faction of the Agency.

She was perfectly professional again, too, and he missed her hand on his arm. "I did. I've gone over them. I think the secretary might be an excellent source if we can convince her to talk openly. Rebecca is almost certain she will. Apparently she loves to gossip, and when the booze is flowing, she's a little loose lipped."

Tag nodded, his lips turned down. "Do what you can. If there's a fount of information in some safe or backed up on a computer at Kronberg, I want to know. According to the reports, Green claims to have a cure. I don't suppose he's going to use that in the manner we would like that to be used."

"He told us exactly how he intends to use it. He's going to reverse engineer it and between that and the notes, he'll figure out how she did what she did to us," Robert explained. Another generation of brainwashed soldiers would be born, this time in service to the CIA. "I think he's also interested in the time dilation portion of her meds."

There had been two parts to Dr. McDonald's torture techniques. The drugs she used wiped clean personal memories but left the patient with full muscle memory and language skills. He'd woken up in a lab with no idea how he'd gotten there or who he was, but he'd known how to fight. He couldn't remember what pizza tasted like, but he knew what it was called.

He'd been a soldier of some kind. He'd figured that much out. He knew far too much about US military-grade weapons to have been anything else.

The second part of her protocols used a drug that tricked the brain into thinking more time had passed than had in reality. She could use that time to punish her men for insubordination. His body hadn't aged during those long periods of pain, but he wasn't sure he could say the same about his soul.

"We have to stop that at all costs," Adam said gravely. "And we have to figure out exactly how Steven Reasor ended up with Dr. McDonald and how they managed to then erase him from existence."

He checked behind him to make sure the door was closed before turning back to the monitor. "I would like to know that, too. There's no record at all of Steven Reasor ever coming into Germany?"

A frustrated sigh came from Adam. "No. And that means someone is working this from two angles. There should be a passport from the US, and it should show Reasor entering Germany. He would have needed a work visa. The German government doesn't have a record of him applying. I can find Rebecca's. I can find Veronica Croft's. Hell, Dr. McDonald has a record, but nothing on this guy. He's a ghost."

"I think there are bigger factions at play, and that worries me." Tag ran a hand over his head before staring grimly into the camera. "We don't understand the past and how Reasor fit in. I'm struggling to imagine Tucker could have been that evil in his former life. I don't know that evil like that can be erased. It's not like all of you came out sunny and happy. Dante came out of it a heaping pile of human garbage, and Sasha's not much better."

"Ian," Ariel admonished.

Big Tag shrugged. "I call it like I see it, Doc, and yes, that's my professional opinion. I've been wrong on occasion. All I'm saying is keep an eye on things. And by *things* I mean Tucker."

They'd gone over this before they'd left London. "I understand Ariel has veto power when it comes to Tucker and his mental health."

But she would listen to him. She knew Tucker. She knew he couldn't possibly be the bad guy in all this even with everything they knew about him. Tag and Adam were right. Something was off and they needed to figure it out.

He didn't know why, but he'd trusted Tucker from the moment he'd met the guy. He was comfortable with him. His every instinct told him that Tucker was a solid guy who would watch his back.

"Dr. Adisa has veto power over everything about this op," Tag corrected. "Everything. If she feels like you're in danger, she can call it off. Hell, if she gets a hankering for Yorkshire pudding, you will all get back on the plane and head to London. Am I understood?"

It was right there, the instinctive need to salute and say "Sir, yes, sir." He forced it down because no matter what he'd been before, he wasn't a soldier now. "Of course. We'll be landing in forty minutes. I'll keep you and Damon updated."

Tag nodded. "And Adam will be in touch if he finds anything further. Tell Peter hello from me. He's a good guy. He'll be your driver and translator, if needed. He's also muscle. He's former German intelligence but now he tours castles or some shit. Hopefully he still knows how to shoot. Not that I want any shooting. This should be a shooting-free zone. The last time we shot up Germany, my ass had to fill out paperwork for hours because Damon was a delicate flower and couldn't hold a pen. Germans are serious about paperwork. They're also serious about not shooting people."

"Damon took most of those bullets," Ariel pointed out.

"Yeah, he still wasn't willing to do that paperwork," Tag shot back. "So don't shoot anyone you don't have to. And if you do have to, hide that body. One of you has to be good at that. Send daily reports and dear god, use condoms. The London team is breeding like rabbits."

He reached over and tapped the button that switched off the monitor because he'd heard this lecture before. "There's a reason I work for Damon."

Ariel turned in her chair. "I thought that was because it was safer in London than Dallas."

"It's safer in so many ways." He glanced down at where she'd been taking notes. "You know Tucker is a good man."

"Of course I do, but I also know he's in a dangerous place. I think our best bet is to keep him as close as possible."

"I think he'll remember the building." It was precisely why Tucker might be invaluable. "Sometimes we don't remember places until we get inside them and muscle memory takes over."

"Let's see how the first forty-eight hours goes." She closed her laptop. "I want to be back in London before the end of the week. We get in, get the intel and get back out, and then we don't have to worry about Tucker. Once we get back to London, we can spend some more time exploring what happened. I would like to talk more to Rebecca about her experiences with Steven Reasor. I'm being forced to almost treat them like two separate entities."

"Can you talk to Big Tag? Can you tell him there's no way Tucker betrayed us?"

She studied him for a moment. "Why are you so certain?"

"Because I know him."

"You know the Tucker who exists now. You can't know who he used to be. Ian is wrong about a couple of things. He thinks a person is born good or bad. He's got a black and white concept of the world. Oh, he knows a good person can do bad things. He's not naïve. But I don't agree with his world view. I don't think we're born with a particular bent for good or evil. I believe in nurture over nature, though sometimes even that goes wrong. A human being is always complex. Some of you handled what happened better than others. The experiences were both similar and incredibly unique."

"You think one of us betrayed the group." He didn't want to believe it.

"I think Levi Green managed to find us very quickly in Canada. I don't know how he does that without inside help."

"There was someone new on the team. Have we looked into Nina?" Nina Blunt was a new operative.

"Absolutely we have," she replied. "I will look at everyone but you have to know Nina couldn't have tipped him off in Colorado."

He'd considered that, too. "According to Jax they were set up with security there. He could have been tapped in. It would have been simple enough to guess we would go for the secret facility. He already knew where it was. It was all a matter of whether or not we could get in under his radar, and we couldn't. It's not Tucker."

"Who do you suspect? Besides Nina, who is easy to suspect because you don't know her."

He didn't want to argue. That was the last thing he wanted to do. "I think Green got lucky. If he truly had someone on the inside, he would have taken us all down by now."

"I hope you're right." She was quiet for a moment. "Why did you change your mind when I got to Canada? I know Big Tag was teasing us but you were different when I got there. We didn't get to talk about this before."

He let all the professional stuff fly straight out the window. If they were going to work together and give a relationship a real shot, they would have to separate the two. "I never changed my mind about you. It was always about me. I knew how crazy I was about you two seconds after we met."

"You were interested in a lot of women."

He chuckled because she was right…and wrong. He pulled her hand into his and brought it to his lips. "I was looking for anything to hold on to. I was especially looking for a woman I couldn't hurt. I had a type right after Tag rescued me. I was all about the tough chick because I thought a woman who was physically strong and well trained might be the only one who could handle what I need."

"What do you need, Rob?"

It was time to be honest with her. "I need to be put on my ass from time to time. I need to break things, though not as much as I used to. I didn't want one of those things I broke to be you."

"And what changed? Was it what happened in Canada?"

He didn't put down her hand. He liked touching her too much. "I'm better. I'm stronger than I was before. You were right. I needed another therapist. Not because you're not good."

"You couldn't talk to me the way you should have been able to because you were emotionally involved with me."

Well, no one ever said she wasn't a smarty pants. "Exactly. Kai's helped me a lot, and one of the things he's helped me see is that it's time for me to start living. There's no grand past out there for me."

"We don't know that."

He'd thought about this a lot. "I've been missing for years. If I had a family, they would have looked for me. That was a fear of mine. What if we fell in love and suddenly I found out I had a wife and three kids?"

"I've thought about that, too, but you're a different person. I don't know that your memories ever come back unless Levi is telling us the truth and there really is a cure. Or Rebecca can find one. We need to consider that. A person is formed by his or her experiences. Getting your memories back…"

"Won't change how I feel about you." Of that he was certain. He couldn't imagine a time when he wouldn't be crazy about her.

"You can't know that, but you also can't live in limbo," Ariel said. "You can't spend the rest of your life trying to get back to your old life."

"I'm more than happy to move on. I really hope you're willing to take the chance with me." He kissed her hand again.

The door came open and the subject of their professional discussion was suddenly there. "Hey, did you know they have an Xbox?"

Sometimes Tucker was exactly what Big Tag called him—a puppy. Of course they were all a little like that, though they were puppies with teeth who sometimes went a bit rabid under the right circumstances. "Let's play then. We've got some time. Any interest?"

He looked at her but she shook her head. "I'm going to stay here and work for a bit. After all, apparently I'm not working this evening."

Because they had a date. Satisfaction settled deep inside him. "No work tonight. I'll come get you before we land. You get immersed in work and Owen still lands like he's setting down on an aircraft carrier."

He winked her way and closed the door. He should spend some time with Tucker and then he would be free to spend all night with Ariel.

He followed his "brother," forcing away thoughts of traitors.

Tonight his life would really begin.

* * * *

Ariel opened her laptop and stared at the screen.

How was she supposed to tell Robert what she was really doing? That she was reporting back to Damon, who was working with MI6? They had to keep the chief updated, feeding him some information so he didn't get tempted by whatever deal the Agency could make. They were walking a delicate line and had been for years. Then there was the fact that she was watching more than just the Lost Boys. She was watching her old friend Kim to try to figure out where she fell in all of this. It was obvious the Agency had factions working against each other. It was her job to figure out who they could and couldn't trust.

And she couldn't mention any of it to Robert.

An alert came across her monitor, letting her know the Dallas office was calling. She knew the drill. If she wasn't alone, she would refuse the call. She accepted it and Ian was there.

"Is it okay to talk?" he asked.

"I wouldn't have answered if it wasn't."

It looked like Taggart had moved out of the main conference room in Dallas to his own private office. He settled back in his big chair, looking very much the king of his personal castle. "Well, you've been out of the game for a while now, Doc. Can't be sure you haven't gone soft."

She'd never worked with Taggart until after she'd left MI6, and she'd always wondered what he'd been like in the field. Ruthless, she would bet, but with an underlying core of humanity not a lot of people would suspect. She felt comfortable working with this man. "I was always soft. That's why I got out of the game. What did you not tell me?"

If he was calling back so soon it was because something important had been left out of the general briefing—something he didn't want Robert to know about.

"Solo's in play," Ian said. "Adam has been monitoring our external players and she flew into Venice yesterday. We lost her from there."

"Maybe she has work in Venice." Having Solo around could make things much more difficult. Not simply because she cared about the woman, but she would have to brief Ezra or keep secrets from another man she respected mightily.

"It's only a seven-hour train trip from Venice to Munich. Or she could have had a car waiting. If she flew, she would show up on cameras unless she's flying private, and then why not fly straight to Munich like we are? I know she could be there for other reasons, but I suspect she's going to show up."

"What do you want me to do?"

Taggart was quiet for a moment as though trying to figure out how to explain something. "How much do you know about what's been going on in the US lately? With President Hayes?"

Everyone knew what had been happening. No US president in the modern era had gotten married while in office. "He recently got married to his former press secretary. It was all over the tabloids. I believe he lost his father as well."

Frank Hayes had been sick for a long time. It had come as no great shock, but there had been some gossip concerning how quickly the president had married after his father's funeral. She didn't judge the man at all. Sometimes grief could be made more bearable by taking positive steps toward the future.

"Yeah, the first father died of 'natural' causes." Big Tag used air quotes around the word *natural*. "Frank Hayes was an ambassador to Russia for years before he got sick. There have always been questions about the president's father's work in Moscow, and I think that finally played out in a big way. I believe the truth about his death was covered up, and Solo's fingerprints were all over that. I've heard some rumors that there was a big cleanup project at the White House the day Frank Hayes died, and they weren't using Merry Maids, if you know what I mean."

She'd stayed out of US politics, but she did remember hearing some rumblings about the president's possible ties to the Russian mob. Or that they were looking for a way to put pressure on him. "You think Kim was involved in covering up something for the president? Did it have something to do with the assassination attempt?"

There had been a lone wolf shooter who'd tried to take out the president the same day his father had passed away. The press had speculated the stress of almost losing his son had done the old man in.

"Absolutely. I think there was a throwdown. Hayes came out on top, and he cleaned house with the help of a few of his friends," Taggart asserted. "I know what Solo's work looks like. She had the press shut down in hours. We've all been wondering who she's working for, and I'm placing a big old bet that it's the president himself. Well, the president and a man named Connor Sparks. If she's working for that team, we need her. Do you understand how much easier our lives get if Solo can get the president on our side?"

A lot of their problems would disappear. At least for however long the president was in power. "How much should I tell her I know?"

"Make that call in the field. You're going to have to make a lot of decisions, and without input at times." Ian was quiet for a moment beforc he got to the heart of why he'd called her back. "I need to know who's working with Green."

That was her real mission, and she felt like she hadn't done a good job of it. She'd spent months with these men. Shouldn't she be able to tell? Logically she knew it wasn't her fault, but that didn't change the feeling in the pit of her stomach. She had to be honest with Ian. "Any of the men could do it given the right circumstances."

He shook his head. "No, Doc. I'm not asking for a shrink talk. I've read your reports. I need to know what *you* think. You're only relying on one part of your skill set. Stop being a shrink and put on your operative hat for me. Going on pure instinct, what do you think?"

Well, she didn't believe in coincidence. Not with something like this. "It's one of three people. It's Dante or Sasha or Tucker. They're the three who aren't honest with me in therapy. Jax is an open book. He's incapable of this level of betrayal. Owen would never have put Rebecca in danger, and I seriously doubt Levi would have shot Rob if he'd been working for him."

Logic told her it was one of the three. Instinct made her want to bring that list down to two.

"Or Levi is really smart and shooting up Robert takes the suspicion off him. He could have killed him. It would have been easy to do it," Ian pointed out.

The idea of Robert being the traitor was completely unbelievable. She would bet her reputation on the fact that the man was exactly who he presented himself to be, with the singular exception of hiding his rage. It was always there, bubbling under his surface, but he tried to hide it from her. From the world. "It would have been far easier for Rob to stop the car and turn us all over. Levi wanted Rebecca. He wouldn't have put her at risk if he'd had another way to bring her in."

"He let his minion shoot Jax, too. Well, I can't wait to see who he decides to shoot next." Ian sat back. "As it happens, I agree with your assessment. Robert is important to my family. I don't know my brother makes it through what he went through if Robert hadn't been there. But the same loyalty he showed Theo is why I can't trust him to see a traitor in his midst."

"He sees the good in people." He often ignored the bad willfully. It was one thing that worried her about him.

Ian stared at her through the monitor. "Tell me why you think it's one of those three. What do you mean they haven't been honest during therapy?"

People tended to start therapy with their walls firmly up. Especially when the therapy wasn't their idea, as was the case with the Lost Boys. Dante and Sasha had seemed angrier than the rest at the outset, but sometimes still waters ran very deep. "All three of them are holding back in our sessions. Every one of them did in the beginning, but the rest opened up after they realized they were safe. Normally I wouldn't worry about it. They went through something traumatic. It could take years to truly open up."

"But we don't have that kind of time," Tag pointed out. "Are you sure you're okay with this mission? I know I joke about it, but I understand you have feelings for Robert and have for a long time. You can't talk to him about this."

Because he couldn't believe his men would betray him, and he might talk too much and too openly with them. "I understand. I don't intend to let him find out what I'm doing."

"Watch all three of our suspects carefully. If you think for a second that things are going sideways, pull the plug," Ian reiterated. "Robert's mission is secondary to yours. He just doesn't know it."

So she had to figure out how to bring a potential Agency plant into the family, figure out who the traitor was, help decide if there was anything at Kronberg worth going after, and keep her primary mission from the man who might be her lover.

There was definitely a reason she'd gotten out of the business. "I'll keep you up to date."

Ian suddenly smiled. "Please do because we've got a bet going."

She rolled her eyes. It was obvious the serious portion of the talk was over. "On what?"

"How fast you end up married and joining the baby brigade."

She laughed because it wasn't a terrible thought. "Well, I'm not getting any younger."

And babies were cute. She was in a place where she could raise a child surrounded by loved ones. She couldn't pretend like she hadn't thought about it.

"Damn it. Theo was right. He bet you'll be engaged before the end of this mission and pregnant before you actually get married. I should have taken the under. Could you do a guy a solid and use condoms for a couple of months?"

He was incorrigible. She shook her head. "Good-bye, Ian."

"Does that mean no? Because Charlie hasn't placed her bet yet…"

She closed the laptop.

The door opened and Robert stood there, a confused look on his face.

"Were you talking to someone? Did Damon call in?" Robert asked.

"Ian wanted to clarify a few things on my end of the job," she replied. "Nothing important. He doesn't always understand my professional wording in a file."

A smile brightened his face. "I'm sure he would prefer you simplify things. Instead of *Dante shows the hallmarks of having several social disorders,* Tag's version? He's an asshole."

"Yes, that's definitely a clinical term we all use." She stood up because she was done working for now. "Is there a bar on this plane?"

"I was coming in to ask if you wanted a glass of wine." He held the door open for her. He was always such a gentleman. He never failed to pull her chair out or offer to pour her a drink.

At first she'd thought it might be a key to his past, but then Kay had told her Robert read books about how to treat a lady. He'd started shortly after he'd met her.

God, she hated lying to him.

"I would love one," she replied.

She followed him toward the galley and hoped it was the last time she would have to lie to him.

Chapter Two

"Hello." A tall blond man stood beside a Mercedes van with a friendly smile. He'd been waiting inside the hangar they would leave the jet in while they were here in Germany. Owen had barely turned the plane off and opened the doors before he was introducing himself. "My name is Peter Bergman and I'll be your host while you're here in Munich. Welcome. We should get in the van as quickly as possible."

He gestured for them to hurry along. Peter Bergman wore a black suit and well-worn loafers. The blue of his tie stood out against the snowy white dress shirt he had on. He looked every inch the gracious chauffeur and tour guide.

Robert wished he was here with Ariel on vacation.

Tucker ignored their guide and walked to the edge of the hangar, looking out at the glorious Bavarian day. The colors here were vibrant, the sky bluer than blue and grass a vivid green. Tucker stood there for a moment, his body still, and it made Robert wonder what was going through his head.

He didn't get out much. Tucker was almost always in hiding. The first time he'd had some real freedom had been in Toronto. His part in the mission had been to work at the company their target also worked at. He'd been cooped up in a medical research building most of the time and then he'd found out that nasty piece of his past.

He wanted to tell Tucker to run free for a while, to go and

explore the city.

But he couldn't. "Time to get to the hotel, buddy."

Tucker nodded and shoved his duffel in the back of the van. "Yeah, we should get going. I bet Dante and Sasha already trashed the place."

"It would have been helpful if someone had warned me how much those two can drink," Peter said, rearranging the luggage. "I've had to send out twice already. They claim they work better drunk. And don't worry. There's plenty of space. I checked myself that we would have enough rooms."

He didn't like the thought of Ariel in a room by herself, but he couldn't assume he would be staying with her. He would make sure they had adjoining rooms because he wasn't about to leave her unprotected.

Dante and Sasha had been sent earlier in the week to do preliminary recon on the building. He really hoped they'd been behaving themselves.

He turned back and helped Ariel down the last few steps as Peter finished packing in their luggage.

Rebecca stepped off the plane with Owen following after. He wouldn't be putting the plane into storage himself, it seemed, since Peter was intent on getting them moving.

"I've got a team coming in to ensure the jet is ready for you to fly out when you're done," Peter said, hurrying them along. "It will be waiting for you."

"Is there a problem?" Ariel asked.

"I think I might have been followed, but I'm not sure." Peter opened the door to the back seat. Tucker had climbed into the front. "I'm out of practice and perhaps a bit paranoid. I'll feel better when we get back into the city."

Owen stopped Rebecca from getting into the van. "Maybe we should think about turning right around and heading back to London then. I only agreed to let Rebecca come because we thought it would be safe."

Robert's gut tightened. They'd barely made it to the ground and someone was already watching them? "He didn't say he was sure he was followed."

"Owen, I need to do this," Rebecca argued. "Someone is always going to be watching us."

Owen's jaw had tightened, but he let go of his girlfriend's hand and then followed her to the third row of seating. It was obvious he wished she was back in her comfy lab at The Garden.

Rebecca was right. Someone would always follow them, and that's how it always would be until they figured a way out of the trap. He settled into the seat beside Ariel and Peter closed the doors. "Let's get going then. Is there a back way out of this airport?"

"I've got a good route," Peter promised, hopping in the driver's seat. "But I'd like to leave quickly just in case. Like I said, it's probably nothing. I quit intelligence a few years back after my partner was killed by a rogue MI6 agent. I left Berlin and moved down here. The pace is much slower. There's bottled waters by your seats and snacks if you care to partake. If we do get attacked, you'll find Rugers and extra ammunition under the seat. There's also some wonderful pamphlets on the history of Bavaria if you are interested. Buckle up."

Okay, the dude was a little weird and dedicated to his new job, but the guns were more than welcome. They could be hard to come by in Europe. In the States he could pick up a dozen like he was ordering donuts. Here, not so much. Peter would help them with that if it came to it.

He reached over and took Ariel's hand in his. "Don't worry. I promise we won't need those guns. It won't be like Toronto. Have I thanked you lately for saving me?"

"It was my pleasure," she responded in that seductive tone that got his motor revving hard. "And it would be nice to keep this whole mission violence free. I actually wouldn't mind doing some sight-seeing if we get the chance."

"I can show you all around the city," Rebecca promised. "Well, I can show you the parts around the medical district. I have to admit I didn't do a lot of touristy things while I was here."

"Workaholic," Owen said under his breath.

"It's true," Rebecca admitted. "But I do know some cafés in that part of town. There are tons of museums, and I've heard there's even a palace."

"Yes," Peter replied. "The Residenz is the largest palace in

Germany. It was once home to the Bavarian royal family, the Wittelsbachs. Fascinating history. I can arrange a tour if it's safe."

Tucker turned in his seat. "Seriously? I don't ever get to see sites. I get to see conference rooms and computer screens, and the only parts of Bliss I got to see were parts where people almost murdered us and a bar where Jax got laid and I did not get laid."

"You should be happy about that since the woman you were potentially getting laid with turned out to be the boss's ex-wife," he pointed out as Peter started driving through the small airport. He seemed to be taking a circuitous route. "Somehow I don't think Ezra would forgive you for that."

"I don't know why. He's not sleeping with her anymore. They're divorced." Tucker made it sound like a simple thing.

"I think it's all for the best that you and Solo didn't work out," Ariel said. "I believe you would have found her hard to handle."

"What's your take on her?" He hadn't asked Ariel her professional opinion. He'd been too busy trying to get his hands on her when she'd shown up in Toronto. After he'd gotten over being pissed she was there putting herself in danger, that is. "Ezra thinks she's the devil. River thinks she's misunderstood and only trying to get back her one true love. I can't really trust either of them when it comes to Solo. Too many personal feelings."

Her eyes briefly looked away and she was right back in professional mode. "I think Kimberly Solomon is a long-term operative, but one who has the best interests of her country and the people around her in mind. She could be quite ruthless when she needs to be, but I think she would have a difficult time hurting someone she liked or believed innocent, even if it meant giving up her mission."

"Levi Green thinks he's doing what's best for his country, too." Tucker sat back. "Every report I read talks about how he spouts patriotic bullshit right before he shoots one of my friends. I wonder if he writes that crap down."

"Oh, I got the same shite when he was trying to convince my Rebecca to go with him." Owen's Scottish accent had gone deeper, a sure sign he was emotional. "He should have been an actor."

"Or," Peter said, taking a right on the highway, "he's a true believer. That's the worst, I've found. I worked with a couple of them. They genuinely believed anything they did was for the betterment of Germany. They're ideologues. You can't argue with them and you can't bribe them because in their head, they're right. My country was led by one once. Did not turn out well. Did you know Bavaria was actually the birthplace of Nazism? It's not something we like to talk about, but it all began here."

"Ideologue. That's a good way to describe Levi," Ariel said. "He's also quite slippery. I wish I'd been able to take him out in Toronto. I worry the next time he'll have us in a position where we can't take the shot."

"You shouldn't have been shooting then." He got sick to his stomach when he thought about the situation she'd been left in. His gentle Ariel had been forced to take a rifle and save Becca and Owen. "You should have gotten the gun to Owen or called in Ezra. I hate that you had to do that."

"I was a bit tied up at the time," Owen pointed out.

"He was. To a chair." Rebecca managed to sound sunny despite how bad the memories must be. "He heroically took down that chair. It will never be used for evil again. So proud of you, babe."

Owen chuckled. "Well, *I* was proud of how Ari came in like an avenging angel and saved us. If she hadn't, it would have been me and whatever piece of that bloody chair I could have bashed Levi's skull with."

A single brow arched over her eyes, the one that told him he'd said something dumb. "Before you tell me I should have handed the gun over to anyone else, I doubt Rebecca would know which end of the gun to point."

"I'm really more of an intellectual," Rebecca admitted.

"I know that one." Tucker held his hand up.

"I wasn't trying to say you're not competent. I know you are." No McKay-Taggart and Knight employee would be allowed to stay incompetent. They were all trained in self-defense, but the non-ex-military or law enforcement employees were also trained to duck if they had the choice. "I'm saying we need better protocols in place. You should never have been left alone like that. He could have done anything to you."

Her expression softened. "But he didn't and we survived. You couldn't help the fact that he shot you, Rob. I was terrified when I woke up and I thought you were dying, but it didn't stop me from acting. I would do it all again tomorrow, though I would take the shot at Green if I had it."

"The good news is you won't have to do it again. Not while I'm here," he promised.

"And the bad news is, I've seen that car before," Peter announced.

Robert didn't glance back. He didn't want to give anything away and he was pleased Ariel seemed to have the same idea. "Can you lose him? When did he start following you?"

"Sometime after I left the city. I stopped by my office to pick up a few things and when I returned to the road here, I noticed that SUV behind me. I made note of the plate," Peter explained. "It's the same."

"We can't let him follow us back into town." He was already trying to come up with ways out of this mess. They couldn't go back to London without some information on Tucker.

"Or we could maneuver him into a position where he's trapped and then I can kill him." Owen sounded bloodthirsty.

"Babe, you can't do that." Rebecca was definitely the reasonable one in that relationship. "We need information from him. Torture him first, find out who he's working for and what he's supposed to do, and then you can kill him."

Or not so reasonable.

"Didn't you take a Hippocratic oath?" Ariel asked, managing to be amused despite the fact that they were being followed.

Were any of them going to take this seriously? Had they forgotten what had happened the last time they'd been in a car together and someone had come after them?

"Hey, it's going to be okay," Ariel said. "Are you honestly surprised someone's watching us? I wish I could get a look at the driver."

He wasn't going to risk it. Not with Ariel in the car. This time she could be the one getting shot.

Up ahead he saw a sign for fresh vegetables and a small roadside stand. "Pull in there. He won't be able to stop without giving himself away. He'll have to drive on and turn around. We can make a crazy dangerous U-turn and drive into town from a different direction."

"When did asparagus go white?" Tucker was staring at the sign for the stand. It was a cute hand-painted sign announcing the stand's offerings. "Is it an albino asparagus?"

"It's called *Spargel,*" Robert replied without thinking about it. "It's delicious. It tastes like sweet corn. It's the only asparagus I can handle. We used to eat it with ham."

He stopped as the car did. He'd never seen *Spargel* before. Not once. The Garden's cooks had never offered anything like it with a meal and yet he could taste it on his tongue. How did he know he ate it with ham, and what had he meant by "we"? It was there, that hint of what lay behind the veil separating his brain from the now and then, the one he could never quite push back except in his dreams when he…

When he wrapped his hands around her throat and knew he wouldn't stop until she was gone.

"Robert? The car's gone past." Ariel had a hand on his arm, concern clear in her eyes. "Are you all right?"

A sharp pain bit through his brain, a clear warning. But it was right there. He could see his hands reaching for a fork, felt the anticipation. It was close, everything he'd worked so hard for.

"Peter, you should get us out of here as soon as you can without killing us."

He could hear Ariel talking, but she wasn't what he saw. He was somewhere else, getting flashes of clear blue sky and the smell of motor oil. Laughter was all around him, and so was a mixture of excitement and dread. It was actually happening. His first…

Pain screamed through him and the world was suddenly far too bright, like the earth had been encompassed in the whitest light.

Someone touched him, a cooling hand on his head.

"Robert, it's all right. Let it go. We'll write it all down and figure this out another way. You have what you need from the memory. Let it go," Ariel said, soothing him. "Let it go and come back to me."

But he was trapped in the moment and the memory was right there. His first what? It was important. He wasn't alone. He was surrounded and he could hear their laughter, feel the camaraderie. He had people who cared about him. Who were they?

"Robert, listen to my voice." Through the haze of pain, he could hear Rebecca talking to him. "I need you to do what we've been practicing. When you get caught like this, you think about something else. Something real."

Rebecca had begun working with all of them to try to better process whatever memories they did get. The first thing they should do was let it go, ride the wave gently and not lock onto it. He'd gone past that now.

"You need to remember something that's happened since you were rescued. Something easily accessible." Rebecca's voice soothed. "Let go of this one and find someplace where her training can't touch you."

Or he would be horrifically ill for days.

Something real. He had to get back.

London, England
2 years before

The drama was a lot to take, and now he'd pissed Erin off. It wasn't his fault he was interested in her sex stories. He envied Theo Taggart for having sex stories to remember. Oh sure remembering this one had sent Theo into a night of puking up his guts and holding his head, but at least it proved he'd had sex.

"I think we should give those two some time," a feminine voice said.

Dr. Ariel Adisa came to stand beside him at the small buffet that had been laid out for this morning's conference. He liked the British team. Not that McKay-Taggart in Dallas didn't occasionally cater in, but it was always something easy like donuts or bagels. Someone had cooked all this goodness and presented them with care. It was elegant and graceful.

A bit like the woman standing beside him.

"Yes, that was a bit uncomfortable, and believe me I've gotten used to the two of them fighting," he replied. Since they'd been rescued in Africa, Theo had been having a hard time fitting in. He didn't remember his previous life, and that included the woman he'd been in love with, Erin. Finding out he had a kid hadn't helped, though Robert didn't see the problem. TJ Taggart was cute as a button and Erin was...he was going to say strong, but that didn't really describe Erin. She was a Valkyrie bitch goddess who could cut a man down to size with her mere stare. What she could do with actual weapons was far worse. He was a little grateful for Erin and Theo's argument now because it gave him a chance to stare at the gorgeous woman beside him.

"He's having trouble reintegrating?"

Robert was having trouble thinking. Words. He was supposed to say words. It was hard when mostly what he wanted to do was get his hands on her. She had the most beautiful eyes. They were big and kind, and he could get a little lost in those. "I think we're both having some trouble. It's weird, you know. I recognize that Danish. I know what to call it, but I can't remember if I ever had one before today."

"Your situation is unique. I've been reading up on it. The closest I can come is complete retrograde amnesia, and even then most of the time someone remembers the victim. They're not left completely alone. They almost always have a family member who can come forward and fill in the blanks."

Like Erin was trying to do for Theo when he wasn't being a stubborn ass. Robert didn't have that. No one had come for him. No one was looking for him. "That's not going to happen for me. According to the Taggarts, they can't tell I existed at all before Moth...Dr. McDonald caught me. I'm trying to view the whole situation as the ultimate do-over. Much of my life now revolves around trying to figure out what foods I like."

"That has to be hard, Robert. I hope you'll let me help."

Robert *was* hard. So freaking hard, and he would love to let Ariel help him with that. When had he turned into this horny as hell asshole who couldn't look at a woman without thinking about getting her in bed? He talked about being horny all the time, but she was the first woman he'd responded to this way. Visceral. Primal. A voice in the back of his head whispering that she could be his if he pursued her, if he didn't give up.

So he was an obsessive stalker. He learned something new about himself every day.

"I don't know how long I'll be here, but I've promised my therapist back in Dallas I would keep up with regular sessions," he explained. He didn't want to talk about therapy. He wanted to pretend for ten seconds that he wasn't some damaged reject who needed daily sessions in order to function. He wanted to be a man who'd met a lovely woman at work and he could spend the day flirting with her and coaxing her into going out with him. He wanted to pretend he could take her out to lunch to one of the cafés that he'd seen from the car, where people sat in the sun and talked and ate and drank a beer and had a life.

He wasn't that guy.

"Excellent," she said. "We can start tomorrow. I think you'll like it here. Are you going to apply for Master rights?"

He hadn't thought about the fact that like the Dallas office, the London team was attached to a BDSM club. He'd seen The Garden the night before but there had been a ton of Erin and Theo drama and it hadn't really hit him that he might be able to play while he was here.

Before he could answer, Ariel was shaking her head. "Or just rights to the club. We can always welcome another submissive."

He felt his shoulders straighten and he was suddenly a bit taller than he'd been before. "I'm not a sub, sub."

Sure enough her eyes shifted away from his. "I'm sorry, Sir. You never know these days."

"No, I'm sorry. We're not in the club. I pulled some Dom bullshit on you and I promised I wouldn't do that. I've met some Doms who need to be in charge all the time and I'm not that type of top." He was still figuring out the BDSM stuff, but he liked it. It had done exactly what Kai had promised. It had helped him find his center in one place in his out of control life.

God, what would this woman look like in fet wear?

Her lips curled up in the most delicious smile. "Then I'll expect to see you on the dungeon floor, Sir. But remember I'm in charge in my office. We'll have to find you the right play partner. I'll think about it. I know all the subs. Lovely women. I'm going to get some coffee. See you later, Robert."

She walked away and he couldn't help but watch her. She was

the only sub he would want.

And naturally she was the one he couldn't have. Because she was going to be his therapist. She was going to listen to all his sad stories and tell him his life would turn out fine in the end if he was simply honest with himself. She would come up with ways to help him cope, and they wouldn't involve shoving his cock deep inside her and riding her until he couldn't any more and he filled her up.

"Uhm, Mr. McClellan, perhaps some ice water for you?" Damon Knight shook his head. "You don't seem to need our coffee or tea to get warm."

Damn it. He turned toward the wall to hide the fact that his slacks were tenting.

Knight chuckled and said something about wouldn't this be interesting.

He reached for the water and took a deep drink. He definitely needed to cool off.

Robert took a deep breath and reality seemed to come back to him. He wasn't where he'd been before. He'd been in the seat beside Ariel. Now he sat on the floor of the van, his head in her lap. She'd used one of the water bottles on him. His hair was wet, but the cool water had likely kept him from throwing up all over the van.

"Hey, are you all right, love?" Ariel stared down at him with worried eyes.

He managed to nod.

"It worked?" Rebecca asked.

"Yes. I'm better. Sorry." He hated feeling vulnerable. He got back to his seat and glanced out the window. They were going super fast down what looked like an ultra-modern highway.

"It was the asparagus," Tucker said. "It makes me sick, too."

"Don't mention it so soon," Ariel admonished.

"Did we lose the tail?" He couldn't think about what had happened or he would be right back in trouble again. He hated Hope McDonald.

"Absolutely." Tucker gave him a thumbs-up. "Peter here is a race car driver and I learned that exits ramps are ass farts."

"*Ausfahrt*, Mr. Tucker," Peter corrected. "And it's good to have you back with us, Mr. McClellan. I'll have us in Munich in no time at all."

Tucker laughed and he noticed Owen was grinning. Morons. But it made him smile.

"Did you find a good memory to hold on to?" Ariel asked.

He reached for her hand. He didn't have to be a macho asshole about this. He'd gotten sick. She'd been there for him. "The best."

He sat back and relaxed. It wasn't how he'd hoped to start the mission, but as long as she was here with him, what could possibly go wrong?

Chapter Three

Ariel stood outside the pretty building that looked absolutely nothing like the hotel she knew Robert had booked their rooms at. They were on a quiet street in the city that their driver had explained was one of Munich's more upscale neighborhoods. The building looked like something out of a movie with its gold and green façade. She half expected a Victorian lady to step out for her daily walk.

Robert had his hands on his hips, staring up at the four-story building. "This is not the Charles Hotel. Is this where Big Tag decided to put up Dante and Sasha?"

Peter nodded and gestured toward the building. "Yes, this is where Mr. Taggart chose to house you. It's mine. Well, mine and Lina's. We don't actually live here, but you'll find the accommodations quite suitable."

She wasn't sure that was a good idea. "I don't know that we should break up the team."

Tucker had his duffel bag over his shoulder as he looked up at the building. "I'm okay with staying here. It looks pretty sweet. Which floor are we on? Are there neighbors? Are any of them women?"

Dear lord. She should have warned their hosts about Tucker's insatiable need to flirt. And do other things with every woman available. Especially hookers. Did she have any cash, and could that be expensed? There was a reason she'd been happy to let Kayla act as mother hen to the lads all this time. "Tucker, try to remember we're working."

He glanced back at her and that grim look she'd seen in his eyes so often lately was back. "I promise I won't forget we're trying to figure out how evil I am."

Yes, maybe she would find a couple of women for him. Perhaps Peter could help. It couldn't possibly be the oddest request he'd ever received.

"We can't break up," Robert argued. "I got us all rooms at a hotel near the city center. I'm in charge of logistics and everything is set up. We'll pick up Dante and Sasha and be out of your hair."

"I canceled the rooms," Peter said as if he were commenting on the weather. "You will stay here. It's much easier. Big Tag told me to use my brain. My brain tells me you should all stay here. We're closer to Kronberg. It makes sense for you to be here if anyone in intelligence discovers you are in Germany."

"You did what?" Robert asked, his voice going icy cold.

She stepped beside him, putting a hand on his arm. Robert was one of the most reasonable men she'd ever met. He tended to be cool and calm under pressure, but he'd had a day. He also took great pride in his work and didn't like having his plans go awry. Peter was pushing some of his buttons and she needed to make sure he didn't explode. "Peter, I think what Robert is asking is what happened that you would change his plans. He does handle logistics for our group and he's excellent at his job."

"I think what Robert's asking is how Peter would like to be murdered," Owen countered with a grin. He looked like he was excited about whatever was going to happen next.

"The answer to this is not at all, though if I had to choose I would pick head shot from a distance and completely out of the blue," Peter replied, utterly nonplussed. "I've thought about this much. It's why I got out of intelligence."

"We're staying here and not the hotel?" Rebecca adjusted her hot-pink cardigan as she slipped her arm through Owen's. "I was looking forward to it. It looked really nice."

Peter frowned. “My place is nice, too. Well, it was before you sent along the slobs. You must tell them they have to clean up after themselves. I am not a maid. And I changed the plans because the hotel isn’t secure enough.”

“They require a key to use the elevators.” Robert had spent time working on the plans. She’d watched him as he’d carefully laid out their accommodations. “Do you think I didn’t check it out? I had us on the eighth floor. You literally can’t get to that floor without a key to a room on the eighth floor, and I reserved them all.”

Peter closed the trunk door with a thud. “And I happen to know that German intelligence keeps an operative at that particular hotel. His name is Sebastian and he’s a bartender. He’s excellent at getting intelligence from the many, many wealthy and powerful people who stay there. They usually stay on the eighth floor.”

“Fuck,” Robert cursed.

“Well, we would have checked for bugs,” Owen pointed out, in sympathy with his brother. “We’re not foolish. We’ve got a full complement of anti-spy tech.”

Robert nodded, obviously strengthened by Owen’s words. “You’re right. We have protocols to deal with this type of situation. And we’ll stay out of the bar. I picked that hotel for a reason. Thank you for letting us know what to look out for. We’ll take Dante and Sasha off your hands.”

Ariel hated the fact that she was going to have to be the bad guy, but in this case Robert wasn’t being reasonable. It was precisely what she’d worried about when she’d made the decision to try a relationship with him. “Peter, would you take the others in and show them around? I’m sure we could all use some time to clean up.”

“Of course,” Peter said, walking to the door. “I think you’ll find we have everything you could need right here. Let me tell you a little about the history of the building.”

Rebecca sent her a sympathetic look as she, Owen, and Tucker followed Peter into the house through what looked to be the back door.

“I think we should talk to Ian about that man,” Robert began. “We don’t need a guide who walks in thinking he’s in charge of this mission.”

She stepped in front of Robert, lowering her voice. "I think given what happened on the highway, we should consider staying here."

"I know your first instinct is to please those around you and you're a bit conflict averse, but I'll take care of this." Robert put his hands on her shoulders. "I think we'll be more comfortable at the hotel. It's only a few days. I promise we'll be careful."

"I'm not at all conflict averse." That might be a lie. She wasn't normally. Conflict was natural, though she didn't want to be in conflict with him. "And yes, I prefer to please, but Rob, I'm not a doormat."

His hands came up to cup her face. "I know that. But I want to make this as easy on you as possible. You haven't really been out in the field, and it can get stressful. I want you to understand that I'll take care of you."

It was sweet of him. "I've been in the field before. You don't have to worry about me. Let's talk about this. What Peter said makes sense."

His hands came down as if he realized affection wasn't going to win this argument. "We don't know this man. We have no idea what his motivations are."

He was trying to save their time together. She knew exactly what he was doing. "Ian knows him, and we have to trust Ian. He told us to listen to Peter. I know you had plans and they were lovely. But we can't take the chance. We have to think about Tucker. If German intelligence figures out who he is, they might decide to use him as leverage to get Big Tag or Damon to share information with them. We need to be as careful as possible."

"I can handle it."

She hated it, but she had to put her foot down. "We're not going to the hotel. We're staying here."

Robert's eyes went stony. "Are you saying that as the head of this team?"

"Yes." She wished he hadn't forced her into this position. "Yes, I am."

"Then I'll get us moved in." Robert turned and grabbed his bag. He picked up hers as well. "Lead the way."

He'd lost his soothing tones. "Robert, we should talk."

"If you're worried about anyone seeing us here, we should get inside. Apparently we have nowhere else to go. I suspect Peter is going to suggest we stay inside tonight, so I'll cancel our dinner reservations."

"Is this some sort of punishment?"

"Would you suggest you and I go out when no one else apparently can without some serious oversight?"

He kept putting her in that corner. "No. I think it would be unfair for us to be the only ones allowed out. But we're not going to hide the whole time. Rebecca needs to be in that café tomorrow to meet with the researcher from Kronberg. Honestly, we should probably spend the evening going over those plans. It might be a good idea to wait until we get back to London to revisit the state of our relationship."

He stared at her with suspicious eyes. "Now that sounds like punishment."

"It's not meant that way. We need to consider what's happening. We're having our first argument and it's affecting the team."

"Not at all. We're doing exactly what you think we should. I'll go find my room." He strode toward the door.

She would have followed him but her mobile vibrated. She pulled it from her pocket and sighed at the text. Kim. It was from a number Ariel knew she kept for personal use.

Smooth moves on the highway, Ari. But we need to talk. I'll be around. And have fun in the sex club!

Sex club?

Today was definitely not going the way she'd planned. She sighed and followed Robert into their temporary home.

* * * *

Robert stepped into the house and looked around. He'd expected to walk into an elegant foyer, but the place actually did look a lot like a hotel lobby. There was a front desk and a sleek laptop sitting on top. There were a couple of seats off to his left and a bar to the right.

What kind of house was this? From the outside it had looked perfectly normal, but most houses didn't have reception desks.

He walked down the center hallway toward the sound of voices but not before glancing back to make sure Ariel had gotten inside.

He could have made it work. She hadn't listened to him at all. The first chance she'd gotten, she'd taken control from him, and wasn't that the way his life went.

They were being too cautious and didn't understand that it was starting to rankle. His men were starting to feel suffocated. It was always the same rooms, same jobs, with no hope for anything changing. It was starting to get to him, too, but he'd had some light at the end of the tunnel with Ariel.

Now he would be lucky if she talked to him about anything but the job.

She closed the door behind her and he found himself at the end of the hall looking into a familiar place.

Tucker stood in the middle of a dungeon, his arms spread wide. "Well at least it feels like home."

They were in a club. Naturally.

"Welcome to Halsbänder," Peter said, back to his normally cheery self. "This is a club my wife and I founded a few years ago. In English, you would call it Collars. It's closed tonight, but tomorrow we're open and we're happy to extend you the same rights you have at The Garden."

"Does Big Tag know anyone who doesn't own a club he can stash us in?" Owen asked. "Surely someone he knows runs a pet store or is an apartment building manager. It ain't normal to know this many perverts."

Rebecca sent her boyfriend a glare. "You're one of those perverts."

Owen shrugged. "Precisely why I can call us all perverts."

Tucker sat down on a spanking bench. "This is normal to me. I could nap right here. This is like a couch to me. There is something wrong with that."

Halsbänder wasn't as opulent as The Garden nor as technologically advanced as Sanctum. It was an old-school dungeon but it was neat and clean, done in lush colors. It seemed to branch off into smaller rooms, likely scene spaces and specific fetish rooms.

Yes, same place, different country.

"The dungeon is obviously here on the first floor. The second floor serves as the club's offices and the research library for my tour guide business," Peter explained. "I have many, many books on the history of Bavaria in there if you should want something to read. Well, and if you can read in German."

"Do you have a bunch of books on spanking?" Tucker asked, making himself cozy on the spanking bench. It looked like it was set up for a scene, or perhaps the intensely large purple dildo on a tray not far from Tucker's head was merely there for aesthetic purposes. Tucker didn't even wince.

"Of course, but those are in German, too." Peter started toward the stairs in the back. "Your rooms are on the third floor. You'll find a fully stocked kitchen there and a media room. My wife and I lived here for a few years, but she now prefers the country."

"Let me guess, all the movies are in German," Owen deadpanned.

"You have not seen the *Avengers* until you've seen it in German. It's an excellent dub," Peter promised. "Come along and I'll show you where I've put you. Mr. McClellan, you'll need to share with Mr. Tucker. I've got Dante and Sasha in one room, Owen and Rebecca in one and Dr. Adisa in her own."

And she would sleep alone because he no longer had a shot at coaxing her into bed.

It might be a good idea to wait until we get back to London to revisit the state of our relationship.

Wasn't that what they always did? One step forward and two steps back. When one of them was ready, the other wasn't.

She moved toward him and took her suitcase out of his hand. "I'll go settle in. I'll see you at dinner."

He watched as she strode up the stairs with Rebecca and Peter.

Owen looked over at Robert. "It's not that bad."

"Of course you would say that." Dante's voice always sounded tortured, like someone had torn up his throat and he'd never fully recovered. They suspected he was from somewhere in the Eastern Bloc. He spoke Hungarian, Polish, and English. "You get to leave The Garden on a regular basis. It doesn't matter to you that we're stuck in a cage again."

He looked to his left and saw what he hadn't before. Dante was standing in the shadows. He peeled away and joined the rest of them. He was wearing his normal uniform of a black T-shirt and dark-wash jeans. He rarely wore anything else.

"I thought we were moving to some swanky hotel." Sasha was with him. He had a beer in his hand. They were almost one hundred percent certain he was Russian. It was hard to mistake that accent. "You promised us this would be a different trip." He gestured around the room. "It looks very much the same to me. Dante and I have been holed up with the German, who is far too invested in his own history."

What was he supposed to say? He didn't hold the power here. He hadn't truly had any power in…ever when he thought about it. Was this the rest of their lives? Shut up in dungeons, hidden from the world as much as possible because the world wanted to take a bite out of them again. "We got followed from the airport."

Dante rolled his eyes. "Of course you did. Someone always seems to know where we are. Have we asked the proper questions about why this is?"

Owen glanced up the stairs like he wanted to make sure the women couldn't hear them. "And what would those questions be?"

Dante looked at Owen, his eyes narrowing. "I think this should be a discussion amongst the four of us. You should go find your pretty girlfriend and make sure she's safe. There are some unsavory elements around here, after all. I would make sure to lock the bedroom door."

Sasha sighed and stepped forward as Owen's eyes flared and he went from happy-go-lucky guy to raging revenge machine in a heartbeat.

"You lay a hand on my Becca and I'll show you the inside of your own arsehole," Owen promised.

Sasha waved a hand. "He didn't mean this, Owen. No one is going to harm the doctor who is trying to help us. That would be rather foolish of us. Let's all calm down."

He didn't feel calm.

"Guys, this place isn't that bad." Tucker had sat up. "They even have a media room, and no one has to clean toilets."

"You might think differently if you walk into one after Dante's morning ablutions." Sasha seemed to think the potential for real violence was gone. He walked fully into the dungeon. "The fridge is stocked with beer. If there's one thing we can get in this country, it's good beer. But Dante is right. Someone is watching us always, and we should figure out why that is. They find us very quickly."

"They did not find us at all, Sasha," Dante pointed out. "It wasn't until the new group gets here that we're suddenly in danger and can't move about like normal humans."

"Do you have something to say to me?" Owen didn't look like he was ready to give up the fight yet.

Robert moved to a place where he could easily get in between the two men. It wouldn't be the first time he'd gotten caught up in a family fistfight.

Of course, from what he understood about the way Tucker, Dante, Sasha, and Jax had been trained, there had been a lot of violence between them. He'd been in what McDonald had called her alpha team. There had only been three men in their unit—he and Victor and Theo Taggart. The rest had been the unit she tested her therapies on before giving them to the alphas. They'd been trained like fighting dogs, and only the strongest had survived.

"Sasha's right. We need to calm down." He knew they'd been moving toward this. What had happened in Colorado and then Toronto had to be addressed. "Our host believes someone followed him. We have a tag and we're going to look into it. This is a couple of days and then we'll head home. I promise I'm going to talk to Damon about loosening up the leash. They're only being cautious."

"That's good, Rob." Tucker always backed him up. "Maybe we can have some boys' nights out."

"Maybe we could have some actual fucking freedom," Sasha said under his breath.

"You know why that's not allowed. You're both wanted by Interpol. The fact that you haven't been turned over is reason enough to know we're safe here." This was the fight he hadn't told Ariel about. It was something between the six of them.

"Or McKay-Taggart is playing a game and we are the pawns," Sasha said. "Think about it…"

Dante's face went tight and he elbowed his partner. "Not here. Not with him here."

"Are you actually talking about me?" Owen asked. "You honestly believe I'm…what? Selling us all out to Levi Green? Selling us out to the arsehole who tried to take my girlfriend from me and sell me to MSS for experimentation?"

"We only have your word for it," Dante pointed out. "Yours and Dr. Walsh. How can any of you trust a doctor again? Any of them. I think we should point out that our kind Dr. Adisa showed up in Toronto just in time for the Agency to make an appearance. I wonder why that was."

Oh, his reasonable soul was being tested today. "What exactly are you trying to say, Dante?"

Tucker was the one moving now. He placed himself between Robert and Dante. "He's being an ass like normal. Come on. We've all had a rough day. Let's settle in and grab a beer."

"Yes, ignoring the problem has worked well to this point." Sasha took a long drag off his bottle. "You know I'm sure the big boys are telling everyone it must be one of us. One of us has to be the one selling out the team, but I think it's one of them."

"Why? Why would anyone in the company sell us out?" He couldn't believe it. McKay-Taggart had worked hard to free them.

"I can think of several reasons," Dante said. "Money being the chief. But there are others. Have we considered that perhaps not everyone cut ties to their former agencies? Perhaps there are some divided loyalties. It's why I feel Owen shouldn't be considered one of us. His ties to the company run deep. He spends as much time with Nick Markovic as he does with us."

"I'm sorry I'm not damaged enough for you, mate." Owen slapped Rob on the shoulder. "I think I'll go find Rebecca. You know where I'll be if you need me. Good luck chasing down conspiracy theories."

He started up the stairs but not before he'd flipped off Dante.

"You can't shut him out because he wasn't tortured as long as the rest of us." Tucker squared off against the duo. "Owen's been through a lot, too, and he's always been loyal to us."

"Says the man who started out as the one who tortured us." Dante stood. "As the first of us, I was tortured more than any of you bastards. I see things you do not. Think about it. Ariel was in both

Toronto and she was here. I happen to know she was kept updated on the mission to Colorado. She knew when Jax went into the woods. Of course, Ezra is an even better candidate. Keeping his old friends in the loop would be an excellent way to get back to the Agency."

"You don't stop at all, do you?" Tucker asked.

"If it's not one of them," Dante began, "then it is one of us. I can handle it from one of them. I would understand if it was one of them. If it is one of us…"

He whistled as he walked away.

Sasha stood. "He's got it in his head that we're being held prisoner again."

"That's ridiculous."

"Is it? We might not be forced to fight each other but we cannot leave and we must do what our betters tell us to do," Sasha said, walking to the stairs Dante had recently disappeared up. "It feels not so different to me."

"Then we remember that time very differently." The situation was getting dangerous if those two honestly believed being safe was as bad as being held by a woman who routinely tormented every one of them. "When we get back to The Garden we'll have a team meeting. We shouldn't do this without Jax."

"Jax knows who he is." Sasha's tone was spiked with bitterness. "And he's got a pretty wife to keep him company. I've got Dante."

"Then let's get the information we need to find out who we are and get some power in this game. I promise you, I won't allow anyone to use us. There's a life for every single one of us when this is done." He had to believe it.

Sasha stopped and emotion tightened his face for a moment. "I will hold you to that."

He held out his hand. Sasha was often the toughest of his "brothers" to get to. Dante would shrug and go back to drinking during an argument, but Sasha would shut down. "See that you do."

Sasha reached out and gripped his hand. "I'll go and see if I can talk to him. Or get enough liquor in him that he's all right to be around. I'll make sure he comes to dinner."

He strode up the stairs and Robert looked to Tucker. He knew exactly the words that had gotten to him. It had likely been a direct hit. "We have no idea if you ever set foot in either of the off-site bases where she kept the men. Where she kept us. We only know that you worked with her at Kronberg."

"We don't know that I didn't," Tucker replied. He shook his head. "I don't want to think about that now. What happened with Ari? One minute she was holding your hand and then she had that blank look on her face women get when they're hurt and don't want to show it."

"I hurt her? She was the one who told me we shouldn't have a relationship while we were working together," he shot back.

"What had you done before she said that?"

Fuck. "I was pissy about not getting to go to the hotel. I pretty much told her she could be my girlfriend or my boss. I was an asshole."

"You had a rough afternoon."

He shook his head. "That's not an excuse. I don't get to have a bad day and make hers bad, too." He thought about the problem for a moment. There was a way to make both their days better. "Hey, didn't Peter say there was a kitchen here?"

"Yeah."

"Show me."

Chapter Four

"She didn't tell me when she would contact me," Ariel said quietly over the secure line. "I think we have more problems than Kim hanging around."

"Solo hanging around might be the best of our problems." Damon's upper-crust British accent came over the line. "Ian and I have been discussing the fact that if Solo is getting cheeky, it might mean she's got more leeway. I agree with Ian's assessment. Solo is likely working for a group that could be very friendly to us."

"Then let me tell the lads." Not telling Robert was killing her. She'd overheard a bit of the argument he'd had with the rest of the Lost Boys. She wasn't proud of eavesdropping but there had been a weird vibe in the room, a simmering anger she couldn't deny.

"And risk one of them contacting Green? I think he's on the ropes with the new developments. I think it would be a mistake to bring this out into the open if what we fear is true and we've got a leak. Look, talk to Solo if she contacts you again. Try to get her to tell you what's happening on her end of this. I don't think she's a physical danger to the lads."

"She's not. She got close in Colorado. If her plans had been to take one of them for physical testing or questioning, she could have done it then."

"Excellent. Then you're not keeping anything from them that could hurt them. This is how this game is played, Ari. We're almost done. I can feel it." Damon was quiet for a moment. "We're close to making some breakthroughs. Theo Taggart won't tell me exactly what he's got, but he thinks he's close to convincing a woman who worked for Hope McDonald's father to talk to us. We believe Senator McDonald used his place as the head of the Armed Forces Committee to funnel soldiers into his daughter's program. I sent you a report on the initial findings. You should feel free to share that. They need to know we're doing everything we can to identify them so once we have the leverage, we can get the charges dropped against each of them. When we do that, they can go home."

The thought of Robert going home made her heart ache. His home was in The Garden. She wanted his home to be with her. "That would only cover the American military."

"We're not sure. McDonald had deep ties across the globe thanks to his connections to The Collective."

The Collective had been an illuminati-like group of corporations who had set about manipulating global governments and systems to enrich themselves. Kronberg had long been rumored to be a part of it. The Collective itself had retreated, but she had no doubt they would simply lick their wounds and resurface some time down the line. "So we might soon be able to give our lads their real names."

"That's the hope," Damon assured her. "Do what you need to do to keep their spirits up."

"It didn't help that we're stuck in a club again."

Damon chuckled. "I've heard it's nice. And the neighborhood is quiet enough that you should be able to have a bit of freedom. They can take walks, go out for meals, but make sure they never go alone. And tell Robert next time he plans to seduce one of my employees he should do it in a hotel that's not monitored by the local intelligence agency."

"I'm certainly not going to tell him that. He was upset enough that his plans got ruined."

"Are you sure you want to jump into this now?" Damon asked. "If Theo's right, we could find his family soon."

It would be smarter to hold off. She knew it logically. She'd spent her whole life being careful. "I think it's safe to say that being stuck in a club with everyone around us successfully put a kibosh on the date."

"I'm sorry, dear. It's probably for the best."

It was and yet she felt lonely at the thought of not spending time with him tonight. Despite today's man fit, Robert was usually the nicest man she'd ever met. Oh, she wasn't fooled by his placid demeanor. She knew there was war going on inside him, but the core of the man was solid.

She wondered if he understood that. She'd always thought his hesitation came from the rubbish idea that he could hurt her physically.

He often forgot who she was. And then there was that part of her he didn't know about at all.

There was a knock on her door. She glanced to the clock. It was getting late. The pizza had likely arrived. She didn't want pizza. She wanted to start the day again and not have any of this hanging over them. When she'd gotten on that plane, she'd been filled with anticipation, and all of it was gone now. She'd expected dinner to be a quiet affair with only her and Robert. Now she would have to referee between Owen and Dante. She needed to get the whole group together for a session to get at the underlying problem.

"I've got to go, Damon."

"Be safe."

She hung up her mobile and slipped it into her pocket before answering the door. She'd expected Rebecca or Owen, but it was Robert who stood in her doorway.

And he looked delicious. He'd changed out of his traveling clothes into a set of perfectly pressed black slacks, a snowy white dress shirt, and blue tie. It should have looked staid. It would have on most men, but on Robert it made her wonder what she would see when she peeled off all those clothes.

She had a damn degree in psychology and it didn't mean anything when her hormones got involved.

"Hey, I know I acted like a massive asshole earlier today." He had a grim look on his face that changed to charming when he brought his hand around from his back and showed her the perfect white rose he offered her. "Would you please let me make up for it?"

There were a thousand reasons to say no. She could do it gently. She could remind him that the first chance they'd had to prove they could manage a relationship and still work together they'd blown. She could point out that there was still the hope of a cure out there.

Or you could live in the moment, my love. You could stop being so in that head of yours and let yourself feel.

Sometimes she could still hear her father's wise voice in her head. He'd done so much, taken so many chances to bring his family to a better place.

"Ariel, please. I'm sorry I treated you like that. I took out my bad day on you and it wasn't fair. I wanted our night together. I planned it all out, but I forgot that the only really important part of the night wasn't the restaurant or the hotel. It was that we got to be together. Be with me for a while."

She took the rose from his hand, all thoughts of why this was a bad idea flying out of her head. "Yes."

But she wasn't nearly as dressed as he was. "Give me a minute to change."

He shook his head. "You look beautiful and we're only going to the kitchen."

"You dressed for the occasion."

"I was also the asshole who challenged the authority of my commander in the field. Trust me, I like this far better than dropping to the floor and giving you a hundred like I…" He shook his head. "Not going there."

She stepped in, putting a hand on his face. "It's okay. Let the visual piece go and tell me what you felt."

He pressed his cheek against her hand. "No therapist stuff tonight. I promise I'll write it down later and talk to Kai about it, but I want you to stop thinking about me as a patient. This can't work if you don't. Please come to the kitchen with me. I managed to shove everyone else in the media room. They're watching a football match. Well, Rebecca is reading on her e-reader and rolling her eyes when the guys yell at the screen, but the kitchen is on the opposite end of the floor. I promise it's quiet there."

She was still in the slacks and blouse she'd worn this afternoon. They were casual and comfortable. Certainly not something she would wear on a date. Robert was far better dressed for the occasion.

A vision of a private dinner where he was in a suit and she was wearing absolutely nothing floated across her brain. Sir wouldn't want her in clothes. Sir would want to see nothing but her own skin so he could touch her everywhere, whenever he pleased. They could spend long hours like that. She wouldn't worry about anything at all but pleasing her dominant partner.

"Come on." He used that deep voice on her she'd heard him use at The Garden. Like her, Robert spent at least one night each weekend playing. She'd seen him paired up with some of her friends, but never had he taken one to a privacy room or up to his flat.

She hadn't indulged herself in sex in a long time.

She followed him down the hallway and sure enough, heard someone yelling from the far end about a ref's call. Poor Rebecca.

Robert led her away from it, his loafers making no sound over the carpet. This part of the club was comfortable, much more like a home than downstairs, and it made her wonder if Peter often had guests he put up here. She'd talked briefly to the man and he appeared to be very interested in teaching and training new D/s couples.

Were she and Robert going to be a D/s couple?

She stopped that line of thinking. This was nothing more than a pleasant way to spend an evening with a man she liked enormously.

With a man she might be falling in love with.

Why couldn't she let things be? Why did she always have to look past the now?

"Hey, if I didn't know better I would think you're the one whose stuck in a nasty memory loop in your head. Are you all right? I'm not frightening you, am I?"

She rolled her eyes. "You have to stop treating me like I'm a delicate flower who wilts in direct sunlight. You don't frighten me at all. You frustrate me at times because I think you hold back on me. You see me as something I'm not, and I worry that could be a problem."

"Something you're not?"

Maybe it was best to get the uncomfortable discussion out of the way. "You view me as a savior."

"I do not."

"It's nothing to be ashamed of, but if we're going to have a real relationship, you have to see me for the woman I am. I'm not delicate. I'm flawed and human. I can't be on a pedestal. Women placed on pedestals always fall off them."

"You think I see you with some kind of halo around your head?" he asked. "You didn't save me. The Taggarts did, and I assure you when I see Big Tag I'm mostly annoyed by his sarcasm. I don't have a deep desire to throw myself at his feet. I'm grateful, but gratitude isn't what I feel for you. If I put you on a pedestal it would be because I could fuck you better there."

Her breath hitched. "Robert."

He shook his head. "Don't. You started this when you accused me of putting you in the Madonna role. I didn't meet you and immediately think 'this woman can fix my soul.' I met you and got a hard-on. I met you and thought 'this woman can fix my cock because she's the single sexiest woman I've ever met.' I don't know about your other patients. I'm sure many fall in love with you because you're an angel, but I want to bring out the devil in you. I want the dirty, nasty Ariel who will rock my world not with the power of her mind—but with every drop of the sexuality I intend to bring out in you. That's the memory I clung to this afternoon. That's what saved me. The filthy thoughts that went through my head seconds after meeting you."

She remembered that moment quite differently. He'd been charming and seemed a bit lost. "But we were at a morning meeting. We were in the conference room."

"And I got a hard-on that Damon told me I should put away because I wouldn't be needing it. I never wanted you to be my therapist. I did it because I didn't think it would be good for you to be my lover. We're never going to work well together. My first thought is always going to be to protect you, and that's not because I don't think you're competent. I know you've had all the classes."

"You know I was Scotland Yard before I joined the team." A lie, but one that had been established before she'd even met him.

"Yes, I do, and they likely gave you all the self-defense training you could ever want, but I'm a man who cares about you. Tell me when I go in the field you're not thinking of me."

She'd been terrified the whole time he was away. "You know I do. I worry."

"I didn't want you to come with us to Colorado because I knew it could get dangerous. After how you took care of me in Toronto, I have to shove that scared part of myself back. I thought I was going to die, and my biggest regret was never taking a chance with you. Let me take a chance with you tonight."

She had to be honest with him about the few things she could. "I just got off the phone with Damon and he thinks he might be close to finding someone who can tell us who you are."

He stared down at her, his hazel eyes warm. "I am Robert McClellan. That's who I am. I'm curious about who I used to be but I know deep inside that I'm not that person anymore. I'm the man you see before you."

"But we don't know if you left anyone behind." It was a thought that kept her up at night, that some other woman was pining for him.

"A wife would have looked for me. No one looked for me. If I left behind kids, would that disqualify me from being with you?"

"No." She would want to know them. "Of course it wouldn't."

"Then let's stop thinking about what might be and make something real. I've lived the last several years of my life not thinking about anything but survival and figuring out my past. I would very much like to have some kind of future, and I can't do that if I'm always looking behind me. Have dinner with me. That's all I'm asking for now. I'll take this hour by hour if I have to."

"All you want is dinner?" That was disappointing, but probably smart.

"Hell, no. I want more but I'll take what I can get when it comes to you. You're the one I want, Ariel. I want the Ariel who bluffs like a pro when we play cards but mucks the best hand if she thinks it would help someone else win. I want the Ariel who's kind to everyone around her but doesn't let them take advantage of her. I want the Ariel who knows what she wants and doesn't hesitate to reach out and take. I want so badly to be the person *that* Ariel wants."

He was everything she wanted. Even that fight they had today proved it. He hadn't sulked in his room, waiting for her to fix things. He'd apologized. He'd taken responsibility and acknowledged what he'd done. He was a strong man who'd seen the worst life had to offer and still come out with kindness in his heart. She wanted him more than anything. She went up on her toes and tilted her head back, offering up her lips. "I would like that very much."

He didn't seem even the slightest bit interested in refusing her. He immediately sighed and brought his mouth down on hers. He brushed their lips together, his hands moving to her hips. "I am sorry about today. You handled the situation quite well, but then you always handle me well. I might have to change that."

She knew what he was talking about. She was in the position of control on the mission. He wanted a little of it somewhere else. She couldn't think of a better idea. "Tell me what you want from me, Sir."

He hissed, like a pot letting off the tiniest bit of steam. "Do you have any idea how long I've wanted to play with you?"

"As long as I've wanted to play with you. You weren't the only one attracted that day." She'd seen him sitting there with Theo and Erin and her hormones had gone into overdrive. She'd been fairly new to the team and had been very much in self-care mode. She hadn't been looking for a man. Not at all, but Robert had shown up and her plans had gone to hell.

"Does anyone care that I'm wearing a suit for this?"

She turned and Tucker was standing in the doorway to the kitchen, a bottle of wine in his hand.

"I'm the only one of his brothers willing to play the waiter tonight and you two are going to make out until all the food is cold and then I won't even get a tip."

One day there would be a woman who would take one look at Tucker and fall head over heels. He was a beautiful man with golden brown hair and a face meant for a movie screen. There was a light about Tucker she'd rarely seen in others. And that woman would have to take on all his crazy, too.

"How about I give you the rest of the night off, buddy?" Robert turned to his friend. "I think Ari and I can take it from here."

She found her hand in his again, the press of it warm and secure.

"Fine, but if the pasta is cold it's not my fault. And I hope you enjoy the playlist I spent all afternoon working on." He shrugged suddenly and grinned. "I didn't really. It's my 'let's get down to business' playlist. Candyee says it's guaranteed to put you in the mood. And she's a pro."

Oh, lord. "Thank her for us."

Robert had a hand over his mouth.

Tucker winked her way and walked back toward the media room.

And she let Robert lead her into the kitchen to start their date. She hoped it ended properly.

* * * *

Robert stared at her across the candlelit table and promised he was going to be way nicer to Peter. Ariel looked gorgeous in the candlelight and she'd relaxed after he'd poured her a glass of Pinot Noir. He'd served her the spaghetti Bolognese he'd put together after Peter had gotten him acquainted with the kitchen. One of the things he'd done while holed up in The Garden was learn to cook. He wasn't handy with a computer like Jax, or as excellent at deductive reasoning as Sasha. He was good at putting a plan together, making sure the team had everything they needed out in the field. He was the logistical guy, but most of the time he wasn't needed. He'd discovered he was excellent in the field at being a bodyguard and had great instincts as to when the shit was about to go down. But sitting around The Garden waiting, working out, and practicing how to kill enemies hadn't been as fulfilling as he'd thought it would be. So he'd learned to cook. He wasn't Sean Taggart level good, but he was competent in the kitchen.

"That was excellent. Teresa taught you well," Ariel said, putting her glass down.

Teresa was kind of the mother sub at The Garden. She did a lot of the cooking and took care of the team. "She was a patient teacher. Most of the people at The Garden have been kind to me."

"Is that why you decided to stay? I know Ian offered you a job."

"I stayed because they needed me." His brothers. "Theo didn't need me after he stopped being a stubborn asshole about his wife. Once he accepted his past, he was good. Think about it like you're the only person in the world with a disease and suddenly you find out that there are five others out there just like you. There's this odd happiness. Then guilt that you feel happy."

"You felt that way because you weren't alone."

"And it was never truly happiness. It was more like a settling deep inside me. They needed me. Being around for them as they adjusted to the world gave me purpose. The first time Damon called me into his office to give a report on my men, that was the moment I found some pride."

And he'd felt…normal again. He hadn't even been sure of what that word meant at the time, but now he knew there had been a familiarity in taking charge.

There was an Army base in Germany. Lots of soldiers moved through there. Had he been stationed here?

"You have a lot to be proud of," Ariel said, pushing her chair back. "We should do the dishes."

He let the thought go. He wasn't going to have another episode tonight. He was going to keep his focus on Ariel. "No, I've got that covered. Owen lost a bet and I finally called it in. Don't worry. Rebecca will help him out. I left them what we didn't eat. They're probably waiting outside for us to leave."

"No, we're not," a feminine voice said from behind the doors.

"Yes, we are. We're hungry and you two are taking forever. Please bang already," Owen yelled from behind the door.

He should really be better about this. Robert got to his feet. "You know I facilitated your relationship with Rebecca. You could be a little nicer."

Owen stepped inside, Rebecca following after. "I'm being very nice. You'll sit here and talk the doc to death if I don't give you a nudge."

"And honestly, if he hadn't spoken up, his stomach growling would have interrupted you." Rebecca moved to the counter where he'd put the rest of the spaghetti and salad. "He can't help it. He's a bottomless pit. There's no satisfying him."

Owen pulled his girlfriend into his arms and waggled his eyebrows suggestively. "You satisfy me quite nicely."

Rebecca laughed as he nuzzled her neck. "Seriously, guys, we can grab a bowl and come back later if you two want to talk."

He didn't want to talk anymore. Not like this. He wanted to be alone with her, naked with her. He'd waited forever, but he wasn't going to push her into this. If she was going to leave him at her doorstep with a kiss, he would handle it.

A gentleman. He would be a gentleman right up until she let him off the leash. Then he would eat her up.

"I think we've had a long day and we'll have a longer one tomorrow," he said, reaching for her hand. The minute she threaded their fingers together he felt something inside him relax. He loved the daily intimacies they'd started to find. Holding her hand, kissing her, those small affections grounded him mightily. "Don't forget the morning briefing. Peter says he's bringing in something called butter pretzels, so we should assume we'll get a lecture on the history of pretzels in Bavaria."

Owen groaned. "We'll be there."

He led Ariel out. Down the hall he saw Dante outside the media room, a beer in his hand. He'd been turned toward the kitchen at the opposite end of the hall, as though he'd been standing there staring at it. Had he been listening to the happy couples?

There was something dark in Dante that always gave him pause.

Dante turned without a word and disappeared behind the doors where he would likely drink himself to sleep. It seemed to be the way he and Sasha operated.

But he wasn't thinking about that tonight. Tomorrow would be soon enough to sit everyone down and talk about the problems they were having. He would get Jax on the phone. He wasn't leaving him out because he was in London.

"Are you all right?" Ariel had stopped beside him. "Is Dante giving you trouble?"

He was glad she'd been upstairs when they'd gone on their rant. "I think the pressure is starting to get to him. But we can talk about that tomorrow. I think after we get back to London we should have a big group meeting and get some things out in the open."

"They think Damon and Ian are keeping things from them?"

No. He did not want to go there. He stopped in the middle of the hall and got into her personal space. She backed up against the wall and he loomed over her. It was time to move from reality to a place where they might be able to play out a few fantasies, if she was ready. "No work talk. If you want to go to sleep, I'll kiss you now and see you in the morning. Tucker and I are in the room next to you. If you need anything I'll be there. If you aren't tired and you want to talk some more, we can go down to the bar and have another glass of wine with the full knowledge we don't have to go any further than that. I'm more than willing to sit up talking to you all night long."

She tilted her head up to him. "And if I want to go to bed but not to sleep?"

His heart rate ticked up, blood starting to thrum through his system as he invaded further, brushing his chest against hers. He reached for her wrists and gently brought them up and over her head, pinning her to the wall. "Then we need to make a few things clear."

She took a deep breath, her lips curling up as though she liked the way he smelled. "Me sub, you Dom. Got it."

He leaned over. "Hey, I'm trying to make sure I take care of you the way you like to be taken care of. I've watched you play. I don't think your play partners realized how much you like being dominated. I think they view you as a woman who enjoys a spanking from time to time. They don't get how much you need to know your partner is thinking about how to handle you. They don't understand that you need to stop thinking. You need a place where you obey your partner."

"In their defense, I had no interest in sex with any of them. I was looking for a spanking, some physical play that wouldn't lead to real intimacy. You watched me?"

"I always watch you," he admitted. "It's why my brothers insist I'm your stalker. I watch you because I can't not watch you when you're in a room. If I thought for a second that it made you uncomfortable, I would make myself stop, but I think you like it."

She watched him, too, and not in a way that made him think she was wary of him. It had always been there between them—the crackle and fire of sexual chemistry.

"You're going to be a talky one, aren't you?" she asked.

And she was going to be a brat. "You're the one who usually makes everyone else do the talking. Yes, I want you to talk to me. I want you to tell me how you're feeling and if the things I'm going to do to your body work for you. I need you to understand that nothing is more important to me for the rest of the night than ensuring that you're well taken care of. So let's set some ground rules. Unless you want me to play this vanilla. I can do that. I can gently take you inside and lay you out on the bed and then I'll make love to you."

Her eyes flared. "Or you could bend me to your will and fuck me so hard I can't think of anything or anyone but you."

He liked how she thought. "Then stop being a brat. And yes, I'm a talkie top. I'll make you talk to me while we're playing. This is my therapy session, Dr. Adisa. You're not in charge. Say that. Tell me who's in charge."

"You are, Robert." Her tone had softened along with her eyes.

"And who obeys me?"

"I do. I obey you when we're playing."

"Tell me your safe word." He had no intention of her using it, but they needed it there between them.

"I've always used red, but I'm not going to use it with you."

"But you have it if you need it. We're going to walk into that room and you're going to strip for me. You're going to present yourself to me. Am I understood?"

Her pupils had dilated and her body seemed more languid than it had before. Him taking control was doing exactly what he'd thought it would.

"Yes, Sir."

"Then kiss me sweetly and do what I commanded."

She popped up on her toes and brushed her lips against his. Heat flashed through him and he had the overwhelming need to press her against the wall and find a place between her legs. He could shove his cock inside her and not stop until they both came.

Or he could make this last for a long time. He could spend hours and hours playing with her because making love to Ariel wouldn't merely be about an orgasm. It would be about exploring the intense emotion that had grown between them.

He released her wrists and she bit her bottom lip as she relaxed back down off her toes. She looked up at him briefly before sliding away and reaching for the door.

"I'll be right in. Don't start without…" He was about to walk the few steps to the door of the room he'd been assigned, but it came open and an arm poked through holding the small leather bag that served as Robert's kit. "Is there any privacy at all in this place?"

He heard Ariel giggle.

Tucker merely shook the bag. "Not when you're out in the hallway. Go do your dirty stuff in a proper bedroom if you don't want me listening in. Also, you know what Big Tag would say."

He grabbed the bag from Tucker. He loved the guy, but Tucker also knew how to act like the most obnoxious little brother the world had ever seen. Tucker was harshing his top space.

"We'll use a condom," Ariel promised, looking far less serious than she usually did. The weight of the world always seemed to be on her shoulders, and now she seemed more relaxed.

This was the Ariel he saw on the dungeon floor. He wanted her to be able to find this lightness in other parts of her life. She could if she trusted him enough.

"Good night, Tucker." He turned and followed Ariel inside her room, locking the door behind him. He set the kit down and stared at her. "I'm waiting."

She held his gaze as she kicked off the shoes she'd been wearing and began to unbutton her blouse, revealing inch after inch of gorgeous skin. She took her time, and this wasn't some shy offering of a woman who hoped her partner accepted her. This woman knew the value of the gift she offered.

"God, you're beautiful." It went beyond the word. Or rather the word went beyond the physical. Ariel was beautiful inside and out, and she'd proven she was a puzzle, complex and fascinating.

She shrugged out of the blouse and draped it over the chair to her left. The room was small, but there was more than enough space for what he intended to do. She eased her slacks off and stood in front of him wearing nothing but a sunny yellow bra and matching panties.

"You know, if I'd had my way we would be in a suite with a view of the whole city. I'd open the curtains and watch the moonlight pour over your skin."

Her eyes lit for a second with mischief, but then she seemed to change her mind. "I'm sorry, Sir. I know you planned everything out carefully."

Such a good sub. He kind of wanted the brat. "Tell me what went through your mind just then."

She wrinkled her nose, a sweet expression on her face. "You would watch the moonlight pour over my skin and German intelligence would help us make a porno."

He growled a bit, but it was all in fun. "I would have made certain there were no cameras, and you're a well-trained sub to have kept that to yourself. Are you not going to give me a reason to spank you?"

She shrugged and reached for the back of her bra. "I'm sure we can play those games at some point. I would like very much to explore with you. It's been a few years since I actually had a D/s relationship that was anything beyond play in a club."

His eyes caught on her breasts and he didn't even pretend he wasn't staring. He didn't have to be polite here. Here he could indulge in her. "You've had a long-term top before?"

"The boyfriend who introduced me to the lifestyle. We worked together for a few years before I joined McKay-Taggart and Knight." The bra joined her other clothes. "Robert, are you sure? We work together. I don't want to jeopardize your position."

She asked him that now? He would have been sure before, but there wasn't a damn hesitation in his head now that he could see how tight her nipples were. "I don't have a position. I don't really work for them. If you think about it, they're working for me. Take off your panties. I'm absolutely sure I want you, and it won't be for one night. I'm not trying to fuck you out of my system. I don't want you out of my system." Of course there was another reason she could have asked the question. "Are you unsure?"

He would slow down. He didn't want to stop. He would take all the time she needed to get comfortable.

She stepped close, her head tilting up and eyes wide as she looked at him. "Rob, I'm sure. I know in the beginning I was worried you weren't capable of having a relationship."

He remembered those conversations quite well. He still cringed inside at the thought of them. "You were worried I was some lost duckling and I imprinted on you."

Her head shook slightly. "I didn't put it like that, but time has passed and I've watched you grow. You didn't move on to a willing woman, and there were many of them."

"I only wanted you. After I met you, you were the only woman I could see." He needed to put all his cards on the table. "I've had sex since I was rescued. I met a woman at Sanctum. A couple of them, actually, but it was never serious and it was more about comfort than anything else. This is different. Since I started living at The Garden there hasn't been anyone else because what I need now can't be filled by any willing woman. What I need can only come from you."

"And I can't hide behind professionalism any more. I felt the connection between us the moment we met. I wanted you to be sure because we're taking a chance here. I wouldn't take it with anyone but you."

Sweet words, but he wanted more. "Then take off those pretty panties and present yourself to me. We'll work out a contract if you want, but not tonight. Tonight, I want you to do what I asked."

She didn't move back, merely let her hands find the waistband of her undies and shoved them off. With her foot, she kicked them out of the way and never once looked down. Her eyes were on him as though watching for his every expression.

She was the sexiest woman he'd ever seen, and somehow he knew deep in his bones that counted his whole life, even the parts he couldn't remember. Ariel Adisa was a goddess, and he intended to worship her tonight.

"How do you want me to present myself, Sir? We don't have any protocols established."

"Turn around for me. Let me see you."

She stepped back and turned slowly.

"Stop." Her ass was stunning. He'd seen her in fet wear before, but never naked and willing to do his bidding.

He couldn't help but move in and put a hand on her. A deep breath filled her lungs and she seemed to relax at his touch. He was anything but relaxed. His whole body felt on edge. His cock was hard and ready, but he wasn't through exploring her yet.

He leaned in and caught her scent. Lavender. That's what her skin smelled like. He ran his nose from right behind her ear to the crook of her neck. A sweet shudder went through her, and she leaned back against him. "Tell me what you like about the lifestyle. I think I know, but I want to hear it from you."

"I'm always in control, always thinking about others. This is the only time I allow myself to let go and think about nothing more than the next moment. The next breath. The next touch. I struggled with sexual pleasure until I found a lover who was also a Dom."

"The one you worked with?" He moved back. Robert clenched his teeth, glad she couldn't see him. He grabbed her hips, holding her still. He didn't want to talk. Not now. But he was afraid if he didn't, he would lose control. God, the beast that seemed to simmer under his surface was pressing hard against the cage.

"Sir?" Gentle fingers covered his where he gripped her hips. "Rob?"

She was using that soft voice that let him know she was going into shrink mode. It was the worried sound of a mother hen. He was fucking this up. Panic and disappointment and lust—raw, hot lust—were vying for control of him.

Her hands stroked the back of his fingers. "What's wrong, love? I shouldn't have mentioned the past. Why don't we sit and talk a bit?"

If he let her she would put him in the patient zone. She would shove him back in the comfortable place where she didn't have to acknowledge that he was a man who could make her feel something beyond sympathy. They would be right back where they'd been before.

Instinct took over. He'd learned to trust his instincts—whoever he'd been before had known how to clean and disassemble a gun, how to block a punch.

For the first time he let instinct take over when it came to sex. When it came to pleasing a woman. When it came to her.

He used his grip on her hips to spin her around to face him. The movement had been sudden, shocking, and she wasn't steady on her feet. Good. He didn't want her steady. *He* wasn't steady. She looked up at him, her eyes wide with surprise and…arousal. That was good. He wanted her aroused, but he wasn't stopping there. He wrapped one arm around her torso, trapping her arms at her sides. The other went around her shoulders, jerking her naked, vulnerable body against his fully clothed one.

Holding her tight, he bent his face to hers and claimed her mouth.

He'd kissed women before. He'd kissed her before. This was something else.

This was possession.

He had her right where he wanted her—he held her hard against him, her neck bent, base of her skull resting on the forearm of the arm he'd wrapped around her shoulders. Her mouth was soft and yielding under his. When he swept his tongue over the seam of her lips, she flowered open, giving him access to her mouth.

A growl of satisfaction rumbled through him, even as he claimed what she'd offered, tongue delving into her mouth, tasting her. Her tongue stroked against his. Tentative at first, and then with a bit of aggression. The kiss became a dance, a duel. He pulled back just enough for them to breathe and then claimed her mouth once again, sucking her tongue, showing her what he wanted, then thrusting his tongue into her mouth.

She did what he wanted, what he needed, and sucked on him. His cock jerked in his pants. It was a pale imitation of what he truly wanted, but now he knew what it would be like when he pressed his cock into her mouth.

Robert's arms tightened around her, and she made a small noise of discomfort.

That sound was enough to break through. He released her and forced himself to step back. They were both panting. He'd planned tonight, knew what he wanted to say to her, how he'd touch her. How he'd take it slow and learn her.

That kiss hadn't been in any of his plans.

Ariel was the picture of desire, lust obviously taking her over. He'd done that to her. She dragged air into her lungs, making her breasts with their tight nipples bounce slightly. He forced himself to look away from all that lovely, naked skin.

He knew he should say something. He'd promised her he would take it slow and they would find their intimacy. For her that meant talking, sharing their feelings with each other. He always had something to say. But right now there were no words, because despite the fact that he'd screwed up, that he'd kissed her and held her so tight he'd hurt her, he didn't know what to say. The months of tension between them, the slow burn of their sexual chemistry, had come to a head in that kiss.

Ariel inhaled, held the breath. A little shiver worked down her body, and he realized he was staring at her naked breasts again. He jerked his gaze to the ceiling.

She took a step forward, hands coming up.

Then she shoved him, hard.

It wasn't a move he'd anticipated, though he should have given what a caveman he'd been. He stumbled back a few steps, his back thudding against the wall.

His heart clenched. He'd hurt her, badly enough that she was fighting him, literally pushing him away. He opened his mouth, but there weren't words enough to express how sorry he was for how he'd treated her.

She looked him up and down, then took two running steps…

…and jumped on him.

He managed to catch her and then she was kissing him. She'd wrapped her arms around him, one hand tangling in his hair. With his back to the wall she couldn't get her legs around his waist, but she gripped his hips with her knees. He felt her start to slide and reached down, grabbing her ass, that glorious ass, with both hands. He squeezed, and she made a little sound, then bit his lip.

She didn't hate him. He hadn't scared her. She'd liked the kiss. Even better, she wanted more.

He would give her more.

He pushed away from the wall, carrying her. The bed was his destination, but with most of his blood in his dick and no way to see, he missed the bed, managing instead to trip on something. He felt himself start to fall and shifted their weight, managing to go down on one knee and then twisting hard. He landed on his back with a thump, Ariel on top of him.

Ariel sat up, straddling him. "Robert, are you hurt?"

He tried to speak but all that came out was a groan.

Her lips parted, eyes rounding. "You're hurt. I'll—"

He grabbed her hips, swallowed, and managed to speak. "Your pussy is right on my dick."

It was why he'd only been able to groan.

They both looked down. Ariel was astride his hips, her pussy hovering only an inch above the tented crotch of his slacks. He could feel the heat coming off her. He could see the way her pussy glistened—she was wet. Ready.

The scent of her arousal was a heady perfume. He wanted to taste her. Needed to fuck her.

Ariel looked at him from beneath her lashes. "I was aggressive. This started out as a D/s scene."

"And I'm the one who kissed you like some manner-less caveman. I ruined it. And you being aggressive is…" He frowned. Hadn't he spent months and months learning this woman, watching her and figuring out what she needed? She needed someone she trusted to take control. "It's not what you want. You need a Dom, you need D/s. I'm not—"

"I don't know what this is." Ariel laid her hands softly on his chest. "But I don't want to stop. Do you?"

"No." That was the biggest understatement of his life. "I don't want to hurt you."

"You won't. I trust you."

Would she if she knew what he dreamed of at night? It was one of the things he'd kept from her, holding on to that nasty vision that came to him like it was gold he hoarded. "You shouldn't."

"I do, Robert. I do trust you."

"What I want right now isn't to be your Dom." He was trying to ignore how much he liked the view from here. Lying on his back, looking up at Ariel's lovely tits, was something he could get used to. "I want to *take* you. I want to *fuck* you. I want to…" He didn't know a way to describe what he wanted that didn't sound like he was an aggressive, violent asshole.

She stared down at him. "And I want you to take me. I want you to fuck me."

This was the woman he needed—the one who challenged him, who forced him to constantly see her anew. He was so fucking in love with her. He let go of all thoughts that this had to go one way. He didn't have to prove anything to her except that they were in this together. He let go of the idea that he needed to be gentle with her. His woman knew what she wanted and it was him.

Ariel's hands were still on his shirt. She closed her fingers into fists then yanked. He lost half the buttons with that first hard pull. She was going for a second when he gave in and once more let pure instinct take over.

They were on the floor a few feet from the bed. Robert sat up, wrapping his arms around Ariel as he did. He claimed her mouth, using one hand to hold her hips, force her to stay straddling him. The other hand yanked his tie off. He wouldn't need it again.

He broke the kiss, her taste lingering on his tongue. The sweetness of her mouth wasn't the only part of her he wanted to taste. "Put your nipple in my mouth."

She leaned forward, fingers sliding through his hair as she pressed her breast to his mouth. His lips parted and he took the tip of her breast. He sucked hard, wanting the contact, wanting to draw blood to the already engorged flesh to make her even more sensitive. He released that breast, taking the other in his mouth, sucking and then nipping her. He heard air hiss from between her teeth. He did it again, gently biting her nipple, but then moved his head back, stretching and pulling on the tip of her breast.

"Did that hurt?" He asked the question but his early panic—the idea that he could ruin everything with one brutish move—was gone. It was an academic question. She wouldn't leave him simply because he'd gone too far. She would talk to him and he would adjust.

It was what couples did. During sex. In their everyday lives. They made accommodations.

"Yes," she breathed.

He gently kissed the nipple he'd abused. He licked her because that "yes" hadn't told him she wanted to stop. "And do you want me to do it again?"

"Yes. Please. Yes."

He switched back to the first breast, capturing the peak between his teeth then slowly biting down, adding pressure until she was moaning, her hips rocking forward onto his stomach. Reaching up he tangled one hand in her hair, making a fist and then tugging. She arched back, his grip on her hair forcing her to offer those sweet breasts and wet nipples up to his mouth.

"Brace your hands on my thighs."

When she obeyed he released her hair so he could get both hands on those breasts. He squeezed, watching the skin plump up between his fingers. Then he took each nipple between thumb and forefinger, rolling and pinching. He watched her neck work as she swallowed, listened to the breathy, desperate sounds she made. He wanted to do this all night—play with her nipples and watch her.

His brain might want that, but his cock, and maybe even his soul, needed more. Needed all of her. Needed to fuck her. To finally take her. He craved possession in the most primal and intimate way possible.

He pinched her nipples, gripping them hard, then pulled, forcing the tips of her breasts to slide from between the vise of his fingers. She let out a breathy sob.

"Tell me what you're feeling." He wanted to hear her say it. He wanted the words coming from her mouth.

"Need," was all she said.

"What do you need?"

"You." A simple word that meant everything. She was finally seeing one of the pieces he'd withheld out of pure fear that she would reject him. She wasn't rejecting him. Not at all.

He looked to the side, and the bed was right there. All he had to do was get them to the bed and then he could take his time. He could fuck her thoroughly and slowly. He could play with her. Worship her the way he'd planned.

"Please," she begged. "Please."

They weren't going to make it to the bed. He was going to fuck her right here, right now.

Robert leaned back on an elbow. Ariel's torso was still arched, her hands on his legs. That meant he had a lovely view of her pussy. He hadn't even touched it yet. Hadn't tasted her there.

Later. It would have to be later because now what he needed, more than he'd ever needed anything, was to wrap himself around her, to feel her arms around him as he sank into her.

With one hand he started jerking at his pants, struggling to lower the zipper. Ariel looked at what he was doing, then pushed up and reached to help him. He had to close his eyes and focus on ripping off the remnants of his shirt while she lowered the zipper of his slacks.

She shifted, swinging her leg over so she was no longer straddling him. His heart almost stopped, but she wasn't leaving him. Instead she grabbed his pants and yanked them down and off.

"There's a condom in the pocket," he forced himself to say. Fucking condom. He didn't want to wear it, but even his inner caveman wasn't foolish enough to go without at this stage.

No one had ever told him how hot it was to have a woman rip his clothes off. There was something unspeakably arousing in the way she moved—hard and fast, as if she couldn't wait to get him naked. As if she needed him as much as he needed her. She tossed the pants away as he shed the last bits of his shirt.

"Put it on, Rob. My hands are shaking too much," she said, handing him the condom. "I know it would be sexier if I did it, but I can't."

He took it from her, forcing himself to open the packet, grip his dick, do what needed to be done. All the while she was watching him, her hands shaking with desire. He couldn't take his eyes off her.

They were both naked and ready, and for a moment they stopped, considering one another. It should have been almost comical—him sitting, her kneeling beside him in the cramped space on the floor beside the bed.

He held out his arms and she fell into them, wrapping herself around him once more. It didn't matter where they were. They had each other.

The first touch of her naked body to his own skin was a revelation—it both soothed him and pumped up the level of his need.

He gripped her knees, forcing her to straddle his legs. He shifted her until she was sitting on his lap, her legs around his waist. He folded his own legs, so he was sitting cross-legged, her ass cradled by his thighs, her legs spread open and ready. They were tucked in together like puzzle pieces.

"Look at me," he demanded.

Her gaze met his. He slid his right hand up her spine, curling his fingers over her shoulder from behind. He reached between their bodies, lining up his cock. He held her gaze as he maneuvered himself into position. The blunt head of his dick slid along her labia once, twice, and then he found the entrance. He positioned himself, then released his cock, grabbing her hips.

He was right there, on the edge of something he'd wanted and needed for so long.

"Keep looking at me," he commanded. "I want your eyes on me."

Ariel clung to his shoulders and nodded.

He flexed his fingers on her hip and shoulder, then jerked her body down at the same time he pressed his hips up.

His cock sank deep with one powerful thrust.

Her eyes widened, her mouth opened, and she seemed to have stopped breathing. He registered all of it, but dimly, because the need to come was an ache in his balls. Her pussy was hot and tight around him, her body seemingly made for him.

"Ariel," he breathed, her name all he could manage.

She leaned into him, running her hands over his hair like he was something precious that she would never let go of.

He pressed his forehead to hers, their breath mingling, his cock still buried in her. For a moment he found peace, a bliss he hadn't expected.

But that pent-up desire, the need that had driven him, wasn't satisfied yet. He released her hip, instead wrapping that arm around her waist, the other reaching up to grip the nape of her neck. He raised her off his cock using the arm around her waist, withdrawing until only the tip was still inside her. Then he slammed her back down.

Ariel sucked in air, then let out a little sob. "I think…I think I'm going to come."

"You're going to come on my cock." Hers had been a bit like a question, but his a statement. A command.

"I've never come from just—"

Whatever she was going to say was lost when he lifted her, then slammed her down again.

And again.

She grabbed his face with both hands and kissed him frantically, her mouth moving over his, kissing the corner of his mouth, sucking his lower lip. A savage satisfaction rushed through him as he felt her thighs start to quake. She abandoned kissing him, instead pressing her cheek to his temple, holding him, but not so tightly that he couldn't manipulate her body, couldn't lift her up and then pull her down onto his cock.

His own orgasm was building. He was both impressed by how long he'd held off and bitterly disappointed this was coming to an end. Out of the corner of his eye he caught sight of his discarded tie, and beyond that his kit.

This didn't have to be over. Maybe he wasn't done with that tie for the evening. God, he hadn't even finished fucking her and he was already thinking of the next time.

For now what he needed was to make her come. She said she might come just from the fucking, though she never had before. He intended to be the first man to pleasure her this way. And the last.

Again and again he brought her down onto his cock, making a place for himself within the warm heat of her pussy.

He cupped her breast, finding her nipple with his thumb. He rolled her nipple then flicked it, listening to her breathing change as he did, learning what she liked.

"Robert, please," she begged.

He didn't know what she was begging for, but he knew what he needed. He needed to hear her cry out in pleasure. He needed to feel her grip him so tight it felt like she'd never let him go.

He fucked her harder, finding a rhythm between his cock and the hand on her breast that ensured her breathing was uneven. He kept it up until she was moaning in pleasure each time he thrust in. Then he took her over the edge, gave her that bit of pain that would ensure her pleasure.

He buried his face against her shoulder and bit her at the same time he pinched her nipple and twisted.

Ariel moaned—a sound of pure desire. Her pussy clamped down hard on his cock, and then he was coming, the pleasure he felt with Ariel making him realize he hadn't really understood the meaning of the word until this moment. They held one another tight as the storm of sensuality passed over and through them.

Ariel slumped onto him, the last of the tension leaving her body. Reluctantly, he pulled her off his cock. He shifted so he was holding her in his arms, then managed to get up, walking the two steps to the bed. He laid her down in the center. He moved to the small bathroom and took care of the condom. He washed up and rejoined her, not bothering with clothes.

When she started to curl onto her side he stopped her with gentle hands.

"No, baby, I want to look at you." He grasped her knees, forcing her legs apart enough that he could see her core. "You're going to keep those legs spread because I want to see your pussy."

Ariel's eyes, which had been half closed, widened.

"Rob?"

He bent and scooped up his discarded tie, holding it up for her to see. "I'm not done with you."

She licked her lower lip, and his dick, which should have been satisfied, twitched.

"That was what we needed. We needed to fuck. I needed to take you hard and fast. But I didn't get to take my time the way I wanted," he informed her. "Now it's time to play."

Chapter Five

Ariel wasn't sure she could take another second of his torture. She wanted to reach down and force the bastard sadist to put his cock inside her and end this desperation.

Which was probably precisely why Robert had used his necktie to secure both of her hands to the headboard of the bed.

"Just a little more."

She bit back a curse as he dragged his tongue over her pussy.

She was on her knees on the bed, her body stretched out for him. She was sure she looked like she was in prayer, arms together in front of her, her breasts brushing the pillows under them. She would look like a penitent were it not for the man on his back between her legs.

She glanced to the side and caught a glimpse of them in the mirror. Yes. They were a perverse version of worship.

No. It wasn't perverse. It was dirty, but in the sweetest way. Nothing the man had done to her had been without love and affection.

Though he was slowly driving her mad.

After he'd dropped her on the bed, he'd made it a point to prove exactly how in control he could be. He'd tied her up and slowly explored every inch of her body. First with his hands, and then his mouth and tongue. She'd thought after that first encounter she would need a little time to recover, but long, languid strokes of his tongue had her in full-on heat again.

She gripped the necktie she'd bought him for Christmas the year before as she let out a low moan of pure pleasure. She could feel his big body between her legs, broad shoulders forcing her knees wide. She wasn't sure how long he'd been down there lavishing affection on her pussy, but the world seemed to have faded in that time. There was nothing left but her and Rob and the slow drag of his tongue, the feel of his fingers parting her core so he could spear her with that talented tongue of his.

He sucked on her clit, his hands moving to the globes of her ass. He wasn't shy or afraid of anything. At one point earlier, he'd parted her cheeks and played with her asshole. When she'd squirmed at the sensation, he'd slapped her ass and held her down.

She'd nearly come just from that.

Something about being dominated during sex flat out did it for her. She could certainly enjoy vanilla sex, but she never got the same soul-deep pleasure she did from D/s sex. If she were writing a paper on the subject she would talk about her strictly regimented childhood and an overwhelming need to both please the people around her and be the absolute best at whatever it was she happened to be doing. At times it was almost pathological. She was always thinking, always trying to improve.

Not once tonight had she thought of anything but being Robert's little fuck toy.

His fingers pressed deep inside her pussy and she was dying. He'd kept her tied up or held down every second. She hadn't even gotten her mouth on his cock. Her Sir knew what he wanted, and he intended to get it any way he could.

What would this man be like on a dungeon floor? He would be commanding, demanding. He wouldn't give her a single moment to think about anything other than pleasing him. He would give her whole nights of pure relaxation.

She needed him so much. She needed him for the simple fact that she could trust this man with her body and soul. He would take care of her and she would be free to find her subspace.

She would repay him with perfect submission in the bedroom.

Even when it drove her to the edge of madness.

Robert's tongue worked her clit while his fingers fucked deep inside her, curling up and finding that perfect spot. She gritted her teeth as she started to approach orgasm. This was when he would pull out and start with the gentle licks again, chuckling when she moaned and begged him.

"Please." The word came unbidden from her mouth. She couldn't stop begging him. She needed to come. She was drawn tight, an arrow that needed to be shot.

"Only because you asked nicely." He whispered the words against her pussy and then sucked her clit hard.

She screamed out his name as the wave hit her.

She was still shaking, the orgasm flooding her system when he slid out from under her, and she heard his feet hit the floor. There was the sound of him opening a condom, and she shivered in anticipation of getting that big dick inside her.

She looked at the mirror again and caught sight of him. Six foot two and completely made of muscle. There was nothing at all soft about Robert McClellan. He was a Greek god of a man, and the fact that he had the sweetest smile only made him all the more gorgeous. She'd always known there was another side to her gentleman, a darker side he tried to hide, but she hadn't imagined he would be so overwhelming.

He stroked his big cock as he looked at her. As much as he'd been in a hurry that first time, he'd taken things slow since, as though he needed to prove to her that he could be in control, keeping her on the edge for hours and constantly bringing her back, making her need him more and more each moment.

Even though she'd come mere moments before, she already wanted him again.

His gaze caught hers through the mirror and a slow, sexy smile crossed his face. He stroked his dick. "Do you see something you like? Because I know I do."

Vain man. "Yes. You're very attractive, Sir."

"I'll try hard to keep my masculine beauty to your high standards because you are beyond attractive." His hand moved up and down his cock and it seemed to lengthen before her eyes. She hadn't thought it could get harder, but it did as he squeezed it in his big hand. His thumb rubbed over the head of his cock and she couldn't miss the pearl of arousal he caught there. He looked down where it gleamed on the pad of his thumb and strode her way. "Taste me."

Oh, she could do that. She couldn't move toward him because he had her trussed up right and proper, but she could open her mouth, let him shove his thumb in. She sucked at it, tasting the salt that had pulsed from his cock. She could use a mouthful of him. "I want to suck you, Sir. You taste good. I want to suck you until you fill my mouth."

His face had tightened, showing off that Captain America jawline of his. He was the all-American boy, and that made his filthy as hell Dom persona all the hotter. She was the only one who got to see this side of the man. This piece of Robert was all hers.

She was getting in deep with this man.

"And you will, but not tonight," he promised. He stepped back and opened the condom, rolling it over his cock in one smooth move. "Tonight, I need to be inside your pussy. Hold on, baby."

She felt the bed dip as he got in behind her, and she was holding on to that tie for dear life because he wasn't waiting. He gripped her hips and thrust up inside her hard.

She was caught between the tie around her wrists and Rob behind her. There was nothing she could do but ride the wave he set off. She turned her head again so she could watch him in the mirror, watch him enjoying her, taking her, dominating her. The picture of him thrusting deep burned into her brain, an erotic image she knew she would never forget.

Then she couldn't think about anything at all except the fact that his hand had moved from her hip, finding her clitoris and pressing down hard.

"I want one more from you. One more before I let myself go."

She couldn't deny him even if she'd wanted to. Over the long hours they'd spent together he'd learned exactly how to make her come.

He bucked inside her and then he was holding her still, pressing himself as hard and high as he could. He lost his rhythm as his body went stiff and he followed her over the edge.

She felt him kiss the nape of her neck before he pulled away from her. He reached up and untied her hands.

"I'll be right back, baby."

She was exhausted but in the best of ways. Sore but happy. It had been a long time since she'd had any kind of sex, much less the athletic fucking Rob seemed addicted to.

She was going to need to up her cardio routine.

She managed to get the covers of the bed turned down while he was in the bathroom. It was chilly at night, but she wouldn't be cold. She would wrap herself around him and sleep like a baby.

Why had she waited so long? She'd known months in that Robert was different. She'd known she wanted him and that his desire went far beyond a need to attach himself to someone. They fit, and tonight proved they fit damn near perfectly. Even their kinks meshed beautifully.

He'd given her everything she needed.

The bathroom door opened and he strode out. The man was simply perfection. She took in his muscular body and couldn't help but stare. He stopped mere feet away from her and smiled.

"Seriously?"

She shrugged and yawned. "Not seriously. But in the morning I'll likely be ready to go again. But gently. It's been a long time for me and you're not exactly a small man."

His cock was like the rest of him, built big.

He leaned over and kissed her. "I'll remember that. Nights are nasty and mornings are soft and sweet and gentle. Good night, Ariel. I'll see you in the morning."

She expected him to get into bed and cuddle her, but he reached for his pants. "Where are you going?"

A little of the glow she'd been feeling fled. He wasn't going to sleep with her? She sat up as he pulled his shirt on. He didn't bother with the buttons since half of them were on the floor because she'd ripped it off him in her haste to touch him.

He slid his feet into his shoes and his smile had faded. "I don't sleep well and I don't want to disturb you. I would hold you until you fall asleep, but I'm worried I'll fall asleep, too."

"I don't mind. I want you with me."

He shook his head. "No, I can't do that. I'm sorry, but I have nightmares and I don't want you to see me like that."

"But I can help you."

He stepped back. "I can't. I'm sorry. You have no idea how much I don't want to disappoint you, but I can't give you this."

Even Doms had hard limits and this was one of his. She wanted to argue and cajole and get him back into bed, but his eyes had gone hollow. She could push him for selfish reasons or she could give him the space he needed. For now.

"Kiss me again, and if you happen to sneak into my bed in the morning, bring coffee with you."

His whole body relaxed and he smiled again. "A little bit of cream and a whole lot of sugar. I promise."

He kissed her mouth and her nose and her forehead and then her mouth again before groaning and forcing himself away.

"Good night," he said with a sigh. He picked up his kit.

She didn't want him to leave. Of course he had bad dreams and she wanted to be there when he woke up shaking. She wanted to take him in her arms and remind him he was with her and not that crazy woman who'd ripped his mind from him. But he wasn't ready for that. "Good night. I'm next door if you need anything. I mean anything at all."

She watched him leave.

It was a while before she managed to get to sleep.

* * * *

Robert stepped out into the hallway, closing the door as quietly as he could. It was late and everyone should be sleeping, but a quick glance toward the kitchen let him know someone was up.

Damn it. He did not have to go down there and figure out what was wrong. He had every right to go to bed and get some sleep so he could climb into Ariel's bed early in the morning and hold her like he would have if he wasn't so fucked up.

Ariel. God, she'd been everything he'd dreamed of. Better, really. Being with her…he couldn't process all of it right now. He needed time to really let it sink into his soul that they were together now.

They were a couple, and he'd been wrong to push her away. He would make this work.

He opened the bedroom door, trying not to wake Tucker, but the light was on and no one was in either of the twin beds that probably wouldn't fit either he or Tucker.

Ariel's bed was a queen. He would fit on that. Oh, he would have to cuddle with her, and he would absolutely take up most of the space, but they could tangle themselves together and they would sleep fine.

Right up to the moment he wrapped his hands around her throat and potentially killed her if he didn't wake up in time.

He tossed his kit and shoes on the bed and changed his shirt. If Tucker was up this late, he likely couldn't sleep and needed to talk.

He wouldn't be able to go to bed knowing Tucker was up. Damn it. It was probably a good thing since if he tried to sleep now all he would see was the look in Ariel's eyes when she'd realized he wasn't going to crawl into bed with her. He walked out into the hall again, passing Ariel's doorway and wishing he'd been whole enough to have stayed with her.

"I don't think that's a good idea." The words drifted down the hallway.

"Well, of course you don't. They care about you."

Robert hurried up. That was Dante and Owen, and he prayed they weren't about to come to blows.

He made it to the kitchen and they were all sitting around the table where he'd spent the early part of the evening with Ariel. It hadn't been the date he'd planned, but it had still turned out to be the best night of his life.

It didn't look like it had been the same for the rest of the group. They all looked up as he walked in, and he couldn't help but notice that every one of them had gone tense and alert the minute he'd walked in the room.

They relaxed when they realized it was him. Tucker sighed and sat back. Owen's hand came off the knife that was sitting next to the remains of the pear he'd been eating. Dante got up and walked to the fridge. Only Sasha remained exactly where he was. His eyes were red and his hair slicked back as though he'd dunked it in water at some point.

Robert knew that look and realized why they were all up. "How bad was it?"

Cooling off with cold water was one of the first things they did when the migraines started to take over.

Dante flipped the top off a beer. "It was disgusting. He wouldn't do any of the things he's supposed to do. It was almost like he wanted to be violently ill."

Sasha shot him the finger. "Fuck you, Dante."

"It's under control," Tucker said. "I got him cooled off. Rebecca gave him some anti-nausea meds and we've kept him calm."

"And guess who is left to clean everything?" Dante complained. "I'm always the one who cleans things up. I'm sick of it and we're doing it for people who lie to us."

"I thought you cleaned up the room so you wouldn't have to sleep in puke," Sasha pointed out, his bloodshot eyes turning to his partner. "I told you I would do it."

"I'm not talking about that, though I suppose it's all part of it. Levi Green says he has the cure." Dante paced. "I want it. I think we should make contact and negotiate with him."

Shit. He'd been hoping it wouldn't come to this. "No one is contacting Green. We can't trust him. We can't believe a word he says."

"And we can believe Damon?" Dante asked.

"Damon took us in." Owen stood up. "I don't know why we're arguing about this. The door is right there. If you two don't want to be here, feel free to leave."

Unfortunately, Owen was right, and they might be at that point. "You're not a prisoner, Dante. If you want to leave, you can head out at any point in time. I'm sure you'll get to negotiate with Levi a couple of hours after you hit the streets."

"Or I would immediately be taken into custody by police who wish to turn me over to Interpol," Dante replied. "Perhaps even Damon himself would call them. Have you ever wondered how they could get the charges dropped for Robert and Theo but not the rest of us? I find it interesting. They've managed to save the ones they like."

"Jax and I still have warrants." Tucker's voice had gone low. "You think they haven't worked on it? They have. I've seen the legal bills."

"You've seen what they want you to see." Dante wasn't moving from his position.

He was done with Dante. "There's no talking to someone who won't listen. I don't think you need to be involved in our operations if you genuinely feel like we're all willing to betray you."

"He doesn't think you will betray us." Sasha sounded weary. "He thinks you are all being naïve, and I'll be honest I think you are, too. I think they aren't telling us things we should know."

"They won't listen, and now Robert will call Damon or hell, he'll tell his girlfriend and I will be out." Dante finished the beer and grabbed another. "Or Damon will put me in some form of jail or turn me over to whoever will pay the most for me."

It was all their fears—that they could be caught and lost in some government program, and that would be their end. They would have no future. No past. Nothing but experiments and pain until they died. No one would come for them. No one would care. It was why they'd stuck together even when they annoyed each other. They were the only ones who understood what it meant to survive Hope McDonald. They owed each other. "I'm not talking to Damon, but Dante, you need to decide if you're in or you're out. When we get back to London, we'll all sit down and discuss this. I don't think we should make any decisions without Jax."

"I will talk about this with you," Dante said, his tone wary. "But something has to change, Robert. We can't go on this way. I'm going to bed. You should be careful around the girl. She's not what she appears to be."

"What?"

"Ariel. I know you're blinded by her beauty, but she's involved with the rest of them," Dante said and for once he didn't sound bitter and angry. He sounded weary. "Ask Owen. He saw her that day. You don't get that accurate from a range. Not when you're trying to hit a moving target."

"Hey." He turned to Dante as he walked out of the kitchen and down the hall. The other man didn't stop and Robert didn't take his eyes off him until he was safely behind his own door. "What was that supposed to mean?"

"It means we're worried about Ariel." Sasha sat back and ran a hand through his hair, forcing it back. He'd lost weight and it was starting to show in the gaunt lines of his face. "I never noticed it before Toronto. She moves like an operative."

"Because she's been trained. Damon and Big Tag wouldn't let her out in the field if she hadn't had some self-defense skills."

Sasha sent a pointed look across the table where Owen was sitting.

Owen huffed and sat back. "It went beyond what a self-defense class could have taught her, Rob. I was there. She was…I would let that woman watch my back in the field any day of the week. Not only did she take out the Agency man, she took down that MSS operative hand to hand, and she didn't even have a spot of blood on her. She used a knife, and not a one of us heard the fight, so I'm thinking there wasn't much of a fight at all."

It was ridiculous. "Ariel isn't some kind of killer. She's a therapist. She's got a PhD in psychology. She helps people."

Ariel was one of the gentlest human beings he'd ever met. It was precisely the reason he'd rejected their attraction in the beginning.

"Hey, assassins can help people if they're killing the right targets," Tucker said, his eyes on the table in front of him.

"You think she's hiding something, too?" He couldn't believe Tucker wasn't on his side. Tucker was always on his side.

"Have we asked her?" Sasha took a drink of the water that sat in front of him. Or maybe it was vodka.

"She told me she used to work in private practice for a while and then wanted to do something more." They'd gone over it before. "She was employed by Scotland Yard and she did some work for MI6 as a profiler when they needed her. That was how she met Damon. And she got lucky that night in Toronto. Yes, she was a badass, but it was fueled by adrenaline. She was the only one left who could save you."

"And she did it with precision," Owen countered. "I'm not saying Ariel's anything but the hero she was. I thank god every night that she was there and she did what she did because otherwise I would be in Beijing wishing I was dead and Rebecca would be Levi Green's personal neurologist. But that wasn't her first time, mate. She's a professional. I would bet my life on it."

They were all paranoid. They needed to get out more or have more work to do because they were all becoming crazy conspiracy theorists. "Have you all discussed this behind my back?"

Tucker finally looked up. "It's not a big deal if Ari used to be someone else. We all used to be someone, and probably some of us weren't good people. Ari is good. I don't see what the problem is. It means you can relax around her. She can handle herself. You don't have to treat her like glass. Tell me why you're not still in bed with her."

He felt his skin heat. "That's none of your business."

Tucker shoved his chair back. "Of course it's not and yet here I am shoving my nose in. You left her bed because of that freaky thing you do in the middle of the night."

"Where he tries to strangle something?" Owen said. "I watched him nearly tear apart a pillow one night. He always looks happy when he's doing it."

"He's afraid he will strangle Ariel?" Sasha asked.

"I'm not putting her at risk." He hated that they all knew about what he went through every night. He hadn't told Ariel about his nightmare for precisely this reason. He hated the sympathy in his brothers' eyes. He couldn't stand the thought of seeing it in Ariel's. Nor could he risk her finding out about it firsthand. "And that's all I'm going to say about it. We should get to bed. We've got to provide security for Rebecca's interview tomorrow. We'll deal with this when we're back in London. Let's just get the job done."

He couldn't deal with it now. And getting back to London would allow him to include Jax. Jax was levelheaded, and he could often sway the others.

"Sure." Tucker grabbed his water bottle. "I would like to point out that no one cares if Rob strangles me. I'm always his roomie and not once has he managed to get his hands around my throat but hey, it could happen."

Owen got up, too. "There are nights I would strangle you myself, mate. 'Night. Sasha, I hope you feel better."

Sasha nodded his way. "Please thank Rebecca for me. I do feel better. I will try to stay away from that memory."

Sasha didn't move from his chair and Robert didn't particularly want to go back to the room he was sharing and face more questions from Tucker. "Did you write down what you do remember? Ariel told me it could help."

Sasha went still, the moment lengthening between them.

"You don't have to, of course." What was going on behind Sasha's cold exterior? He almost never talked about anything personal. Sasha had always held himself apart. Even when they were in custody, Sasha had seemed to greatly prefer to be alone.

"Do you get flashes from your life?" Sasha asked the question with a tentativeness Rob hadn't heard from him before. "They're like little moments in time that almost feel like a movie except you know it was real and it happened to you?"

"I see my mother. I'm young and she's holding my hand. We're walking across the grass and she looks down at me, but I can't ever see her face because the sun is behind her." He wanted to see her face because he knew she loved him. He knew because he could feel how safe he was with her.

What was Sasha's memory? Was it of torture and pain? Or worse. Did he remember doing something he wished he hadn't? Some memory that would have been best left in the past.

"I see a child. A baby. They put her in my hands and she's small. She's tiny. I'm afraid I will drop her." Sasha's head fell forward. "I think I have a child. I don't know her name. She's wearing a pink blanket. That means she's a girl, right?"

The words were a shock to Robert's system. Sasha had a kid somewhere in the world? It was almost unthinkable. "If you had a wife don't you think she would have looked for you?"

Because he had to think if someone out there had cared for him, they would have looked for him. Wouldn't they? If he'd had a family, they would have moved heaven and earth to find him.

Sasha shook his head and finally pushed away from the table. "I don't know. I would think so. Perhaps the child is not mine. Perhaps the child is somewhere safe and couldn't care less about me. I can see that happening. All I know is this is the vision that I can't resist, the one that I know I should. I would do anything to see how it ends."

Wasn't that what they all were looking for? What the hell they had been doing before they'd been nothing at all? What they'd left behind.

They were wrong about Ariel. They were paranoid and expecting everyone around them to be lying because that was all they'd ever known.

Ari was the best woman he'd ever met, and he wouldn't insult her by asking her to prove herself to him. She'd done that over and over again. She did it every time she helped one of them.

He didn't want to live in a world where Ariel Adisa betrayed him.

"Come on," he said. "I think we should go to bed and start all over again in the morning."

Tomorrow is another day. It was good enough for Scarlet. It's good enough for my boys. No matter what happens tomorrow, you get a new start and you always have each other. It's enough. I promise you. It's enough.

He stopped and let the words flow over him, but he didn't try to catch them. That way led to exactly what had happened to Sasha. The sweetness of it pierced him. Her voice. He could hear her voice. It was throaty, with a Western twang. It was magical to his ears.

It skidded away into the slipstream of his mind, but he'd heard it.

His mother.

"Are you all right?" Sasha asked, sounding like he actually gave a damn.

He nodded. "I'm good."

He started down the hallway. He wanted more than anything to open Ariel's door, to wake her up and make her hold him, but he didn't.

He walked into the room he shared with Tucker because no matter what the rest of them thought, she couldn't handle him and he couldn't accept the thought of hurting her.

Still, as he lay down, he couldn't get the words out of his head.

It's good enough for my boys. You always have each other.

At some point in time, he'd had a brother.

Chapter Six

Ariel glanced behind her at the table where Rob sat with Owen. They appeared to be studying the menu, but she could feel his focus on her. But then he'd been focused on her all morning.

He'd slipped into her room before dawn and she'd found herself woken with kisses and his big body wrapped around her. He'd made love to her and then taken her to the shower where they'd gotten more dirty than clean. She'd felt like the world had changed, become something better and brighter.

Then they'd joined the others for breakfast and she'd reevaluated her optimism.

Something was up with the lads. Oh, they'd seemed normal. She'd expected their good-natured ribbing about her relationship with Rob, but there had been something underneath it that she couldn't quite put her finger on.

"Would you like some more coffee?" Rebecca asked from the seat beside her. They were in a booth in a small café on the edge of the medical district. According to Rebecca it was where many of the researchers at Kronberg had breakfast or lunch.

They'd been sitting for half an hour with no real information surfacing in what seemed to be a never-ending recitation of medical journals and who'd published what and when and which prestigious medical position they'd moved on to.

This was yet another reason she was happily in private practice, and one where she didn't have to run to conference after conference. The social side of business had been dissatisfying.

Rebecca seemed perfectly comfortable with it.

"Sure." She could use a little caffeine boost. Despite how exhausted she'd been she hadn't been able to go straight to sleep. She'd lain there in bed thinking about how Robert had walked away.

They all had bad dreams. How could they not? He would likely never get over it if he didn't try. Did he expect to not ever sleep with his lover?

Rebecca poured her coffee from the small carafe the waitress had left for them.

Dr. Arthur Dwyer was in his mid-thirties, his entire life devoted to climbing up the ladder of corporate medicine. According to all the information she'd been given, he was brilliant and likely lonely since he didn't date or go out with friends. He worked and worked, and when he wasn't working, he wrote for a journal devoted to pharmaceutical research.

No wonder he'd immediately said yes when Rebecca had called to ask him to brunch.

Arthur looked at her as though remembering she was there. "You said you were in the medical field, too?"

He hadn't been pleased when he'd realized Rebecca wasn't alone. She'd decided to go in with Rebecca when the other woman had mentioned Arthur had been known for getting a bit handsy. Ariel was there to make sure Rebecca didn't have to deal with unwanted advances and to save them all the trouble that would come when Owen murdered the man for the aforementioned unwanted advances.

"I'm a clinical psychologist," Ariel replied.

"She's been helping me with my protocols." Rebecca had told him a little about the work she was doing. Not that she was working with a group of mind-erased soldiers, but she'd talked about helping recover memories.

"I'm sure she is." He'd been utterly dismissive of anything that wasn't drug therapy. He was a true believer in better living through pharmaceuticals. "I can't believe I'm seeing you again. I didn't think you would ever come back to Germany. You left so fast. That was such a crazy time. First you and then Steven walked out, and then Dr. McDonald transferred like overnight. I'm glad that's never happened to my team. We've only had to replace one junior member over the last couple of years. Stability is important. I always wondered what happened."

"I wondered what the rumors were," Rebecca replied with a hint of mischief in her eyes.

She was good. She might be a doctor, but she'd caught onto the spy thing quickly. That look in her eyes said she was curious but that it was all in fun. No danger here. It's nothing more than a spot of gossip.

Arthur took the bait. "Oh, there were all kinds of rumors flying around. You know no one can come up with a conspiracy theory like a bunch of researchers."

"Really? I would think you would be quite serious." Ariel recognized the kind of man he was. The key to a man like Arthur was to challenge him. He was the kind of man who couldn't stand the thought of being wrong.

"Oh, we can come up with some crazy stuff." He looked around before leaning in. "There was a rumor that Dr. McDonald caught you and Reasor having an affair."

Rebecca shuddered. "No. Never. I was married, and even if I hadn't been I wasn't attracted to him."

Rebecca had gotten comfortable with Tucker, but Ariel had noticed she still didn't like to be alone with him. She understood he wasn't the man he'd been, but there was an ugly history there. One only Rebecca remembered.

Arthur shrugged. "I never bought that one. The two of you were complete opposites. My favorite theory was that McDonald was working on something dark."

Yes, this was one of the things she would like to know. How much had gotten out? How careful had McDonald been? "Something dark?"

Arthur's voice went low. "McDonald was an odd one. I'll be honest she always…what is the word you Americans use? She creeped me out. I'm a very ambitious man. It would have been easy to get on her team, and yet something about her always made me pause. I didn't like to be around her, but I wouldn't go so far as to say the woman was capable of trying to invent a way to give people Alzheimer's. That would be evil, and what would the purpose be?"

Oh, it wasn't as simple as that, but someone had known at Kronberg. Someone had an inkling of what Hope McDonald had been doing there. If the rumors had filtered down to Arthur's level, a lot of people had to have known.

"I miss the rumor mill. The people here could come up with some doozies. At least it's not aliens. Well, I assure you everything I worked on was to cure the disease," Rebecca managed with a laugh, though Ariel could see the way her shoulders had tensed.

"Of course it was. I actually thought she might be close given how Kronberg treated anything coming out of that lab."

"I never worked anywhere else in the company," Rebecca said. "There was a difference in security procedures? I would have thought there would be a single protocol."

"There was for everyone else. Dr. McDonald's research was treated like pure gold," Arthur said with a long-suffering sigh. "While she was working there the rest of the teams were definitely not as important as hers. If McDonald needed a piece of equipment, she got it. They would take money from other budgets to give her whatever she requested. As for security, someone came into her office at the end of the day and downloaded whatever she'd worked on. It wasn't allowed on the shared network. We take pains to ensure our research can't be hacked, but they were overly concerned with McDonald's. I had a friend who worked in tech support who said no one was allowed to work on McDonald's systems. She had her own tech and no one else touched her systems."

"I know. I was surprised to find out the other teams didn't have a dedicated tech," Rebecca said. "And then I decided Dr. McDonald was merely eccentric. And filthy rich, of course."

"Yes, the woman did have an entitlement problem," Arthur replied. "But then she also spent more time with the board of directors than any other doctor here. She and the head of research and development were close. I was surprised she left the way she did."

"How did she leave? I'd already gone back to the States at that point," Rebecca admitted. "I left because my husband and I were having trouble. Not that going home worked. We still ended up divorcing."

Ariel knew the real reason Rebecca had left. She'd been terrified by Steven Reasor, the man they now knew as Tucker. Someone had used the time dilation drug on Rebecca and she'd spent a night in hell. She always said "someone" because she had a hard time believing it had been Tucker.

Arthur shook his head. "It's a mystery. I think it's probably why there are so many rumors about her. One day she up and left, her lab was completely cleaned out, and we never heard from her again. They were all gone. All her researchers, not that the team was ever big. She kept her team small because I don't think she trusted many people. Funny thing is from what I can tell, most of the team is gone now."

Ariel knew what he meant but wanted him to talk more. "Gone?"

Arthur leaned in, his voice going low. "Dead. They're almost all dead. Reasor had that car accident. The tech who worked with her was killed a few years back in a mugging. Dr. McDonald died under mysterious circumstances. Even her dad passed. Cursed group of people, if you ask me. You were lucky."

"Yes, I guess I am." Rebecca had paled slightly. "Did anyone ever find out what happened to Veronica?"

Arthur shrugged. "Oh, I heard she got out of the business, but I don't know where she went. I know she upset the big bosses for some reason. She requested to move teams and when she was denied she walked out without notice. It was a couple of days before Dr. McDonald disappeared. It's good she didn't want to work in medical research because I don't think she would be able to find a job again. The bosses were upset with her."

"Rebecca left the same way," Ariel pointed out, turning to her friend. "You never mentioned Kronberg tried to blackball you."

"They didn't," Rebecca replied. "I didn't give notice at all, but they've never given me a bad reference."

"Well, they know you're going to move on to bigger and better things. Veronica wasn't in your class, dear. They wouldn't mess with the darling of neuro. I'm sure they wanted a chance to hire you back someday. No one cared about Veronica. She should have been grateful for the job, but she was a foolish girl," Arthur said with irritating authority.

"That's sad," Rebecca replied. "I was hoping to catch up with her. I always liked Veronica."

Arthur glanced down at his watch. "Well, this has been delightful, but I have to get going. I have a meeting soon. And you know I never believed any of the rumors about you and Reasor. Now the one about him and Veronica, that I did believe. I always thought the lady did protest too much, if you know what I mean."

Veronica and Reasor? Rebecca had never mentioned a romantic connection between the two.

Rebecca looked as surprised as Ariel felt. "I don't. I knew Veronica pretty well. She and Steven never got along. She never once mentioned she had a thing for him. Quite the opposite."

"Well, I do know that they went away together the weekend before Steven left," he admitted. "I was at the airport and I saw them get on a plane together. I assumed when he left that the weekend didn't go well and that was why he requested the transfer to Argentina. He didn't even come back to the office from what I understood. He simply went straight to McDonald's secondary lab."

"Where did they go?" Ariel asked. "Steven and Veronica, that is. Sorry. I've heard so much about these people from Rebecca that I feel like I know them."

He pushed back his chair and stood. "Paris. They boarded a plane to Paris. Like I said, I guess the city wasn't kind to them because Veronica came back alone, and shortly after, she left the company. Rebecca, it was good to catch up with you. Please keep in touch. We've all missed you. I would love to hear more about the private group you're working for. I thought you were crazy to leave Huisman, but then I heard about the foundation's troubles. If only we weren't reliant on foundations for money."

Rebecca stood, too, offering her cheek for a kiss. "Wouldn't that be lovely?"

They said another few words of good-bye, but Ariel's attention had caught on a woman walking toward the bathrooms. Tall and blonde, there was something about the way she moved that gave her away.

Kimberly Solomon. She was chic and lovely in white slacks and a crisp green top, a Chanel scarf around her neck.

Ariel glanced back and Robert and Owen were eating their lunches, seeming to pay no attention to anything but their burgers and beers.

Had they seen Kim? What the hell was she doing here? She didn't have permission to let anyone else know the fact that they might be working with the Agency in a small way. She wasn't sure how Robert would handle an operative walking into the middle of their mission. After the morning she'd had with the Lost Boys, she wasn't sure she should tell them at all. They were suspicious, and a faction of them were starting to question the status quo. That much was obvious. The question was would telling them they had Solo in their corner hurt or help the situation?

"I'm going to visit the loo," Ariel said, standing. "I'll be back in a minute. Arthur, it was lovely to meet you."

Rebecca nodded her way as she and Arthur were exchanging cards. Robert glanced her way but seemed to be mollified when she nodded toward the ladies' room. She took her purse and quietly stepped away.

She opened the door and Kim was sitting there like she'd been waiting, but then she likely had.

"Hey, Ari. You have a little glow about you. Come on, dish. How was it?" Kim asked, looking like they were nothing but a couple of girlfriends gossiping about their love lives.

"What are you doing here? Owen and Robert are sitting right there in the dining room. They could have seen you." She knew exactly what was at stake, even if Kim didn't seem to care.

Kim waved that worry off. "They didn't even look at me when I walked by. They were far too busy pretending like they weren't obsessively watching their ladies. They didn't do a particularly good job of it. When that dude showed up and hugged Dr. Walsh, Owen nearly came over the table after him. That research dude was lucky he managed to stop short of touching her ass or I don't think anyone would have kept Owen off him. Such a caveman, that one. I wish I didn't find it sexy. I should be more liberated, right?"

"You should be more careful." She moved the small trash can in front of the door so at least they would have a heads-up if they suddenly weren't alone. "What if I'd brought Rebecca back here? What if she walks in?"

"She doesn't know who I am." Kim sighed and put her Louis Vuitton handbag on the counter. "I'm sorry but I couldn't help it. I needed to talk to you."

"You could have texted. You seem good at that." How long had Kim been watching? It seemed to Ariel like Kim had some superpower where a person could only see her when she wanted them to. A handy thing for a spy.

"I wouldn't risk sending this information to your phone because I don't know who to trust on your team. I know I didn't tip off Levi in Colorado. If I hadn't been following Levi's man, things would have gone differently. If it wasn't me who tipped him off, it had to be one of them. You've either got a mole or Levi is way better than I give him credit for."

She'd thought this through about a million times. She lay in bed at night worried whoever was willing to betray the team would come after Rob. "We're working on the problem. I think I've got it down to two men, but I need more time to figure it out. This is a fact-gathering op. It isn't dangerous or I wouldn't be out in the field with them."

Kim frowned. "It might be getting dangerous. Levi is on the move. I have intelligence that places him on his way here."

Levi was the last thing she needed. This was supposed to be simple. "I'll let Damon and Big Tag know. Maybe we should pull up stakes and go back to London."

Kim's gaze turned distinctly calculating. "Or you can let me try to figure out who's communicating with him. Pretend nothing's wrong. Let me watch and track. I can figure this out. Once we know who our mole is, I can work more freely. I'm afraid if I show up again, the mole will dive deep and we'll lose our chance to catch him."

That had been exactly Big Tag's plan, too. "All right. I'll run that by the bosses, but for now I'll watch and wait. But I have a question for you. Who are you working for?"

"I'm not really supposed to say, but they have your best interests in mind," Kim said. "I promise you. The faction I'm with is working toward the same objectives you are. They want to shut down the elements inside the Agency that want to continue McDonald's work. Beyond that, part of my mission is to figure out who all was in on it. We want to know the names of the companies and individuals who funded her work and any person who was complicit in what happened to those men."

"They don't want the information for themselves?"

Kim shook her head. "No. They know better than anyone that some knowledge is best left unused."

She was done playing around. "Why can't President Hayes just fire the bastards?"

"I'm not confirming or denying anything, but if I was working for the president, I would tell you he's in a sensitive position. The politics of it could cause a scandal that would rock the Agency. We need firm proof, enough that if it gets out to the press, there's no question we did the right thing. The man I'm working for has been set up before, and he can't let it happen again."

It was as close to a confirmation as she would likely get. "All right."

"I'm working hard to get the smoking gun we need, but you should understand that Levi has some finely honed survival instincts. He has to know the tides are shifting and once his bosses are out of power, he'll be out of a job."

"Good. He shouldn't have one as it is. The Agency should have backed Ezra."

"Well, my ex wasn't the best at politics," Kim admitted. "He never was good at playing the game, and Levi is a master. I knew if it came down to a choice, they would back Levi. I had to do a lot of work…"

Kim had gone pale.

"What kind of work? Did you try to save his job?"

"No. I had to work hard to make sure his job was the only thing they burned." Kim shivered. "He knew too much. I had to play dirty to make sure he stayed alive."

"Kim, what did you do?"

Tears shimmered in her eyes. "I did what I had to do. I would do it again. And again. I won't ever stop protecting that man. Not even if it kills me."

She hated how vulnerable her friend looked. Kim was always so strong, always in charge. It was easy to forget she was simply a woman who loved a man. "Let me talk to Ezra."

Kim laughed, though there was no joy in the sound. "The very fact that you call him Ezra is proof enough that he won't want to talk about me. It doesn't matter. We all make our choices and we have to live with them, but by god I'm going to make sure that man doesn't go down on my watch."

"Does he know?"

"Again, it doesn't matter. Just take care of him for me, Ari. I'm going to settle things on my end once and for all, but I need time. Levi hates him."

"I think it's more a case of Levi wanting you."

She shook her head. "I'm a symptom, not the disease. Levi wants me because Beck had me. I don't know why, but Levi's hatred of Beck runs deep, and I worry about what he'll do if this shit goes down and I don't take him out fully. Do not underestimate him. I'm going to be in and out of Munich for a little while, but you can call if you need me. I might have a lead on your girl."

"On Veronica?"

"Yes, and don't ask me. I can't take you with me. If I can find her, she might be the key to what really went down." Kim settled her bag on her shoulder. "I'll be in touch. And maybe I can come out of the shadows and we can get a drink. I don't have a love life. I need to live vicariously through yours. I miss you, Ari."

"I miss you, too." She suddenly wished she could do exactly that. She wanted to go out to the bar and talk about what had happened the night before. She liked Rebecca, but there was a necessary distance between them. Kim knew everything about her. There weren't secrets being kept from Kim.

There was a knock on the door and then a masculine voice. "Ari, are you all right in there?"

Robert.

Kim gave her a wistful smile and then disappeared behind the stall door.

She hurried to open the door or her personal caveman might bust in. "Sorry."

He smiled down at her. "Are you all right?"

She nodded and took his hand. "I'm good. That was a lot of information to process. We should get back to the club. I need to write it all up."

Robert stared at the door and for a moment she worried he might still go in. She held her breath.

And then he turned and started to lead her out.

She prayed Kim worked fast because she couldn't keep lying to a man she was absolutely certain she was falling in love with.

* * * *

"Paris?" Tucker paced the floor of the kitchen.

The minute they'd returned to the club, Robert had called a meeting. If he could have kept the news from Tucker he would have, but it was too important.

Ariel had been contemplative the whole ride home. He knew the expression on her face well. She was worried about something and it was probably Tucker and his reaction to the news. Now she was occupying herself by making tea.

Robert didn't want tea. He wanted to be alone with her, but that wasn't happening anytime soon. "That's what this Arthur person said. He told Rebecca he saw you getting on a plane to Paris with Veronica Croft shortly before you transferred to Argentina and she quit Kronberg all together."

"This should be easy enough to check." Dante sat behind a laptop. "I don't suppose he gave you the name of the airline?"

Rebecca shook her head. "I didn't think to ask him that. I should have. Damn it."

Owen slid an arm around her shoulders. "You did everything perfectly, love. You were great out there. If you'd pushed him he would have gotten suspicious."

"He wasn't suspicious at all." Peter stepped into the kitchen. "When he left, I followed him a few blocks and he called someone, a friend I suppose. Said he'd met with you and that you were still pretty but…well, he's not a particularly nice man. He called you an ice queen."

"I'll show him what I can do with ice. I'll stuff his dead body in a bloody freezer and then we'll see how he likes it," Owen muttered.

Rebecca merely sighed and leaned into him. "He was always a douchebag, but he was friendly. I'm glad I got good information. I think we'll have better luck with Louisa. I knew her better. I can be a little more open."

"We'll go over all of it," Ariel promised, pouring out the tea. "I'll make sure you're prepped and I'll be with you the whole way. We're meeting her at an outdoor café, right?"

Rebecca nodded. "It's one in the Marienplatz we always used to meet at. She's kind of a bitch but she's in on all the gossip."

"I want to know everything about this Veronica person." Tucker couldn't seem to stay still. "Was she my lover? Was she my victim?"

"Well, you didn't do a good job with her since apparently we don't think she's dead," Sasha replied. "Next time you need to be better."

"Hey." He'd felt some slight sympathy for the man the night before, but Sasha was still a massive asshole. "This is serious, and Tucker is asking the same questions any of us would in his situation."

"I don't see how Tucker getting laid in his previous life has much to do with this. I'm more interested in the fact that they changed their security protocols surrounding McDonald than I am in finding out Tucker here had a woman he didn't have to pay," Dante said.

"I'll get on the Dark Web and see if I can find anyone willing to talk about the protocols," Peter offered. "I'll pretend to be a corporate spy. I've done this many times to get information, though usually I had government backing. This time if I get caught, I will have to hope Ian is up for a jailbreak."

"We'll take care of you," Ariel promised him. "It would be good if we could have some understanding of their protocols. If Kronberg still has that information…"

Robert shook his head. He'd thought this through during the car ride back. "It would be old intel. We all know she made her biggest findings after she went on the run. After she left Germany she wouldn't have been held in check by their protocols. I doubt she shared her findings with them after she left Europe."

"It would still be helpful to know what her first formulary of the drug looked like." Rebecca thanked Ariel for the tea and turned back to Robert. "If I know where she started from, I might be able to better extrapolate where she went. I might also be able to figure out if it's even possible she also made a cure. If Kronberg has her early research, I would love to see it. I want to see how she took the work I did here and twisted it. I want to know how much I'm responsible for."

"You're not." Owen shifted so he could look in her eyes. He caught her face between his big hands. "You are not responsible for any of this, my love. You were trying to help."

"I should have seen something was wrong," she insisted.

"You did," Tucker said. "You knew I was wrong. It wasn't your fault. It was mine."

"God, we're full of martyrs today," Dante said with a huff. "If only Ezra would show up we would have the holy trinity."

"Fuck you, Dante," Tucker said.

"You keep offering and I might take you up on it one day," he said under his breath. He stood and closed his laptop. "I'll be in the office. The Wi-Fi is better in there. I'll let you know if I find anything about the flight. I might be able to track them around Paris if I can find the plane they took."

"Maybe if I look at some pictures of Paris," Tucker offered.

"No," both Ariel and Rebecca said at the same time.

The last thing they needed was Tucker making himself sick.

Sasha shook his head. "I would not recommend this. Haven't we had enough puking? Leave it be, brother. Let Dante and I see if we can find a paper trail. I think this is one of those stories it's better we tell you than you live through."

Because he'd already lived through it once.

"I think that's a perfect idea, Sasha. You two work on that," he said. The faster they got the information the faster Tucker might calm down. Unless they found out something else terrible about him. "We also need to look into the Argentina flight. If Reasor went to Argentina, there should be some records."

"I'll look into it. If Jax has some time, he could help, too." Sasha stood up. "I'll give him a call. I'm going to work for a while. Is the club open tonight? I wouldn't mind some time with a Domme. Do you have any here who would scene with me?"

Peter nodded. "Of course. You're more than welcome. Unless someone thinks we shouldn't be open. I don't see any reason. We're a private club and we'll have security."

He wasn't going to shut down the club. He wanted to spend some time with Ariel. If they shut the club, they would spend the evening working, and they could all use some time off. Sasha definitely needed to scene after what had happened the night before. If he didn't, Robert was worried he would let off steam in other ways. "Please do stay open. Several of us will likely come down and play."

"I would love to see it when it's open and full of people. It looks so different," Rebecca admitted. "I've only seen The Garden before."

Owen leaned in close. "One day I'll take you to Sanctum. I promise. Come, love. Let's rest for a bit and then we'll walk the dungeon tonight. Hopefully Sasha doesn't convince his Domme for the night to torture his balls. It's hard to watch that."

"Speak for yourself," Sasha said. "It's a beautiful thing."

Owen shuddered. "We speak two different languages, mate."

The three of them walked off.

"Is he all right?" Peter asked. "Perhaps he shouldn't play. I heard there was trouble last night."

Ariel sat down beside Robert. "Sasha needs to scene. He's a switch, but he only tops when he's feeling good about himself. He often bottoms. It's part of his therapy. He never pushes it too far. I would select a Domme who's worked with masochists before in case he does tonight."

Peter pulled out his cell phone. "I have one in mind. She's good. I'll see you two this evening and I'll let you know how it goes on the Deep Web."

"Thank you, and thanks for following up with Arthur." It was good to know Peter was doing his part. This was why Big Tag had wanted the man around. He could work more quietly than the rest of them because he fit in here, knew the language. And he was the type of man who might go unnoticed.

"I'm happy to help. I will say though that there was a woman at the restaurant today who I swear I've seen before. I'm putting a description of her in my report. I could be wrong, but she's a striking woman. I will be on the lookout for her," Peter said. "I'm going to file my report now. I'll see you all this evening."

"Do you think it's Solo?" Tucker asked.

Ariel seemed to stiffen. "If she is here, we can't know she's not here to help us. I thought you liked her."

"I did," Tucker replied. "But that was before I knew who I was. Maybe she's here to bring me in."

"She's not going to take you in. If she wanted to do that, she could show up with the authorities and we wouldn't be able to fight them." But he would try. He'd thought that scenario through. He couldn't let them take one of his brothers. He couldn't trust anyone in the government.

"Maybe she *should* take me in," Tucker said. "I don't think I want to know what I did in Paris. I don't even like saying the word. Something happened to me there. Or maybe I did something. Veronica Croft was alive after we went to Paris?"

"Yes," Ariel affirmed. "She was alive. She came back and quit her job and that was the last we know of her. You didn't kill her."

"We can't know that." Tucker had his hands on his hips, his face tight. "Maybe I waited until I got back."

"I don't think so. You went to Argentina before she quit," Robert pointed out.

"We'll figure it out, Tucker," Ariel promised. "Please come out and play tonight. If you're not feeling like topping, you can bottom for a change. Or I can find you a sex worker. I think you should indulge yourself. It's perfectly legal here. It won't be hard to find someone."

"You know sometimes I don't even have sex with them," Tucker said, his voice hollow. "I sit and talk to them. I lie in bed and wrap my arms around them. God, I'm fucked up. I'll come downstairs and see what happens. I'll be okay."

Tucker turned and walked out.

Robert reached for her hand when it looked like she was going to go after Tucker. "Don't. He needs some space. He'll talk when he's ready."

"But he needs to talk now," Ariel insisted.

How hard was it on her? She wanted so much to fix them all, to put together their pieces and make them whole again. It wouldn't happen. They were irrevocably broken and no amount of talking about their feelings would fill the empty holes. But they could learn to live with them. They could find their way. "He needs to know that we're here. I know you're the therapist, but you've gotten too close to us."

Her eyes had filled with tears as she looked up at him. "I know I have. I've lost my objectivity."

He pulled her close. "We need you to be involved with us. Tucker needs it desperately. I wasn't saying something bad about you. In this case, I do know what he needs and it's space. Let's give it to him."

She nodded and wrapped her arms around him, laying her head on his chest. "All right."

It felt good to be able to hold her. He stroked his hand down her back, happy that she relaxed against him.

He couldn't help but think about how odd it had been at the restaurant today. She'd left Rebecca alone, and that had seemed out of character for her. Yes, he and Owen had been sitting at a table close to them, but Arthur hadn't left and she'd been there to give her impression of the man. "You would tell me if something was going on, right? Something we needed to know about."

"I would if I could."

He held her close and tried not to think about the fact that he'd seen a woman go into the bathroom before her. A blonde.

Ariel wouldn't lie to him.

He forced the thought from his head and started planning the evening.

Chapter Seven

Ariel scanned the dungeon floor, taking in the scenes in front of her. She'd dressed in the locker room, helping Rebecca into her corset and talking about how they wanted the evening to go. That was usually her transition time. Putting on fet wear helped her move into her submissive persona. Not tonight. Tonight she couldn't seem to shut her brain off. The problems they were facing churned in her head.

Tucker had decided to stay upstairs. Dante was keeping him company. When she'd left the two had been murdering each other in some video game. Should she have stayed with him? He'd seemed perfectly happy, but she knew Tucker's emotions ran deep.

Sasha had gone into a privacy room with the tall, beautiful Domme Peter had selected for him. Rebecca and Owen were happily wandering the dungeon.

Everyone seemed to be taken care of, at least for the night. Hopefully they would all find some peace. She glanced to her right and suddenly wasn't thinking about her problems. A woman was bound face-out to a St. Andrew's Cross. She was topless but far from naked. A miniskirt of what looked to be hot-pink faux fur covered her hips. A long pink and white-striped tail hung between her legs. She was fairly confident the tail was held in place by a plug in the sub's ass. The woman's hands were encased in gloves that looked like large cat paws, done in the same pink faux fur as the miniskirt, accented with white, and what appeared to be real metal claws. The cuffs holding her to the St. Andrew's Cross wrapped around her wrists just below the point where the gloves stopped. On her feet she wore wedge boots covered in stripes of pink and white fur.

The most bemusing part of all of it was the large costume cat head that completely hid the woman's face, head, and neck. Like any good therapist who lived and worked in a sex club, Ariel had a vast knowledge of most kinks. Germany was the epicenter of furry culture. The Garden didn't have any "furries," as members of the community called themselves, in the club. While the woman wore a partial fur suit, her Dom wore a full suit that turned him into a towering gray wolf. He'd made some concessions in his attire—he'd taken off one paw glove, probably because he couldn't hold that crop with it on.

The crop struck the underside of the woman's left breast. She yowled, a distinctly feline sound, then struggled against the restraints, hissing. The wolf reached out with his still-gloved hand and petted her from shoulder to waist. The cat calmed and relaxed back against the cross.

She studied the couple, fascinated by the intimacy playing out in front of her. There was an artistry to any BDSM scene—even the furry ones. Maybe especially those. It took bravery and a deep sense of self to allow one's fantasies to be played out in public. This couple obviously had an enormous amount of trust between them. It would be challenging for the Dom to read the submissive's reaction when they weren't speaking, and he couldn't see her face or hands. There were plenty of BDSM masks or hoods that could be used in scenes, but those were usually formfitting to the sub's head, and still offered the top some opportunity to read facial expressions. A good Dom or Domme could also read body language, but again, the hands were a key part of that—fists versus relaxed hands, fidgeting fingers versus clinging to ropes or restraints.

Perhaps The Garden needed to invite a Furry Dom to teach an advanced class on reading a sub's body language. She would enjoy that. Even experienced couples might find themselves at a loss if they were prevented from communicating via words, expression, or hand signals. Or perhaps this was more about creating a unique language that both parties understood, even if that language didn't use words. Communication was key to BDSM play and—

A hand wrapped around her waist from behind. Pure instinct moved her. She stepped back, using her shoulders to shove the person who'd touched her without permission. She brought her foot up and smashed it down, her heel to his toes. She twisted slightly and brought her elbow up and back, catching him in the solar plexus. He doubled over, and as she completed her turn to face him, she raised her arms, right hand wrapped over her left fist, prepared to smash the back of his head with her elbow.

A familiar brown-haired man was doubled over, hands on his knees. Robert.

She'd attacked Robert.

She blinked and dropped her arms. Not only had she attacked him, she'd nearly incapacitated him. A friendly, approachable psychologist shouldn't be able to take down a trained super-solider in hand to hand, especially when she was barefoot and wearing nothing but a corset and G string.

"What the fuck?" Robert wheezed.

She dropped to her knees beside him. "Rob, I'm sorry."

He sucked in air, then raised his bowed head enough to look at her. With her on her knees and him bent over, their faces were close together. Close enough that she could kiss him.

"How did you…" He frowned at her, and Ariel's stomach knotted.

"Are you alright?" She'd acted purely on muscle memory. She hadn't been thinking at all. She was on edge after the meeting with Kim and being forced to lie to Rob. "I'm sorry. I was watching a scene and you startled me."

A brow rose above his eyes. "I…startled…you, and you nearly put me on my ass?"

There was another way to distract him. She was already on her knees, so she spread her legs, resting her hands palm up on her thighs. "I apologize, Sir."

"Is there a problem here?" Peter was in a set of dark brown leathers, showing off his lean and muscled frame and looking far from the mild-mannered tour guide he was during the daylight hours.

Everyone was watching them. She'd interrupted the scenes. Damn it.

"No, Sir. I was distracted when my Dom touched me, and I reacted." She forced out a chuckle. "I was trained in self-defense by some of the best in the business, and I think I hurt him."

Robert got to his feet.

Peter winced. "Ah, I see. Master Robert, do you need something? Ice?"

"No ice." He rubbed his stomach, then looked down at her. "Remind me to compliment whoever handled your self-defense training."

She straightened her back and lowered her gaze to Robert's knees. "I will, Sir. I'm so sorry."

"I'm sorry for startling you, sweetheart." Robert held out a hand. "And I'm sorry for disrupting the scenes, Master Peter. We're a new couple and learning all sorts of things about each other. Come with me. I have our scene ready. I think my gorgeous sub here could use some stress relief. I know I could."

She placed her hand in his. Robert gripped her fingers and raised her to her feet. Awareness and desire, woken by that single touch, pushed away all of her previous worries. In his boots and leathers, Robert towered over her, broad and strong. She wanted to feel that strength, wanted him to use that big body to make her submit.

And maybe, deep down, she wanted him to punish her for lying to him. Wanted him to offer her absolution through pain.

"How about I greet you properly this time." Robert slid one hand around the back of her neck, pulling her to his chest, then holding her still as he bent his head and kissed her.

Her whole body went soft, molding against his. She wished she wasn't wearing the corset. Wished he wasn't wearing the leather vest.

He deepened the kiss, nipping her lower lip then thrusting his tongue into her mouth. This was what she needed. She needed this man dominating her in the dungeon and being her partner in the outer world. She needed him by her side. She'd never really believed in the mystical, magical "one," but this had to be what it felt like to find a missing piece of her soul.

Robert broke the kiss, still holding her by the back of the neck, his thumb below her ear. "I'm going to push us tonight."

A thrill went through her at the thought of seeing where he would want to go. "Yes, Sir. I want that. I…I need it."

Because I'm lying to you.

"I want to do things to you…" The words seemed to rip from him. "Things that are too hard. Too rough."

Robert taking her roughly. Robert letting go and unleashing on her. The thought of it made her ache with need. "I can take it."

"No, you're soft." His thumb stroked the skin of her neck below her ear. "You deserve to be worshiped."

"Worship doesn't have to be soft. This is fantasy and I need it rough tonight." Their bodies were still pressed together, and she felt his cock harden in his leathers. She rubbed her hips against him. "I want you to take me. Dominate me. Fuck me. Help me find the pleasure that can only come when I give up control. When I trust you with my body—" *And my soul.*

He was waiting for her to finish, but she couldn't say the last part out loud. When they got back to London, she was going to have a long talk with Damon. She needed to tell Rob everything, the whole story of her life so this lie wasn't between them.

She didn't want to talk any more tonight. Her blood was humming, her skin tingling in anticipation of his touch, and she didn't want to wait a second longer.

Ariel slowly turned her head to the side, his hand sliding against her skin. She parted her lips and took the thumb that had been stroking her neck into the wet warmth of her mouth. She sucked on it the way she'd sucked at his tongue, the way she wanted to suck his cock.

With his thumb still in her mouth she raised her gaze to meet his. His eyes were hazel and bright, focused on her with an intensity that made her want to push him further. She nipped him, hard enough that his nostrils flared. Then she drew back slowly, her lips sealed in a ring around his thumb as it slowly emerged from her mouth.

"You're deliberately being a brat."

She tilted her head back, allowing his thumb to slide down her chin, then along the underside of her jaw, leaving a damp trail.

"Please." She didn't want to talk. It was time to play, time to find the Ariel she could only be here and with him.

He swooped down, planting a shoulder against her waist then straightening up. Her world upended and she braced her hands on his very nice, leather-covered ass as he strode across the dungeon floor. It was hard to compete with the furry scene, but she felt eyes on her as they went past, and that only added to her ever-heightening arousal.

The world spun, and then she was standing, Robert's hands on her waist keeping her steady until she found her balance. They were toward the back of the club, near a wall.

They weren't near any of the main pieces of equipment, but his kit was on the floor not far away.

Robert took a step back, putting space between them but not distance. He'd only stepped back so he could watch her. "Take off your clothes. I want you naked."

She relaxed, grateful they'd moved past the time for questions. She reached for the closures on the front of the corset. The laces at the back allowed it to be adjusted and tightened, but the hook and eye closures on the front were how she actually put it on and took it off. She started at the bottom, undoing the lower third. Then she went to the top, sliding her thumbs under the corset and undoing the closures one by one. When there were only a few middle hooks holding the corset closed, she dropped her hands. She knew what she looked like—the top of the corset was flowered open, her breasts straining to be free. A triangle of skin between the top of her thong and the inverted V of the partially removed corset would also be visible, drawing his attention down to the scrap of fabric that concealed her pussy.

She felt powerful, beautiful like this.

"Spread your legs," he commanded.

She didn't think, merely obeyed. She stepped wide to give him a better view of what he wanted.

"You're aroused. I can see how wet your pussy is. You soaked the fabric." His voice was dark and deep.

"I'm ready for you, Sir," she murmured. Beyond ready. If he wanted to fuck her that minute, she could handle him. No one had ever gotten her ready for sex merely by being in her space.

His gaze slid up her body to her face. "I assumed part of being ready meant obeying me."

She frowned. "Sir?"

"I told you I want you naked. You're gorgeous and wanton but you're not naked." His voice deepened. "You know exactly what you're doing. Topping from the bottom."

She hadn't thought of it that way, but he was right. She had been trying to tempt him. He knew her well.

She released the last closures of the corset, letting it fall. Her breasts felt heavy with need. She drew her shoulders back, offering herself to him, begging him to touch her. "That wasn't my intention, Sir."

"I think you're lying to me."

Her breath caught, and the whole world seemed to freeze. She looked at him from beneath her lashes, but for once his face was unreadable.

"Take off the panties," he commanded. "And that's two."

She stripped off the thong, losing a bit of her grace in her haste to obey. "Two what, Sir?"

He stared at her, determination clear in his gaze. Robert was indulgent. In the vanilla part of their world, he would be gentle. A thrill went through her that he could let loose this piece of his soul. It was only for her. "My plans for you included a bit of pleasure, a bit of pain, but no true punishment. Now we have to talk about discipline."

She bowed her head submissively. "I'm sorry, Sir."

"Are you?" He cupped her chin with his hand, forcing her head up. "I don't think you are. I think you want…no, you need…something more tonight. I was going to give that to you, but now I'll have to stop and punish you, too."

She winced. She had been topping from the bottom. "You're…you're right, Sir. I'm sorry."

"You thought I wouldn't give you what you needed."

"You don't see all the different parts of me. You think I'm made of glass or something. You don't see the part of me that isn't soft, the part that needs you to be rough." She hadn't realized how much she needed him to see past her outer trappings. His belief that she was soft had been the very reason he'd pushed her away before. She'd prayed after Toronto that he would see her differently.

"You are soft. Wonderfully soft." He palmed her breast.

Thank god, he was finally touching her. Her skin sang wherever their skin met. That moment of relief changed to one of arousal when his thumbs danced over her nipple.

"And I *will* worship you. I will worship you with my lips." He kissed her forehead, then feathered a kiss over each cheek. "With my hands." He squeezed her breasts. "With my teeth." His lips trailed down her neck to her shoulder and he bit her, hard enough that she jumped.

That flare of pain made her nipples tighten against his palms, sent a bolt of arousal through her.

"I'll worship you when I turn you over my knee and spank your ass. When I tease your clit or torture these sweet tits." He released her breasts only to pinch her nipples, rolling and plucking. "I will worship you, but most of all, I will dominate you. When we're playing, you will submit to me. You will trust me to give you what you need."

There was nothing she wanted more. She let her head fall back, exposing the line of her throat. "Yes, Sir. I trust you."

He brushed his lips over her skin, working his way from the notch in her collarbone up her neck. He nipped her chin before retreating. "Move against the wall."

She obeyed, taking small steps back until her shoulders hit the cool stone of the wall. She realized why he'd chosen this spot. There were chains bolted high on the wall dangling down, like some medieval dungeon.

He took leather buckle cuffs from his kit and strode over to her. He crooked a finger and she held out her wrist. "I plan to keep you chained up all night. If your wrists start to hurt or the cuffs pinch, you will indicate so, either by telling me or by holding up three fingers."

He finished buckling her wrists into the restraints.

A shiver of trepidation went through her. They were using nonverbal protocols? Was he going to gag her? It was surprising since Rob liked to talk. He was keeping her off balance, mindfucking her. Yeah, that did something for her, too.

"Show me," he demanded.

She held up three fingers. He nodded in satisfaction, then took her cuffed wrist and brought it back against the wall. He used a carabineer to clip the cuff to a link of the dangling chain. When both hands were restrained against the wall, he stepped back, and she couldn't mistake the look of deep satisfaction on his handsome face.

She tested her bonds. Her arms weren't raised overhead, which made sense if he planned to keep her like this for some time. Arms up was a tiring posture, and there was a limit to how long a sub could stay like that. Instead, he'd restrained her with her wrists level with her shoulders. She had some mobility, enough that when he stepped close again she was able to reach out just enough to brush his shoulder with her fingertips as he knelt.

He spread her legs, wide enough that her pussy was open, vulnerable, but not so wide that she couldn't maintain the posture, then added cuffs to her ankles, and attached those to two of the closest O-rings bolted into the bottom of the wall.

She was utterly restrained, and he could do anything he liked with her. She wasn't sure why this always did it for her, but it did. This had always been her fantasy and she'd long since given up on feeling anything so useless as shame about her sexuality.

He paused, still on his knees before her, and brought his face close to her pussy. He breathed deep. "You're hot, so ready for me."

"I am, Sir."

Robert went back to his kit and pulled out a large plastic bag. She blinked, staring at what he had in his hands. Maybe it was the somewhat dim light of the dungeon, but that looked like a big bag of—

"Clothespins." Robert showed one of his prizes to her and one side of his mouth tugged up in the most heartbreaking grin. She loved his dirty Dom, but the playfulness got to her, too. "I was planning on using clamps on you, but I couldn't decide what kind. Trust me. I've spent hours thinking about this. I couldn't decide where I would put them." He rattled the bag. "Now I don't have to decide. I get to put them everywhere."

"Everywhere?" she asked.

"Everywhere." He opened the bag and clipped a dozen or so clothespins to the bottom of his vest.

Ariel had a vivid memory of her mother doing the same, clipping clothespins to the bottom of her shirt so she could easily get them as she hung out the washing to dry.

After tonight, she was sure she'd never be able to look at a clothespin without thinking about him.

He held up one clothespin, a devilish smile quirking his lips. "Where to start?" He ran the tip of the pale wooden clothespin along the inside of one arm to her shoulder. She caught her breath as he hesitated at her breast, then let out a noisy sigh as he kept going, across the top of her chest to her other arm.

He was the one teasing now. And it worked. She wanted that stupid clothespin. Her breasts ached with need.

He repeated the motion, and this time she thrust her breasts toward him. He paused, the clothespin at her collarbone. "You want me to clamp your sweet nipples?"

More than anything. "Yes, Sir. Please."

"What if I make you beg?"

Begging wasn't something she would do with anyone she didn't trust. But here it was all simply part of the game. "Then I'll beg. Please, Sir. Robert, please. I need you."

"It will hurt. This clothespin will bite down hard."

He was making her crazy talking like this. "I know, I know. I want it."

He trailed the clothespin down the center line of her body, between her breasts, over her bellybutton, to her pussy. "And what if I want to start here?"

"Then I'll beg you to clamp my pussy, Sir."

"Your clit?" He rubbed her clit with the clothespin. The wood, which had felt smooth against her flesh before now, felt hard, the edges sharp, the metal of the spring cold. "Would you beg me to clamp your clit?"

She whimpered.

"Answer me," he commanded in his deep Dom voice.

"Yes, yes." She rocked her hips forward, sliding against his hand. "I would beg you to clamp my clit. I would beg you to torture my pussy."

"Excellent."

She heard the clothespin clatter to the floor, but before she could get too disappointed, he bent his head and sucked one nipple into his mouth. The sensation sent a jolt of desire through her. Her body went taut and she found herself on her toes. She tried to grab his head, to hold him to her breasts, but the chains wouldn't allow it. She moaned in pleasure and frustration and he drew his head back, nipple sliding from between his lips. He treated her other breast to the same delicious tug as he let it slide from his mouth.

He was breathing hard when he cupped her breast, lifting it. She looked down and saw the hard bulge his cock had made in his leathers.

His thumb brushed her nipple, bringing her attention back to her breast. He plucked a clothespin from his vest and squeezed it open. She held her breath, her heart hammering in her chest as he lowered it toward her.

Only for him to veer away. He instead pinched the underside of her breast with the thumb and forefinger of his other hand, then attached the clothespin there. She let out the breath she'd been holding, only to gasp. With each inhale the clothespin jiggled, sending fresh bolts of sensation the short distance between the clothespin and her nipple.

He added a clothespin to the same spot on the other breast, then stepped back. "How does that feel?"

It hurt, but she was extremely aroused, so the pain fed her wanting. "Odd. It's not what I expected."

He nodded as if that's what he'd thought she'd say and selected another clothespin. Again, he clipped it to her breast, this time beside her nipple. Ariel closed her eyes, concentrating on the feeling of his hands on her. Again and again he pinched the skin of her breast, then snapped a clothespin into place. It had been a long time since anyone had paid this much attention to her breasts without touching her nipples. She hadn't realized how hot it would make her, how much she would like the short burst of pain, followed by the lingering warmth from the pinch of the clothespins.

She heard Robert step back and opened her eyes. He was watching her with a hungry gaze. She looked down, examining his handiwork. A ring of six clothespins circled each breast. Her nipples, untouched in the center, were ruched up tight.

She licked her lower lip and brought her gaze to meet his. "More, please, Sir."

Robert growled and lunged for her. She arched her back, offering her already wonderfully abused breasts, but he didn't wrap his arms around her or reach for her nipples. He hit his knees, grabbing the inside of her thighs and forcing her ass back against the wall. He spread her open, then leaned in and licked her pussy, one long stroke up to her clit. Her breath fled as his tongue glided over her. She'd hadn't expected it, hadn't had time to prepare herself mentally for how desperately aroused—and therefore wildly sensitive—she was. She tried to clamp her thighs around his head, but he held her open. He nipped the flesh at the top of her pussy, his lower teeth and lip almost brushing her clit.

She wrapped her hands around the chains, needing the balance they provided. "Sir, please. I need to come."

"You don't come until I give you permission." He smacked the inside of her thigh, sending a delicious thrill through her. "Look at me."

She looked down, past the clothespins, to where he knelt between her legs. Holding her gaze, he stuck out his tongue, flicking her clit.

She could have come then—she was ready. The bondage, the clothespins, every delicious word he'd said…they were enough. They'd brought her to the edge.

But her Dom had told her she couldn't come until she had permission. The part of her that needed to submit, that needed to not be in control, forced her to hold back the orgasm.

"I want to come, Sir," she begged.

Robert surged to his feet. "Open your mouth."

Eagerly, she obeyed, hoping he'd kiss her, or maybe he'd loosen the chains, lower her to her knees, and slide his cock into her mouth.

"Stick out your tongue."

Again she obeyed.

"This is your punishment." He raised a clothespin, squeezed it open. He positioned it on her tongue, then released it.

She whimpered as the clothespin bit down. It hurt, and not with the sweet arousal-tempered burn of the ones on her breasts.

He raised a second clothespin and her eyes widened.

"You earned two," he reminded her softly.

She shook her head. Robert looked pointedly at each hand. He'd given her a signal she could use if this was too much.

She kept her hands wrapped firmly around the chains. Though her job was helping other people express their feelings through words, she wasn't sure she could fully explain what she felt in that moment. Robert, who acted like her boyfriend, worshiped her to the point she felt like a goddess around him, was now punishing her.

This was a real punishment, a bite of pain not softened with pleasure. A sign that he was able and more than willing to truly top her in the club. To correct her behavior, to control and command her even while taking care of her. The dichotomy of this man was fascinating. Robert, who had so little control in his own life, had complete control of her.

She dropped her gaze to his chin.

"Good girl." He raised and applied a second clothespin to her tongue. "Two."

Again she whimpered. She could no longer close her mouth, and she could feel the saliva beginning to pool against her lower lip.

Robert kissed her forehead, then dropped to his knees once more. Ariel wanted to look down at what he was doing, but she stared forward, letting the sensation roll over her. She couldn't think about anything but what he was doing to her body. The clothespins pinched, but they were doing their job. They were forcing her to stay in the now, to concentrate on him.

His fingers slid along her labia. He stroked every plump, damp fold of her pussy with his fingers, as if he were memorizing her by touch. She sighed in pleasure, her breath catching when he came close to her clit, but he never touched it. He took his time, playing with her as if she were his favorite toy. And as he did, her need grew and grew, swelling inside her so that with each breath she was aware of every inch of her own skin.

Then he tugged on her labia. "This isn't punishment. This will hurt, but it's not punishment. It's pain because you need it." There was a pause, and then she felt the open clothespin slide over one side of her plump pussy. She held her breath.

Robert released the clothespin. It bit down, pinching hard and tight. She shrieked and danced onto her toes.

Robert switched to the other side of her pussy. Again she felt the clothespin slide into place. "You need it, and I need to give it to you."

He released the pin, and a fresh wave pulsed through her, centered on her wonderfully tortured pussy.

"And," he growled, "I like playing with and tormenting this sweet pussy."

The sharp, stinging pinch faded to a warm pulsing that was neither pleasure or pain but both. Ariel shifted her hips side to side, feeling the clothespins clack against one another. Robert tugged one gently and she thrust her hips out. "Beautiful," he murmured.

She felt the tug as he unclipped her ankle bindings from the wall.

She let her mind float, finding that wonderful peace where she didn't have to make any decisions, where she didn't have to try and decipher another person's actions or words. There was no ambiguity here. He ordered. She obeyed.

"Look at me."

Ariel lowered her chin, wincing as a bit of saliva spilled down onto her chest.

"God, you're gorgeous. I don't know why I was worried about this. You like it. You like it rough and I like giving it to you. Baby, you are the single sexiest thing I've ever seen." Robert reached up, sliding his thumb through the moisture, then rubbed it over her nipple. When he withdrew, the air on her wet skin was cold, making her nipple ache for his touch. He repeated the caress on the other side, dampening that nipple too.

"Brace yourself." Robert grabbed ahold of her hips.

Unsure what he was about to do, but trusting him fully, she adjusted her grip on the chains and held tight.

Robert lifted her hips up and away from the wall, her feet leaving the floor. For a moment she was suspended in the air, her bodyweight supported by his massive, muscled arms. Robert adjusted her so that her thighs were on his shoulders, her back resting against the wall.

"Don't try to hold yourself up," he ordered. "I've got you. Trust me."

Ariel relaxed her shoulders and arms, letting her weight settle on him. His hands were on her ass, supporting her from below, his face only inches from her pussy. She was completely dependent on him.

"I'm going to eat this sweet pussy. You come as many times as you want. I want to taste you when you come. Then, no matter how many times you've come, I'm going to make you come again when I fuck you." His words were a promise—a dark, wonderful promise.

She nodded, wanting to let him know how much she needed him. Wanted to beg him for more, but she couldn't.

She was being punished because she hadn't trusted him, and she welcomed that punishment, even as she swore she would never fail to trust him again. When they were in a club, they were solid. They were together. This was finally their time and she wouldn't let anything come between them. She would quit if she had to. Robert was the important thing.

He used two fingers to spread her pussy open, pressing the clothespins against the inside of her thighs. "These will help keep your pussy open for me, so I can taste every inch of you. Next time I'm taping the clothespins in place, so your pussy will stay spread. So I can see your clit at all times."

She came close to orgasm right then. The man liked to talk, and he was very, very good at it.

He buried his face in her sex and proved that there was something he was better at than dirty talk, and that was eating pussy. The clothespins bit deeper into her labia as they were squeezed between her thighs and his cheeks. The fresh spikes of pain only made her hotter, and when his nose bumped her clit as his tongue thrust inside her she came.

She'd been hovering near orgasm since he'd put the clothespins on her tongue. Now she had his permission to find release, and his face buried in her pussy was all she needed to fall over that edge.

Every muscle in her body tensed for a moment, that sweet peak of pleasure holding her like a vice. Robert thrust his tongue deep inside her, and that tension broke. She screamed in pleasure. Normally she didn't. Normally she would have clenched her teeth, but he'd made it so she couldn't do that. She couldn't hide the sounds she was making. Everyone around them would look over and know what he was doing to her.

Robert's tongue swept up to her clit and she sobbed. She was so sensitive it was as if he'd touched her with a live wire. Every nerve ending jangled. It was too much, and she had no way to tell him that.

Robert paused, his mouth still against her, and then stopped. He kissed her clit, the soft pressure of his lips a shockingly intense sensation. He kissed her again and again, laying almost chaste kisses over the swollen pearl as she came down from the first orgasm.

Her breathing steadied and softened, but his mouth never stopped, and soon those closed-lip kisses became an open mouth. Each time he kissed her she felt the edges of his teeth and tongue dance over her. She started to rock her hips forward and back, needed to move, needed that primal thrusting motion.

Robert drew back. She looked down at him. Their gazes met. Held.

He reached up between her legs from below, grabbed both clothespins, and yanked them off.

She gasped as pleasure-pain raced through her. Robert pounced, his mouth covering her clit. He licked her with rhythmic passes of the broad flat of his tongue. She came again. Forgetting about the clothespins on her tongue she bit down, adding a fresh layer of pain over the wave of pleasure she was riding. Her thigh muscles trembled, as did her arms.

Each exhale was a whimper of pleasure, each inhale made the clothespins still on her breasts jiggle, and her nipples were diamond hard and aching to be played with.

Robert lifted his head from her pussy, examining her with a dark intensity that made her shiver. He kept his gaze on her as he lowered her back to her feet. The moment lengthened between them, the intimacy almost too much to take. He looked down at her like she was a work of art he'd had a hand in creating.

And then one long arm slid up her side to her breast. He cupped her, the edge of his index finger and thumb nudging the clothespins.

Ariel looked at him, eyes widening as she shook her head. She couldn't come again. Not so soon.

Robert swiped his hand across both breasts, knocking all the clothespins off with one sweep.

Her breathing was hard, fast, and a bit shaky. She looked up at him, mute and pleading. Robert released one of the clothespins from her tongue. She screwed her eyes closed in pain as her tongue throbbed. He released the other and she closed her mouth, swallowing hard.

"You took your punishment well," he murmured. "Good girl."

She rubbed her abused tongue against the top of her mouth, easing the ache.

"Open your mouth," he commanded.

Ariel looked at him, eyes wide. She didn't want those clothespins back on her tongue. That had hurt and she hadn't liked not being able to talk. She didn't want to open her mouth. Didn't want to obey.

But he was her Dom, and she trusted him.

She stopped herself from whimpering, but she did as he'd ordered, opening her mouth. Robert's cock twitched against her pussy.

"Do you know what it does to me when you obey?" He kissed the corner of her mouth, then sucked her lower lip. "It makes me want to fuck you."

He captured her mouth with a kiss. Ariel kissed him back, nipping and licking.

"Please." She breathed the word against his lips. "Please." She rubbed her cheek against his, feeling the stubble there.

"Are you sure?" He stared into her eyes. "I can grab a condom."

They'd had this discussion before they'd come down to get ready. He had medical tests constantly. She was on birth control. Neither had any desire to play around. They were going to be monogamous. "I'm sure. I want you."

"I've never wanted anything the way I want you." He worked the ties of his leathers, shoving them down and freeing his cock. He moved into her space, pinning her to the wall and reaching down to haul her thighs up. "Wrap your legs around me. I want you to come again."

She held on tight, gripping his waist with her thighs. "Even if I don't, this has been—"

Robert took one of the clothespins recently liberated from her tongue and snapped it onto her right nipple.

Her vision went blurry as pleasure-pain lanced through her. She'd thought she was done. That she had nothing more to give.

Robert proved that wrong. He applied the other clothespin to her left nipple. She buried her face against his neck and bit him, needing to give back a bit of what she felt, needing to mark him as he'd marked her. He growled, and then he was holding her hips, lifting her up, his cock nudging her thigh before sliding against her pussy.

Ariel let her head fall back against the wall. Robert shifted his grip on her hips, freeing one hand to come up and cup her head, protecting her from whacking against the stone.

It was such a sweet, caring gesture that her throat tightened with tears. This was what she'd been waiting for all her life. This man. He was everything she needed.

God, she was in love with him.

Robert's cock slid into her, and there was no more room for soft emotions. His cock filled her, opened her body, which was tight from the orgasms. When he was fully inside her he paused, his breath hot and damp against her neck. She shivered, the tremble working its way down her body. Her nipples were burning from the clothespins, her pussy was pulsing around his cock. She'd thought she couldn't come again, but she would.

Robert lifted his head and kissed her softly, sweetly.

Then he adjusted his stance and began to thrust in hard.

Ariel felt as if she could fly away or fly apart. Pleasure pulsed through her each time he shoved that big cock into her body. Her mouth felt swollen from his kisses. Her aching tongue reminded her of his punishment, and her nipples burned within the vise of the clothespins.

She hovered there, on the edge of a final orgasm. He thrust in, lifting her body with the force of it, his hand protecting her head, his cock so deep inside her that his groin rubbed her clit.

"Together," he panted.

Together. Yes. They were strong together, better together. She was caught between his body and the wall behind her, and there was no place else she would rather be.

Robert reached between them and yanked the clothespins from her nipples. Her eyes rolled back in her head, her pussy clamped down on his cock, and she came. Every muscle went taut, and she wished she could hold him, wished she could cling to him as a storm of pleasure and feeling washed over her. She couldn't wrap her arms around him, but she clung to him with her legs and buried her face in the curve of his neck, tears dampening his skin.

Robert thrust once, twice, and a third time. He whispered her name, and the way he said it, with such gentleness, made her heart ache.

They stayed that way, intertwined, for the longest time. Finally he set her back on her feet.

Robert stared down at her. For once, neither of them had anything to say. He kissed her softly then went about releasing her from her bondage. He was still wearing his vest and tucked his cock away in his leathers. She was naked and trembling both from the intensity of what she'd experienced and the chill she felt after the loss of his body heat.

When she was free, Robert scooped her up in his arms and she settled in, one arm around him, head on his shoulders. There were plenty of other scenes still going on, but they were done. In silence, he carried her out of the club to their room.

Chapter Eight

He was stuck in the dream again. The world here seemed dark, made of nothing but shadows. He could hear someone talking but couldn't make out what he or she said. He didn't even know who they were. Sometimes the fog would lift and he would get a glimpse of a face. Men. He was surrounded by men, but she was the one he wanted to kill.

She'd betrayed him. She'd hurt him. She'd taken everything of his past and twisted it into a lie.

He could feel his hands grasp her throat. Her skin was warm. He wasn't going to let go until it went cold, until he felt her neck snap.

"Rob?"

She was still talking. Every word that had come from her mouth was a lie. She'd only told him the truth this evening. The truth about herself. About who she really was under the mask she wore. He would rip it off and see how ugly she was underneath.

He would make her pay for everything she'd done to him.

"Rob, it's time to wake up. The pillow is perfectly dead, love. You've killed it right and good."

Ariel. Her lyrical voice cut through his anger. That voice didn't belong here. Ariel didn't belong in his nightmares.

He opened his eyes, daylight causing him to blink, and she was kneeling at the side of the bed, a smile on her face. She'd put on his T-shirt and wrapped herself in a robe. She was soft and sweet and so pretty it almost hurt to look at her.

He'd fallen asleep. He hadn't meant to fall asleep. He'd promised himself he would hold her until she dozed off and he'd gotten caught in the trap of her warmth. He had his hands wrapped around her pillow. It was the one she traveled with, the one made of silk.

He sat straight up in bed. "Did I hurt you?"

He knew what he was capable of. He had no idea what he would do if he'd tried to hurt her.

"Do I look hurt? Or worried and frightened? Although I do have some spectacular marks after last night, but those were fun. So no, I'm not upset. Though if you mangle that pillowcase we'll have to go find another one. My hair looks dreadful if I sleep on cotton." She picked up the pillow and fluffed it before placing it back on her side of the bed. "See. All good. I brought you some coffee."

He shook off the last remnants of the dream. "Ari, I'm sorry. I didn't mean to fall asleep."

She tossed her robe aside and climbed on the bed with him, straddling his thighs. "And yet you did, and you slept all night."

It was shocking. He never made it through a whole night without something waking him up. "Did I disturb you?"

She framed his face with her hands and looked at him like he was something precious. "You did. You're a furnace, Rob. You wrapped yourself around me like I was a teddy bear, and I swear you give off so much heat. We need a fan. I'll see if Peter can find one for us. Though I suspect I'll love it during the winter. I'm quite cold natured."

She was missing the point. "I had your pillow between my hands. That could have been you."

She shook her head. "You won't hurt me and if you start to, I know where your balls are located. I assure you once I've twisted your bollocks into a pretzel, you'll wake up. Stop being pessimistic. You slept with me and we were fine. I loved having you in my bed. Now kiss me. I have to get ready to interview someone Ezra's sending over. She's going to be here in an hour."

"Who is this again?" He was having a hard time keeping up with everyone Ariel was supposed to meet with and decide whether or not they had any information.

"Someone who came up in the investigation. Her name is Emily Seeger. She worked with Hank McDonald on several projects and her name came up in some of Hope McDonald's old notes. The Dallas team looked into her and contacted Ezra."

He didn't like the sound of that. "Ezra is sending her here why?"

"He wants me to interview her. There are a couple of odd things about her that aroused his interest. She works on an Army base here in Germany. She's a nurse and military family advocate. That's how she knew Senator McDonald. She testified a couple of times before the Senate Armed Forces Committee. She agreed to come down for the day."

"Does she understand why we've asked her for an interview?" He suddenly didn't want to work. He wanted to strip off the T-shirt she wore and see those marks he'd left on her. The night before had been beyond satisfying. It had blown his damn mind and rocked his world. She'd been everything he'd ever wanted in a woman.

The memory of the way she looked when she came was burned onto his brain.

She brushed her hands across his chest, staring at him like she could eat him up. "She's talked briefly to Theo and Erin. She knows I'm with a private investigation firm looking into the death of Senator McDonald. She doesn't know why."

"I want you to be careful."

"It's an hour interview at the worst. Basically I'm going to decide if she's worth talking to further. We know she did some work for Hope McDonald. McDonald had a couple of projects going on before she had to go underground. I don't think anything's going to come of it. I'm much more interested in Rebecca's friend, Louisa."

"I'm more interested in getting back to London." Where he would start thinking about moving in with her. She was right. He had made it through the night and she was far stronger than he'd given her credit for. Maybe they could have some normalcy. He needed to trust her. She was smart and she knew what she could handle.

She stared down at him, a thoughtful look on her face. "Come on.

Don't you want to know?"

He wanted to know if she was already soft and wet and wanting a little morning hello from him. "Know what?"

She sat back, her luscious ass right on his dick. "Have you thought about the fact that if Tucker really did travel to Paris with Veronica, maybe they were lovers. They wouldn't be the first pair of employees to cover up their affair."

"Rebecca said she couldn't stand him."

"And yet they snuck off to Paris together. I know Tucker's worried about it, but I think she's the key. I think she cared about him. She knew what he was doing there. Why else would McDonald wipe his memory unless Tucker was trying to do something good?"

He could think of a hundred different reasons McDonald might have done it. According to Rebecca, Reasor had been ambitious. The most obvious reason he could think of was Tucker trying to take more credit than McDonald was willing to give him. "You are an optimist."

She shrugged. "What's there to be pessimistic about right now? I'm afraid you've caught me in a thoroughly good mood. Someone seems to have taken all my stress away."

When he'd taken her to bed, she'd looked peaceful. He'd felt the same peace. It was likely why he'd fallen asleep. "I still want you to be careful."

"I promise," she vowed with a smile. "Peter's picking her up from the train station soon. If you want to sit outside my office and make sure she doesn't try to murder me, you should feel free."

"I can do that. And maybe later on we can sneak out for a walk. Just you and me. There's a park a couple of streets down and it's a beautiful day." He wanted to pretend for a while.

She kissed him, a sweet, affectionate brush of her lips over his. "Take a shower with me."

That he could do.

Twenty minutes later, he watched through the big back windows as Peter helped Emily Seeger out of the van. Peter was talking and gesturing around, likely telling her the history of the neighborhood. She was pretty, with dark brown hair and big eyes. He put her at five foot three or four, and she maybe weighed a hundred and ten pounds.

She wasn't something to be afraid of. And yet he was. Something about the woman made his muscles clench.

"Rebecca is doing some therapy with Owen, and Dante and Sasha are still asleep. What's on the schedule today? Another long day of staring at a computer screen and pretending we're not hiding out from the cops?" Tucker nodded toward the door below. "She's cute. This is the woman who worked for the senator?"

"According to Ari."

Tucker leaned against the wall overlooking the first floor. "Meeting new people scares me now. I always wonder if I tried to assault them at some point in time. It's kind of playing hell with my game. How can I pick up women if I'm always afraid they'll slap me for something I did years ago? I liked it better when I thought there was an evil twin version of me out there somewhere."

"Who says there isn't?" If Ariel was going to be optimistic, he could be, too. "It's not like evil twins haven't popped into our lives before. Kayla's came back from the dead."

"I don't think I'm going to be that lucky," Tucker replied. "I've been dreaming about it at night. Just flashes, but I can see McDonald, and she's not treating me like she did as Mother. We're in a lab and she's handing me work."

He turned to Tucker, a little surprised. They'd been given two different versions of the drug. He and Theo had a slightly milder drug. They'd been rescued before Dr. McDonald had perfected her treatment. Dante, Sasha, Jax, Tucker, and Owen had been given the final drug, the one that had supposedly wiped their memories for good. "You didn't tell me you were getting flashes."

"I think we're all having them," Tucker replied. "You know Rebecca said it could be only a matter of time before the memories started to come back if her therapy worked. I'll admit, though, that I had a couple even before we started working with her. They were weird and not very focused. They were more like feelings. After I started working with Rebecca, they got clearer. I hoped mine would be of my childhood or something. Not a reminder that I worked with McDonald. Are we going to parade me by the new girl and see if she smacks me? That should be fun."

"It would be informative," he mused. "Did Ariel ask you to stay in your room?"

Tucker shook his head. "She did not. Of course, no one told me they were bringing in a woman who could be from my past, so I expect the timing doesn't mesh. If they thought she might know me, I would be locked away somewhere. Damon's careful about those things."

Something about Tucker's tone worried him. "Are you starting to have doubts about Damon and the McKay-Taggart crew?"

He seemed to carefully consider his words. "No. I think they have our best interests at heart."

"But?"

Tucker sighed. "What happens when the pressure is really on? How long can we maintain this? At some point the wrong person is going to see one of us. The Agency still thinks we were the only ones who broke into The Ranch."

The Ranch had been a secret testing facility in Colorado where McDonald had done some of her early research. It had been shut down quickly and they'd found a lot of her work still sitting there in the empty facility. Unfortunately, they hadn't been alone there. "There are people in the Agency who know damn well who got away with the majority of that research."

Levi Green had left Jax alive, but he'd taken almost everything Jax and River had found.

"Yes, but we all know they won't talk about what really happened, and if it comes down to it, we'll be the ones to take the fall," Tucker pointed out. "What happens if they decide to implicate McKay-Taggart? Have we thought about the authorities raiding The Garden? Or the Dallas offices?"

The door below came open and Emily walked in with Peter.

"I have to think Big Tag and Damon have thought this through." The pressure seemed to be building among his men and he had to find a way to solve the problem. It was probably time to talk to Ariel about it.

"I've spent a lot of time in Germany. My husband was stationed here for a couple of years and we fell in love with the place," Emily was saying. She had a husky voice.

"It's a beautiful part of the world," Peter said. "Ah, here's Dr. Adisa."

Ariel stepped out into the hallway. She was wearing a pretty green dress he'd zipped her into an hour before. She held her hand out and shook the other woman's. He couldn't see her face but knew she would have a professional smile on her lips. Not the one she saved for him. The smiles she'd started to give him were intimate, a promise between the two of them.

What would he do if his brothers wanted to ditch London and go off on their own? He couldn't leave her.

"Why don't you join me in the office? It's upstairs. I'll have some tea brought up," Ariel was saying.

"I would love that. I'm intrigued by what Mr. Fain told me. I'm going to be honest with you. I never liked the senator. I worked with him because he could actually get things done, but he always seemed sketchy to me. I assumed it was because he was a politician and they all seem sketchy." That was the moment Emily Seeger looked up. She stopped, her hand on the railing. "Oh, my god."

She seemed stuck there, her body going completely still.

Robert wondered if that was how Rebecca had looked the first time she'd laid eyes on the man she'd known as Steven Reasor. He hated that this would push Tucker further into his shell.

"Shit," Tucker said under his breath. "Ariel's going to kill me."

Something seemed to break Emily out of her statue-like state. One minute she was standing there staring at them and the next she was striding up the stairs, her eyes wide. Her hands had started shaking and there was a wild look on her face. He stepped in front of Tucker. No matter what he'd done in the past, he couldn't let this version of Tucker pay for those crimes.

"Maybe you should go back to your room and let me sort this out," Robert offered. He would explain to this woman that the man she used to know as Steven Reasor wasn't the same man today. He looked to Ariel, who was following Emily up the stairs.

"Russell? I can't believe it. I'm dreaming. I have to be dreaming."

"I have another name?" Tucker asked.

"Ms. Seeger, perhaps we should talk about this," Ariel was

saying.

Emily Seeger stopped right in front of Robert and tears streamed down her face. "Russell? I don't understand. You died. You died. We buried you."

A chill went through him. She was talking to him. She was calling him by another name and looking up at him like he meant something to her. "I'm sorry. We've never met."

"I'm your wife."

The room threatened to spin and he looked at Ariel, whose eyes had gone wide.

His past was here and nothing would be the same again.

Chapter Nine

Robert felt sick. This couldn't be happening and yet here he was with a crying woman in his arms, and it absolutely wasn't the woman he wanted in his arms.

Emily Seeger had practically collapsed, and he'd caught her out of pure instinct. She hadn't seemed capable of walking on her own, so he'd picked her up and carried her into the communal space where they usually spent their time playing video games or watching TV.

"I don't understand." Emily wouldn't let go. When he'd tried to set her on the couch, she'd wrapped her arms around him and refused to move. She stared up at him, tears streaming down her face.

"Maybe we should talk for a moment or two." Ariel's voice was shaky.

Ariel was here and he had his hands on another woman. He didn't want them there, didn't want Ari to think for a second that he wasn't fully hers. He took a step back. She tried briefly to keep her hold on him, but he gently broke it. He turned toward Ariel, who shook her head.

Damn it. Nausea threatened. He needed to talk to her, but she was clearly not ready for that. Calm. He needed to find his calm and deal with this the way he'd been trained.

This woman had information. That was how he needed to look at it. But first he needed to ascertain if she was even telling the truth. It wouldn't be the first time he'd been lied to. He looked up at Tucker, who was watching the whole scene play out. "Could you go and update the rest of the group on what's happening? They might want to start gathering some data for me."

"You want me to leave?"

He was not about to put up with Tucker's love of drama. Not now. "Yes, I need you to do your job."

Tucker's eyes turned somber as he glanced at Ariel and he nodded and left.

"I'll be outside if you need me," Peter said before he followed.

"Ariel, I would like for you to stay." He didn't want her walking out until he could walk with her.

Emily looked from him to Ariel. "What's going on here? I was told this was some kind of query into how Senator McDonald died. I thought you people were investigators, and then I walk in here and my dead husband is standing there looking at me. Don't try to tell me you're not Russell Seeger. You look exactly like him. You sound like him. I know my husband. What kind of game are you playing with me?"

Ariel shook her head. "It's not a game. The man standing before you has severe retrograde amnesia. He can't remember anything about his life before his traumatic brain injury."

That was one way to put it, but then Ariel was telling him they were going slow with this woman.

He stared at her. He felt absolutely nothing for the woman with tears in her eyes. He didn't have any sense at all that there was something between the two of them. All he wanted was to haul Ariel off and tell her that nothing had changed.

"Amnesia?" Emily wiped the tears off her cheeks. "I don't understand."

Ariel found a box of tissues and handed them over before settling herself in the seat across from them. "Why don't you tell us how Robert died?"

"His name is Russell," Emily insisted.

"He knows himself as Robert." Ariel had gone straight into

therapist mode. He'd seen her do it a thousand times when emotions were running high. A placid mask came over her and her voice took on a soothing tone. "He doesn't remember anything about his life before. You need to understand that he's spent the last several years as Robert McClellan."

"Well, his name is Russell Seeger." Emily took a shaky breath. "This is surreal."

"And we are investigators," Ariel explained. "You can certainly talk to my bosses if you would like. We're investigating the senator, but also the senator's daughter."

Emily paled. "Dr. Hope McDonald?"

"Yes," Ariel replied.

They were in synch on one thing—this was surreal. "From the information we've gathered, you did a little work with her."

Emily nodded. "Yes, I did. When you were stationed here in Germany, I took a job at the military base's hospital. She came through a couple of times with her father. She did some training sessions with the doctors. I wasn't exactly sure why she came in so often. I got the feeling she was working on something."

"Did I know her?"

"You met her," Emily replied. "She was flirty with you. I thought it was creepy, like there were two sides of her. There was the cold and dismissive one I saw, and then she would turn to you and giggle like a teenaged girl. That happened at a reception we attended for her. We had a fight about it that night because you didn't think she was flirting."

A shudder went through him. From what he understood, she'd behaved in a similar manner with Theo Taggart before she'd kidnapped him. Despite the sick feeling in the pit of his stomach, he was curious. "I was stationed here in Germany? I was in the Army?"

"Yes. We met about a year after you joined up. We were stationed on the same base in North Carolina and we fell in love. We got married and they let me follow you when you got stationed here. It's pretty easy for nurses to move around. Not so much for Army Rangers. They tend to need you in very specific places. We were lucky we got to be together even though you were often deployed." Her hands were in her lap and she stared down at them. "I don't know how to feel right now."

"I'm sure you have a lot of feelings," Ariel started. "And they're all valid."

Robert held up a hand. "One of my feelings is suspicion. It's a smart feeling to have at this point, don't you think? She can't come in here with no proof. If she's my wife, why didn't she question my death? You don't think there would be some kind of footprint out there that Adam would have found?"

"Who's Adam?" Emily asked.

"Adam is the incredibly brilliant investigator who has spent the last several years of his life trying to figure out who I am. So you walk in and I'm supposed to believe we never posted on social media?" Now that he really thought about it, this was impossible. This was some kind of trick. He wasn't going to fall for it.

"One of the reasons they asked me to interview her was the fact that she's listed as a widow, but Adam couldn't find anything about her husband. His records have been erased," Ariel replied.

"We did have a social media page." Emily's eyes were red with tears. "I didn't post a lot of pictures because you didn't like to have them taken. And it wasn't smart given what you did for a living. Half the time I wasn't sure where you were. I have pictures though. I have our wedding picture at my place."

"I'd like to see it." He would see the pictures, then let Jax see them to prove they hadn't been doctored in any way. He stood up. There was no need to listen to her until they'd proven she was who she said she was. "Ms. Seeger, I apologize if I seem cold, but I really don't remember you and I'm in a position where new people could be dangerous to me. I'm going to inform my team of the new developments and we'll be in touch with you."

"What?" Emily stood, her eyes on him.

Ariel followed suit. "Robert, we need to talk to her."

"Not until I'm sure she's not tricking us." Robert walked to the door.

"You have a scar on your back, right above your left butt cheek," Emily said quietly. "You got it when you were twelve and wrestling with your brother. You broke the kitchen table and fell on a vase. You had to go to the hospital. You have another scar on your right thigh.

You took a bullet in Afghanistan when you were escorting some politicians around. You have a birthmark on the back of your right calf. It's faded now. When you have a tan you can barely make it out."

He went cold. He had all of those marks. But then Dr. McDonald would have known that. She would have taken copious notes. "Did you work for her?"

"Did I work for who? I work for the US military." Emily's shoulders straightened. "I'm not on trial here. You're the one who has questions to answer. You're the one who left me alone all these years. How do I know you're not lying about the amnesia?"

"The door's right there," Robert offered. "Feel free to walk through it."

"Robert." Ariel was looking at him like she didn't know who he was in that moment.

Robert took a deep breath. He wasn't handling this well. "Ms. Seeger..."

"My name is Emily," she insisted. "You call me Em. You call me *baby* when we're alone."

"I'm sorry. I don't remember any of that. Ariel, I need to talk to you." He couldn't sit there and pretend that this was okay.

Ariel's expression was tight but she gestured for him to move. "I'll be back as soon as I can, Mrs. Seeger. As you can see, we've all been thrown for a loop."

"Please do come back because I'm not leaving here until I understand what happened to my husband." Her gaze moved between he and Ariel as though she was starting to figure out there was something between them.

Good. She should know. His heart pounded in his chest as he followed Ariel down the hall. She walked in front of him, her heels clacking on the floor. Her head was high and she didn't look back.

She wasn't going to shrink her way through this. He wasn't about to let her distance herself. He reached out and hauled her around, and his heart nearly stopped.

Ariel was crying, tears streaming down her face.

He softened, pulling her into his arms. "Baby, this doesn't change a thing."

She pushed at him. “Don’t call me that. That’s what you called her.”

His gut twisted. “I don’t know who she is. Even if she was my wife, she isn’t now. She hasn’t been for a long time. I am not the man she knew. I’m the man *you* know. I’m the man who loved you from the moment he saw you.”

“Please, Rob. I need some time to process this.”

“You don’t need any time at all because nothing has changed between us.”

“You haven’t even asked her if you have children.”

He hadn’t thought about children. “I don’t. She would have said something. Ari, this should show you how much nothing has changed. I’m not some cold bastard. If I thought I had kids out there in the world, I would want to take care of them. But I feel nothing at all for this woman. She’s not my wife. She might have been Russell Seeger’s wife, but I’m Robert McClellan.”

“And what happens when you do remember her? What happens when you wake up one day and have a vision of marrying her or the first time you kissed her? God, she said you have a brother. Don’t you want to know about him?”

He did, but he couldn’t think about that now. “You are the most important person in my life. My other brothers, the ones I went through hell with, are checking into this right now. They’ll figure it out and if I do have a family out there, I’ll deal with it. But it won’t change a thing between me and you.”

“It changes everything.”

He tried to reach for her again, but she backed up, putting a hand between them.

He watched as she disappeared behind the door of her office.

Robert stood there completely at a loss for how to fix things.

“If it were later in the day, I would offer to sit and drink with you,” a familiar voice said. Tucker came out of the kitchen to stand beside him. “That seems to be how Dante and Sasha fix everything. But it’s early and it looks like it’s going to be a long day for you. So I think I’ll stand here and if you want to talk, we can talk.”

“I don’t want to talk.”

Tucker nodded. “Then we’ll just be. But you should know

whatever you decide, I got your back. And if you want to go talk to this woman, I'll go with you. If you want to run away, we could do that too. Join the circus. Do they still have circuses?"

Despite the ache in his soul, at least he had *this* brother.

He had a family. He didn't need another.

He was Robert. He was going to stay Robert. Finding out about who he used to be wouldn't change a thing. Not one damn thing.

* * * *

Hours later Ariel was still shaking on the inside as she walked through the Englischer Garten. To her left, the Isar River wound its way through the city, and it seemed like the place was teeming with families out enjoying the day.

Families like Robert's? Had he and Emily strolled this park, their fingers tangled together as they felt the sun on their faces?

She was not going to cry again. She wouldn't allow it to happen.

Yet she could feel sorrow pressing against her like she would explode if she didn't let it out.

They'd been close to having a future. So bloody close.

She gripped the shoulder strap of her purse because she needed to have something to do with her hands. Ezra would be here in hours and she would have some cover then. He'd promised to get on the first available plane when she'd called and told him what had happened. He was going to update Damon and Big Tag then come down to meet the woman for himself.

But until then, she needed to talk to the only other person she knew who might be able to shed some light on the situation.

She glanced around because she'd reached the section of park she'd been told to come to. The Steinerne Bank. It was a semicircular bench made of stone. When she'd asked where to find it, Peter had explained that it had once been a temple to the Greek god Apollo. The temple had been made of wood, and over the years had not been well maintained. In the 1800s an architect had built this stone bench over it. Peter had said a lot of stuff she hadn't really heard. All she'd been able to think about was the fact that Robert's wife was here.

She glanced down at the words carved into the bench. She did remember this part.

Hier wo lhr wallet, da war sonst Wald nur und Sumpf.

Here where you meander was once only wood and marsh.

This whole park had been wood and marsh once. The whole city. They'd built something beautiful. They'd created all of this, like two people in love created a life together. They worked hard and built something lovely.

She'd convinced herself it wouldn't happen to them, that Robert's past wouldn't drive them apart. It had been so long and no one had come forward. There hadn't been any movement at all on Robert's identity. Hell, she'd convinced herself deep down that his past wouldn't come up. Like he'd truly been born in that lab and he was all hers.

Even the file they believed was his had perpetuated the lie. *Ex Novo*. McDonald had used Latin to conceal the names of the men she'd experimented on. They believed Robert was the file marked *Ex Novo* because of his blood type and other markers. *Ex Novo* was a Latin term meaning built from nothing. She was sure McDonald had thought it a fun inside joke.

But Robert hadn't come from nothing. He'd had a life and a family before he'd been turned. He had people out there who cared about him.

She could still feel his arms around her, holding her close all through the night. Had he been that tender with his wife? Had he made love to her like she was the last woman on earth?

"Hey, got your text." Kim Solomon strode up wearing a sundress and strappy sandals, her designer bag thrown over her shoulder. "I was in the middle of something, but I always have time for you. What's up? You said something big happened."

"First of all, you should know Ezra's on his way from London. I expect he'll be here sometime this evening." She took a seat on the bench. Despite the fact that the park was packed, this particular section was quieter than the rest.

Kim sat down beside her, and the smile had left her face. "All right. Then something big happened. Is everyone okay?"

There wasn't an easy way to say it, so she simply put it out there. "Robert's wife showed up this morning."

Kim gasped. "What the ever fuck? You're joking. Robert has a wife?"

She was telling Kim because of her connections. That was all. This wasn't a desperate call to a girlfriend for sympathy. They were in the middle of a mission. She had to shut the emotional stuff down. "Yes. Her name is Emily Seeger. I need you to find out everything you can about her. I've already got McKay-Taggart working, but it would be helpful to know if the Agency has anything on her. She's a nurse at Ramstein. I was planning on interviewing her because at one point in time she had business dealings with both Senator McDonald and Hope McDonald."

Kim shifted her bag to her side and moved closer. "Ariel, are you okay?"

"I'm fine. I'm worried about how Robert is handling this. He doesn't seem to want to have anything to do with her. He's in denial."

Kim nodded slowly. "Yeah, he's obviously not the only one. Talk to me. Or at least tell me you're talking to your other girlfriends. You're close to Penny Knight, right? I know Kayla Summers moved, but she can pick up a phone."

This was exactly what she wanted to avoid. She didn't need more reasons to get emotional. "I was surprised by her appearance, but I'm going to be fine. I knew this was a possibility. We know very little about them. It's actually shocking that it hasn't happened to one of them yet. Jax didn't have anyone left alive he was close to in his family."

"So everything's fine?" Kim asked. "You're not freaking out and doing something stupid like giving him up to some chick who walked through the door after years of not looking for him, right? You and Robert are cool?"

"Of course we're not. We're…he has a wife. He has a life waiting for him."

"He doesn't have to," Kim pointed out with a smile. An evil smile.

Ariel knew that smile well. "You can't assassinate her."

"I don't see why not," Kim said with a shrug. "Look, I'm a problem solver. She's a problem. We go together like peanut butter and jelly. And that jelly is going to be red, if you know what I mean."

"You can't kill her." She had to reiterate the command because sometimes Kim could be stubborn. If she thought assassinating her friend's boyfriend's inconvenient wife would make her friend happier, she might do it and then go out for mimosas afterward. She had a big heart and a surprisingly malleable conscience.

"I don't see why not. This is why you guys get in trouble. We can do an awful lot of cleanup after she's dead. Unless Rob already has feelings for her. Damn. I hadn't thought about that. Is he like all over her? Maybe I should kill Rob."

"Stop." But she was smiling because she knew Kim was joking about that. It was her friend's way of trying to get her to open up. Ariel had made it through the call to Damon and Ian. She'd managed to talk to Peter without breaking again. She wasn't sure she could do it with Kim. Which deep down might have been why she'd called her. "I have to be professional now. I screwed everything up by letting the personal stuff in. I knew better. I knew this could happen."

"You knew his wife could come back?" Kim asked.

"I knew he might have one out there."

"Then why wasn't she looking for him? I know if Beck went missing I would move heaven and earth to find him, and we're not even married anymore," Kim said. "I would do it because I still love that man even though he hates me. So where has this chick been? Who's she been doing since her beloved went missing?"

"She thought he was dead," Ariel explained. "I don't have the whole story yet, but I believed she was told by the military that he died in combat. You know that was very typical of the way the McDonalds worked. We think they had a network of loyal people in the military who helped cover up their crimes in exchange for money, or perhaps they simply blackmailed them. It's what they did to Jax. If you look up Jax's military records, they show plainly that he died in a helicopter accident. I can't help but consider the fact that she could be telling the truth."

Kim seemed to think about it for a moment. "So her husband dies in combat. The military could tell her anything they like as long as the report is good enough. I guess they could have told her there wasn't enough of his body left if he was trapped in an explosion or a fire."

"See, you can't kill her." She knew Robert thought something was amiss, but when she considered it, Hope McDonald sometimes got obsessed with a subject. Like she had with Theo. She'd met Robert and decided she'd wanted him. She'd used her father's connections to bring in her subject.

"The jury's out on that, but I certainly will look into his records," Kim offered. "Have you thought about pulling up stakes? I don't want you to do that. It fucks with my mission, which is mostly to see if your mission leads anywhere. But I also don't like wifey showing up at a terribly inconvenient time. Toss in the fact that Levi's somewhere in Europe and maybe you should head back to London and figure everything out from the safety of The Garden. Or better yet, I've got a place in Rome I could stash you and Robert. It's super romantic."

Had Kim heard a word she'd said? "I can't be romantic with Robert. He's got a wife."

"He's got a wife he doesn't remember. Did he ask you to back off?"

He'd come after her like a caveman who wasn't going to let go of his prize. Or a man worried he was going to lose someone he loved. Tears were back, pulsing behind her eyes and threatening to make the world hazy. "No. He told me nothing had changed."

"Then believe him." Kim put a hand on her shoulder. "He's in love with you. Not her. He's not the man she married. I don't even know if he needs a divorce if we've got his death certificate. You know, he definitely wouldn't need a divorce if you hand everything over to me."

"You can't kill her. You really need to find some new ways to solve problems."

Kim wrinkled her nose. "Why when what I do works so well." She sat back. "Trust me, at some point soon, I'll be able to deal with Levi permanently. Then everyone should watch out."

"So you've thought about it?" In some ways she was surprised Kim hadn't already tried to kill Levi. She really was the kind of woman who plowed through a problem. Sometimes literally.

"Of course I have. Especially after he tried to kill Beck in Mexico. I've been asked to let the situation play out."

"By the president."

Kim merely smiled. "By someone important, but if Levi tries to physically harm Beck again, no one will be able to hold me back." She sighed as though coming to a decision. "I'm going to tell you something that is highly classified."

"Don't put your career on the line."

Kim shook her head. "I'm not. I've got some leeway when it comes to this op since it's not exactly on the books, if you know what I mean. I'm not working for the Agency exactly. I'm doing a little oversight on them from an interested party."

Namely the president and his men. "All right. But you have to know I'm going to tell my boss."

"I understand. Tell him if he wants to talk to me, I'm more than willing. I think we're looking for the wrong thing. I've had some feelers out at Kronberg," Kim began. "They said there was a break-in three days before McDonald left for Argentina. Someone downloaded the backup files and disappeared with them."

That made sense. "McDonald, obviously. She knew she was leaving."

"I don't think so. Do you know what Veronica Croft's minor was in?"

"No." She wasn't sure what a minor in college had to do with anything. Veronica's major had been pre-med.

"Computer engineering," Kim replied. "She was considered quite the hacker at one point in time. It explains how she's managed to hide all these years. The question is, why would she need to hide. No one went after Rebecca Walsh."

A few things fell into place. "They didn't go after Rebecca because she didn't know anything. You think Veronica did. You think Veronica is the one who stole those files. Why? Why would she take them and not try to sell them? Or turn Kronberg and Dr. McDonald in?"

"These are questions only Veronica can answer," Kim said mysteriously.

"So you don't think there's anything left at Kronberg? That would be a reason to go back to London. If Veronica stole the backup and McDonald took her original research with her when she left, then Kronberg has nothing we need."

"Or what they have is even more valuable, and I need to know if it's really there."

Now they were getting to the heart of the matter. "What are you looking for, Kim?"

"I think Kronberg was smart and knew exactly what could happen to the company and the board of directors if it ever got out that they knew what McDonald was doing. I think they kept a comprehensive record of everyone who had anything to do with the project, and that includes certain members of the government who knew exactly what was going on. I'm talking senators. I'm talking cabinet members."

A chill went through her. "President Hayes wants to know the names of everyone who was involved."

"If I were President Hayes, I would want to prosecute everyone involved," Kim said with grave intent.

"What do want me to do?" That kind of knowledge would give them a lot of leverage.

"I need you to talk to Louisa. She's worked there for a long time and she'll know where the secrets are kept."

"All right. That was what I was planning on doing anyway," Ariel admitted. "Only the information we're looking for has changed. If we can get this, you can come out of the shadows?"

Being able to bring Solo in would take a lot of the load off her shoulders. She could be honest with Robert and his men about working with her.

"If I can get my bosses proof, we'll all come out of the shadows," Kim affirmed. "I'm talking full pardons for any man who was subjected to this kind of experimentation."

They would be free. All of them. They wouldn't have to hide. "I'll find us what we need."

"Just give me a best guess as to who I need to lean on." Kim stood up and glanced around. "I don't want you to put yourself in danger. I'll be in touch and know that I'm still looking for Veronica Croft, too."

"I'll let you know what we find out." She stayed where she was. She needed a few moments before she went back to the house. "Thank you, Kim."

"No, thank you. And call me if you need to talk. I know you have other friends in your life now, but…well, you're pretty much still my girl. Listen to Robert. He knows what's in his heart. And if this chick gives you trouble, I'm more than ready to handle it." Kim winked and walked away.

Ariel sat back. It could all be over soon, and she wasn't sure where that would leave her. If Robert had a home to return to, would he even want to stay in London?

A shiver went up her spine and she suddenly knew she was being watched. She wasn't sure where the person was, but there were eyes on her. She glanced down the way Kim had walked, but she was already gone.

Maybe she was paranoid.

She took a deep breath and started back toward the club.

Chapter Ten

"You should talk to her," Sasha said. "She's still in the living room."

"He should talk to her so she gets out of our living room," Dante grumbled.

Robert turned and gave Dante the same stare he used to give the guys in his unit when they were assholes.

Pain flared through his brain. God, he wanted to reach out for that memory, but he let it go. It was nothing more than a thought in his head, the remnants of another life. The trouble was Emily Seeger was more than a mere thought.

Dante shrugged. "I think if he talks to her for a few moments perhaps she realizes he's annoying and she no longer wants to be married to him."

"We don't know that she *was* married to him," Tucker pointed out. "It could be a lie. She could be a plant."

"You think Levi Green planted her in the Army a decade ago, made sure she met Senator McDonald so one day she could do what?" Owen asked. "Look, I'm all Team *Ariert* here, but I'm not sure how sending Emily in here works for the people against us."

"That's terrible." Tucker sent a dismissive look Owen's way.

"*Robari* is the only way to go here. You don't get to make power couple names."

"Says the man who came up with *Jiver*," Owen shot back.

"Well, Jax wouldn't let me call them *Rax*," Tucker replied. "You know I call you and Rebecca *Owbecca*."

"That's terrible, man. It sounds a bit like Chewbacca."

"Stop, both of you." Dante shook his head. "You're both idiots. I'm going back to work. Robert, you should handle this situation and quickly. Everything Sasha and I have found makes me believe she's who she says she is."

"I find it interesting that there's no mention of Russell Seeger and yet I can find you on her social media. There are some pictures of you buried on her Facebook. She posts something about you every year on the anniversary of your death," Sasha explained. "I'm sure it's something Adam's new facial recognition would have eventually picked up, but her page is set to private. Naturally knowing what to look for means I can hack into it. I can't guarantee they're not manipulated, but you look happy."

He wasn't happy now. Emily was still waiting for him and Ariel was gone. Peter had told him she'd gone for a walk. By herself. It made him sick to think that she was out there alone.

Ari didn't believe him. She had some bullshit thought that he would magically look at a woman he couldn't remember and fall back in love with her.

Still, if Emily did have any information about him, he needed to know. If she was some kind of plant, he needed to know what she wanted and why she was here.

And if she was real…well, he had to deal with that, too.

"Keep looking into her. I'll go and talk to her. Don't forget we're meeting with the administrative assistant this evening. This mission doesn't stop simply because my world blew up." He strode down the hall, not looking back. If they could find the information they needed, he would talk Ariel into going home and letting another team deal with retrieval. Once he had her at The Garden, he would prove to her that nothing at all had changed.

Except he had a wife.

His "wife" sat on the sofa, staring at the big TV screen, though nothing was on. She looked lost. Kind of the way he felt.

She blinked and seemed to realize she wasn't alone. Her jaw tightened as she looked up at him. "Hello, Russ…Robert."

It was obvious she wasn't going to leave until he talked to her. And what else would a wife who'd recently found out her husband had come back from the grave do? Was he being too hard on her? Owen had been right. It was a stretch to think someone had planted her long before McDonald had actually started her experiments. There was such a thing as coincidence.

"I'm sorry I left the way I did before. I wasn't polite and I apologize."

"Well, your girlfriend was upset. I'm not wrong about that, right? There was a lot of emotion between the two of you. She's good at covering it, but she was upset, and not for professional reasons."

He hadn't meant to hide this from her. Not from anyone. "Ariel is important to me. I've been in love with her for a long time. I'm sorry if that hurts you."

She pursed her lips and seemed to think about what she wanted to say. "Well, apparently you didn't remember me at all. I suppose it's not surprising you would find someone else. I should point out that you were in love with me for much longer."

He hated the fact that he was obviously hurting her. "I don't remember. Do we have kids?"

He should have asked right away, but he was scared of the answer. How would he feel about kids he didn't remember? He wouldn't be able to walk away from them.

"No." There was a wealth of sorrow in her tone. "We put it off. I didn't want to be alone with kids while you were deployed. And then we ran out of time."

He managed to not breathe a sigh of relief, but it was there. "You said something about me having a brother. Just one, or did I have a big family?"

She stared at him for a moment. "You really don't remember anything, do you?"

He shook his head. "As far as I know I woke up in a medical facility a few years ago. All of my memories are from there on."

He didn't tell her about the feelings he had, the vague shadows of the past that sometimes played along his brain. Or the ones that kept him awake at night.

"You were born in Wyoming. You lived on your grandad's ranch. Your father walked out on your mom after your brother was born. You were the oldest." She spoke as though going through a report for school. There was no emotion in her voice. She was trying to get through it. "Your brother's name was Timothy. I'm so sorry to tell you he died in a car accident after you died. He was drinking and he lost control of the car."

"And my mother?"

She shook her head. "Cancer. A couple of years ago."

So he didn't have a family. That must have made it easier to erase him from existence. "I need names and dates."

"Of course. I'll help out in any way you need me to." She turned to him. "I'll answer all your questions, but you have to talk to me, too. I know you don't remember me, but I've spent years thinking about you. My life ended the day you died. If you're back, I want a chance with you."

That wasn't going to happen. He felt bad for her, but she was missing the point. "I'm not the man you married. He really did die. He might not have gone the way the military told you he did, but he's not here anymore."

"What happened? Your whole squad was lost in a bombing," she said, the words seemingly tortured. "There were ten of you who they couldn't even find enough body parts to bury."

"Ten of us?" He'd always imagined he'd been alone.

She nodded. "I went to ten funerals. You loved those men. I made sure I went to all of their ceremonies even though I was aching inside. I needed to honor you by being there. We still talk. I'm still close to some of the wives."

"Emily, it's important that I have those names." Had they been placed in McDonald's program, too? Were they some of the men who'd died under her tender care? Were their secrets contained in those files they'd found?

"Of course. I'll give them to you but you should be able to look it up. I can't imagine the reports aren't available to the public."

"I assure you they are not."

"Why wouldn't they be?"

He wasn't ready to trust her with the answer to that question. "Did you get my insurance and the death gratuity?"

She nodded. "Yes. The military sent me everything they owed me. Insurance paid out quickly. Russ…Rob, I didn't have any reason to think you were alive. You were a soldier and you died in combat. Why would they lie to me? This is what I don't understand. Do they know you survived? Did anyone else survive?"

The enormity of what had been done slammed into him. McDonald had taken a whole team. He'd handed them all over to his daughter to play around with, like they were toys and it didn't matter if they broke. He would simply find her new ones.

"I don't know." He had to tell her something. It honestly didn't matter. If she was bad, she already knew it anyway. "There wasn't an explosion. I was part of a medical experiment. The experiments involved memories and behavioral control in an attempt to create super soldiers."

Her eyes had gone wide. "They experimented on you? The Army did that?"

He shook his head. "No, though I'm sure there are some factions in the military who know exactly what happened. There have to be. It's why we wanted to talk to you."

She gasped. "Because I worked with the McDonalds. Oh, god. It was her. She did this to you and I introduced you. I made you come to that party with me. I did this."

He hadn't expected her to take it that way. Not that he should expect anything at all. He definitely didn't expect to feel a tug of compassion for her. She looked genuinely upset. If she was real, he couldn't be angry with her.

Why wouldn't she be real?

"It wasn't your fault." His voice softened. He was angry that her appearance had upset what he had going with Ariel, but he shouldn't take that out on her. "Dr. McDonald decided I would be a good candidate. She would have found a way to take me no matter what you would have done."

It was what she'd done with Theo. If Hope McDonald had worked the same way she had when she'd taken Theo, she'd likely taken him to the primary site and moved the other men in his team to the secondary. He needed pictures of them to see if Tucker or the others remembered their faces. They still talked about the other members of their team, the ones who had died that final day.

"I can't believe this is happening." Emily started to sob and she leaned into him.

He didn't want to touch her, but he put an arm around her shoulders.

She shuddered as though relieved and wrapped herself around him as she cried.

How would he feel if he'd lost Ariel and found her years later? He would have mourned. He didn't think he would have moved on. She was in his soul. He would be devastated.

"Please let me stay for a couple of days," Emily begged. "I understand that you have a life, but I need some closure. You need answers. I can help you with that. Your group called me in for a reason."

He wanted to tell her to go. He wished she'd never shown up. He wasn't sure why, but he didn't like being near her. It didn't feel right to even hold her while she cried.

He was a bastard.

But he was a bastard who needed information. "I'll see if Peter can find you a room. We do need to talk about what we do from here."

She looked up at him, tears in her blue eyes. "I just want a little time."

That would be all he had to give her.

* * * *

The Marienplatz was filled with people enjoying the early evening. The city center was a vibrant combination of shopping, cafés, and gothic architecture. Ariel would far rather be exploring St. Michael's Church or the Rathaus-Glockenspiel than sitting here with Rebecca and her friend Louisa. Instead of enjoying the end of the day, she was gently herding someone into telling her information that could endanger her life.

There was a reason she'd gotten out of MI6. She hated all the lies.

They sat in a small café across from St. Michael's. Somewhere near the church, Robert and Sasha were watching them. Tucker was "shopping" at the H&M next door. Peter sat on one of the benches, reading a magazine. Any one of them could be there in a few seconds if something went wrong. Not that they expected Louisa to attack them. She seemed more than willing to talk.

Dante had offered to stay behind and watch the new girl. She assumed he would really be diving into the shipment of beer Peter had recently had delivered. She did feel better not leaving Emily alone in their safe house. She'd placed her computer in the safe, and there were security cameras to catch her if Emily snuck around the club.

She hadn't needed security cameras to catch the tender moment between Robert and his wife. She'd decided to check on the woman when she'd returned from her meeting with Kim.

He'd been there. He'd had his arms around her even though it was obvious he was uncomfortable with touching her. Would he feel the same way in a few months? That was why she had to keep her distance. His memories could come raging back, and she couldn't be the reason he stayed away from a wife he loved.

"I'm trying to understand what happened to Steven and Veronica." Rebecca's words cut through her misery, reminding her she still had a job to do.

"I don't know why you would care," Louisa replied. Her English was excellent and she spoke it with a light German accent. Ariel would bet she'd spent a lot of time in other countries. She was a bit younger than Rebecca. She was the assistant to the VP of research for Kronberg Pharmaceutical, and if Rebecca was right, also slept with her married boss. "Steven was an ass. Veronica wasn't as sweet as she seemed to be."

"How do you mean?" Rebecca was getting good at interrogation. She had a friendly style that brought people in. "She was always nice to me."

"I don't trust anyone that nice. Veronica seemed like a scared little mouse, but then I would get security reports about her being in sections she wasn't supposed to be in," Louisa replied. "I have no idea why she liked to prowl around the lab at night. And I don't need to tell you Steven was terrible. You were the only one worth anything and Dr. McDonald knew it. Is Steven the reason you dragged your therapist all the way to Germany?"

It was their cover. Ariel was helping Rebecca confront what had happened to her here in Munich. "She doesn't completely understand what went on and why Dr. Reasor attacked her that day. It's helpful to hear from people who were there. There were events going on around the same time and she needs to know if they're connected. It would help her put the episode behind her."

A cunning smile crept across Louisa's face. "But no one is exactly sure what happened. You're right. There was a lot of drama surrounding your departure."

"I figured if anyone knew, it would be you," Rebecca said. "You know everything about the company. Everyone talks to you."

Louisa took a drink of her beer and sat back, looking satisfied with the compliments. "It's because they know to get to my boss, they have to get to me. All right. I'm interested in helping you. You weren't obnoxious. I don't know the whole story. There are things the boss doesn't tell even me."

And that bothered her. Louisa thought she should be in the middle of everything. Being shut out would upset her. It always helped to know what motivated a person. Louisa needed to feel like she was the center of attention. It was an easy thing to offer. "That doesn't seem like a smart thing to do. You're a team. I've always found the support team for a boss is usually smarter than the boss."

"He's practically a senile old man," Louisa said with a dismissive wave of her hand. She was on her third beer and they hadn't been here very long. Louisa took the term "happy hour" seriously. "I run that office, but old men need to keep their secrets. What do you want to know?"

Rebecca leaned forward. "The last time I saw Steven, he told me I didn't understand the scope of Dr. McDonald's research. She'd asked me if I wanted to go to Buenos Aires with her. Steven didn't want me to go and that was when he...well, I won't go into the details, but he was why I left. He scared me."

"He must have since you never looked back." Louisa glanced

around. "Look, I don't know everything about it, but I know she was doing something the big bosses didn't want the press to find out about. I assumed it was something about her testing. She wouldn't be the first to ignore protocol in search of a breakthrough. She was likely using testing methods the world wouldn't approve of and that's why they were so careful with her. My boss personally looked at her daily reports."

"We were working on a cure for several degenerative brain diseases," Rebecca said. "I was in that lab every single day. I was responsible for a lot of those protocols. I never saw anything that would worry me."

Louisa tipped her beer Rebecca's way. "Well, I think you were brought in for different reasons than Steven. You had some incredible instincts and she was working on a problem. You were working on the same problem in your own research. Dr. McDonald always could find bright minds to steal from."

"I thought Dr. Reasor was quite smart." According to Rebecca he'd had a brilliant mind. It was the only thing she could believe Tucker and Reasor had in common.

"Oh, Steven was smart, but that wasn't why she hired him. Maybe it was in the beginning, but he was more like her defender, if that makes sense. What's the term I'm looking for? Second in command? He made sure she got what she needed. He scared all of the employees. He kept copious records and investigated everyone who came in contact with him. If he found dirt, he would use it as leverage to do her will. I thought when you left that he'd found something on you."

Rebecca shook her head. "No, he made me run for different reasons."

From what Ariel had learned, she believed Steven Reasor had used the time dilation drug to torture Rebecca. He hadn't physically harmed her, but the drug had made it seem like he had. She would have been extremely open to suggestion. She'd been so frightened by the experience that she'd left the country and her job behind. She'd buried the memory deep and it had only come out when she'd seen him again in Toronto.

It hadn't been long after Rebecca had fled that Steven Reasor himself had disappeared. Not that they had proof he'd ever really existed.

"What do you know about how he died?" Rebecca asked.

"I know the rumors and I know what I think is true." Louisa sat back and looked completely serious for once. "The rumor is he went away with Veronica Croft for a weekend before he left for Argentina. Some people say he blackmailed her into it. He was obviously into her. If you were in a room with the two of them, his eyes were on her. She might have been attracted to him, but his behavior put her off. At least that was what she said. I wouldn't put it past him to blackmail her into his bed. He didn't come back to the office after that. I assumed he flew directly from Paris to Argentina. That was where her other lab was."

"And that was the same time McDonald cleared out her lab here?" Ariel asked.

Louisa nodded. "Well, she cleared out far more than that. You can't tell anyone I told you this, but shortly after Steven and Veronica took their trip to Paris, it was like the world exploded. My boss got called in and everyone was here. There were some people I didn't even know were associated with the company. Wealthy, influential people. I wasn't in the meeting, but no one was happy when they came out."

Rebecca's gaze was steady on Louisa. "What do you think happened?"

"Well, the project was shut down immediately," Louisa explained. "I was never told exactly what it was about. I was only the secretary. But it wasn't hard to figure it out. Someone found out what McDonald had been doing. Whoever it was confronted her and she ran. Or she caught wind of what was happening and she ran. She took everything. The night that she left the country, the Kronberg executives worked overtime to cover their asses, as you Americans say. They cleaned it all up and we're stronger than ever. And if anyone comes after us, well, my boss taught me how to handle that. He's a bit like Steven in that way."

So he did keep a file. Somewhere in that building was the information Kim needed to jump into the game and free the men. This was exactly what they needed.

"He kept some leverage?" Rebecca asked.

"Always, but I think this was serious leverage. Let's just say there's a safe in his office that not even I know the code to." Louisa looked up and a waitress was approaching with their food. "Rebecca, I hope this brings you some peace. You need to know that even if Dr. McDonald was doing something she shouldn't, it won't ever get out. My boss will make sure of it. You're safe. As for Steven Reasor, well, you're safe from him, too. I wouldn't be surprised if the company had a hand in that. Like I said, there were many people in and out of the offices after she left, and I would bet some of them were connected to powerful agencies. You're safe, my friend."

The waitress set down the tray and started passing around the food.

Ariel glanced at Rebecca, who was smiling at Louisa.

"That is exactly what I needed to hear. Thank you so much," Rebecca said before looking down at her plate. "Schnitzel. Oh, how I have missed you. Why don't we talk about happier things? Tell me all the gossip."

Ariel looked down at her own plate. She wasn't hungry at all. She looked back, hoping to get a glimpse of Robert. He'd been standing outside the church with a camera around his neck, looking every inch the curious tourist.

He wasn't there now. Where had he gone? She started to pull out her phone to text him. If something had happened…

The door to the church came open and he slipped back outside. His shoulders were straight, and even from here she could see the way his jaw was tense. He took up his place again, but he wasn't pretending to be a tourist. He simply stood there.

She could feel him staring at her.

She took a sip of her wine and tried to force herself to listen to the conversation.

All the while she wondered why he'd gone into that church.

Chapter Eleven

Robert stared across the plaza at the restaurant where Ariel and Rebecca were sitting down with the target. He probably shouldn't think of her as the target. He should call her the witness or something, but he was in a nasty place and even the words in his head seemed to have sharp edges.

He knew Ari needed time to process what had happened earlier today. Hell, he knew he needed time, but he didn't want to take it. He wanted to get her in bed and reassure them both that they belonged together.

He wasn't Russell Seeger. He wasn't going to let himself be treated like his body belonged to someone. His soul was completely different and it belonged to Ariel. She had to see that.

"If I were a murderer I could kill you now," Sasha said. "You need to get your head in the game. Not that I expect any excitement. Do we really need four of us out here in a public place? I think Tucker is only here because he wants to buy clothes. I pray he finds socks that can handle his stink."

"You know why we're here." Though he would admit that there was some truth to what Sasha had said. It felt good to be outside, to breathe fresh air and remind himself there was a sun in the sky.

"Yes, we're here because Damon and Big Tag told us to be here."

He didn't want to have this fight again. "If you want to go back, feel free. You can catch a cab at the entrance."

"You must truly be off your game if you're not going to give me one of those *rah-rah* speeches of yours." Sasha leaned against the white wall of St. Michael's church, watching the tourists go in and out of the massive wooden doors.

It was a gorgeous day and he wasn't sure he'd ever seen a sky that same color of blue. The plaza was packed with shoppers and tourists. This part of the city center was pedestrian only, all the streets blocked off to traffic. It was where the city held its festivals and Christmas markets.

Had he come here with Emily?

Why did the thought of him walking through the Marienplatz holding Emily's hand make him vaguely nauseous? Who had that man been? Obviously he'd been a soldier, but why had he gone into the Army? Had it been because he loved his country or because he hadn't had any other prospects?

"Hey, stop thinking about it or you'll be sick right here," Sasha said. "Do I need to punch you? I don't know how they will take it here. If we were in Russia no one would care, but Germans tend to follow the rules of society."

He shook it off. Sasha was right. He'd been about to dive down that deep hole. "I'm fine. I'll concentrate on the job."

"Have you thought at all about what Dante and I said the other day?" Sasha stared out, his eyes on the café across the way.

"I have, but I think we need to wait until we get back to London so we can all be together to discuss it." He turned and looked up at the statue that stood between the two big doors. It was a bronze work depicting St. Michael defeating Satan. The saint held his long spear to the devil's throat.

Sasha's voice went to a whisper. "You haven't thought at all about the fact that we're more closely watched in London? If we want to do anything at all about it we should do it while we're here."

Robert turned to face him. "What the hell are you talking about doing?"

"Has it occurred to anyone that we were trained for this?"

"Trained for what?"

Sasha's eyes rolled. "Dr. McDonald trained us. She taught us how to rob a bank. Why don't we simply go into the place and take what we need? You might not want your memory back, but I do."

"We don't even know where it is or if it's there," Robert shot back. "We have no idea if there's a cure at all."

"But that data could give me my name," Sasha argued. "It could…never mind. You think getting your memories back means losing Ariel. Jax doesn't care. Tucker really doesn't want to remember who he was."

He hadn't realized how isolated Dante and Sasha must feel. When they'd first come out of McDonald's lab, they'd been matched pairs. Dante and Sasha had been close and Jax and Tucker had stuck together. Over time Jax and Tucker had integrated with the rest of The Garden, but Dante and Sasha had held themselves apart. "I promise I will do everything I can to reunite you with whoever is out there. I promise. I won't let you down."

Sasha's jaw went tight. "I know you will. You are a good man. And I know Damon is, too, but there are higher powers in play and being good doesn't always work out. We should know that more than any others. You're being naïve. You want to be one of them, but you are not. We are not. We're still merely a job for McKay-Taggart."

His cell phone buzzed in his pocket. "Give me a second."

Sasha said nothing, simply took out the camera they'd given him and started taking pictures. He moved around the front of the church, blending in with the rest of the tourists chronicling their adventures.

Robert pulled out the phone and swiped the screen to get to the text that had just been sent.

Hello, Rob. I'm happy you're back to fighting shape after our last round. Sorry for shooting you, but I had to slow Ariel down. I'm sitting in the back pew on the right side if you would like to discuss the situation. Don't forget we're not alone.

Fucking Levi Green.

He looked over at Sasha. Peter was across the plaza. He couldn't even see Tucker.

He could text Ariel and let her know. Another ping let him know Levi was still texting.

Don't keep me waiting, man. Come on. I'm not here to fight. How about I give you a gift?

He knew he should ignore it, but he'd had a day. He quickly texted back.

How about you fuck off?

How many men did Levi have hanging around? He'd selected a very public place so the likelihood of a firefight wasn't high. It didn't mean Levi couldn't drag him into the shadows, but he was ready for that. If he were going to arrest them all, wouldn't he simply do it?

The screen flickered and then a picture filled it. Robert stopped, staring down in disbelief.

It was a picture of Ariel. She wore the same clothes she wore right now, the dress she'd put on this morning when she'd gotten ready for her meeting with Emily. He would have known since he'd been the one to zip her up. She had the same white Prada bag over her shoulder and her hair was in a halo around her head. She was sitting on a stone bench and she wasn't alone.

Kimberly Solomon sat next to her.

She'd met with Solo today?

She hadn't mentioned that piece of news to him. The Agency was here and she was meeting with them. Had she met with Levi, too?

Every little whisper he'd heard lately rained down on him.

What if he was wrong?

"Damn it, Robert. I'm not cleaning up after…" Sasha set the camera against his chest again. "What's going on?"

"Levi Green is in the church."

Sasha's brow rose. "Is he planning on killing us here?"

"He wants to talk to me." He should shut down everything right now, but that picture…

"I'll back you up." Sasha looked behind him, staring at the table where Ariel and Rebecca sat gathering information. "They're fine. Peter and Tucker are still watching. No one will notice if we slip away. I'll have your back if you want to talk to him."

Ariel was talking to Solo. Why shouldn't he do the same?

Because Solo never shot you, moron.

He wasn't listening to reason.

Come on, Rob. I'm offering you knowledge they won't give

you. Ten minutes. It's all I ask and I'll tell you exactly who your girlfriend is.

Robert turned and walked in the door.

He went from the bright light of day to the shadow of the vestibule, from the vibrant sounds of the Marienplatz to the hushed murmurs of a working church that also functioned as a tourist site.

What the fuck was he doing?

"I'm going to keep my eyes on you," Sasha promised. "I won't be far away. You're doing the right thing. You're being our leader."

He wasn't sure about that, but he knew he had to face the man. He had to ask him about that picture. He had to know what Levi knew about Ariel.

He walked into the church, his sneakers thudding along the white marble of the floor. The high altar was the focal point of the building and there were hundreds of tourists walking around the sanctuary, taking pictures of the stained-glass windows and the reliquaries, but he had one focus.

The sanctuary was in three sections. He moved past the candles toward the far side of the church. The middle section of pews ran all the way back, but the sides were shorter. He had to make his way around and through the crowds.

A dark-haired man sat in the last pew, his arm casually around the back. He looked like he was simply studying the great altar, perhaps contemplating the nature of God.

Or thinking about his sins.

"I'm here."

Levi looked up. He was wearing slacks, a white dress shirt, and a black vest. His hair was still done in that manner that looked like he'd just rolled out of bed but had likely taken the man an hour to perfect. He should have been in a café somewhere complaining about how the eggs weren't organic and how music was better on vinyl. "I always knew you were the reasonable one. Have a seat."

"I think I'll stand."

"Then you'll attract attention and we shouldn't talk because I know Solo's around and I can't be sure she isn't here right now."

Fucker was right. He slid onto the wooden bench beside him, keeping as much space as he could between them. "I want to know about Ariel."

"Do you? Some things are better left behind us," Levi mused. "I'm sure you wish *your* past hadn't come back to bite you in the ass."

He already knew about Emily. "I suppose I can thank you for that gift. You should know I'm not stupid. I don't believe she's my wife simply because you sent her in."

Levi held his hands up, an innocent look on his face. "Oh, I didn't send you that particular gift. I believe you can thank the Taggarts for that one. They've been scouring the globe for any scrap of information they can find. I believe they were interviewing Nurse Emily because of her connections to the McDonalds. I don't think they understood who they were dealing with, but the Taggarts are deep ones. If they thought sending in your wife would give you a shock that might end in them getting much-needed information, they would do it."

"Or you sent her in and she's lying. You're once again putting us all in a position where we'll get the intel you need and you'll run off with the prize." It seemed to be how Levi liked to work. "This Emily person is nothing but chaos to throw us off."

Something like sympathy hit Levi's eyes. "I wish that were true. If only for your and Ari's sake. What? I like true love. You think I'm some kind of monster, but I really was pulling for the two of you. Ariel deserves someone like you. Which is precisely why I gave you that distinctly nonfatal gunshot wound. You're welcome."

"I'm walking back out of here in ten seconds if you don't tell me what you know about Ariel. Why the hell would she meet with Solo?"

One of Levi's shoulders moved in a casual shrug. "They've been friends for years. Ever since Ariel worked for MI6."

The man was supposed to be some kind of ace operative and he didn't have his facts straight. "Ariel didn't work for MI6. She worked for Scotland Yard."

"Yes, that was her cover, but I assure you she absolutely was MI6, and she was good at her particular job which wasn't sitting in a therapy room getting men like Damon Knight to talk about their feelings. She was an assassin."

Robert laughed. Did everyone in the world underestimate his intelligence? "You must be getting desperate."

He pulled a tiny drive out of his vest pocket. "This is a thumb drive with Agency intelligence files on her. Have Jax verify them for you. Hell, let Jax off the leash a little. Have him hack MI6 and what you'll find is that Ariel and Damon are still in bed with them. They're feeding the Agency a bit, too. Not enough to get me off your ass, but enough I'm not allowed to simply arrest you all."

Almost as if it moved of its own volition, his hand opened and Levi dropped the drive on it. He should shove it back at the asshole. "Damon would have told us."

"And yet he did not." Levi relaxed against the pew, looking perfectly comfortable. "I will tell you everything, Robert. You're afraid that I'm going to turn mad professor on you all and vivisect you or something. That's not the case, man. I want to help you, and not in the sit-on-my-hands way Big Tag is working. Have you thought about the fact that the Agency could use your team for something beyond medical experiments?"

"No." He knew damn well he should shove that thumb drive up Levi's ass, but he found himself placing it in the pocket of his jeans.

"Well widen your horizons, Rob. Tag and Damon want to keep you hidden. I wouldn't do that. Come in with me. You'll do a couple of interviews, figure out what you do and don't know, and then we'll get you on the payroll. All of you. We'll clear your names. I can do that but you have to trust me. Imagine it, being free and clear of every warrant out there. You could come back to the States."

Ah, now he saw what the man was doing. "I could come home and settle in with the little wife?"

"I would actually suggest you don't do that," Levi said with a mysterious smile. "You're in love with Ariel. I hope you still are after you read those files on her. She was only doing her job. If she didn't tell you it's because Damon asked her not to. She's used to obeying orders. It's kind of a necessary thing in our line of business."

Ariel would have told him. She was his lover. She'd been pretty much his everything since the moment he'd laid eyes on her.

So why hadn't she told him she was meeting with Solo? It wasn't like they hadn't talked about the woman.

"All I'm saying is maybe you should put the blame where it belongs, and that's on the big guys." Levi sat forward. "I'm going to admit something to you that I haven't before. I've been in this game for longer than anyone knows. I was working to find out what McDonald was doing long before Ezra or Big Tag got involved. This is *my* case. I know more about it than anyone. I didn't get involved because my brother got taken. I got involved to help my country."

"Yes, you've made it clear that you think McDonald was doing good work."

Levi shook his head. "No. That is not true. She took good soldiers and messed them up. Now I'm a realist. I know bad things happen when we put our soldiers in the field, and sometimes you have to sacrifice a few to save the many. But what she did was monstrous. However, there is nothing gained by throwing the knowledge away. The pain has already been had. There's no way to give that time back to you, but I can make it worthwhile. Your pain could mean something."

"Yes, it could mean other people have to endure it," he shot back.

"Or it could lead to someone like Rebecca Walsh finding a cure for Alzheimer's and dementia." Levi sounded altogether too reasonable. "The time dilation portion could mean a prisoner could serve his time and not lose a whole life, a young man dying of a cancer we can't cure might live a life in his head. You see the bad, but I see a wealth of possibilities."

He was being far too optimistic. "And it could be used for bad."

Levi leaned forward. "Everything can. It doesn't mean we don't try. Look, my time is running out. The truth is Solo's getting the upper hand and I've got one last shot at making this thing work. I'm offering you and anyone who wants to come with me knowledge. I know who you are, Robert. I know why you were placed in the program. And I know a few things about Tucker, too. If I can't get your cooperation, I'll have to play my final card and I would rather not do that."

"I suppose your final card would be a fatal gunshot wound."

"Not at all. I don't plan on killing any of you. You're important to me. Think about it. Talk to the guys about my plan. I can open up the world for you in a way your current keepers can't. Look through the material I sent you." Levi stood up and straightened his vest. "Text me back if you want to talk further. Obviously I can't come to your place, and you might have trouble getting out. They watch you pretty closely. I find it interesting Ariel doesn't have the same restrictions. By the way, she knows I'm in town. Solo knows so I'm sure she talked to her bestie about it. You have to wonder, if Ariel was so scared of me why she would take a walk through a park without any backup. Either she's not scared or she knows she can handle anything I throw at her because she's a badass. I wouldn't mess with her. You've got a couple of days before I have to make a decision."

His decision was already made. "I'm not going to willingly come with you."

"Read those files. Talk to the others. I suspect they might be getting tired of being shut away. After all, *they* haven't been shut away with a woman like Ariel. Tell Tucker I have an even bigger hooker fund than Tag," Levi said with a smirk on his face that faded as he glanced around the church. "You know there are a bunch of people buried down in the crypt."

"If I want a history lesson, I'll talk to Peter."

"But this one is important," Levi insisted. "One of the men buried here was King Ludwig. He was one of the last kings of Bavaria. He was…inconvenient. The people loved him but the government at the time found him troublesome. They had him declared mad and took him off the throne. When he agreed to live quietly, they still had him killed. Oh, history questions it, but I know a coverup when I see it. If Solo gets her way, if the people she's working for cover up everything McDonald did and hide her work, you and your men are the only pieces of evidence left that prove she existed."

The church suddenly seemed colder than it had been before. "What is that supposed to mean?"

"It means the factions I work with want to use her research. You're important to that. You can take what happened to you and turn it around. You can be the hero. If Solo gets what she wants, you're nothing but evidence of something they want to cover up. Something a lot of people will want covered up. Think about that. The people she's working for, well, I don't even think Big Tag can protect you from them. Know that I'm somewhere in the city, eagerly awaiting your text. You're their leader, Robert. It's time for you to make the decisions and stop letting McKay-Taggart lead you around by the nose."

He moved to the end of the pew and Robert had the strongest instinct to go after him. He could beat the fucker until he got the truth out of him.

Or was the truth in his pocket?

"Don't attack him here." Sasha was suddenly standing in the aisle, his eyes watching the retreating Levi Green. "There's a lot of security and many cameras. We need to be careful leaving. I wouldn't like our faces to show up on the evening news. We should go. You can tell us what he said when we get back."

"He said the same bullshit he always says." Except it had been different. "We'll have a meeting this evening."

Sasha nodded and they carefully made their way out the doors they'd entered through.

Robert blinked in the bright light of day. He glanced over to see if he could catch a glimpse of Levi in the crowd, but he was already gone.

He went back to his job and wondered if the thumb drive in his pocket would change everything.

* * * *

Ariel knew that something was wrong. Very wrong. It was there in the harsh set of Rob's jaw, in the way he wouldn't quite meet her eyes. During the trip back to the club, he'd said all of three words to her, and she was almost certain he'd lied. He'd told her he thought he'd seen someone suspicious go into the church.

Peter closed the door behind them. "I'll go and get the recording transcribed. I think you got a lot of information out of that. And I noticed Robert and Sasha took a quick tour of the church. You should have waited. I could have taken you through the whole thing. *Michaelskirche* is a stunning example of a Renaissance church. Did you take note of the organ?"

It was easy to forget that Peter used to work intelligence. Which was probably why he'd been good at his job. He was handsome but not in a showy way. He was the guy next door, the one who would check on your pets if you needed him to. He was also incredibly observant.

"I thought I saw someone suspicious," Robert said.

Robert wasn't a good liar.

But then she'd always known he wasn't an operative. She'd always thought it would turn out that he'd been a soldier, the kind who did heroic things and didn't sneak around in shadows to do his job.

Why would he lie to her?

"We are very paranoid." Sasha was much smoother. He stepped in beside Robert. "And have terrible memories. Robert thought he saw someone from our days with McDonald. I followed him in. It was nothing but a tourist. Sorry. You know how paranoid he can get when he thinks you're in danger."

Sasha, on the other hand, was an excellent liar.

What had happened in that church?

"Are we going to debrief?" Robert asked.

"Yes, give me some time to bring Ezra up to speed. He texted me to say he's here." She nodded toward the rest of the team. "Why don't we meet in the conference room in an hour?"

They broke up and she found herself alone with Robert.

"We should go upstairs." Robert gestured for her to go first. "It's been a long day."

It felt like an endless day. Had it really only been this morning that she'd woken up happy and warm in his arms? It had been mere hours before that she'd known he was the one man in the world for her.

But she wasn't the one woman for him. Once, he'd made vows to another and they hadn't broken up. There hadn't been a divorce. There had been a tragedy, and she worried she was going to add to that.

Robert stopped at the top of the stairs. "Is Ezra here to talk to her?"

"Yes," she replied. It was hard to look at him when all she wanted to do was wrap her arms around him. She couldn't be a coward. They still had to work together. She joined him on the landing. "I'm too close to the situation to be professional about it. I can't be the one who figures out if Emily is telling the truth."

His eyes seemed darker than normal. "Funny, it felt like you weren't close to the situation at all."

She moved away from the stairs since this was a very personal conversation. "How can you say that?"

He followed her, stalking like a hungry predator. "You dropped me pretty damn quick the minute she showed up. It was almost like you were waiting for a reason to drop me."

Was he insane? "She's your wife, Robert. What am I supposed to do? You have to figure out who she is to you, and don't tell me she's nothing. You can't know yet. You need time, and the fact that I want nothing more than to get into bed with you and pretend none of this ever happened won't change the fact that it would be wrong."

He moved into her space. "I don't love her. I don't know her."

She reached up and put her hands on his arms to steady him. "But she apparently knows you. Think about it. What am I supposed to do? Should I pretend none of this matters? What happens when you start to get your memories back? What if being around her would be the key to opening up your whole life?"

His hand wound around the back of her neck, forcing her to look up at him. "Then fuck my memories. Ariel, run away with me. Go to your room, get your things, and let's just leave. All that will matter is the future we can have together."

It was so tempting. They could leave and not look back. She had plenty of money she could access. They could find a place on the beach and hole up and hide away from the world. They could be their own world.

But it would always be waiting for them—the world he could have had, the one that might be real.

"You need time. Running won't solve anything."

He took a step back and all that heat she'd felt coming from him had gone to ice. "I suppose you're right."

Why couldn't she make him understand? She was so articulate at expressing herself, at helping people through their feelings, but she was failing when it was most important. "I am not rejecting you. I'm in agony over this."

"Then I should step back and leave you in peace."

She couldn't stand the tension between them. "Have you thought about calling Kai?"

"Of course. I should do that." His face was a polite blank. "I'll try to get him on the phone."

He wouldn't. He was placating her. This was the way Robert worked. When he was done with a conversation, he wouldn't argue. He would say anything he needed to say to extricate himself from the situation. She reached out to touch his arm. She couldn't let him walk away. He had to understand that she still cared about him. "Rob, please don't leave like this."

He stood there, not breaking her hold, but he didn't look back at her. "There's no other way to leave it. I have to wonder if it was ever real. If you were ever real."

She let him go. "What is that supposed to mean?"

He turned and his eyes were stark as he assessed her. "Is there anything you want to tell me about your past?"

Fuck Levi Green. "So Levi was the one in the church."

"Why should I tell you anything, Agent Adisa? Maybe he was. Maybe he wasn't. Answer the question."

This was the fight she'd been trying to avoid. "If I've kept anything from you it was because it wasn't important. Whatever I did before I met you doesn't matter."

"Ah, but my past is everything, isn't it?" Robert asked, the words thick in his mouth. "My past is something you want to crack open and force on me. Yours gets to be a secret."

"I don't know what he told you, but he did it to turn you against me. Can't you see he wants you alone and vulnerable? He shot you. He nearly gave Owen over to the Chinese. Do I have to go through the litany of his crimes against us? You can't trust him." It didn't matter that he hadn't acknowledged that Levi had been the one he'd met. Only one person in the world could have turned everything upside down. Levi could have easily gotten her records. It would be unethical to use them, but no one ever accused Levi of having ethics.

"Maybe he's not the only one I can't trust." He gritted his teeth and took a step back. He seemed to take a steadying breath. "I'm sorry. I'm angry and too emotional right now to do my damn job. I got a text while I was doing the surveillance at the meeting with the assistant. Obviously it was Levi and yes, he's trying to create chaos. I'll write up a report."

She managed to catch a breath. He was being reasonable. She could work with that. "Why would you lie about it? Sasha did, too."

"Because I don't know who to trust anymore," Robert admitted. "I thought I knew everything about you. Why would you lie about MI6? Were you or were you not an assassin?"

"I can't talk about my work in the past. It's classified." Her gut was in knots. He knew and he was definitely angry about it. "You have to understand."

"I understand that I'm an open book and you haven't bothered to tell me the basic truths about yourself. We wasted a lot of time. I pushed you away because I thought you were far too delicate for me. If I'd known you were some kind of super assassin, I would have hopped into bed with you the first day. Tell me something—all this time have you used my attraction to you to control me? I've been thinking about this a lot. I'm the leader. The men tend to do what I tell them to do. It wouldn't be a bad play to keep me on your leash."

Anger rose. He was the one manipulating things now. "No. I didn't sleep with you so I could control you. I was an assassin not a whore."

He paled and his next words weren't as solid as the accusations from before. "I didn't call you that. I didn't…god, I didn't mean to do any of this. I'm so angry with you and yet I meant what I said. I would run away with you right now. I would do it without taking anything with us. I want you."

"And I want you, but, baby, you have to remember what happened with Theo and Erin." Her anger had fled in an instant and she was all tears and heartache again. "He didn't want her and then he remembered how much he loved her. What if he'd found a woman and she came between them? That wouldn't have been fair. Not to anyone concerned. I've seen this happen before."

He shook his head. "No, you haven't. You might have heard about it, but I watched it up close. It is not the same. Theo was attracted to Erin the minute he saw her. No matter what McDonald did to him, he still dreamed about Erin. He might not have remembered her name, but he remembered how he felt about her. He saw her in a bar and wanted her immediately. I do not want that woman. I'm not attracted to her. God, I'm vaguely repulsed by her and I can't figure out why."

"Robert!"

She gasped and turned because that had been Ezra's voice biting out the command. Robert's face had fallen and he stepped back. Ariel turned and it was worse than just Ezra standing there. Emily was at his side, a hand over her mouth.

"I'm sorry, Ms. Seeger, you shouldn't have had to hear that," Robert said.

"Maybe you shouldn't have said it," Ezra shot back.

Robert shook his head. "No. I'm not a piece of meat to get tossed around. Look, I understand that everyone wants me to take one look at a complete stranger and get my life back. I was supposed to run to her and have my soul magically healed, but that's the thing. The healing already happened. I'm in love with Ariel. I'm not going to fall out of love with Ariel. Although I might walk away because she's been lying to me, and that means you have too, Ezra. So maybe I should think about this for a while. Or maybe I'll just go drink. Enjoy the debrief. I don't think I'm needed there."

He turned and walked down the hallway.

"I think I need a moment. Please thank Peter for the lovely room. It's very comfortable. And Dante was quite the gentleman." Emily turned and moved toward her room at the end of the hall.

Ariel's stomach churned. She'd hoped Emily wouldn't find out about her connection to Robert. Maybe it was cowardly of her, but if Robert eventually went back to Emily, Ariel wanted to have a spot of dignity left. That plan hadn't worked, but then none of her plans seemed to work out lately.

Ezra stepped up, his blue eyes staring down at her with sympathy. "Are you all right?"

She had to force down her pain, focus on the job. "Levi apparently paid a visit to Robert. He knows about my work with MI6. I'm sure Levi sent him whatever files he has on me, so Rob is probably finding out exactly how bloody my hands are right now."

Ezra looked down the hallway the direction Robert had gone. "I can stop that."

She put a hand on his arm. “Taking those files away would only make things worse at this point. Who knows. Perhaps him knowing who I used to be will change his opinions of me. Maybe he’ll be more open to giving his wife a chance.”

“Or maybe he knows what he wants,” Ezra replied, his voice softer. “I only heard the end of it, but I think I got the gist. The two of you finally took the plunge and then his wife shows up and you stepped back. Are you sure you want to do that? You love him. Everyone knows that.”

She loved him so much it hurt, and now it felt so wrong that she hadn’t told him, that she might go to her grave never having said the words to him. “It doesn’t matter now. He’s not in a position to make this decision. Unless you found out her story is complete rubbish.”

“I wish I could tell you that, but she checks out. Once we knew where to look it was easy to find her pictures of him. Now according to all records, Russell Seeger doesn’t exist, but we know McDonald always did a hell of a job getting rid of a person. They were particularly thorough with Robert.”

“Why? Why not report him as killed in action and let it be?”

“I think by then she realized what could happen if he showed up on a camera somewhere,” Ezra explained. “She talks in her diary about being more careful with her subjects, especially the ones she thought she would be able to put out on the streets. You know she had several teams she used to rob banks to fund her after she fled from Kronberg.”

Which was precisely why several of them still had warrants out for their arrests. “Yes, I suppose she was an excellent tactician. What did you think of her? Emily, I mean.”

Ezra sighed as though he didn’t want to leave the personal talk, but he seemed to accept the inevitable. He turned and walked to the kitchen. “I think she’s upset and off balance, but I would expect that from a woman whose husband came back from the dead.”

She followed him, more than willing to get out of the hallway. “Yes, I imagine it was quite a shock, and then he wasn’t happy to see her.”

Ezra strode to the fridge and pulled out two beers, offering her one. “He wasn’t happy because he knew how you would react. I think you both need to take a deep breath. We know she is who she says she is. We don't know that their marriage was happy. We don't know that Robert will ever get his memory back and want to fly away with her. We need more time. We need to get boots on the ground and ask some questions."

She took the beer and twisted the cap off. She didn't even think about refusing it. She settled into the chair across the table from Ezra. What would she do if she wasn't involved with Robert? If this was Tucker or Dante's wife, how would she handle it? "We should talk to people who might have known them, get a feel for what Russell Seeger was like."

"*Was* being the most important part of that sentence." Ezra sat back. "He is not the same person. None of them are the people they used to be. I think you two need to cool off and then sit down and talk. Now tell me why you're okay with him reading whatever bullshit Levi gave to him. Also, why I don't ship his ass back for meeting with Levi and not bothering to mention it until later. He should have immediately reported in and given us a chance to take the man down."

"I think shipping him back like a naughty toddler would do a lot of damage."

"He deviated from protocol and we're looking for a traitor."

"The group is in a very tenuous state." She had a lot to tell him, and he wouldn't react well to most of it. "I think if we push them too hard right now, they'll break. I told you they would only be able to stay in this state for so long."

"Who's having trouble?" Ezra asked. "Because Jax seems perfectly happy. Owen got emotional after he went to Scotland with Rebecca that weekend, but I thought that was a good thing."

Owen had taken his girlfriend to his old home and finally faced his past. "It was healing for him. Jax and Owen are balanced by their partners. Robert was balanced by his position in the group. Leading the men has given him grounding, a grounding I'm worried he's going to lose if the group splits."

"I think he'll lose it if you walk away from him."

She couldn't let this get back to her screwed up personal life. "I'm going nowhere. Ezra, this is serious. Tucker hasn't been stable since Rebecca positively identified him as Steven Reasor. And Dante and Sasha have started to question whether or not we're taking the best course of action."

Ezra's brows rose. "Well if Dante and Sasha want to leave, the door is open. It might solve a whole lot of our problems."

Because like Ian, he thought one of them was the traitor. "I think any of the lads leaving would harm the group."

"And if one of them is talking to Levi Green?"

"I think that could be devastating to them all." She hated to even think about what morale would be like if one of the Lost Boys turned out to have betrayed the group. "They know we've kept things from them."

"Things they didn't need to know," Ezra argued. "You know why I asked you to keep your prior work from them. You weren't burned by your group. You're still friendly with them, and Robert and the others have a whole lot of reasons to be wary of any intelligence agency. It's why I agree with Damon about not telling them we've cooperated with several agencies. It's the only thing that's kept us all safe. Levi hasn't raided The Garden because we've kept certain parts of the Agency fed."

"I think they'll understand our reasoning. Keeping it from them is far worse." There was more to the story. "And you should know I met with Kim earlier today."

Just like that all of Ezra's casualness was gone. His every muscle seemed to tense and his eyes focused in. "I knew she was in town. She called you again?"

This was the bad part of Ezra being here. He couldn't be reasonable about his ex-wife. "No, I called her. I wanted her input on Emily Seeger. You know she's got better contacts than anyone else. She can get us information not even Big Tag can."

"If she's telling us the truth and she's not simply trying to beat out her boyfriend to get to the prize. She always was competitive that way."

"I'm not Damon, Ezra. I know he puts up with your prejudice against her. And I'm not in a good mood. I know Kim. You can't get away with that shite with me. If you don't want to work with her, maybe you should go back to England and send Damon down.

Believe me, I'm considering benching myself after today's revelations. I'm wondering how fast we can get Kai here. Or Eve McKay. I don't need your jealousy further endangering these men."

For a second she thought she'd pushed him too far. His jaw tightened and she could see the way his hands fisted. But then he relaxed, sitting back and taking a deep breath. "I'm not good when it comes to Solo. I'm still…how can it be so raw after all these years?"

"Because you still love her. It doesn't do you any good to fool yourself because you're literally the only one who believes it."

He was quiet for a moment. "You don't think she's working with Levi?"

It took everything she had not to roll her eyes, but at least he was asking the question. "I think she hates the man. I believe her when she says she made a mistake. I believe her when she says she was drunk and depressed over the divorce. She's not dating him."

"He always wanted her."

"And he took advantage of her. Ezra, have you ever considered that? She was vulnerable and he moved in on her."

"She shouldn't have been drinking. I'm sorry. I don't mean that. I hate myself for even thinking that. God, I don't like who I am around her." He took a deep breath and schooled his expression to something like professionalism. "I know what the boss thinks. Do you believe she's working for the president?"

"I do. I think she's on our side. If we can get the right data, the president can clean up the Agency. If you want to take down Levi Green, Kim is your best shot."

He took a long swig of beer. "How is she doing?"

He'd never asked the question before. Not once. Even after she'd been shot, he'd ignored her. "She's good. She's…she's Kim. She offered to handle Emily for me."

Ezra snorted. "I can imagine. Do I need to get the woman a bulletproof vest?"

"You should know she told me she's planning on taking out Levi."

A grave look came over his face. "We'll see about that. Does she want to come in?"

"I think so, but she's worried if she hasn't got solid proof of what she's looking for, you'll throw her out."

Ezra growled, a sound of deep frustration. "She can come in, but she can't stay here. She can talk to the men if she wants to, but she can't sleep here."

And why was that? Did the great and mighty Ezra Fain think he couldn't control himself if his luscious ex-wife was underfoot? "I think she'll be fine with that. If I know her, she's probably in a much nicer place than this. I'll give her a call."

He nodded. "Do it tonight and we'll bring her in tomorrow morning. We need to figure out what our play is. We'll hold the debrief then. I don't think I can face her until I've had some sleep." He stood and finished off his beer, dropping the bottle in the recycling bin. "And I don't think you should give up on Robert. I think you distancing is more about your fear than wanting to save his marriage."

She didn't want to save his marriage at all. She wished his marriage didn't exist. "I'll think about it."

It would be all she would be able to think about.

She reached for her mobile and dialed Kim's number. At least she could make one person happy today.

Chapter Twelve

Robert stared at the Scotch in front of him. It was late and he should go to bed, but he couldn't quite make himself get off the couch. He could hear the thud of music from downstairs, but he wouldn't be going down to the club either. He would have. If his world hadn't gotten turned upside down he would have been downstairs with Ariel sitting on his lap as they watched the scenes. He would have felt the anticipation of playing out their own.

He wouldn't feel this emptiness, the utter hollowness that came from knowing she hadn't walked away with him. It was funny. He'd read the file Green had given him. He'd gone through all the surveillance shots of Ariel meeting with Solo. It hadn't had the effect he was sure Green had hoped for. Those shots of her in the park had contained a few where he'd been able to see the pain on her face. In that moment she hadn't been a ruthless operative, conspiring with another. She'd been a woman in pain, confessing to her friend.

He didn't even question it. She'd been talking about him, about the fact that their relationship was threatened.

And the rest of it? He didn't even fucking care. She'd identified threats, some of the worst of the worst, and she'd taken them out when the legal system couldn't. He didn't care that she'd killed some terrorists, a couple of cartel heads, a dictator who practiced genocide.

As he'd read about her skill, he'd kind of wished someone had sicced her on McDonald. He'd had a brief fantasy of Ariel being the one who'd come for him that day. She would have brutally murdered Hope McDonald and in all the chaos, the smoke would part and he would see her. She would have been a vengeful goddess until she caught sight of him. Their eyes would lock and she would fight her way to him. She would carry him out of that lab like he was payment for all her hard work.

Yeah, he'd had a lot of Scotch.

He heard the floor squeak and sighed. They'd all come in to talk to him. Tucker had offered to sit with him. Sasha had wanted to talk about what had happened with Levi Green. Owen and Rebecca tried to get him to eat dinner. Even Dante had come in. He'd talked about spending time with Emily and how it must be nice to have a lovely wife.

He didn't want to deal with any of them.

"Well, you always did like Scotch," a feminine voice said. Emily walked around the couch and picked up the bottle, noting the label. "Though you're drinking a better brand now."

Damn it. He forced himself to sit up straight. She was the last person on earth he wanted to see, but he'd been quite cruel to her earlier. "I'm not the one buying it. My bosses have high standards."

"You work for Ian Taggart and Damon Knight," she said, sitting on the chair across from him. "I talked to Dante this afternoon. He explained about your job. Well, he said mostly your job has been trying to figure out who you all are and what exactly was done to you. I need you to understand that I plan on telling you everything I know. I'll help in any way I can."

"Thank you for that." He was so uncomfortable with her. Shouldn't he feel something for a woman he'd married? "I'm sorry for what you overheard earlier."

"But you weren't sorry for saying it."

"No. It's how I feel. I can't even wish I felt differently."

"You're in love with the doctor. She's stunning. I can see why you would fall for her."

Ariel was more than a gorgeous body and beautiful face. "She's one of the kindest women I've ever known."

"In my defense, you haven't known many. You're kind of a toddler, and a sheltered one at that."

He should have been offended but he laughed because it was pretty much bang-on true. "Yeah, that has been pointed out to me on occasion. By more than one person. You want a drink?"

It was the least he could do. He didn't know if she did drink but she probably needed one after the day they'd been through.

"Yeah. I'm usually more of a vodka girl, but you don't remember that." She gave him a half smile as he poured her a few fingers of the eighteen-year old Scotch. "It's so weird to think that you have no idea who I am. Most of my adult life you were the one who knew me best. I'm really sorry for what you've been through. It must have been terrible."

Terrible didn't begin to cover it. He passed her the glass and sat back. He didn't want to talk about that part of his life. "It's over."

"It doesn't sound like it's over. It sounds like you're still having to fight for your life." She took a sip. "You should know you were good at that. At fighting. You were an excellent solider and all your men loved you. If you ever want to know about them, I've got some pictures back at my place."

"Could you tell me about my family?" It was the one thing he did want from her. "Sometimes I think I remember them."

Her eyes widened. "I thought you didn't remember anything at all."

"I don't really," he admitted. "I get flashes of what seem like memories. I get brief glimpses and feelings. It's hard to explain. The strongest are about holding hands with a woman. I have the sensation of warmth on my face and I know I'm safe with her. She's taller than I am and I feel love for her, but not desire. She's my mom. I'm almost certain of it."

He'd gotten used to that memory. He was able to let it flow over him like a warm blanket. It was a good part of his day.

She sat back, a frown on her face. "I'm not sure how to put this. You weren't close to your mom. Maybe you were when you were young. I never met her. You left home because you didn't get along with her or your brother. I want to candy coat it. I really do, but you were always a man who valued honesty."

That hadn't come close to the feelings he'd had or that voice that sometimes whispered through his brain. "What did we fight about?"

"You didn't talk a lot about your family. I know your father wasn't in the picture. You didn't talk to either your mother or your brother the whole time we were together. You went into the Army to get away from those problems. We became your family and you were happy with us," she said, her tone wistful.

It hurt something deep inside him to think he didn't talk to his brother. His brother was nothing more than an idea in his head. A whisper across his brain. And yet the thought that he was gone and they'd parted badly made Robert ache. He'd liked thinking there was someone out there he'd shared a childhood with. "I was close to my unit?"

"You were really close to a guy named Bill Barrows, though you called him Happy. He got that nickname in boot camp because he always had a dumbass grin on his face. Even when he was doing pushups or running until he got sick. You told me the only time he wasn't smiling was when you got into a firefight." She was much more animated now that she was talking about the past. "Happy was your closest friend, but you had a ton of them. Jimmy Collins would come over every Sunday because he knew I made a roast. He would show up and find a reason to stay until we pretty much had to invite him for dinner. I would make the roast because you liked roast beef sandwiches. I mean, you craved them."

He still did. When they made roast at The Garden, he would always go back for seconds or thirds. "So I was a private?"

"You were when I met you. When you...well, you were an E-5 when you went missing."

"I was a sergeant." That felt right to him. Somehow he knew what it felt like to stand in front of his team and give out orders. Happy would smile even though he was telling them they were likely going to see heavy fire...

He let it go.

"You were so proud when you got your promotion. I always knew you would go as far as you could. Our plan was to put in your twenty and then figure out where to go from there. We were pretty happy to go with the flow, if you know what I mean. We didn't need a ton of money. We had each other."

He heard her words, but he was thinking about other ways to jog his memories. "I wish I could read my records."

"Yeah, apparently those are all gone. I guess having a senator for a dad helped Dr. McDonald out. He could get rid of all those pesky records."

"She needed to hide what she was doing but still be able to have us go out into the world. It was precisely why she never worked in the States. She preferred South America and Asia. If she'd worked in the States, someone could have seen our faces and potentially asked why we weren't as dead as we were supposed to be. My mother…did she come to my funeral?"

"I'm sorry. She didn't. She cut off all ties with you when you left Wyoming," Emily explained. "I called to invite her but your brother told me you died a long time ago."

He nodded. He needed to stay away from those questions. Especially since it seemed like there was no one left to answer them. "I understand. We should talk about Dr. McDonald."

Her face flushed. "I still feel guilty that I introduced you to her."

"How did you meet her?"

"She did some work at the hospital I was stationed at, taught some classes," Emily explained. "We thought it was amazing to have someone with her reputation willing to come into a base hospital and give us her time. Now I realize why she did it. She was a sick woman. Dante said this Rebecca person thinks she might be able to cure you. Is that true? You might get your memories back?"

He didn't want to give her hope. "Rebecca worked with patients who have Alzheimer's and dementia. She believes with therapy and some drugs in the pipeline she might be able to reconnect the neural pathways Dr. McDonald broke in our brains. But that doesn't mean it's going to happen tomorrow. It could be years down the line."

"Dante mentioned there's a man out there who claims to have a cure."

"Dante talked a lot today."

She shrugged. "We were the only ones here. He was nice to me."

"That doesn't seem to bother him most of the time. And he's not known for being nice. You should be careful around him. He's been through a lot." He should have thought about that when he'd walked out the door. He shouldn't have left her alone with him. He should have insisted Tucker stay behind. Even Sasha would have been better.

"You all have been through a lot. He told me a little about it."

"Some of us handled it better than others. Dante's got a dark side. I don't think you should be alone with him."

A smile came over her face. "You were always protective. It was one of the things I adored about you."

He didn't want her to get the wrong idea. "I would say that about any woman. I'm not trying to hurt you, Emily. I'm not. You need to understand that even if I do get my memories back, it won't erase what I feel for Ariel."

"She seems to think it might," she gently pointed out.

"She's wrong."

"I didn't come here to fight," Emily insisted. "Look, I can help you. I can talk to you and tell you about your life. Believe it or not, we were good friends before we got married. It's why I think we worked so well. I get that you're not attracted to me anymore."

He hated the fact that he'd hurt her. "I'm sorry. That was a harmful thing to say. You're obviously very attractive."

"But I'm not your type." A rueful laugh huffed from her mouth. "You pretty much told me that the first time we met. I won you over in the end."

He had to admit, he was curious. Now that he was settling into the new reality, he had to wonder about his past. "How did we meet?"

Her lips curled up. "How do privates and nurses usually meet? The private was a dumbass and needed the nurse's attention. You were super flirty and I accused you of hitting on me. You weren't very smooth at the time. You told me I wasn't your type and then still asked for my number."

He winced because that sounded about right. "What had I done to end up in the hospital?"

"Well, you'd managed to make it all the way through boot camp without a single injury and then you decided to show everyone that you could break dance." She shook her head. "You could *not* break dance. You were, however, excellent at breaking your big toe."

"Is that the reason it hurts from time to time?" It was an

annoyance and one he'd never figured out. He'd decided he'd likely gotten it in one of the many fights he'd been in during his time with McDonald.

She nodded, grinning his way. "Yeah. You would always think you could do things when you got a little tipsy. Sometime I'll tell you about the great juggling incident. You promised me you knew how and decided eggs were the best way to go. That was a nasty cleanup." Her smile faded. "It was also the first time you kissed me. I'm sorry. That memory was overwhelming. I know you don't want to hear about those things."

"I do need to know about my past." He would have to listen to her stories. She wasn't so bad. She seemed quite nice. He supposed a nurse would have to be a person who cared about other people. She might be able to help figure out how McDonald's network had operated. He'd always had questions. "What did I like? Sorry. That's a pretty broad topic."

She leaned forward, an eager look on her face. "You loved baseball. You would watch football, but it wasn't your favorite. You were on a team, too. Center field for your high school. You played a lot of video games, but I think that was more about spending time with your friends than the actual games. You were good at fixing things. I would want to throw something out and you would always find a way to fix it. Like our old toaster. I wanted a new one so bad but you just kept that sucker running. Your favorite subject was history. You liked to read nonfiction. I've still got a bunch of your books. I gave away your clothes, but I kept some of the books."

"And you said you had pictures." It would be surreal to look at himself in a picture and not be able to remember anything of the hows and wheres that it was taken.

She bit her bottom lip. "Some. A lot of them got ruined when I got water damage in the apartment. The upstairs neighbor had an overflow and it dripped down and wrecked a lot of my keepsakes."

He wasn't terribly upset by that, but he had to say something. "I'm sorry to hear that."

"It forced me to move," she admitted. "I needed that push. I think if I hadn't I might have stayed there and mourned you for the rest of my life. I wouldn't have ever dated again."

"It's good for you to move on. It's okay if you have a boyfriend." He would be more than happy if she'd found someone.

She seemed uncomfortable with the shift, but she plunged ahead anyway. "I dated a couple of guys. A doctor. A guy who works in admin. But I haven't taken things past dinner and a movie. I haven't cheated on you."

"It wouldn't have been cheating," he said gently. "That's the whole point. You didn't know I was alive."

Her chin came up, a stubborn expression on her face. "But now I do. I know you think you won't remember me, but you can't be sure."

"Like I told you, there's a very slim chance of that. The only one of us who's managed to get back his past is Theo Taggart. He wasn't in the program as long as I was."

"I still think you should try," she implored. "Come back to the base with me. It might jog your memory. Did coming to Germany make you feel anything at all?"

He didn't want to admit that it had, but he owed her an answer. "I remembered *Spargel*."

She dropped to her knees in front of him. "Yes, you loved it. I would make it for you and I would make a ham."

She reached up for him and in his mind she shifted. She was different, her hair up in a ponytail, her eyes desperate and beseeching. She was afraid. The memory was right there and he couldn't stop himself from chasing it. This was important. Why was she afraid? He had to know.

His head started to pound, but he knew there was something important about that memory, about Emily looking up at him from her knees. He was angry. So fucking angry. He could feel the volcanic rage in his gut but he had no idea why he was upset.

"What's wrong?" Emily's voice sounded far away.

She knew what was wrong. She fucking knew.

Why couldn't he remember? He could see the carpet underneath her. It was basic beige, the same as every other unit in their bland apartment building.

Light flared, making the world a stark white place. He was going to lose it if he didn't stop. He would puke all night and he would be vulnerable. He was alone with her. He couldn't be alone with her.

Find another memory, one you don't have to fight for. Throw yourself into it, love.

Ariel's voice came to him, clear as day. He clung to it and did as she asked. In an instant he was back in time.

Loa Mali

He liked the ocean. He liked the feel of sand beneath his feet and the way the air smelled. He definitely liked the sense of peace he found here.

But he wasn't staying.

"I thought I'd find you here."

He turned and the reason he wasn't staying was strolling down the beach wearing a flowy white dress. Ariel. He could see the thin strings that held her bikini top in place. Thank god she'd covered up or he would have a hard time looking at anything but her body, her gorgeous curvy body. Now he could concentrate on her beautiful face. "I thought I would take a walk before the evening's festivities begin. Who would have thought getting married was such a social event?"

Her smile was brighter than the sun. "I think it's supposed to be a social event. And Erin and Theo have been through so much that they deserve a bit of indulgence." She moved to stand beside him, the tide brushing against her feet. "Are you not having a good time?"

"Of course I am, but it's more change. Now it's good change, but a whole lot of it. I'm going to miss Theo." He'd known Theo Taggart as Tomas. He'd been there when Theo had been "born" into the family. That had been McDonald's euphemism for wiping their memories. Reborn again and again into a world where she'd controlled everything.

"I don't think you have to miss him. I heard Ian offered you a job." She turned and started walking in the same direction he'd been going.

He fell into step beside her. "He did. I was also offered a job here with the king of Loa Mali. He's in need of a new bodyguard. I turned them both down. I'm staying in England. I think Damon is going to need a hand with the new kids."

And he couldn't quite bring himself to leave her. He'd only been living at The Garden for a few months, but he already wanted to be around Ariel every moment of the day. It was precisely why he should have taken either of the jobs he'd been offered. He couldn't have her. He wasn't in any kind of place where he could be in a relationship, and he was pretty sure casual sex was off the table. Mostly because it wouldn't be casual at all. But he'd found himself turning down every offer.

"I'm so glad, Rob. I will admit that I think they need you. You handle them so well. Even Dante, who I can't get to say a thing in sessions. He seems to respond to you."

Dante was a bit of a mystery. He hadn't spoken much at first. He'd seemed more dazed than the rest of them, and Robert worried his abuse had been worse. "I think he's settling in. I'll reiterate the need to open up in therapy."

She shook her head. "He has to come to that conclusion on his own. For now I'll keep our sessions light. I think he might be feeling shame. I've talked to the others and apparently Dante was frequently violent with them. McDonald used him to punish the others at times."

"She did that to all of them, I believe. She wanted to see if she could get us to go against our better natures. She often gave us the choice. We could be the one doing the ass kicking or be the one getting our asses kicked. She tried to pit me and Theo against each other several times."

"And what would happen?" Ariel asked.

"Well, there was a third guy in our group, and Victor liked using his fists."

"But you wouldn't hurt Theo and Theo wouldn't hurt you."

He'd never been about to bring himself to that point. He'd always taken the beating. "No. I couldn't do it. Even when I knew it would cost me. I think I had to hold on to some piece of myself no matter what."

Ariel nodded as though he'd made her point. "Yes, and Dante did not from what I can tell. He did her bidding."

"He was in there for a long time," Robert replied, needing to explain. "Longer than most of us. It's hard to tell. She wiped our minds so many times, but most of them remember Dante being there."

"Still, shame is a hard thing to deal with. From the outside it can look like he feels nothing, but I think he's afraid he won't be accepted given the fact that he was brutal in the past."

"I'll talk to Sasha," he promised. "He seems to get along with him better than the others. I'll see if he'll spend some time with Dante."

"Good, because I'll be honest, I'm a bit worried he might run."

"Where would he go?" Where would any of them go? They had no homes. There were warrants out for their arrests. They were trapped.

Ariel gasped and stumbled. He caught her before she could hit the ground, dragging her against his chest and twisting so when they fell, he bore the brunt of it. He turned to try to see what had caused her fall. A tiny crab raced away.

"I'm sorry," she said, her voice breathless. "I'm not much of a nature girl, it seems."

She was so close. All he had to do was lift his head slightly to brush their lips together. His arms were already around her. It wouldn't take much to flip her over and be on top of her, their bodies nestled together in the sand.

He released her because he wasn't good for her. He was one of the sad-sack men who she had to sit and listen to. She deserved far more. She deserved a man who could give her everything.

He got to his feet and helped her up. Her fingers tangled in his and she didn't let go.

She blinked up innocently at him. "In case there are any other wild creatures who try to attack me."

Her hand in his gave him the warmest feeling in the world. He could give her this. They started down the beach, talking about absolutely nothing meaningful.

It was one of the best days he could remember.

He was shaking when he came out of the memory. It was odd how they hit him when he got to this state. They were like dreams. He was fully inside them, as if he were living it all over again.

"Oh, I was so worried about you." Emily was looking down at

him.

His head was in her lap and she brushed a hand across his hair. He felt so sick he couldn't move.

"Here, I've got a cool rag." Ariel's voice hit him like a slap in the face.

He had to get up.

Emily gently pushed him down. "You've had an episode. You need to move slowly or you'll get sick again. Ariel heard me shouting and came in to help. She said this happens when you're trying to remember. I'm so sorry. I did this to you."

He wanted Ariel, but Emily was correct. If he moved right now he would get sick and make it all worse. He was forced to lay there, his hands shaking as Ariel handed Emily the towel.

"Do you want to talk about it? I can write down what you remembered." Ariel's gorgeous eyes were staring down at him.

He didn't want to write anything down. He wanted to go to bed with her. He wanted to shake off this horrible feeling and lie in her arms until he felt human again. The last thing he wanted to tell her was that he might have abused his wife. She'd been scared of him in that memory.

And he'd been so angry.

"He doesn't need to write anything down. He needs to forget," Emily insisted. "If this is what happens when he tries to remember, then I want him to forget. Babe, you don't have to do what she tells you."

Ariel started to stand again, but he reached for her hand, stilling her.

"I was in Loa Mali with the magical attack crab," he said.

Her eyes softened and she smiled at him. "You were my hero that day."

"What are you talking about?" Emily asked.

"When he starts getting caught in a memory that's hurting him, I've trained him to find a memory that's one hundred percent his, that no one ever tried to take from him. It grounds him and allows him to find his way out again." Ariel took a deep breath and stood. "Though we're lucky he was sober enough to do it. I remember how full that bottle was, Rob."

She sounded like a disappointed wife.

"Tucker helped with some of it." He was feeling good enough to sit up. "Though I should go and take a cold shower. That will shake off the rest of it."

"You should take some more time." Emily moved in beside him. "I'm a nurse. I should stay with you tonight."

"And Rebecca is a doctor. A neurologist. I assure you, she can handle Robert's needs." Ariel held a hand out and helped him stand. She sounded awfully territorial, and he liked that. Despite everything they'd been through today, he wanted her so badly.

"It's not a problem. Rebecca is right down the hall," he assured her. "But I'll be fine. I won't go down that road again. At least not tonight. I'll be a good boy and get some sleep."

"Excellent because you should know we're going to have a guest tomorrow. Kim is coming in. She's going to be with us for a while," Ariel said. "She's going to explain quite a bit tomorrow."

That meant they were in for some drama. His men would be nervous about having the Agency involved. Two members, really. Sometimes he felt like the bone two dogs were fighting over. "All right. I'll get some sleep then. Emily, thank you for the help. I'm sorry you had to see me like that."

"I would do anything to help you." Emily got to her feet.

"In the morning you can sit down with Ezra and tell him everything you know about McDonald. That's how you can help." He wanted so badly to not feel like she was smothering him every time they were in a room together. It was a sick feeling in his gut that had nothing to do with the memory he'd tried to catch.

Or did it?

"Can I see you again?" Emily started to move toward him.

He took a quick step back. "I'm sure we'll see each other. We have a lot of things to decide on. But I need some sleep. Good night."

He walked away and forced himself not to look back.

* * * *

Ariel watched Robert leave and her heart ached. Was she making the right choice? It was obvious he was in turmoil. Robert was the calmest of the men, the one least likely to make himself sick chasing a memory. He'd learned that a long time ago, but from the moment they'd set foot in Germany he'd been on the edge.

Should she go after him? Should she accept that they were different and had to deal with things differently? She hadn't forgotten what Ezra had said. She was cutting the relationship with Robert off more out of fear for her own heart than for his good.

"I would like to read any and all medical records you have on my husband. I want to speak to Dr. Walsh as well."

Ariel turned Emily's way and the woman's whole demeanor had changed. She was staring at Ariel with a haughty look on her face. She'd gone from soft and sweet and pleading to full-on cast-iron bitch. Wasn't that interesting? "That's up to Robert."

"He's my husband. I'm a nurse. I have the right to know what's happened to him and whether or not he's ever going to be able to remember his past. I'll float that question by the neurologist."

Ariel squared off with Robert's wife. "You can certainly speak to Rebecca, but I think she'll have the same rules as the rest of the medical world. His medical records are private unless he chooses to share them with you. I'll ask him if he wants to assign those rights to you."

"He assigned them to me when we got married," Emily insisted.

"That was another man in another life. He'll have to make that choice again, and trying to force yourself on him will only make things worse. Robert is a kind man and for the most part he's perfectly reasonable, but he can be stubborn."

Emily sneered her way. "You don't have to tell me who my husband is."

"That's what I'm trying to explain. He's not the same man. After what he's gone through, how could he possibly be the man you married? I was told Ezra explained the program Robert was a part of?" She'd hoped she wouldn't have to go over this with Emily.

"Yes, the disgraced CIA agent talked to me. Quite the team you have around you."

That was interesting. "Somehow I don't think Ezra discussed his status with you. So that makes me wonder how you know."

"I talked to Dante this afternoon. He was very open about how bad things are here." She stared at Ariel for a moment, her arms crossed over her chest. "I thought you were planning on doing the right thing."

"The right thing?" Ariel's mind was working overtime because there was much more at play here than she'd thought.

"Obviously you're involved with my husband. Anyone with eyes and ears can see that. I thought you had decided to do the right thing and back off. You need to stick to that plan because I have no intention of giving my husband up."

"He doesn't remember you," Ariel replied despite the fact that she was fairly certain the other woman wouldn't listen to a word she said. "He might never, and it's his choice as to what he does with the rest of his life. And who he spends it with."

"I'm not leaving here until I convince him to come home with me. He needs to be with me."

"He'll make that choice. He's not a child."

"No, but according to Dante you treat him like one," Emily accused. "He's your lapdog. It makes me sick to think about it. You were supposed to be his therapist. He was vulnerable and you took advantage of him. You're still doing it."

It was time to extricate herself from this conversation because her anger was rising. "I'm not having this conversation with you, Ms. Seeger."

Emily pointed a finger her way. "You'll be having it with a lot of people because I intend to find out what really happened. You're keeping him locked up. You won't let those men out in the world. That sounds like imprisonment to me."

"That's not my call, but I can put you in touch with someone who can help you." She knew exactly who to throw this problem to. "His name is Ian Taggart. You can call him and tell him everything you hate about me. And you would have done better to have stuck with the wounded wife play."

Emily's gaze turned distinctly wary. "What is that supposed to mean?"

She shoved down her anger. She needed to be calm and truly assess the situation. "I was off my game. You walked in and I panicked. You are everything I was afraid could happen. I love

Robert. I've loved him for a long time, but I didn't take the chance because I was terrified that you would be out there somewhere. Naturally you show up just as we've gotten comfortable. I wasn't thinking straight. I put myself in your shoes. How would I feel if my husband was back from the grave? You've taken it quite well."

"How can you say that? You don't know what I feel." Emily finally looked less than confident.

It was absolutely true that she could never know what another person felt deep down, but beyond the first tears, Emily had been calm. According to Ezra she'd listened to everything he had to say and hadn't asked many questions. "You've been very accepting of the situation."

"I'm still in shock," Emily replied.

"Have you called anyone? Your mother? A friend?"

She shook her head. "No."

"So you haven't told anyone at all what's happening?" No one had taken her phone. She could have used it at any time.

"I don't know how to tell them yet." She seemed surprised by the question. "It will be shocking to them, too."

She'd been so upset about Robert's wife showing up that she hadn't taken the time to ask pertinent questions. "Robert's whole team died. Now we know his death was faked. Yet, you haven't asked about them. Did it not occur to you the rest of the team might have survived, too?"

That seemed to shake Emily. Her jaw went slack before she answered. "I assume they used the bombing as a way to hide the fact that they took him."

"Ah, logic is hard, isn't it? You think Senator McDonald somehow managed to know that there would be a bombing, Robert's whole team would perish and he would survive, and then somehow managed to have someone waiting there to scoop him up? No. The logical conclusion is that bombing was staged and McDonald took a whole team. She needed subjects, after all. Yet you didn't ask about any of the other men." She knew she wasn't being kind, but her mind was rapidly filling with suspicion.

"I'm too concerned about my husband. And I didn't consider the rest of it. You're right. They could be alive, too. Another thing you and your group have to answer for." She moved closer, her eyes lit up with something like righteousness. "You should have had his face out on the news. You should have been looking for his family. You didn't want that because you wanted him. That's why. You've kept him all to yourself."

"I'm going to assume Ezra explained the situation to you. If you try calling the press, I'll have to handle you myself. You will put them all at risk if you do that, and I won't stand for it."

Emily looked her up and down and obviously found her lacking. "What are you going to do? Talk me to death? I doubt it. I will be speaking to Mr. Taggart, and I assure you when we're done here, Russell will come home with me. He loved me. Underneath it all he still loves me. You're a bump in the road."

In some ways, it was good her past was out in the open now. "You're going to be a body in a bag if you don't back off. And as to what I'll do to you, I'll use my skills as a former British Intelligence agent. My specialty was wet work. I was very good at it. Do you know what wet work is, Emily? It means I'm very good at solving problems. Permanently. Are you going to be a problem for me, Emily?"

Emily's eyes narrowed, but she took a step back. "I don't know that I believe you."

"Good, then that makes two of us." It was time to really figure out who Emily Seeger was and what Robert's life with her had been like.

"Hey, uhm, I know that I should run and hide because I am seriously scared of the violent estrogen raging through this room right now, but I also promised Rob that I would make sure you're both okay." Tucker stood in the doorway. "Ari, are you going to kill her now?"

Emily rolled her eyes. "I'm going to bed. Tell my husband I'm fine despite the fact that his side piece insulted me."

"I am not going to tell him that." Tucker shook his head.

"Well, you're useless as ever then." Emily breezed by.

"It's good to know my reputation precedes me. And, dude, that was some serious intimidation you had going there." Tucker walked in and picked up the Scotch Rob had left behind. "She's not as sweet as she seemed. She's one of those chicks who's super nice if she wants you and ugly to everyone else."

"Or she's hiding something. Pour me a glass. What did she mean you're useless?"

Tucker picked up two glasses and poured them each a drink. "She does not like being in the same room as me. Seems to adore Dante and Sasha though. Didn't have a problem with Owen. I guess it's just me. I'm okay with it. She gives me the creeps for some reason."

Ariel took the glass he offered. "I want to know more about her."

"And I want to know about you," Tucker said with one of his heartbreakingly handsome grins. "Assassin lady. I like it. Tell me all."

She sighed. It was going to be a long night.

Chapter Thirteen

"You did what?" Robert stared at Sasha, his gut twisting at the words he'd just heard come from the other man's mouth.

Sasha sat across the kitchen table from him. They weren't alone. Dante had a mug of coffee in front of him but had so far been silent.

"I read the files Green gave to us." Morning light filtered in but it did nothing to soften Sasha's harsh features. His eyes were always bloodshot, his face marked with the scars he'd taken during their time with McDonald. "I took the drive from you because I knew what would happen. I knew you would rethink things the moment you laid eyes on Ariel again and then you wouldn't share it."

Sasha wasn't wrong. He'd opened the files and browsed through them, but he hadn't called the guys in for a meeting. Ariel hadn't tried to take it from him, hadn't denied her former occupation. And he'd decided to think the whole thing over. Then the scene with Emily had happened and he'd known he would wake up in the morning and give the drive to Ariel. He'd allow her to share what she felt comfortable sharing. He'd intended to give her the power back because deep down he trusted her.

Her past was over. She was a therapist now and on their side. She'd quit MI6 a long time ago, and surely the meeting with Solo was about finding out how she could help them now. He'd justified all of it in his head this morning.

"You had no right to do that." The words came out of Robert's mouth in a harsh grind.

When had Sasha taken the thumb drive? He'd kept it on him the night before. Or he'd thought he had. By the time he'd gone to bed he hadn't been thinking about the drive, and this morning when he'd woken, it had been gone. He'd come out to accuse Ezra of taking it, but the boss had already left. He and Ariel and Peter were on their way to pick up Solo and bring her back for a briefing. He'd come to the kitchen to prep his men and found out they were the very ones who'd taken the drive.

Sasha frowned his way. His laptop was open in front of him. "I had every right. That information was given to you but it affects all of us. Do you know they're bringing in Solo?"

"Yes, I know. They're picking her up because they don't want her coming here on her own." At least that was what Ezra had told him over the phone. "They should be back in half an hour or so."

"And you're all right with that?" Sasha asked. "You know what's going to happen. She's going to come into this club and start dictating how we live. I thought we were trying to avoid becoming CIA stooges."

"Or they just wanted to string us all along until they could find a way to use us to get what they want," Dante said. "They seem to have found the right combination now. I never thought Ezra would be the one to bring in his ex-wife. Perhaps they have lied about their animosity."

"Why would they do that?" He was sick of this. They needed to have it out and it wouldn't wait until they were back in London.

"To keep us off balance." Sasha shook his head and looked at him like he was a pathetic, naïve child. "We are inconvenient to them now. I'm sure they started this with the thought to help out, but as you Americans say, the shit is getting real now. We know too much and so does McKay-Taggart. If the Agency decides to come down on them, the best play they have is to give us up. Not Owen and probably not you. But the rest of us are fair game, and this is not a game I wish to lose."

"No one is selling you out to the Agency. If they'd wanted to do it, why wait? And why sell us at all?" Robert asked. "We all know that Levi got an enormous amount of data from Colorado."

"It wasn't enough," Sasha replied. "It couldn't have been or they would leave us alone. And we're dealing with several different factions within the CIA. If Solo can be trusted, she claims she's working for someone who is diametrically opposed to Levi's bosses."

Dante shrugged. "I don't know why they do anything. I only know that they are lying to us. They are covering up their dealings and I'm done. I say we go to Kronberg and get this intelligence ourselves. Then we will have power. Then we can force them all to do our bidding for once."

"You're talking about the file Ariel thinks Kronberg is holding on to?" Owen walked into the room, followed by Rebecca. "I read her memo this morning. Apparently we're saving the briefing for later."

"Ariel is bringing Solo in to talk to us." He felt a weird numbness. "We'll have a briefing then."

"Well, we'll hear what the Agency wants us to hear," Dante grumbled, his accent thick. "Has anyone thought about the fact that yesterday we find out there is some kind of blackmail documents out there, a file that ties powerful people to Dr. Walsh, and today Solo shows up? Do you understand what we could do with that file?"

"What's going on here?" Owen seemed to be figuring out that this wasn't a casual breakfast conversation.

Sasha's brow rose and he looked directly at Rebecca. "I think this is a meeting for the men."

"Sexist much?" Rebecca asked, going to the cabinet and grabbing a coffee mug.

"If you were a woman who McDonald had erased, you would be more than welcome, so really the misogyny was on her," Sasha quipped.

"I think we should have this meeting in private," Dante insisted.

"If something's going on, Rebecca's affected, too." Owen stood in front of Dante. "I'm sick of all this shite about who's a real member of this team and who's not. We're all in this together."

"Are we?" Sasha asked. "Then why has Ariel been meeting with Solo and not mentioning this fact to us? Solo is the one who followed you that first day. Ariel knew that, too. She did not mention this to me. Did she to you? Or did she keep it to herself so we would be afraid of leaving the club?"

She'd known who'd followed them?

"She doesn't keep her phone as private as she thinks." Sasha's jaw tightened as though he knew he was in for a fight. "I duped it two days ago when I got seriously worried we were being placed into a position we can't get out of. Solo texted her shortly after we got to the club. They've been talking regularly."

The betrayal hit him like a kick in the gut, and he wasn't sure which betrayal was worse. Ariel hadn't mentioned she'd been talking to Solo. "You duped Ariel's phone?"

"Someone had to." Sasha turned the laptop around. "Someone has to make you see what's happening."

"Rebecca, I think you should come stand next to me," Owen said slowly.

"I think I'll wait for you in our room," she replied.

Dante stood. "If you're thinking about calling your friend, you should know she's out with Ezra. They're picking up Solo and bringing her back here where I'm sure we're going to get a bunch of crap about how the Agency wants to save us all. She'll ride in on a fucking unicorn and we're supposed to believe everything she says."

Rebecca had left her coffee mug behind. She joined Owen and quickly found herself placed behind him. "I wasn't planning on calling anyone."

He needed to ratchet down the emotion. "No one is going to simply buy everything Solo is selling, least of all Ezra. I think when they get back, we should all sit down and figure this out. We won't do anything else until we're one hundred percent certain we know what's going on. Okay? I'll go wake up Tucker and we can sit down and discuss the situation."

"Of course you want to talk," Sasha said, frustration in his tone. "Talk is all you want to do. Ariel will walk in and she'll work her magic on you. She figured out very quickly that you were the one to manipulate. We all follow you so she made sure she could lead you around by your dick."

"Stop talking about her that way." He wasn't going to let anyone insult Ariel or the relationship he'd had with her up until now. "I understand she didn't tell us the truth about what she used to do for a living. She's a different person now and her records are obviously classified."

"Used to do?" Dante asked.

"Maybe we should slow down, lads," Owen began.

Sasha wasn't listening. He turned the laptop around. "She still works for them. Do you remember all those trips to Paris? She says she's going off to meet with a girlfriend. That girlfriend is Solo. Ariel was working at The Garden at the time. And surprise, there was a rumored terrorist killed in the streets that same weekend. I wonder how they celebrated."

"She did not." Maybe he should have read all the files. She wasn't still working for them. Her past was one thing. He could understand that, but actively working for an intelligence agency and not telling him?

Sasha seemed to know he'd just gotten the upper hand. He calmed visibly. "She did according to the later records. You should read them. She's even given MI6 reports on her progress with us."

She wouldn't do that. God, he might be sick again. "We can't trust any of this. Levi Green sent it."

"But we can trust Solo?" Dante asked. "Wake up. We can't trust any of them. We need to get out of here while we can. We've been lucky so far, but now we're here in a place where it would be easy for them to turn us over. We need our own leverage."

"Or you could come with me," a new voice said.

Robert tensed. Emily stood in the doorway dressed in the same clothes she'd worn the day before. Her hair was up in a neat ponytail and she looked young and pretty.

So why did the sight of her turn his stomach?

She walked in and there was determination in her eyes. "I know people, too. I have a place where we can all lay low while you guys figure out what's going on. We can get on a train and get the hell out of town."

"We're not going anywhere." He needed to slow this down.

"If you stay here, they'll keep you dumb, Russ…Robert." Emily moved toward him. "I know the doctor has made you believe you're a completely different person, but I can still see the old you. Have you thought about the fact that she wants to keep you here for another reason, one that has nothing to do with helping you?"

"You don't know Ariel," Rebecca said. "And you don't know this group of men."

"I know her type," Emily replied. "She's an opportunist."

"She's also an assassin," Sasha pointed out. "I bet you didn't know that about her, Rebecca."

Rebecca's eyes flared. "I know she saved me and she saved Owen. She didn't have to. It would have been so easy to not come after us."

"I'm sure she had her reasons." Dante shook his head.

"You've made up your mind." Owen's hands were on his hips. "No one is holding you here. I don't think there's a reason to talk. I think anyone who doesn't want to be here should go."

"And have Ezra call the police on us?" Sasha asked. "We've always known they had that to hold over our heads."

"Ezra didn't cause the problem," Robert argued.

Dante didn't back down. "But he can certainly use it to make us do what he wants to. I can't believe you didn't learn. Years you spent with Dr. McDonald and you're still letting yourself be manipulated. I think she wiped your memory far too many times."

"And I think you're far too cynical. Ariel…I need to talk to her." He couldn't simply believe some files. He needed to listen to her.

"You think she can honestly love you after everything you've done?" Sasha asked. "She knows the things we've done. Owen and Jax managed to find women who they never have to tell the truth to, but Ariel knows."

"Rebecca knows everything I've done," Owen replied.

"I'm going to go downstairs for a bit. I think you guys really do need to work this out." Rebecca reached into her pocket. "Look, I'll even leave my cell phone behind. I'll wake Tucker up because he should be here. Emily, I think the guys need some time."

"I think they need to start thinking about their own futures," Emily replied.

Rebecca shook her head and walked out.

Robert turned to Sasha. "You need to back off. I don't want to talk about Ariel right now."

Sasha leaned against the counter, obviously settling in for a long argument. "She is the only reason we're still in this position. You won't see what's going on."

Emily put a hand on Robert's arm. "I know you've been through hell. I don't care what you've done. You did it to survive. We can get through this."

He ignored her. It was time for him to take charge. "I am the leader of this group. You two stand down. We're going to talk about this after we hear what Solo has to say."

And he would talk to Ariel.

Dante shook his head. "Why would anyone follow you? This is what I have been telling Sasha for months. You are nothing. You are weak. Even with your so-called brothers."

"I have been beside you all this time. I could have gone anywhere else." He didn't have warrants out on him. He'd been offered other jobs, a more normal life. "I chose to stay with you. To fight with you."

A derisive laugh came from Dante's throat. "God, why would anyone fight beside you? Why would they trust you? Everyone here thinks you're such a good man, that you will be the one to save them. Did you save Theo Taggart's face? What did you do when they were carving him up? Nothing. You sat there and did exactly what McDonald told you to do. You're nothing but a piece of shit like the rest of us."

The whole room seemed to go cold. Robert knew what had happened to Theo's face only because Tony had told him. Tony had been the man who disciplined them. He'd worked for McDonald. Theo didn't remember how he'd gotten his scars.

"You know there wasn't anything he could have done," Owen argued.

Sasha had gone still, his eyes on Dante. "How would you know? How would you know what Robert did or didn't do?"

"It doesn't matter what happened when he was with that woman," Emily said. "Come on. We need to cool off. It seems like you guys are saying things you really don't mean. Why don't we take a few minutes?"

Sasha was shaking his head and looking at Dante like he didn't know the man. "No. I want to know how you would know what happened to Theo."

"I do, too, since I didn't even know I was there when Theo got that scar," Robert said. He and Dante hadn't been on the same team. They hadn't even known each other until Taggart had found the secret lab.

"Tony told me," Dante said with a shrug.

"What's going on?" Tucker walked in, yawning.

Sasha ignored him, choosing to turn on the man who was so frequently his partner. "Tony died long ago. You would have had your memory wiped after he died."

"I read about Tony," Tucker said, heading for the coffee pot. "He sounded like a dick."

"Yes, but no one but Robert should remember him." Sasha's stillness had taken on the air of a predator.

"Then I must have read it in the reports we got in Colorado," Dante replied. "Or I'm being fanciful. The point is Robert isn't perfect and he needs to stop pretending to be our leader."

"No." The significance washed over Robert like cold rain. "You knew what happened. That wasn't something you made up in your head. You were very specific. You knew what happened even though you weren't there. Or were you? You're the one talking to Levi Green. You're the traitor."

"Dante's the traitor?" Tucker yawned again. "I need to wake up."

"He's more than a traitor." Owen stood in the doorway as if he felt like he needed to block it.

"Were you ever one of us?" Sasha breathed the question.

"No." Robert could see the truth plainly now. It all made sense. "He was the plant. He was always the one who did her bidding. He was the one who told her when we were remembering. I wouldn't have given myself away, and yet according to those notes, she knew when the drug was losing its control. You were her man in the trenches."

"You never had the fucking drug in the first place," Sasha accused.

There was suddenly a gun in Dante's hand. "Don't move. Not

any of you."

"Rebecca woke me up for this?" Tucker complained.

Yeah, it might have been better if they'd all stayed asleep.

* * * *

"We are not going to mention where we picked up Kim to Robert." Ariel watched as the gorgeous blonde stepped out of the Charles Hotel and waved. The door was held open by a uniformed bellman. The whole place looked elegant and expensive. "Ever."

Would things have gone differently if they'd ended up at this beautiful hotel instead of staying at the club? Probably not, but their drama would have played out in more romantic surroundings. She would have cried it out on thousand thread count sheets.

Peter got out of the van and opened the door for her. Despite the fact that there was plenty of room in the back, Ezra was sitting in the front with Peter. Coward. He'd been sitting in that chair long before Ariel had even been ready to go, as if he wasn't taking any chance of having to sit next to his ex-wife.

"Morning," Kim said with a sunny smile. She was chic in tailored slacks and a blouse that showed off her curves. She'd likely spent the better part of the morning deciding what to wear given the fact that she'd known who she would be seeing. "Peter, it's good to see you. Been a long time. Ari, not so long." She stopped as she realized who was sitting in the front seat. Her smile dimmed and for once she seemed less than confident. "Beckett. I wasn't expecting to see you until we got to the club."

"Solo." He didn't turn to look at her. Not that she could have gotten anything off his expression. He'd had his poker face on all morning and his eyes were covered in mirrored sunglasses. He was fully armored up.

Kim stepped into the van and the smile was back on her face. "Thanks for coming to get me. It would have been very difficult to get a cab or take public transportation or even rent a car in a major European city. They're so behind the times, you know."

The sarcasm was going to be flowing. If she could ever get these two on her couch…

"You're lucky I don't blindfold you and drive you around for a couple of hours before I allow you into the safe house," Ezra shot back.

"I know where the club is," Kim replied as the door to the van closed and she clicked her seatbelt into place. "So I would have to suspect that you just want to spend time with me."

"Which shows how bad your instincts have gotten." Ezra kept his face forward.

Ariel sighed. She would bet a lot that he was staring at Kim through the rearview mirror, and that was precisely why he'd worn the sunglasses. So his ex-wife wouldn't know he was staring at her while he was pretending to ignore her. "Are you going to bicker like children the whole time?"

Peter slid into the driver's seat. "They sounded more like an old married couple to me."

"We're not married." Ezra slapped the denial out as quickly as he could.

"I was going to say we're not old." Kim sighed and settled into her seat. "And no, we're done bickering from my end. I promise to be perfectly pleasant. I can't say the same for Beck."

"Did you realize you're staying in a hotel German intelligence has under surveillance?" Ezra asked.

It was precisely why they hadn't been able to stay in the luxury hotel. Of course if they'd stayed at the Charles, she and Robert wouldn't have had that insanely wild night at the club. She could still feel the pinch of those pins against her skin, remembered the rush of ecstasy as he'd brushed them off her body.

And she could still see the look in his eyes when he'd asked her if she'd lied to him.

"Of course." Kim waved off Ezra's worry as Peter pulled the van out of the circular drive. "I love the Charles. Bastien makes the best martinis. Seriously. I think half of why he's so effective a spy is his restraint when it comes to vermouth. And I got a hell of a deal. Someone had booked the eighth floor and then canceled at the last minute. Who does that? I've got a sweet balcony. By the way, that balcony has an incredible view, Ari. You parade your little problem anywhere close to this hotel and I can take care of it for you."

Ariel glanced up and didn't miss the way Ezra's lips quirked before he managed to school his expression again.

"Somehow I don't think sniping Emily Seeger is going to fix the problem," Ezra said.

"Though I do have an excellent rifle." Peter made a left, his cyes on the road. "And there's a long history of assassinations in Bavaria."

She needed to head off the history lesson. "I think we should talk to Emily. She might actually be able to give us something, though we need to treat her carefully. She's not what she seems. I'm starting to get suspicious."

"I am, too," Ezra agreed. "Though I'm also suspicious about where the tip about her came from. Big Tag said he's gotten several leads from sources he wasn't willing to name."

"Well, if you had known it came from me, you wouldn't have listened. And that's precisely why I went around you." Kim turned to Ariel. "I got a tip about some people who worked with McDonald before she went on the run. I sent it to Big Tag. He had his brother run down a couple of people, but I guess he decided Seeger was the best. I had no way of knowing she would turn out to be married to Robert. He couldn't have either. McDonald did a spectacular job of getting rid of evidence. I suspect it was actually her father's office who did that."

"Come on. We both know it was someone in the Agency." Ezra's words came out with a bitter huff. "No one else could erase a person so thoroughly. It was one of ours. Well, one of yours."

"I called in a couple of favors and I'm trying to run down some info." Kim frowned. "I didn't know. About the wife part. You have to know I would have given my friend a heads-up. Well, maybe I wouldn't have. I would have just taken care of it. I hate that it surprised me. I'm off my game."

"Kim, you can't murder people to solve my problems." Sometimes having Kim Solomon for a friend could be scary.

"You wouldn't have known." Both Kim and Ezra managed to say it at the same time.

Kim blushed but went on. "I believe in true love."

Ezra coughed.

"I do. I have way more faith than other people," Kim continued. "But sometimes true love needs a little help. I think of myself as a cupid."

"A psychopathic cupid," Ezra said under his breath. He sat up straighter. "I do accept that you didn't know about Emily's connection to Robert. Did you know Levi Green turned over files on Ariel's previous work?"

"What?" Kim slid the sunglasses off her face and looked genuinely shocked. "To who? Why would he do that? He's an asshole but he's never put an operative in danger before."

"I've got a bullet wound that proves you're wrong, and Kayla Summers still has problems taking baths." Ezra's voice had gone arctic. "You know he had her waterboarded, right? He did it so she would tell him how to get into The Garden. He wanted to steal one of the Lost Boys and do god knows what to him."

"She wasn't working for the Agency," Kim replied. "And there was nothing about that in his report."

"Surprise, he lies." Ezra's mouth had turned down. "Stop trying to justify Levi's actions. Or just come out and tell me you're working with him."

"I'm not." Kim's hands had fisted. "I was only saying he's been careful up to now and I don't understand what he's doing. Why would he out Ariel? Everyone already knows."

"Robert didn't." She hadn't talked to Kim about what had happened.

Kim sighed. "Of course he didn't. You wouldn't want him to worry about divided loyalties. There's a reason we work in secret. I will definitely report Levi to the Agency for outing you. Those files are classified. It's a gross violation of his job."

"He'll have someone cover it up for him," Ezra said. "And the only person who can confirm it was Levi is Robert, who we rather want to keep out of the Agency's clutches."

"No, that's the thing." Kim sounded hopeful again. "The tide's turning and that's probably why Levi's getting desperate. He got the notes Dr. McDonald left in Colorado, but the formulary wasn't in them. He understands the basic protocols but without the formulary, there's not a lot he can do. I think he's put his whole career on the line to deliver this to his people. The heat is on now, and if he doesn't find something soon, they'll have to let him go."

"You mean fire him?" Ariel asked.

"Or worse." The smile was back on Ezra's face. "The group he's working for is very aware of what could happen if it got out that they've been trying to gain access to highly unethical medical research. The easy play is to say they knew nothing about it and Levi was acting as a rogue agent. It's the way the game goes and Levi knows it. You're right. He is getting desperate."

"And a desperate man is a dangerous man," Ariel pointed out.

"I have to ask, why would Robert or any of the men be shocked that Ariel used to work intelligence?" Peter stopped at the light. "Almost all of the company's employees used to work for some form of intelligence agency."

"Robert has an emotional attachment to Ariel that comes from her ability to empathize," Kim began.

"Yeah, it's got nothing to do with her boobs." The eyeroll from Ezra was implicit. She didn't need to see it to know it was there.

"Beck." Kim could still sound like an embarrassed wife. "Though they are nice. Have you shown them to Robert lately? It could be the distraction you need."

"Could we stop talking about my breasts?" She needed to steer the conversation back to the professional. "What Kim is trying to say is I've forged meaningful ties with these men on the basis of therapy. They trust me. I didn't tell them I used to work for one of the agencies that's very interested in them. I certainly haven't told them I'm still in touch with the same agency. It's going to cause trouble."

"Yet you didn't stop him from looking at the files." Now Ezra took off the shades and turned to look back at her. "I could have ordered him to give it up. He told us flat out what he had. He didn't have to keep it."

"And that would have made things worse." She'd sat up all night thinking about it. Even after she'd seen him with Emily, she'd wondered if he was awake and reading through every bloody thing she'd ever done. "It's better to get it out in the open. Let's hope Levi gave him the real files and not something he's doctored. Reality is bad enough."

"You were working in the best interests of your country. Hell, in the best interests of the world." Kim put a hand on her arm. "You did nothing you should be ashamed of. Lives were saved. He's going to see that."

She shook off the thought. "It doesn't matter. Robert has other things to worry about now. And we've got to figure out if we should take the risk and try breaking into Kronberg to see if there really is proof of who all worked with McDonald. That could be leverage."

"That could be everything," Kim corrected. "It could be exactly what I need to give my boss the broom he'll use to clean up the Agency, and then Levi won't have any power at all. We can work toward getting the men pardoned. If that file exists, it could give them all their lives back."

Ezra's eyes narrowed. "You can't expect us to do all the work and hand over the prize to you."

"You can't do anything with it. I can. It's not like I wouldn't give you a copy. And honestly, I expect you to come in with me. We can show my boss together," Kim offered.

Ezra stared at his ex. "Somehow I don't think the president is going to want a disgraced CIA agent in his office."

"You won't be disgraced when I'm done," Kim promised.

Ariel noted she hadn't argued about who her boss was. "None of this is meaningful if we can't find that file. Do we think Veronica Croft might be the key?"

Ezra sat back again and shook his head. "She's the key to who Tucker used to be. We can't think that means she knows about Kronberg's internal processes. According to Rebecca she was an intern. I seriously doubt she knew what McDonald was doing if Rebecca didn't. We still need to look for her, but I think we should shift our immediate focus to the potential list of people who actively knew what McDonald was up to."

"And we need to figure out who the hell Emily Seeger is." That was Ariel's focus. What would she do if Robert decided to go home with the woman? She knew it wouldn't be for anything beyond a curiosity about his past, but after the night before she couldn't trust him to be alone with her. Something was off. Maybe she was simply being jealous, but there had been something threatening about the woman the night before.

Emily wasn't going to go away until she got what she wanted, and what she wanted was Robert. She'd been very concerned about his memory. Of course she would be, but she kept harping over the chances of him getting it back. Rebecca was probably being deluged with questions at this very moment.

"Well, she's not afraid of Dante, that's for sure." Peter turned again, finding one of the main streets in town. It would take them the few miles to the club.

"Why would you say that?" Ariel had been curious about how the afternoon had gone between the two of them. She'd expected they wouldn't speak at all. Dante rarely talked. He was the most introverted of all of the men.

"I think she should be very afraid of Dante. Every woman should be." Ezra crossed one leg over the other. "I did not think it was a good idea to leave him behind, but he insisted he wasn't feeling well and didn't want to go out. Not that he would let Rebecca examine him."

"I always glance at the security tapes in the mornings," Peter explained. "Something tripped the one in the yard yesterday afternoon. I thought it was probably one of them sitting outside for a bit. I noticed Tucker seems to enjoy being outside. But it was the two of them. Ms. Seeger went out first and then Dante followed her. They seemed to have some kind of argument, but I guess they worked it out because they were perfectly pleasant to each other this morning before we left."

Why on earth would those two have been fighting? "You got the argument on tape?"

"Yes, most of it. They went back inside after a bit. But it did not turn violent." Peter slowed as they approached a red light. "I would have come straight to you if that had happened. It seemed more like Ms. Seeger was upset and Dante was trying to calm her down. Given what had happened earlier that day, it seemed a reasonable response. I would have been upset if I'd learned my husband had come back from the dead."

"But Dante wouldn't care enough to comfort anyone," Ezra pointed out as the van came to a stop. "It's not in his nature. Do you have access to the camera feed on your phone?"

"Sure. Though my tablet will show it better." Peter reached in the console between the front seats and pulled out a tablet. He opened the cover and used his thumb to activate the device. "It's under the security app. It's the last segment I watched. I'm sorry. I didn't think it was important."

"I would very much like to see it." She would be able to tell a lot about how Emily reacted when she wasn't around. "Does it have sound?"

"No. I'm sorry. It's video only. I got out of this game a long time ago. The system is only there for basic security. Because of the club, I like to know who is coming to either door." Peter handed over the tablet as the light turned green and he started down the street again.

"Solo, if you don't mind." Ezra passed it off. "One of Solo's many talents is the ability to read lips."

"Hey, it's come in handy over the years. I don't speak all the fancy languages you do." Kim pressed *play* on the recording and leaned in so Ariel could see.

On the screen Emily strode out into the yard, a hand on her head. She wasn't angry. Her body language told Ariel something else was present. "She's afraid."

"Wait for it," Peter promised. "She is not afraid for long."

Emily wiped tears from her face and then took a long breath.

That was when Dante walked out.

"He's telling her to stay calm." Kim's eyes were intent on the screen. "He says we'll know something's wrong if she doesn't stay calm and think about every single word coming out of her mouth."

"What the fuck does that mean?" Ezra's whole body had gone tight. "What would be wrong?"

Ariel looked back to the screen in time to see the moment Emily went from afraid to angry. She turned to Dante and pointed a finger at him.

And what Solo said next made her heart race.

"We have to get back," Ariel said.

Robert was in danger. More danger than she could have imagined.

Chapter Fourteen

Robert took a long breath and wished he was a more paranoid person. He didn't simply strap on a weapon after he rolled out of bed and went looking for coffee, but Dante did.

Dante, who wasn't one of them. Dante, who'd lied the whole time.

Owen had his hands up. "Hey, mate. There's no reason to get violent. No one else here has a weapon."

"Oh, there are more weapons than mere guns," Dante said bitterly. "You will use everything you can against me now."

"I certainly will." Sasha's stare could have burned a hole through Dante. "He is the traitor. He's working with Levi Green. You bastard. I thought you were my brother. I thought you were the only one I could trust."

This could get bad fast if he didn't do something. The ramifications of Dante's betrayal would have to wait. He needed them all alive at the end of this. "Hey, you worked for McDonald? She wasn't any nicer to you than she was the rest of us. When Taggart came through you had two choices. You could out yourself and go to jail or come with us. I understand that."

He would kill the bastard, but he understood the choice Dante had made.

"He lied to us?" Tucker had put the coffee mug down.

He wasn't carrying either. None of them were. If Sasha had a piece on him, it would have shown up by now. Instead his hands were in fists, and Robert wasn't entirely certain he wasn't about to launch himself bodily at Dante.

"He lies about everything it seems," Sasha said between gritted teeth.

"You're one to talk," Dante bit out. "Sasha has been with me this whole time. You think I'm the only one who has betrayed you? He's been talking to Levi Green, too."

"Because I thought he was the best move for us to make. Because I thought he would clear our names and get us out of limbo," Sasha argued. "He says he has a cure. He can give it to us and I can get my life back. A life you helped her take."

Emily was standing across from him and she'd gone still. He held out a hand, trying to get her to move behind him, but she was watching Dante with wide eyes.

God, he was glad Ariel wasn't here. He would be so worried about her because there was no way she hid behind him. Ariel would be out there trying to solve the problem. And if she couldn't solve it with words, she would solve it another way.

He glanced around briefly, looking for any kind of weapon.

"Owen, move out of my way," Dante said. "I'm leaving. If any of you tries to stop me, I'll kill you."

"Just go." Not that he would actually allow it to happen. Dante knew things. Things they needed to know. He wasn't about to let him walk away, but they were at a disadvantage. Sure they had Dante outnumbered, but the room wasn't large enough for any of them to maneuver their way behind him, and Dante had that gun. If one of them rushed the man, a brother was going down.

That wasn't going to happen on his watch.

"Just go? I'm not letting this fucker go. Do you know the things he did to me? I could forgive it because we were all under McDonald's boot, except he was getting a fucking paycheck." Sasha's hands were shaking.

"You're not so innocent, Sasha. Move, Owen, or I'll shoot you. Get over there next to Tucker." Dante moved in tandem with Owen, sliding closer to the door as Owen moved away from it. "Think about it. Think about how Sasha has been trying to manipulate you all. Wasn't he the one who encouraged you to talk to Levi Green the other day? Sasha is as bad as I am."

"Sasha wasn't the one who worked for the doctor who tortured us." Tucker's eyes had gone bright. "Sasha didn't pretend to be one of us. Sasha didn't report back to McDonald."

Dante chuckled. "No, Sasha is the one who got his memory wiped time and time again because he was too stupid to realize every time he talked to his 'friend' about how he was starting to remember, I would tell McDonald. I got a bonus every time I caught one of you starting to remember."

"Tucker, stay calm. Don't forget, we have a civilian here." He might not think he was her husband, but he didn't want to be the reason Emily got shot.

Emily finally looked at him, her eyes widening. "Yes, we should all stay calm."

Calm. The word coming from her mouth sparked something deep inside him. She'd wanted him to stay calm that day, too. She'd begged him.

You don't understand, Russ. It's a good thing. She's trying to make a breakthrough. It's only some people who don't matter. Do you know how much money we've made? We need it. I did it for our future.

Their future. God, it hit him like a sledgehammer.

He caught her gaze. "You worked with her, too."

All the blood left Emily's face and she went a ghostly pale. "What are you talking about? Russell, stay calm. I think he just wants to get away. Let him go and then we'll be okay."

"Did you sell me to her?" The memory was vague, a hint of what had happened. He questioned it, but didn't force it. He wasn't questioning the memory. He was questioning her.

"What are you saying, Rob?" Tucker asked.

"Owen, if you reach for your cell phone again, I'll shoot you." Dante reminded them all that he was the snake in their midst.

Owen's hands came up.

But his had gone down that day years ago. His had gone around her throat. He'd reached for her even as the drugs had kicked in. He'd fought through them because destroying her had been the only thing that mattered.

It had never been McDonald in his dreams. It had always been her. Emily was the woman from his nightmares.

"So you've finally figured it out?" Dante's laugh was cold. "I can tell you my sphincter has been clenched since the moment that bitch walked in the room. I was certain you would remember that your dear wife was the one who sold you to McDonald."

"I didn't sell him," Emily said between clenched teeth. "Or at least I didn't mean to. He found out what I'd been doing."

Yes. The vision of a laptop screen floated through his head. He'd found the proof on her laptop and asked her about it. "I was investigating you. I got onto your computer."

Her whole demeanor changed, and he realized he was finally seeing the real Emily. "You were a self-righteous moron. Do you have any idea how much that money was going to change our lives? But no. You had to play the good guy. Good guys finish last in our world. Haven't you figured that out yet?"

The memories banged through his head like buckshot caught in a ricochet. He couldn't catch them.

Standing proud with his men. These were his men, his first team. He wouldn't let them down.

Sitting in the sun with his face turned up. It was his day off and he was out in the world. If only his brother could see him now. Tim would love this, but he was stuck in school. He was so damn smart.

Kissing Emily. It would be all right. She'd convinced him that getting married was the smart thing to do. He had never felt that crazy rush his mom had told him love felt like, but he liked Emily. It was comfortable. If only she got along with his brother…

His brother. The face was right there.

Something hard smacked him right in the arm. Pain flared and he looked to see Tucker standing beside him. "Don't you fucking leave us right now."

He forced down the bile that threatened.

"No, please do that sad-sack thing where you whine and cry and can't quite remember." Emily had moved closer to Dante. She frowned his way. "I was out of all this. When McDonald died, I was supposed to be safe."

"And I wasn't supposed to be left behind, stuck in this stupid role she put me in," Dante shot back. "We don't get a choice in this. I told you it was probably time to run. They're closing in on her whole network. Do you have the gun I gave you?"

Naturally all the bad guys were prepared, and the good guys were armed with coffee mugs and cereal bowls.

Rage swamped through him. It took everything he had not to jump on her and finish what he'd started all those years before. But Owen and Tucker needed him. Hell, Sasha needed him. He would beat the holy shit out of Sasha later, but Sasha needed him now.

Emily reached behind her and pulled a small pistol out. "I do. They'll tell everyone if we leave them alive."

"No, if we leave them alive, they'll get us the information we need to buy our freedom," Dante explained. "I've been watching the German. He's made contact with a few people over the Dark Web and concluded that he knows where the secrets are kept at Kronberg."

"Why would we give you anything?" Owen asked.

"We won't," Sasha snarled. "I won't give him anything but a bullet."

"Ah, but our Miss Emily has information that Robert would do anything for," Dante crooned.

Emily held the gun like she knew what she was doing. "God, I never thought that asshole would be my only bargaining chip."

"What are you talking about?" He needed to figure out how to get that gun out of Dante's hand.

"I lied about your brother. He's alive. So is your mother. McDonald hid all evidence of them, but I know the truth. If you want to ever see them again, you'll get us the data from Kronberg," Emily explained.

She was a liar. She was probably lying now, but he needed to get them out of this room. He was fast. He could get to his room and his SIG and be on them again. Ariel and Ezra and Peter had taken the car. What was the plan here? Run through the streets of Munich? This wasn't a video game where all they had to do was evade the cops until the stars on the screen disappeared.

Levi. That would be Dante's play. He would find Levi and Levi would give them cover because he wanted that intel, too.

They might be pulling one last heist, but he wasn't going to give up the data. He wasn't going to believe his viperous ex-wife.

Not that he would let her know that. "Of course. I want to know where my brother and mother are."

Tucker looked at him and seemed to understand the play. "Yeah, we'll get it."

"I'm going to leave now." Owen kept his hands up. "I'm not calling anyone or getting a gun. I'm going to find Rebecca. She's downstairs and I won't have you shoot her. I'm going to get my girlfriend and you're going to let me."

"You'll stay right where you are," Dante said.

"I can't let you run around down there without securing her. If she comes around a corner, you could kill her." It was obvious Owen was trying to keep his cool.

"Or I can prove to all of you that I mean business." Dante pulled his hand up and the world seemed to go into slow motion.

Robert heard himself shout, felt Tucker start to move beside him.

Owen. Dante was going to shoot Owen. He'd always hated Owen, likely because Owen had a place among them and he'd been on the outside. Owen had found some happiness that Dante's dark soul never would.

Owen was going to die.

And then Sasha was there, throwing himself in front of Owen, taking the bullet meant for him.

Bright blood bloomed across Sasha's chest as Owen's arms went around him.

"*Prost*," Dante spat in Romanian. "You are such a fool. I'll be in touch. Don't follow me or you'll end up like your brother there."

Emily went first and then Dante, running out the door and toward the stairs. Owen eased Sasha to the floor and Tucker sprang into action, but there was already blood seeping from Sasha's lips.

"It's bad," Tucker said. "We need an ambulance."

Sasha shook his head. "No. Too late."

"I've got to go find Rebecca." Owen looked tortured. "I have to get my gun first."

Robert nodded. "Grab one for me and I'll go with you. And I'll call."

Sasha reached out and grabbed his hand. "Robert, I'm sorry. I only wanted…I wanted a life. I thought…I betrayed you. Please forgive…"

Owen ran from the room, but he couldn't leave Sasha yet. He dropped to one knee. In the end, they were all just doing what they could to survive. They'd been placed in Hell and had to figure out how to escape the maze of pain and loss and emptiness. "I forgive you…brother."

They'd been forged in fire. Sasha had done something terrible, but Robert couldn't withhold those words from him.

He had to choose who he would be.

"But there will be no forgiveness for Dante." Or his ex-wife. None.

A smile lit Sasha's face, blood streaked and savage. "None, brother. Give him hell." He coughed, a rattling sound that seemed to come from his chest. The hand in his weakened its grip. "Promise me."

Oh, god. He knew what Sasha was asking. "I'll do everything I can to find her."

The child he thought might be his.

"It was worth it." Sasha coughed again. "It was worth it because I can die with my brothers around me. I will see them all again and this time, they will welcome me home."

"Rob, we have to go," Owen was saying. He had two guns in his hand. "Sasha, I'm so sorry, brother."

Sasha's eyes went blank.

"It happened too fast." Tucker was shaking. "There wasn't anything I could do. It must have hit an artery."

Robert let go of Sasha's hand and stood up. He would mourn later. He took the gun from Owen's hand. "Call Ezra, Tucker. Let's go secure Rebecca and then I'm getting a permanent divorce."

Owen nodded and they took off. They had work to do.

* * * *

Ariel held tight as Peter turned onto the street the club was on. German intelligence trained that man well.

"She knew Dante. Emily Seeger knew exactly who Dante was." Ezra seemed to be processing the information they'd received from the security cameras.

"And Dante knew her." Kim already had her Ruger out. "*A* plus *B* leads to one of us killing that asshole, but only after we torture him for information. And don't you tell me we can't, Ariel. You know what he did."

Dante had been McDonald's man on the inside. He'd pretended to be one of them and reported back to her. He'd been used to torture the others and they'd forgiven him because he'd been in the same position as the rest of them. They'd all been trying to survive and they'd bonded. But Dante's betrayal was bone deep. "Oh, I'm not telling you to do anything. I'll torture him myself if it helps the lads out. And you know what I'm going to do to Emily Seeger."

"Sister, I will help you clean up when you're done," Kim promised. "And don't worry about burying the body. We can do a lot with acid."

"There's a big shower unit at the club," Peter offered helpfully. "Perfect for taking apart a body. And honestly, on the right night we won't even have to close the club down. Everyone will assume it's a very heavy scene playing out."

"We need to talk to her, too," Ezra pointed out. "She recruited for McDonald. She sent her own husband in. It makes me wonder if she didn't send the whole team in. We need to ID these men and give their families some peace."

Naturally Ezra picked this moment to become the bloody voice of reason.

She forced herself to calm down. Robert and the lads were likely all sitting around the breakfast table talking about what they needed to do today. They would be prepping for the briefing, and they wouldn't have any idea that those two snakes were amongst them. Robert couldn't know that the very woman who'd sent him to be tortured and twisted into a tool for McDonald's use was probably sitting across from him batting her eyes his way.

"I'm going to kill her." She couldn't stop the words. She'd

promised she wouldn't use those skills again, but Emily Seeger deserved her avenging angel side.

"Of course you are," Ezra replied. "But we need to know who else she worked with."

"She didn't know what she was walking into." Kim unbuckled her seat belt. They weren't far now. "She had zero idea her husband was still alive. From what I could tell, she was angry and upset Dante was there. She thinks he's going to blow her cover. He said something about playing it cool, called us all idiots."

"Well, we kind of are," Ezra admitted.

"How could you know?" Peter was completely cool under pressure. "The way McDonald used Dante, none of the men knew he was a plant. It would have been easy for him to blend in with the rest of the group because they accepted him. To the outside world, he was one of them."

"She had him accompany the men on their robberies," Solo pointed out. "He was there to keep them in line, but to our eyes he had the same warrants as the rest of them. You couldn't possibly have guessed he wasn't exactly who he seemed to be."

Ariel's mobile trilled and she reached for it. Another three minutes and they would be there, but it was Tucker calling and she could give him a heads-up. "It's the lads." She swiped across the screen to accept the call. "Tucker, I need you to listen to me and not give away what I'm saying."

"No. You have to listen to me, Ari. Sasha's dead. Dante killed him. Dante betrayed us all and he's got Emily with him."

Her heart was suddenly in her throat. "Are they in the house? Where's Rob?"

Peter sped up and Ezra and Kim were suddenly looking her way.

"Rob and Owen are going after them," Tucker said. "We don't know where Rebecca is. I'm following. I just wanted you to know what's happening. There wasn't anything I could do to save Sasha. I'm so sorry."

Panic started to rush through her system. "Dante has a gun?"

"Everyone has a gun," Tucker replied. "We don't know where he is. He's somewhere in the club. I've got to go. I have to help the others."

"We're almost there," she promised before the line went dead.

"Stay calm, Ari. He doesn't need you to panic. He needs you calm," Kim said. "I don't know the layout of the club."

"You'll come with me," Ezra commanded in a tone that brooked no disobedience. "You'll watch my six, and I swear to god if you go rogue on me you won't like the consequences."

"When you get inside, there's a panic switch behind the counter that puts the whole club in lockdown," Peter explained. "Hit it and they won't be able to get out until you put the code in. The code is on the back of the book lying on the table. It's the registry number of the book. I'm going to stay with the car and guard them from getting away through the back. I'm out of practice."

She wasn't so sure about that, but she definitely didn't want them fleeing by hot wiring the van. She checked the magazine on the weapon Peter had left for her under the seat. "Don't risk yourself. He's already proven he'll kill. And we know where they'll go."

"Straight to Levi," Ezra said under his breath. "They'll run home. But not if I get to them first."

"He's got a tracker, but he'll cut it out." It was exactly what she would do in the same situation.

"If he gets away, we might still have a chance if I can get online fast enough." Ezra's jaw tightened as Peter pulled into the driveway. Tall hedges granted the drive and the backyard plenty of privacy. The alley was used only by people on the street, so they had a chance to come out of this without involving the police. The walls of the club were soundproofed, and they were likely about to test how well that worked.

Peter put the van in park and they were out in a heartbeat.

Ariel held her weapon at her side, following Ezra and Kim. "I'll go in the back. You two take the front. They could come at us either way and one of us needs to put the club in lockdown."

Ezra nodded and he and Kim peeled away, going around to the front of the building.

It was eerily quiet, the morning only disrupted by the sound of a dog barking somewhere in the distance. Her heart thundered in her chest. Rob was in there and he was vulnerable. Had he been forced to watch Sasha die?

She had to stop panicking. Kim was right. Rob needed her calm. She moved quietly toward the house. The backyard was an oasis of green that wound around to the front of the building. There was a fence, but massive shrubs turned the place into a private playground complete with a hot tub and small gazebo. The stairs leading up to the door were roughly twenty feet away. She started to move toward the door when Rebecca walked around the back of the house.

Rebecca had a bottle of water in her hand and she sighed as though relieved when she saw Ariel. "Thank god, you're back. It's bad upstairs. Something's going on with the guys. I decided to get some air because they have some serious stuff to work out."

She started to walk by the gazebo when a dark shadow peeled away and Ariel brought her gun up. "Rebecca!"

Dante was faster. He had his gun to the back of Rebecca's head and was using her as a shield before Ariel could get a shot off. "Don't even try, Ariel. I've got this right at the base of her skull and I won't hesitate to pull the trigger. Set that gun down now."

If he killed Rebecca, he was dead. They were at a standoff. "I can't do that. If I put the gun down, you'll kill me or her. That's not acceptable."

"Or *I* could kill you." Emily stepped out of the gazebo. "I would love to do that."

Oh, she'd picked the wrong direction to go in. Tucker had just called. They were still in the club, looking for these two, and if Ezra did what he was supposed to do, they would all be locked in and she would be out here. "Dante, you don't want to do this."

"I've wanted to do this for a very long time," Dante replied. He had an arm around Rebecca's throat. "Break free, that is. The fact that this bitch walked in and screwed up everything just facilitated my jailbreak."

"I didn't screw anything up." Emily's arms were shaky. She wasn't used to holding a gun for so long.

Luckily Ariel was. "I think Rob would argue with you."

"Russ was a bright-eyed idealist." Emily was moving slowly, following Dante as he crept toward the path that led to the driveway. "He found out what I was doing and he was going to turn me in. Luckily, the senator had people to help with that. And then the senator was happy because he had ten new men to hand over to his daughter."

It made her sick to her stomach to have to deal with this woman. "You were a nurse."

"Do you know what they pay nurses?" She shook her head. "Look, I didn't understand what I was getting into and then I had no way out. No one was happier than I was when that bitch died. I didn't walk in here thinking my husband was alive. I hoped he was dead. Now I have to run."

"I told you, we have a place to go and now we have someone the boss wants. Get a move on. We need to take the van." Dante kept his back to the house. "Rebecca, if you try anything, I'll put a bullet in your brain and still use your body as a shield. Do you understand me? If you stay calm, you'll survive this. I need you to get Levi to take me in."

Her stomach knotted, but she could see the logic there.

Rebecca simply nodded.

Dante was too big and Rebecca had only started self-defense training. "Stay calm, Rebecca. I'll find a way to get you out of this even if they take you to Levi. You do everything they tell you to."

She glanced back toward Emily and saw Robert standing in the window. A look of horror crossed his face as he realized what was happening right in front of him. Owen joined him and immediately lifted his gun to take off the back of Dante's head.

The windows were bulletproof. Peter had told them when they'd taken a tour the first day. Robert yelled something and Owen's face fell. He turned and started running, likely toward the back door.

It was only mere seconds later that she could hear Owen pounding on the door that would have led him outside.

They couldn't get through. They'd misjudged the timing and now they were trapped until Ezra could get the code in and release the lockdown.

She had to do something. God, it was so different when she cared about the people around her.

Emily started at the sound of the door. "They're coming."

Dante laughed. "The dumb bastards put the club in lockdown. Good-bye, Ari. You weren't as smart as you thought you were."

"No, she's not." Emily looked behind her and Robert was trying to break the window. Dante disappeared with Rebecca. When Emily looked back, she had a smirk on her face. “Not at all.”

Emily pulled the trigger. Ariel moved to her left, hitting the ground and rolling. She heard the windows shake with the force of Robert hitting them, trying to find a way to get to her. She twisted and came up to her knees and fired on pure instinct.

Emily looked down at her chest where the bullet had lodged. The gun in her hand fell to the ground and she dropped.

Ariel couldn’t think about it. She moved. Dante was still alive and he had Rebecca. She ran, praying Ezra was getting the doors opened again. She hit the pavement that marked the driveway and stopped. Peter was in the van. He sat in the front seat, his hands on the wheel. Rebecca was slumped on the seat beside Dante. He’d knocked her out and had a new victim. His gun was to the back of Peter’s head.

“I’m out of practice,” Peter said, his voice shaking. “Tell Tag I’m sorry. I really just wanted to show people around my country.”

“Drive or you won’t see another day,” Dante said as the door closed.

Peter put the van in reverse and it moved, jerking out of the driveway.

She didn’t have a car to follow them with. She couldn’t fire at the van or they might lose Rebecca and Peter. She was fucking helpless.

“Rebecca!” Owen screamed his love’s name as he sprinted past Ariel. He ran down the street, chasing after a car he would never catch.

“Ariel.” Robert was breathless as he spun her around. “Ariel, are you hit?”

They all came out of the house now, but she was numb.

She’d lost Rebecca. She’d lost Peter. She hadn’t seen through Dante’s lies.

Tucker ran after Owen, but it wouldn’t matter. Owen wouldn’t catch them. Owen would keep running, keep trying until Tucker had to pick him up.

All because she’d failed.

She felt Robert’s hands on her body, heard Kim trying to talk to her, but none of it mattered.

She’d failed.

Chapter Fifteen

Robert could still remember how utterly helpless he'd felt when he'd realized he couldn't get to her. Ariel had been on the other side of that bulletproof glass and the doors had been locked. He'd stood beside Owen as both of their women had been placed in danger, and it had been the single worst moment of his life.

He couldn't imagine what Owen was going through, how he'd felt as he'd run like a madman after a vehicle he could never catch. How he'd run until he couldn't anymore. Tucker had found him lying in the grass having chased that van until he'd thrown up and passed out.

"We should move and now," Ezra said. "I want us on a plane back to London as soon as possible."

They were sitting around the conference table but there were way too many seats empty. The ones that were filled contained shocked and numb people. People who wouldn't forget what had happened that day.

It was early evening and the morning felt like it had happened years ago. They'd been forced to regroup, assess, clean up. Plan.

"I know you do, Ezra, but we've got to get a pilot to you first. Owen can't fly at this point." Damon was on the left side of the split screen. "I can't trust hiring someone local."

"I can get Si there but it's going to be eighteen hours or so. I'm sorry. It's the best I can do." Big Tag's face took up the right side of the screen. He looked haggard, and early morning light streamed in behind him. It looked like he was still at the office in his house. "I'll have you out of there and another team in place sometime tomorrow afternoon."

Tucker's eyes came up, staring at him from across the table. That stare told Robert everything he needed to know.

Tucker wouldn't be leaving Germany. Not until the job was done. The mission parameters had changed, but they still would finish. And they would never leave a man behind. Or a woman.

He understood what Big Tag was trying to do. He thought they were far too close to this problem, but he was wrong.

This was *his* problem, their problem. The Lost Boys would handle it.

They were coming out of retirement. While they'd been cleaning up and dealing with the bodies, he'd also made a couple of calls. He'd put the plans in motion. In the end it was a fairly simple job.

"Then I think we should move safe houses." Ezra had been perfectly calm through the last several hours. He'd stood in the yard and looked down at Emily Seeger's body and merely nodded to his ex-wife as though giving her some silent permission. He hadn't even seen the moment Solo had dragged the body away and started her incredibly thorough cleanup procedures.

"I don't think there's a need for that," Big Tag replied. "Look, I know you're nervous, Ezra, but if you haven't gotten a visit from the police so far, you're not going to. Moving the team at this point could cause more trouble than staying in place. The club isn't open again until next Thursday and I've already talked to Peter's wife. Can you give me an update? Have we recovered the van and Peter's body without incident?"

No incident besides Peter's murder.

They continued on, but Robert couldn't get his mind off what had happened this morning and how it had changed everything. Ezra had immediately started tracing Dante's subcutaneous tracker. He'd taken the only other vehicle at the club, a motorcycle. Solo had hopped on the back, wrapping her arms around her ex-husband, and they'd gone after the van.

The wait had taken forever.

It had been even worse when they'd returned with Solo on the motorcycle and Ezra driving the van.

"I found the van left outside the city in the parking lot of a secluded park. Dante had cut the tracker out of his arm. I found the body of Peter Bergman slumped over the front seat where it was obvious he'd been shot in the head by whoever was sitting in the backseat." Ezra's words came out in a dull monotone. "There was no evidence of Dr. Walsh or Dante. I have to assume Dante had one of Levi's men meet them there and they fled."

"I've got someone working on the CCTV cameras around the area." Damon leaned forward. "How is Owen?"

"Owen is sedated." He'd been forced to do it because Owen had lost his shit. "He'll hate me for it later, but I couldn't let him go running through the streets of Munich with a gun looking for Dante when we have no idea where he is."

"You made the right call, Rob." Ariel spoke for the first time in an hour. She'd said very little since she'd been forced to kill Emily Seeger. She'd been an automaton, going through the motions, doing her part in cleaning up the mess that had been made, but it was obvious she was still in shock. "Owen wasn't capable of making proper decisions. He was too… God, I don't even know what to call it."

Grief. Fear. Guilt. The horrifying helplessness that came from knowing someone he loved was in danger and he couldn't do anything about it.

Big Tag's hand ran over his head. "I'll be on that plane. Charlie's packing me up right now. I promise, I'm going to fix this. Well, what I can fix. I can't bring Peter back. God, I'm sorry. *I* made this call. I knew we had a traitor and I let you work with him."

"And I agreed with you," Damon replied. "I thought it was worth the risk to figure out who the traitor was. I didn't realize there were two of them, nor that Emily Seeger would show up and flip the balance we had."

"If it means anything at all to you, I would have made the same call." Solo was sitting across from her ex. She'd been serious and professional, her normally cheery disposition dimmed in light of the tragedy of the morning, "Dante had done nothing at all violent before this."

"Speak for yourself," Tucker said. "He was pretty fucking violent to me when he was working for McDonald. And Jax and Sasha. Fuck, you can't ask Sasha."

Sasha's body was wrapped up and stored in the big freezer unit alongside Peter's for now. They would find a way to carry Sasha back to London and Peter would be given to his people here so he could be buried in his beloved homeland. They would not do the same for Emily Seeger. Solo had promised she could handle that particular job.

"I know," Damon said, his tone solemn. "If we'd had any idea that Dante was capable of this level of harm, we would never have left him in. We didn't know who the traitor was. We had suspicions, but we couldn't know for sure."

"We thought this particular op would be an excellent way to figure it out since this was supposed to be nothing more than a fact-finding mission." Big Tag sounded weary. "It wasn't supposed to end in a bunch of bodies. And Robert, you have to understand that we had no idea Seeger was anything but a nurse who'd worked briefly with McDonald. I've got everyone I can trying to run down your family."

He shook his head. "Don't. We have no idea if she was lying or telling the truth. I tend to think she was lying. We can worry about my past later. We need to find Rebecca. She's the only thing that matters now."

Because Owen wouldn't be able to handle it if they lost her. Rebecca had come into this life because she loved Owen. Rebecca had given up a remarkable lifestyle, put her meteoric career on hold to help them.

Owen would burn down the world if he lost her.

The way he would if he'd lost Ariel.

He stared at her across the table. She wouldn't look him in the eyes.

"Have we had any contact with Dante?" Damon asked. "He obviously took Rebecca with him."

Or they would have found her body.

"It's a good plan. She's an excellent way to gain access to Levi Green," Ezra pointed out. "That's our working theory at this point. It would have been easier to kill her and leave her behind the way he did Peter, but she has value to Levi."

"I've got some people looking in to where Levi is," Solo promised. "I've also written a report that will bring down the wrath of God on him if I can ever get that fucker in the right position. If I can prove he kidnapped an American citizen, I can burn him. If I burn him, well, I can really actually burn him. I've got plans."

"I need you to find a way to talk to him," Big Tag said. "He'll meet with you, Solo."

Levi Green had an unhealthy fascination with the gorgeous operative. He likely would use the opportunity to meet with her, but Robert doubted he would handily bring Rebecca with him so they could nab her.

"No." Ezra shook his head. "I'm not sending my…I'm not sending Solo in to deal with Levi. He's proven he'll do anything. Why should we give him another captive to hold over our heads? He could be anywhere. I think we should go back to London and start searching from there. We'll get in contact with Green and we'll negotiate. We do have something he might want more than Rebecca."

"Beck, you are not trading yourself for her," Solo hissed. "You are not going to be a martyr."

Ezra gave her a smile that could only be described as predatory. "I promise I'll take him with me."

"I think you're right and everyone should come back to base," Damon pronounced. "Ian is sending a team in and they'll start an investigation. They'll be on the ground sometime tomorrow. You'll come back to The Garden. I know he won't want to come…"

"I'll make sure Owen gets where he needs to be," Robert promised. Where he needed to be might be up for debate, but he wasn't having one now.

"Thank you. I know this is hard on you, but I truly believe this is the best way to protect you all." Big Tag sat back. "I'm going to take care of this personally, Robert."

"I know you will, sir." Sometimes it was good to be thought of as the reasonable one. They bought every single thing he was saying.

They had no idea what he'd really been doing during the cleanup. No idea he'd already planned a mission.

A mission he might not return from.

"I disagree about Owen," Ariel said. "He needs to stay here. I'll talk to him, but if you try to drag him back to The Garden, I think he'll find a way to leave again. I understand that you're trying to protect him, but would you honestly sit in an office while your wives were being held by an enemy?"

"No, of course not." Big Tag seemed to think for a moment. "All right. He can stay, but he can't be in charge of this op."

Ariel nodded. "I'll make sure he understands. You might send Kai Ferguson, if you can."

"I was actually going to ask you to remain there. You know what's gone on and you can help with Owen," Damon replied.

Ariel's head came up. "No. I think I should come in. Honestly, Damon, you should fire me."

"I'm not going to fire you." Damon took a long breath. "But I do understand why you're upset. Perhaps it's best if Ian sends in another psychologist. Come home, Ariel."

She thought she should be fired? Why the hell would anyone fire her? He held the question, though, because it seemed like something they should talk about in private. And he was definitely going to be private with her. He had things to tell her, things she needed to hear.

Before he blew their world up.

"I will certainly come back to London," she agreed. "But we're going to have to talk. And I think it's time to tell Tucker and Robert the full truth. I won't hide it anymore." Her eyes flashed, the first fire he'd seen in hours, and she turned to them. "I didn't work for Scotland Yard. That was my cover. I was recruited into MI6 during my last year at Oxford. I thought I would be an analyst. It turned out I had innate skills I was unaware of, and MI6 trained me and sculpted me."

"They turned you into an assassin," Tucker said.

"Hey, that's a rough word to use." Solo crossed her legs and sat back. "She's not some instrument of evil. She was doing necessary work."

Tucker held his hands up. "Hey, not using the 'e' word here. I'm not judging her. I wish she'd been around earlier so she could have assassinated Dante. It would have solved a lot of our problems. And we knew about Ari's past. Levi made sure we did. He sent Rob that report on you and Sasha made sure we read it."

"He thought Levi could get the warrants off you and him and Jax." Robert felt the need to defend Sasha since he couldn't defend himself. "I know what he did was wrong. He was passing along information to Green, but he was desperate. He'd started to have memories of a child."

"What?" Ariel turned shocked eyes his way. "He never mentioned that to me."

"He was closed off. He didn't trust anyone." He wanted to reach out to her, but he stayed in his seat. "He only recently told me about it. He thinks he might have a daughter. I promised him I would try to find her."

He had no idea how he would do it, but he would.

"I'll let Adam know," Ian said, his voice hoarse with emotion. He knew what it meant to have children.

Could he and Ariel have had a family? Would she have wanted a couple of kids? She would have been a wonderful mother.

His mother would love Ariel. His horny-ass brother better keep his hands off Ariel. Tim would think she was gorgeous.

He shook it off. He couldn't get sick now. Hopefully, there would be time later to find out if Emily had been lying and his family was out there somewhere.

Ariel stood up, her eyes bright. "I'm going to go pack and make sure everything is cleaned up. I want to be ready to go."

She strode out and Solo started to get up to follow her.

Robert held out a hand. "Let her be for now."

Solo's brows rose. "Are you going to take care of her?"

"Yes." He would have one last night with her because after what he was planning on doing, she might never be able to trust him again. "I'll take care of her, but she needs to cry and she doesn't like to do that around other people. Besides, we need to talk about what the Agency is planning to do with us. I suspect since Ariel has been meeting with you that we're more entangled than I've been led to believe."

"We've been working with friendly parts of the Agency and some of Damon's old contacts at MI6," Tag acknowledged. "I decided it was the best way to keep them off our backs. It was originally why we allowed Ezra in to interview you. We kept up the contact even after Ezra got burned. We've shared information about our progress."

"And our files?" He understood the razor-thin line Big Tag had been walking.

Tag looked at him straight through the monitor, his eyes gleaming with will. "No. I would never share those with anyone without your permission. I swear it."

The words settled something deep inside. There were reasons to work with intelligence agents, and Tag and Damon would know who to trust. "And why wouldn't you tell us?" The answer was self-evident. He'd lived through this morning. "Because we had a leak. Of course."

"No one wanted to deceive you, and certainly Ariel didn't," Tag went on. "But you run that group, and you don't always see the worst in people. You're not the same as the rest of us. We were operatives. We were trained to keep secrets, to always suspect. You were a soldier. I knew that before anyone confirmed it. You take care of your men and you do whatever you can to make sure they get what they need."

"You thought I would tell the rest of the men." It was a possibility. "You're not my commanding officer, Ian. I can't tell you what I would have done. Knowing what I know now, I hope I would have made the right call, but I can't say it for sure. I would have trusted them and I would have been wrong."

"Then don't blame Ariel," Solo said, her eyes somber. "She wasn't allowed to tell you, and Big Tag pretty much *is* her CO."

"I told you, I'll take care of her." He would take care of them all. "Now we should go and pack, though I was hoping to talk to Jax."

A little lie, but a necessary one. He might be a soldier, but he'd been around the operatives long enough to have picked up a few tricks.

Damon's gaze was grim through the screen. "Jax was very upset when I told him about what happened. I'm afraid he and River took a sabbatical. They're at a friend's country house. The service isn't great there. I'll send a note that you're wanting to talk."

"Or I'll go out and see him myself when I get there. Give him some space, too," Robert said.

"You seem very calm." Big Tag's eyes had narrowed, and even with thousands of miles between them, he could feel that man's suspicions.

He had to allay them and quickly. Ezra wasn't as centered as he normally was because Solo was here. Ariel was lost in her own guilt and grief. It gave him cover. He couldn't have Big Tag start looking at him hard. He couldn't have anyone know he'd gone into Peter's office and taken all the information the man had found out about Kronberg's safes. "I have to be. Look, I was holding Sasha's hand when he died, and I'm the one who held Owen down and stuck a needle in his arm. It's been one of the roughest days of my life, and if I don't hold it together I'll fall apart utterly."

Tag nodded. "Yeah, I do get that. I'm in the same position. I…well, let's say I feel responsible for everything. Peter Bergman was a good man. He was an excellent intelligence officer who served his country well and was a friend to ours. All he wanted to do was retire and study history and now…well, sometimes it doesn't pay to do a favor for me."

He understood the way Tag felt. Peter had been his friend, a nice guy, and now he was dead when he should have had a long, happy retirement. He should have been playing in his club and enjoying life.

Sasha should have had a chance to redeem himself, although in Rob's mind he'd done that when he'd saved Owen's life. Sasha should have had his brothers beside him as he tried to figure out if he had a daughter out there in the world. He should have stayed in therapy and found himself again, but he wouldn't get the chance.

Rebecca should be cuddled up with Owen. She shouldn't be…he didn't even know where she was.

"I'll be there as soon as I can. Let me know if Dante or Green make contact," Tag said. "And Rob, Tucker, I'm sorry about Sasha. Please tell Owen that we won't stop until we get Rebecca back." Tag reached out and the screen went dark.

Damon nodded. "And I'll be waiting here for you. We'll put

every resource we have on solving this problem. See you soon."

Ezra stood. "Rob, I assume you're going to go talk to Ariel. Tucker, can you sit with Owen until he wakes up and explain what's going on? Big Tag will be here soon and all he has to do is stay calm."

Tucker nodded. "Of course."

This was where none of them was thinking. He and Tucker would *never* leave Owen here alone. They were all considering Owen one of theirs since he'd originally been a McKay-Taggart member, but the minute Owen had taken that damn needle of McDonald's, he'd become a Lost Boy.

And they did not leave each other behind.

"Beck, I need to talk to you," Solo said. "I've got to call in and I need to go over what you want my bosses to know and what you don't."

Ezra looked surprised.

Solo rolled her eyes. "I told you I'm always on your side. We'll talk and then I have a body to dispose of. I'm going to make sure no one ever finds that bitch."

"I'll help you," Ezra promised.

They walked out, talking quietly.

And he was left alone with Tucker. "When will Owen be awake?"

"In an hour or two." Tucker looked to the door. "Are we on? What did that fucker say?"

He'd gotten the text from Dante right before the conference call with Big Tag and Damon. "Dawn tomorrow by the Chinese Tower in the Englischer Garten. I've figured out where that is. It's not far from here."

"But we won't get there, will we? That's all one big lie. He'll be there at Kronberg," Tucker said. "He'll show up with Levi Green and try to take it all."

"And we'll be ready." They had to be.

"We'll be outgunned."

"Our other option is to turn it all over to Ezra," Robert offered, though it wasn't an option for him. "That means the Agency gets involved. No matter what Solo says, if the Agency is involved there's a chance she gets overruled and the Agency takes whatever we find. They could let Rebecca rot in order to get that data and beat whatever faction Levi's working for. There's a war going on in the CIA and we can't let Rebecca be a casualty."

It was what he'd realized after he'd come down from his fear. They couldn't leave this to anyone else. They couldn't let Tag and Damon take the responsibility. This was up to him and his men.

That was when he'd started planning.

"I'll sit with Owen." Tucker stood, looking perfectly resolved. "I'll explain it all to him when he wakes up. He'll be ready to go. I'll make sure of it. And the rest?"

"I've got it. I promise. I won't let you down again."

Tucker stood in front of him, putting a hand on his shoulder. "You've never once let me down. From the time I met you, I knew I could trust you. I knew… I don't know why, but I knew you. Let's get this done and get Rebecca back."

"They might never trust us again," Robert warned. "We might get that data and really have to turn it over to get her back. We might not be welcome at The Garden again."

Tucker grinned. "Then we'll figure it out. We'll go to Bliss and hide out. They'll take us in. Jax is family. I'll find some weird dude who hunts sasquatches for a living, become best friends, and we'll find a wife to share. Hopefully not a sasquatch wife. But it won't come to that because I think Big Tag will yell and scream and threaten to do things to our entrails, and then he'll understand. Because he's family, too, and that's what family does. But if it goes bad, we're with you, Rob. Now go and spend some time with Ari. Make sure she comes with us if everything goes to hell."

Tucker walked out. Robert looked toward Ariel's bedroom door. She wouldn't be going with them.

But he would have one last night with her.

* * * *

Ariel stared at herself in the mirror through the mist that filled the bathroom. She recognized the face, but there was something older about the look in her eyes. Not even a hot shower seemed to have washed her clean. How could she go back to The Garden and take her place there again? After everything that had happened, how could she pretend she knew what she was doing?

She should never have left MI6. She was good at shooting people from a distance and getting away with it. Not so great at her actual job.

She would go home, make her report to Damon, and then…

Deep down she knew she needed time. She should take a couple of weeks and let it settle, but what she wanted to do was run. It wasn't even running. It was punishment.

There was a knock on the door and she sighed. Kim. Or Robert. She rather hoped it was Kim because she wasn't sure what she could say to Rob now. There was a part of her that hoped he was so angry he couldn't deal with her. She slipped into her robe and went to answer the door because if it was Kim, she wouldn't simply walk away if no one answered. Kim would break the door down and get the answers she wanted.

I'm fine. Still in shock but fine.

That was what she would say. She would nod and listen to everything Kim told her and ease her friend's mind. When she was alone again she could go back over all the ways she'd fucked up and cost several people their lives today.

Tomorrow she would get on the plane beside Robert and try to explain to him how sorry she was.

She opened the door and he was standing there, leaning on the doorjamb, his kit in his hand.

Her heart threatened to stop. He was safety and comfort wrapped in a gorgeous masculine package, but she didn't deserve him. After what she'd allowed to happen, she didn't deserve any of this.

"Rob, I…"

He brushed past her, walking into her room. "Take off that robe and find your position."

The impulse to obey him was almost overwhelming. She could throw off her robe, kneel before him, and let him take control. Nothing else would matter but pleasing him and finding her own release. She could forget about the fact that Sasha was dead and Peter was gone. She wouldn't have to think about what Rebecca was possibly going through or how tormented Owen was.

But those things weren't going away.

"I think we should talk." She needed to clear the air with him. No matter how she felt about herself, no matter what guilt weighed her down, she wasn't about to allow him to use her for some kind of revenge fuck.

He dropped his kit on her bed and strode back to her. He very gently eased her hand off the door and shut them inside. "And I think you will say all the wrong things."

"Yes, I seem to do that quite a lot lately." She stared up at him. His shoulders were stiff but there wasn't a hint of anger in his eyes. "I need to apologize."

He moved in close, bringing his face to loom over hers. "For following orders?"

"For lying. I lied to you."

"And still I love you."

Oh, this was worse. Tears pulsed behind her eyes, making the world blurry. She shook her head, unable to form words.

"That's better," he said, his hand brushing the line of her jaw. "Don't say anything. Just cry for me. You need to let all this poison out of your system. You did not cause what happened today."

"I was Dante's therapist all this time."

"And you knew something was wrong with him," Robert said quietly.

"You're not listening to me."

"No, you're not listening to me. And I don't think we can move forward with this conversation unless you do as I asked you to." He leaned over and kissed the bridge of her nose. "Do you really want to leave it like this? Us? Do you want to end this horrible day with me in another room thinking about you and you in here alone?"

No. She didn't. "Rob, I killed your wife today."

His lips curved in the most decadent and malicious smirk. "Yes, and I haven't thanked you for that." He sobered and dropped his forehead to hers, his eyes closing. "Damn it, Ari. I was so fucking scared that she was going to kill you. I wouldn't have been…I never want to go through that again. I know you think I'm angry, but I could kiss every single person who taught you, every mentor you had who turned you into a badass assassin because what happened today turns out differently if they hadn't."

"I am everything that report says." She wasn't sure what Robert had read, but the truth was bad enough.

"You're everything and more. And still I love you." He stepped back. "Should I stay or leave you to yourself tonight?"

The Dom was in the house. It was there in the polite tone of voice he used, the one that let her know she was in charge of making the decision, but that would change if she said yes. If she asked him to stay, he would take control. He would take command of her body, and he wouldn't stop until they both had what they needed.

She knew she shouldn't, but he'd said the words she'd wanted to hear forever. *I love you.*

She moved to the center of the room. Maybe they did need this. She let the robe drop and she was naked in front of him. Ariel took a deep breath and fell to her knees, the carpet softening the blow. She'd taken a lot from him today. She'd taken the chance to get to know anything about his past. In her logical mind she understood that it had been her or Emily. Taking out a dangerous threat was something she'd done a hundred times before, but this threat had been important to Robert. This threat had held the keys to his past, and Ariel had taken it all away from him.

A big hand palmed her head. "I'm so glad you made the right choice."

"You might not after I tell you what I'm going to do." She had to be honest with him about everything now.

"You're going to quit," he said simply. "You have got it in your head that you fucked up, that you missed something and that's why Sasha's dead. I've spent all day thinking about this. Why should you have known him better than me?"

"I was his therapist." She'd been hired to help the men McDonald had tortured. She'd also been expected to identify whether or not one of them could be a threat.

"And Dante was an accomplished liar. He was excellent at his job. Tucker and Jax and Sasha lived with him for years and they never suspected."

"Well, if they had suspected, McDonald simply erased their

minds. You can't compare the two," she pointed out.

His eyes narrowed. "I think you should get on your hands and knees. You're not listening to me."

"You think you can spank your will into me?"

"I think I can spank you until you finally cry and then maybe we'll get through this. Tell me you don't need it. If you don't, I'll be more than happy to spend the night holding you and kissing you and loving you."

But he was right. She needed something more. She leaned forward, getting on her hands and knees. She locked her elbows and braced herself, the muscles of her legs tight and tense. That would make the spanking hurt more, get her more quickly to the place she needed to be.

Robert hunkered down next to her, eyes running over her face. "Ari, you need to let go."

"I am." She shook her head. That was wrong. "I mean I will be, once you start spanking me."

Robert rose and walked to the bed, sitting on the side. "Come here."

It wasn't the voice of her Dom, but of her lover, and she shook her head. "Please, I want the spanking."

She wanted to feel his hand smacking her. It might be the only connection she could handle right now. Her emotions were dangerously close to overload. It was precisely why she'd isolated herself these last few hours. She knew damn well Ezra and Solo were taking on the bulk of the burden of cleaning up her mess, but she wasn't sure she wouldn't lose it if she had to look at the faces of the others.

"You'll get your spanking when I'm ready to give it to you." The words were hard with command, and she sucked in a breath.

She pushed to her feet and walked over to the bed, keenly aware of being naked. She had no problem with nudity, but this wasn't merely about her lack of clothing. She felt emotionally naked too. After the day she'd had, she had no more masks to put on. Sorrow and guilt hung on her and they gave her no cover.

"I missed you today."

She shook her head. "I don't think I can do this right now."

He didn't move, merely sat watching her. "I thought you wanted to talk."

"We need to." She couldn't take her eyes off his, felt caught by them. "We need to talk about what happened today."

He reached out and his hand ran from her shoulder down to her wrist. He ran it down slowly, as though relearning the texture of her skin. It struck her that though it had been little more than a full twenty-four hours since they'd last made love, it felt like forever. It felt like there was a chasm between them and he was trying to breach it.

When he reached her wrist, he slid his hand around it, manacling her. "I think you want to talk and you want me to listen. I don't think you want to hear what I have to say."

"I don't think you've had enough time to process what happened." It had gone so fast. He couldn't possibly have thought it all through, have considered the ramifications of what had taken place.

"I'm perfectly fine with what happened between you and the woman who handed me and my whole team over to McDonald for experimentation," he said evenly.

"This is what I mean." She started to pull her wrist away, but he held her tight.

"I understand fully what you mean. Let me summarize all of this for you. You think it's your fault Sasha is dead because you magically should have seen Dante's betrayal. You are a psychic and you simply ignored that particular superpower of yours. You were reckless and that's why Dante was able to take Rebecca. And then when the woman my former self foolishly married threatened to murder you, you shot her first. You didn't let her kill you so maybe we could find her later on and I could reconcile with her because I don't understand my own feelings. Or you think she might have given me information on the family she claims I have. That's why you should have allowed her to kill you."

He didn't understand. "You're simplifying things."

"No, you're simplifying them." He tugged on her wrist and drew her between his legs. She could feel the fabric of the black pants he wore against her thighs. He released her wrist and his hands found her hips, sliding down her torso and lighting up her skin. "It's a complex problem and you're ignoring the fact that you are human and you can't know everything. I don't care if you spent a million hours in therapy with that man, you couldn't have known his true motivations."

He was starting to get to her. "I did know something was wrong with Dante. I still told Big Tag and Damon to go through with this mission."

"Because it seemed like an excellent way to figure out who was betraying us," he pointed out. "I agree. It went to hell. That's what happens sometimes. We're dealing with it the best way we can. This was not your fault."

She went still, not quite able to reply in any way she knew would satisfy him.

Robert sighed and wrapped his arms around her, dragging her close to him. His cheek rubbed against her chest as though he found deep satisfaction from being close to her. "Like I said before, I've missed you. I'm going to spank you now."

As miserable as she felt, those words sent a thrill through her, and her nipples hardened.

"This isn't punishment." Robert released her and looked at her with the calm, controlled intensity that let her know he was totally in Dom mode. "What I'm going to do is about giving us both what we need. You need release, and I need to take care of you. I need my hands on you."

She had to make a decision. She could stay here mired in her misery or she could accept what he was offering. It might not change the outcome of the day, but it would help her find some peace. "Yes, Sir."

He made a sexy noise low in his throat and slid his hands up her torso until his thumbs nudged the underside of her breasts. "I'm going to take you over my knee for this spanking. And it's not going to be playful. This is going to hurt because you need a bite of pain."

"Yes, Sir." This time the words were a sigh of relief. She was aroused—she always would be around Robert—but she was also relieved. As long as he was in control, she might be able to let go of her guilt for a few moments. She could stop going over and over what happened. She could simply let go and be with him.

Robert shifted back a few inches on the mattress. He was so tall that even seated on the mattress he had both feet on the floor.

He patted his knee. "Over my lap for your spanking."

She laid herself over his thigh, her knees, shoulders and head resting on the bed. She turned her face toward the edge of the mattress, looking out.

"No, turn your head the other way. I want to see your face while I spank you."

Arousal pulsed through her as she obeyed.

Robert took her arms, pulling them to the small of her back, crossing one wrist over the other and then manacling them there with one of his big hands. His other hand held onto the outside of her thigh as he shifted.

One of his legs was under her hips, the other under her ribs. He raised the leg under her hips, propping his heel against the bedframe. That lifted her ass, making it a nice target for him to spank.

Ariel squirmed in anticipation. She wanted him to get on with it. But the devious man wasn't done tormenting her. Her sight was limited with her cheek pressed to the mattress, but she could see him in her peripheral vision. The arm holding her wrists at the small of her back was thick with muscle, and the hard line of his jaw was dark with sexy scruff.

His other hand smoothed over her upraised ass, and she saw the corner of his mouth quirk up in a smile. "You're beautiful. I know I keep telling you that, but I need you to understand I think you're beautiful inside and out. The reports that fucker Green sent didn't change my opinion of you, and now that I've had time to think about it, I understand why the bosses wanted you to keep your past from me."

"You do?"

"Yes," he said gravely. "They did it because your past doesn't matter. You were beautiful then and you're beautiful now. You were mine then. You just didn't know it yet."

The first smack caught her by surprise. His hand struck the center of her ass, fingers smacking one cheek, palm landing on the other. A startled yelp escaped her, and a moment later she felt the heat spreading through her.

"Do you want me to count?" Ariel asked.

He caressed her ass. "No, because I'm going to spank you for as long as I want. I'm going to spank you until you can let go. I'll do it until you understand you weren't responsible for what happened today."

His palm smacked against her ass for a second time, followed quickly by a third. She had no leverage, no way to control the spanking. All she could do was lie over Robert's lap and accept what he was giving her.

Smack, smack.

The blows were harder now, making her flesh quiver, and heat was spreading through her. He kept going, steady and relentless, yet never striking the same spot twice in a row. His hand spanked her from the top of her thighs to the top of her ass.

Her chest worked, dragging oxygen into her lungs. The pain was now omnipresent, fading to a dull ache between blows but never entirely disappearing.

He smacked her left cheek, right on the sensitive sit spot. It was a harsh blow, and he held his hand there, trapping the heat against her skin. Ariel cried out as pain burned through her. The cold guilt that had gripped her all day was burned away by the heat.

She'd distanced. She'd put things in intellectual terms and come to a conclusion without ever considering the human emotions that had gone into every decision that had been made.

She'd pushed Robert away because she'd been afraid.

She hadn't been willing to listen to his feelings because she'd feared loving him would mean losing him.

She'd wanted to believe none of the men she'd spent so much time with could possibly betray them. She'd wanted each of those men to find happiness, and that wasn't going to happen.

It wasn't her fault. That was what each smack of his hand stated plainly.

Another hard spank, another wave of heat sweeping through her. Ariel cried out, her feet beating against the bed. Robert held her down, his mastery of her body complete. She couldn't get away—not that she wanted to—but she couldn't. She had no choice but to feel.

To accept.

And to let go of all the things she couldn't have changed.

The first sob escaped when he once more smacked her burning ass. He paused, and she knew he was looking at her.

Ariel drew in a shuttering breath. "Please."

Please don't stop. Please don't leave me. She needed him so much.

Robert raised his hand and spanked her again. Ariel thrashed in his hold, her feet drumming the bed as he spanked her with rapid hard smacks that peppered her cheeks.

The damn inside her broke and the sobs took over. She barely noticed when the spanking stopped and his hand was skimming over her sensitive flesh. He'd spanked her long and hard, and that meant that while the stinging pain had faded, the deep, aching heat remained.

Ariel knew she wasn't crying prettily. The sobs came from her soul.

She couldn't have stopped Dante. She wasn't a superhero. The problems of the world didn't fall on her shoulders. She wasn't responsible for what Robert's wife had done. He wouldn't have wanted her to change a thing about how she'd handled that moment in the yard. Robert wanted her alive more than he wanted to know about his past.

She'd tried her hardest, and with every good intention, and she'd still failed. It was the way of the world sometimes, but she only lost if she didn't get back up and try again.

She wanted so much to try again with this man.

She cried until there were no more tears, only dry, gasping breaths.

The world spun as Robert lifted her, turning to lay her on her side in the center of the bed. He lay on his side facing her. Ariel blinked tears from her eyes and looked at him. Her ass ached, her blood strumming through her system.

"Do you forgive me?" She needed to hear it though she knew what he was going to say.

He brushed back her hair, a look of infinite tenderness lighting his eyes. "There's nothing to forgive. Not when it comes to your past.

Now we should talk about the fact that you pushed me away the first time our going got tough."

"We found out you were married." She felt the need to argue her point. "It wasn't some minor argument."

"No, there was no argument at all. There was you shutting me out. There was you making decisions for me." He put a finger on her lips when she was about to reply. "No. You did those things. *You* decided I needed time. I knew what I wanted all along. I could have gotten every single memory back and they wouldn't erase the ones I've made with you. I told you nothing would change, and it hasn't. I love you. I will always love you. I want you to remember that."

He seemed almost grave as he rolled her onto her back, spreading her legs. Ariel hissed as her backside came into contact with the bed. She was so focused on the quick shock of pain—a sensation that made her pussy pulse and her nipples tight—that she didn't notice him buckling the cuff around her right wrist until the deed was done. Warmth encased her wrist and she realized these cuffs were padded with some supersoft material.

When had he pulled out cuffs? He must have done it while she was on her hands and knees waiting for him.

"What are you doing?" she asked.

Robert arched a brow. "You want to try that again?" That was his Dom voice.

"No, Sir."

He brought her left arm up and out, sliding the cuff around her wrist and buckling it in place. She heard a little click and glanced up. There was a small lock on the cuffs.

"You don't think the lock is a bit of overkill?" The cuffs would strap her in. She wouldn't be able to get out.

He tied red nylon rope to the D-ring on the left cuff, then fed it around the back of the headboard and tied it to the other cuff, which also had a small padlock on it. Robert stepped back after pressing the lock in place, staring down at her.

"I like the way the locks look. Spread your legs," he commanded.

Ariel felt lighter after her emotional release, but the heat was still present. She tipped her head back on the pillow, exposing the line of her throat, and arched her chest, offering her breasts to him.

"You're so fucking beautiful," he whispered.

He made her feel beautiful. And worthy.

Robert pulled his T-shirt off, tossing it to the side, baring that glorious chest. He put one knee on the bed, grabbed her right ankle and lifted it. He kissed her instep, her ankle, then propped her heel on his shoulder.

She moved her toes across to his sternum then slid her foot down the midline of his body, watching his muscles twitch and relax as she caressed him. She didn't stop when she hit his belt but kept going, thrilled at the noise he made when her toes found his cock.

He was hard, hot even through the barrier of his slacks.

"I'm going to make you understand that there's nothing you can do that will make me stop loving you. There's nothing the world can do that will stop me," Robert said. "If you quit and move away from The Garden, you better be prepared for me to follow you."

He grabbed her ankle, lifted it away from his crotch. He nipped at her toes, then lay her leg on the bed before quickly shucking the rest of his clothes. She bent her knees, heels on the bed, and spread her legs, creating a place for him.

Robert didn't hesitate. He climbed onto the bed, between her legs. She was so ready, so in need of his big hard body covering hers.

"Please," she said. It was only a single word, but he knew what she needed.

Or maybe he needed the same thing. Needed to feel connected to her. Needed to remember what it felt like when they became one.

He eased on top of her, his chest pressing against her breasts, his hips in the cradle of her thighs. His cock settled against her pussy, and when he flexed his hips the hard, veined underside slid along the valley of her labia, caressing her clit.

She wrapped her fingers around the ropes and arched up, trying to wiggle into place so she could allow his cock to sink inside her. Robert bent his head and nipped her right where her shoulder met her neck, a small punishment for trying to take control.

Then his tongue swept up her neck to her ear. He sucked her earlobe as he lifted his hips, his cock sliding into place. Ariel strained against her bonds, hugging his hips with her knees.

Robert was so deep inside her that for a moment she forgot

everything but him. For a moment there was only Robert.

"Ari." He breathed her name, the word hot against her neck.

He started to thrust, and she could do nothing but feel—feel his cock inside her, his chest rubbing her nipples. His breath on her face and neck, and the heat from where he'd spanked her.

"I want you to come for me. Together. I want it to be together," he whispered.

He adjusted the angle of his hips, so that each time he thrust in his lower abdomen rubbed against the top of her pussy. Close. She was so close to where she needed to be.

The next time he thrust his pelvis bumped her clit. She wrapped her legs around his hips, heels digging into the flexed muscles of his ass. "Do that again."

"That sounded like an order."

"It was. Do that again."

He chuckled and thrust in. Ariel's whole body tensed.

"I'm close. Robert, I—"

"I love you," Robert said. "I love you, Ariel."

That was all she needed. The orgasm overtook her, pulling her up and over a soft, rolling wave. She clung to him with her legs as Robert thrust once, again, and then she felt him shudder as he found his own release.

Ariel sighed in pleasure as his weight bore her into the mattress. She wanted to wrap her arms around him, but she was stuck in his cuffs. She kissed his temple, where his silky hair was damp with sweat. A moment later he rolled off of her but didn't go far. He lay beside her, his head pillowed on her breast, one big thigh across hers. The other hand came up, casually yet possessively cupping her other breast.

She closed her eyes. The moment couldn't last. Soon enough reality would crash down around them, but they had this moment, and she would accept the peace he'd given her, accept it for the gift it was.

"So can we agree to put the idea of you quitting everything you know and love on hold?" Robert asked. He stretched like the big gorgeous predator he was. "I seem to remember this very smart lady telling me I shouldn't make big life decisions when I was emotional."

"And yet you tried to."

He shook his head. "Nope. Being with you was a decision I made a long time ago. I was sticking to my decision. I recall offering to go anywhere with you. Deep down I knew something was wrong with Emily. She's the reason I have those dreams. I think I'm remembering the night she had McDonald's men come pick me up."

Now she really wanted her arms around him. "Let me out of the cuffs. We should talk about this." And make love again. They could do that all night. She would make love to him over and over until he could sleep. "I know how hard tomorrow is going to be for you."

Because it would be difficult to leave the problem in Big Tag's hands. It would be hard for him to leave Owen behind.

He wouldn't leave Owen behind. God. How could she have thought for a second he would leave Owen behind?

She pulled at the cuffs. There had been no real reason to put her in them. And he'd put padlocks on them so she couldn't use her teeth to work the straps and potentially get out. Those little locks would ensure no matter how flexible she was, she couldn't get out.

"You have no idea. Tomorrow isn't the problem. Tonight is going to be hell on me." He kissed her cheek and rolled off the bed, walking toward the bathroom.

"Robert!" She shouted his name. Kim and Ezra were gone, dealing with the Emily situation. "Let me out."

He couldn't be doing what she thought he was doing. He couldn't have made love to her and then restrained her so she couldn't stop him from doing something phenomenally stupid like going after Dante and Levi on his own.

Except he wouldn't be on his own. He would have Tucker and Owen.

They could all die together.

"But you look so pretty the way you are." Robert's voice floated out from the bathroom.

She managed to move enough that she could see he'd gathered up his clothes. He wasn't washing up and getting ready for round two. He was getting ready to leave. "Please don't do this. Please. Wait for Ezra to get back. We can talk about this."

She was starting to panic.

"There's nothing to talk about." He stood in the doorway of the bathroom, and now she saw what she should have seen before. He was dressed in black from head to toe. He had on a T-shirt and tactical pants, his boots on his feet. This was the way he dressed when he thought things could go wrong.

"You can't go after him by yourself." She pulled at those stupid cuffs but the headboard held firm.

He crossed the space between them and covered her with a blanket. His eyes were gentle as he stared down at her. "You know Owen would do it if we were talking about you. He would never let me go in alone. He would move heaven and earth to help me get you back."

"I promise you we won't leave Rebecca behind." He couldn't walk out of here.

He leaned over and kissed her forehead. "I hope you can forgive me. We have to do this tonight. We don't have another choice."

"Yes, you do. You can wait. Levi won't kill Rebecca." She kicked at the blanket, trying to move herself up.

Robert merely readjusted the blanket. He slid his hands between the cuffs and her wrists as though checking to make sure he didn't have them too tight. "I can't wait. We have to deal with this tonight. Are you thirsty? I can try to get a straw and some water, but I don't want you to knock it over and be cold. Is the temperature okay?"

"No. It's not. And yes, I'm thirsty and hungry and I need to use the bathroom." If she could get out of the cuffs, she might have a chance to put him on his ass and stop this whole thing from happening.

"I love you." He kissed her again. "I'll be back if I can. If I don't come back, know I don't regret a thing. Not even what happened to me with McDonald. I wouldn't change it because it made me the kind of man you might be able to love."

"Rob, don't do this."

"Could you say it? Just once?"

She shook her head. "No. No. If you want to hear me say it, you get these cuffs off me."

She wasn't going to give him permission to walk into a trap. Tears had started to roll down her cheeks.

"Then I'll have to love enough for both of us. I'm leaving the keys to your cuffs on the kitchen table. Good-bye, baby. I hope I see you soon. I love you. Never forget."

He stood and walked out the door.

And she was left alone.

Chapter Sixteen

Robert watched from the shadows. The security guard was making his rounds, strolling through the parking garage, his feet slapping against the concrete and making a racket. For that guard it was just another night to get through. Nothing special. No great thrills except sneaking out here to take a cigarette break.

He was about to take a nice nap.

A figure dressed in all black rose like a shadow given substance from behind one of the company vans parked in the lower level of the garage. Sound echoed here, but the shadow was silent. Robert held a breath as the shadow wrapped an arm around the man and shoved something into his arm before dragging him behind the van again.

"He hasn't lost a step," Tucker said quietly.

"Does he have the key card?" Owen's voice was tight, but then he'd been nothing but a mass of anxiety since he'd regained consciousness. Though he was hiding it pretty well. Owen had woken up, punched him in the face, and gotten down to work.

Rob's nose still ached. But it was nothing compared to how he felt when he thought about the way Ari had cursed him when he'd left her.

He felt hollowed out inside at the thought that he might not see her again, that those might be their final words to each other.

"He'll get what we need," Rob promised, shoving aside those dark thoughts. He had to concentrate on the job at hand.

The dark figure moved again, coming out from behind the bank of company vehicles. He crossed the space between them, pulled up his balaclava, and grinned. "You guys ready? I already put the security cameras on a time loop. That guy won't be expected to check in with the security office for another forty minutes. Even then they're pretty lax, from what I can tell. Still, we should get moving."

Jax.

He'd hopped on a plane the minute he'd found out what had happened. When Robert had called him, he was already on his way to the airfield. He'd known damn well they wouldn't be coming back to The Garden.

Robert moved, holding his hand out to his friend. "You can't know how happy I am to see you. How was the flight?"

It was roughly a two-hour flight from London to Munich, but Jax had still been lucky to get into the city so quickly. He couldn't simply fly commercial.

"Ungodly expensive," Jax admitted. "I had to use a guy who typically works for the mob. Real mercenaries charge out the asshole, but I got here and I'm not in Interpol custody, so I'm calling it a win."

"And River's okay?" Owen asked.

Jax grew solemn, putting a hand on Owen's shoulder. "River is safe at a friend's country house with Buster. Damon thinks I'm there, too. He won't for long. River knows if this all goes south, she's supposed to head to Bliss and we'll meet her there."

Whoever was left would. If they couldn't go home, they would head for the small town in Colorado where River had lived before she'd married Jax. They would be safe in Bliss.

"All right, do we know where this asshole's office is?" Owen glanced down at his watch. "We've only got five hours until dawn. We can't be late."

Tucker glanced his way, but they didn't have to say a thing. They both knew there was very little chance they would be making the exchange in the park. History had proven that Levi Green always had something sneaky up his sleeve. What was going to happen would go down here in the Kronberg building. They would either leave here with Rebecca or they wouldn't leave at all.

And they had other things to worry about. "You get rid of your tracker?"

Jax winced. "Yeah. I had River cut it out. She was not happy with me, but she's now got it glued to Buster's collar. So I'll be seen moving around a lot if anyone cares to look. He'll be pooping in my name all over the English countryside."

"Oh, they'll be looking." Robert started to walk across the parking garage. He had clear access now that he knew Jax had taken over the cameras. "Ezra will be back at the club any minute now, and I'm sure Ariel will let him know we're no longer in the building."

He'd had Tucker pull out his tracker, and he'd done the same for Tucker and Owen. Though he wasn't fooling himself. She would know where he'd gone. There was a possibility that Ezra simply called the cops on them. It would be a good way to foul up their plans.

"I'm surprised she didn't come along." Jax fell into step beside him.

"Oh, she did not have a choice in that," Tucker said. "Robert left her cuffed to the bed where I believe he had recently finished expressing his love for her."

Jax didn't miss a step, but his head shook and there was no way to miss the surprise on his face. "Dude, she's going to kill you. You're going to owe her so much oral after this. It's really the only way to pay a woman back. At least that's what Kay says, and River has never complained. About the oral. She complains about other things."

"Ariel should thank him." Owen strode ahead of them to the elevators that would lead them to the upper floors where they needed to go. He'd taken the key card from Jax and used it to call the elevator down. "He's trying to keep her safe. I didn't protect Rebecca well enough and look where we are."

He hadn't done it for exactly those reasons.

"Rebecca isn't a highly trained operative," Tucker pointed out. "I wish Ari was with us, but Rob is afraid she'll shut the whole thing down or try to turn it over to Solo."

"I'm afraid she won't understand, and I didn't have the time to explain it to her in detail. She's already feeling guilty. I can't put more on her." He strode straight onto the elevator as the doors opened. "And I couldn't risk the chance that she would put this in Damon or Big Tag's laps. This is our mess and we need to clean it up. It has nothing to do with me being scared for Ariel. Hell, at this point, I wish she was here watching my back, but I can't put her in that position."

"She's still going to kill you," Tucker said, checking the magazine on his SIG before settling it back into the holster on his side.

Jax had come bearing all the techie stuff he used to gain control of security systems, but they'd found the real goods they would need had been right there at the club. Peter might have been out of the business, but he'd still had a nice stash of weapons and explosives and tactical gear. It made Robert wonder exactly what else Peter had been doing at that club and whether or not Big Tag had a whole system of his own. Did Big Tag have his own intelligence agency running through clubs across the globe?

It was an intriguing idea and one he would have to think on later. "It doesn't matter as long as we get Rebecca back. Is our secret weapon in place?"

"Yep," Jax said. "Placed it myself. Hopefully we don't have to use it. There's a lot of wild shit in this place. There's some security even I had trouble getting through. But I've figured out where the safe is. I know where the office is. The safe is in there."

"It's on twenty-two." Tucker reached out and pressed the button that would take them to the twenty-second floor.

Robert looked to his friend. Tucker was calm, but he'd paled as though the mere act of walking into the building had cost him. "Good. We thought you might remember some things when you got in here. Don't get lost in trying to remember. Let it come to you if it will. If it won't, don't push it. We can't afford to have you sick."

The elevator stayed where it was, the door opening again as though offering to let them all go.

"What's wrong?" Owen asked, his voice tight. "Why won't it

move?"

Jax frowned and pushed the button again. It didn't light up. "Try the key card again."

Owen swiped it over the panel. Nothing.

"Shit," Jax said, setting the black bag he wore over his shoulder down and starting to go through it. "I'm sorry. I didn't think there was a code required for that floor. It must be only after hours. I screwed up. I'll fix it."

Tucker reached out and quickly input a six-digit code on the keypad offered under the floor buttons. He then pushed twenty-two and the doors slid closed again.

"How did you…" Owen began. "Muscle memory. You probably had an office up there."

"But he's been gone for years. Wouldn't they have cleared his code?" Despite the fact that the elevator was moving, Jax plugged his tablet into the computer that ran the system. He went to work, making sure they wouldn't need a code for the rest of their stay.

"They should have but they wouldn't have prioritized it if they knew he wasn't coming back." Robert noticed how tight Tucker's shoulders had gone. "Stop. You don't need to remember. Everything that's good in life is out here. Not in there. There's only pain in there, brother."

Tucker took a long breath. "I don't like this building. It doesn't feel right."

"I know," he agreed, though for very different reasons. He'd never been in this building, but Tucker had. Tucker had a life here, and it was likely the place where he'd lost that same life. "We're going to do the job, get Rebecca, and get out. If Jax can get us a copy of whatever we're going to have to turn over to Dante and Green, he will. But this is almost over."

"And now we don't have to worry about codes." Jax unhooked his tablet. "I've got control of the elevators. We won't get slowed down like that again. You okay, Tuck?"

"I'm good." Tucker stared at the doors like something was going to attack him when they opened. "We'll get through this. We go straight when we get to the twenty-second floor. I don't know why, but my instinct is telling me there's going to be something on our left that we need to handle."

Owen pulled the rifle off his back. "I'm ready. I've got enough tranquilizer darts to bring down an army. What was Peter doing with all these darts?"

"I found a flyer for a furry hunt," Robert admitted. "I think they were actually having play parties where they hunted the subs. This is a different world, my friends."

The doors dinged open and Robert moved out first, Owen to his left. Robert turned and saw what Tucker had been talking about. There was a security guard on this floor. He sat at the reception desk and he was staring at his laptop, earbuds in his ears.

Owen sighed and lined up his shot. The guy went down without ever looking their way. "They need better trained guards. Where's the office? I want this done."

Tucker walked straight ahead. "It's this way."

This floor was different from the other parts of the building Rebecca had described. This was lush and expensive. Not that the labs were cheap, but she'd described them as industrial at best. This was the floor where McDonald's office had been. She'd walked these hallways, smiling and networking, never talking about the men she had in cages.

Or maybe she had and none of the people who worked on this executive floor had cared. Maybe they were too happy in their posh offices to care where the money had come from.

They moved down the hallway, the four of them a unit in a way they hadn't been before tonight. They'd worked together but they hadn't been so united in a cause. They hadn't been asked to sacrifice for each other until this moment, and it hadn't even been something to think about.

His brothers needed him. He would be there.

They came to the end of the hall, past the luxurious lobby to a set of doors that looked like someone had stolen them straight out of Versailles. They were French doors, elegantly paneled, and the gold name plate proclaimed this was the office of the vice president in charge of research and development.

"Is the door locked?" He was good at picking locks. He'd brought along a torque wrench and a pick. He'd stuffed them in his bag along with the more dangerous pieces of equipment he would need.

Owen simply kicked it in. The door gave way, pieces splintering off. "Isn't now."

It was a damn good thing Jax had control of the alarms. And that the doors had been in the French style. Easier to kick in. He knew that because this wasn't his first robbery. Not even close. French doors were perfect because the weak point was in the middle, and no amount of dead bolts could stay a well-placed kick.

Tucker went first, assessing the room quickly. "We're clear."

This was where he came in. Robert set his pack down on the huge desk in the middle of the room. How many times had he done this very act? He could only remember a few times, but he knew he'd done it more than a dozen. The bank robberies had been traumatic, heart pounding, anxiety-inducing events, but the few times his team had snuck into quiet spaces had been different. There had been an odd freedom in those moments.

And he'd been good at it.

He pulled out the small amount of C-4 he would need. The key was using only enough to blow the door. Any more and he threatened to destroy whatever was in the safe. Any less and the thing stayed locked, but they'd alerted anyone who could hear that they were currently being robbed.

"Found it." Owen had a hand on the large painting that dominated the wall across from the desk. It was a large landscape showing the Bavarian Alps. It was a peaceful painting that hid a safe he hoped was filled with the secrets they needed.

"I remember this room." Tucker was standing in the middle of the big office, a haunted look on his face. "I remember a woman. Not McDonald. She's pretty. She's crying. I think I made her cry."

He had to shut this down. He hated to do it because Tucker needed some of those memories, but they had very little time. If there was any way to get out of this building with the goods and force the dawn meeting, they had to take it. The likelihood of them walking away with Rebecca went way up if they made it to the park. "Hey, I know it's hard, but I need you to think of something else."

"Think about what we're going to do when we get out of here."

Jax stood in front of Tucker. "We'll get this job done, grab Owen's girl, and get back in time for waffles."

Tucker's lips ticked up. "I don't think Ari's going to make us waffles. I think she's going to yell at Robert. A lot."

Jax gave Tucker a slap to the shoulder. "That's right. Think about all the ways Ariel's going to kick Rob's ass. That'll be fun to watch."

Jax was handling Tucker, which allowed Robert to examine the safe. He ran his hand over the cool metal. It was an old-school safe, oddly incongruous with the sleek modern technology of the rest of the building.

"You worked with one of these before?" Owen asked.

He knew the model well. "Yes. It's fireproof and has three sliding bolts."

"It's electronic." Jax had joined them, Tucker standing beside him. "I could probably break the code. I've got a routine for that."

Jax's routine would try to crack the code basically by entering all the possible combinations. It could take hours. Hours they didn't have.

"No, I'm going to blow it." He examined the door carefully, estimating what he would need.

"Are you sure?" Owen asked. "If the data gets damaged…"

They would lose Rebecca. "I've done this before. I promise I can do it again."

It was the one thing McDonald had taught him that would come in handy.

He gently manipulated the C-4, taking the small amount he would need. Three small sections to blow each bolt. He worked quickly and before he knew it, he was ready.

"Get back," he ordered.

They moved out of the office. Robert eased behind the door before blowing the safe.

Owen practically tackled him in his haste to get to that safe.

"Hey, be vigilant. Take everything and we'll figure it out later." They would go over whatever they found in the van Jax had rented. They'd ditched the car they'd been forced to steal since Solo and Ezra had taken the van because they didn't think the body they needed to dispose of would fit on the motorcycle.

Luckily Tucker was damn good at stealing cars.

Owen pulled the safe door fully open and exposed the secrets it held. There were files and drives, none of them labeled. Owen took them all.

They loaded up and turned to go.

"Good work, gentlemen." A voice came over the loudspeaker. Fucking Levi Green. "Now, if you'll come down to the Blue Lab, we can finish our business. Dr. Walsh, could you please give our boys proof of life?"

"Levi Green is an asshole," a snappy female voice said.

Owen breathed a deep sigh. "That's my girl."

"I'd like for Tucker to bring me the bag and I'll release Rebecca. Robert, you can come and escort her back to Mr. Shaw. You'll forgive me if I don't want to greet him personally. Owen, you should know that no harm was done to any lovely doctors during this kidnapping. It actually wasn't my idea at all. Minions. What are you going to do? Can't live without them. Can't shoot them while they're still useful."

He hated Levi Green.

"And don't think for a second that I'm alone. I've got a team placed around the building," Levi continued. "This doesn't have to go bad. I promise you if I get what I need, you'll all walk out of here. If not, we'll make other arrangements. I don't want to kill anyone. Go down to the fourth floor and we'll have a chat. Jax and Owen can surrender to the team waiting for them. They'll be released when we're done."

Jax frowned. "This is a trap."

Yep, and they'd walked straight into it. He had to hope his own trap sprang at the right time.

* * * *

Ariel stared at the ceiling and vowed bloody vengeance on her lover. Except she wouldn't really hurt him. But she could find ways to make his life hell.

If he had a life when he was done doing whatever the hell he was doing.

Meeting with Levi Green was what he was doing. She'd been so mired in her own misery that she hadn't seen Robert was planning a whole mission under her nose.

One more thing she should have seen.

Stop. Stop. Stop.

She wasn't going there again. She was a therapist, not a bloody mind reader. Rob was right about that, and guilt didn't solve a damn thing. It definitely wouldn't save her love.

She hadn't told him she loved him. It was all he'd asked from her and now he could die and she hadn't given him the words.

He could be dying right now.

Panic wouldn't help either. She had to think, and the good news was she'd had plenty of time to do just that since those cuffs weren't going to open themselves and the bed was remarkably well built. Thank you German engineering.

He would be at Kronberg. He would almost certainly have cut out his tracker so they wouldn't be able to rely on finding him that way. He would have gone straight to Kronberg to try to get the files that named all the people who ever supported McDonald's work. He would use those names as leverage to get Rebecca back.

He was walking into a trap. It didn't matter that he knew he was walking into a trap. He would still do it, and no matter how prepared he seemed, Levi would have something nasty up his sleeve.

She squeezed her eyes closed and tried not to see his dead body laid out on the floor.

How much time had passed? How far had he gotten? They would have to have stolen a car unless they'd decided to take public transportation to their robbery. She could see that. Tucker would find a pretty woman and try to flirt. He could get very distracted by a shiny object.

A frustrated scream came from her mouth and she pulled at the damn cuffs again. She couldn't even cut herself and use the blood to try to slip her hands free because Robert had used padded cuffs. He'd very gently made it so she couldn't get away.

She was right back to thinking about violence. She could do it without actually doing permanent damage. Attaching electrodes to his balls wouldn't kill him.

"I don't know if we should open that door," a feminine voice was saying. "I mean screaming in this place usually means do not disturb."

But she needed to be disturbed. "Kim! Kim! Get in here right now!"

The door came open and Kim rushed in, Ezra behind her. Ezra stopped and his eyes went wide when he saw her.

She'd kicked the blanket off in her futile attempts to get out of the cuffs. So she was pretty much out there for all to see.

Kim stared at her for a moment. "Uhm, did Robert get lost or is this some game you guys are playing? Because I did not see him when we came in."

Ezra had turned, giving her a bit of privacy. "I think I'll go look for him and have a talk. This isn't the time for punishment play."

"He's gone." She didn't even care that Ezra had seen her *au naturel*. If he'd ever come down to play at The Garden, he would have seen most of it anyway. "He and Tucker and Owen are trying to get Rebecca back. I don't know the whole plan, but I think Dante contacted them at some point and he's willing to trade Rebecca for the files at Kronberg."

Ezra's shoulders straightened. "Damn it. Do we know where the keys to those locks are? Please tell me he didn't swallow them."

"He left them on the kitchen table," she said. They needed to get moving. They had to get to Kronberg.

"I got this." Kim pulled a pin out of her hair and had the cuffs unlocked in seconds.

"Of course, you do," Ezra said with a sigh. "Get dressed. I'm calling in to update Damon and Big Tag and then we'll go after them. You're sure they're at Kronberg?"

She sat up, pulling the blanket around her. "It's our best bet."

"I'll check the trackers." Ezra had his phone in his hand, staring down at the screen. "Unless they're hanging out two blocks away, I would bet they got rid of their trackers. I'm going to kill them."

"Not if Levi kills them first, you won't." She stood and walked to the closet. "I'm going with you. Someone needs to make sure they didn't completely clear out the armory."

Ezra groaned and put the phone to his ear. "I'll check. Hey, Damon. Yeah, I know it's late but we've got a bunch of puppies who've slipped their leashes."

She dropped the blanket and reached for her clothes. The good news was she always carried a pair of athletic pants, a black T-shirt, and black hoodie. It was a force of habit left over from her MI6 days and one she was thankful she'd never gotten out of.

"So this is exciting," Kim said. "I thought burying Emily would be the funnest thing I did all day but now I might get to kill Levi."

She shimmied into her underwear while giving Kim her sternest side eye.

Kim shrugged. "I'm a 'look on the bright side' girl. I can't help it. I feel super bad about all the dead people except Emily, because she was a ho-bag, but this job is all about making lemonade. It looks like you and Robert are solid now that his wife is permanently gone."

"He left me handcuffed to a bed."

"Did he take care of you beforehand?" Her eyes narrowed. "Dude, if he stripped you down and handcuffed you and didn't get you off, I will help you take his balls."

"We had a perfectly fine time up until the moment he decided to go and do something spectacularly stupid."

"So you two are okay now?"

"Our relationship doesn't..." She'd been ready to say their relationship didn't matter, but it did. "I love him. I'll very likely forgive him completely if he finds a way to survive. He wouldn't be Robert if he didn't go. I wasn't thinking straight or I would have suspected what would happen. There's not a chance Rob leaves Owen here alone. They're family and he takes that seriously."

"Yeah, well, you had a day." Kim grabbed the trainers she'd left by the door and tossed them to Ari. "You can't blame yourself. We couldn't figure out if it was Dante or Sasha. Turns out it was both. Beck's feeling guilty, too. Not that he talked to me about it, but he did talk to me. This has been the most the man has talked to me in years. Oh, sure it was mostly him bitching about my grave digging techniques, but there's progress there. He let me in the same car with him even after we finished putting Emily in the hole. I was kind of worried he would get in the van and leave me out in the middle of the forest, but he didn't."

It was sad that not being left behind to walk fifty miles back to town was a relationship goal for Kim.

Kim held up the cuffs. "He padded them for you so you couldn't nick yourself and use the blood as a lubricant. That's super romantic when you think about it."

"We need to retrain your brain." She pulled the T-shirt over her head and started working on the trainers.

"Or I need to understand that it's over," Kim said wistfully. "He's not the same man and I'm not the woman he married. I'll always love Beck, but it might be time to let him go."

Ariel pulled on the hoodie. "It's past time." She wanted the best for her friend and Ezra was toxic around her. He was a lovely man until the minute Kim walked in the door, and then he turned into something else. "I promise if we get through this, I'll set you up with a nice man."

"Really?" Kim asked as she grabbed Ariel's backpack and held it out for her. "Big Tag's actually got a couple of pretty cute guys. I wouldn't mind being introduced to Michael Malone."

It was good to know Kim used CIA files to pick out potential dates. "I can make that happen."

"If you two are done setting up Solo's Tinder profile, maybe we should get down to the armory and suit up. They took some of the C-4, so I think you're right. They're going after the safe. Before he died, Peter wrote up a memo about a man who'd contacted him on the Dark Web. He said that's where the secrets were kept." Ezra's expression had gone arctic. "Or you can plan your double dates."

Kim's face went stony. "We're ready to go whenever you are. I've already got the building mapped out. I was planning on stealing that data if I had to."

"Of course you were," Ezra replied before nodding to Ariel. "Damon told us to stay put. We're going in anyway."

"I'm sure it was more of a suggestion." Damon couldn't honestly believe they were going to sit on their hands while their men were out there in danger. He'd been behind a desk for far too long.

"It was a lot of yelling in that weirdly polite British way, and I think he promised to go medieval on me if I get in trouble." Ezra turned. "You two grab another couple of pistols. We'll talk about plans in the van."

He strode away.

Kim tossed her the backpack. "Let's get you loaded up. I think he might have been jealous."

Ariel followed her out the door.

It was time to save her man.

Chapter Seventeen

Levi Green hadn't come alone, but the team surrounding him was different this time. When Robert and his team had walked out of the office door, they'd found themselves completely surrounded.

"Mercenaries?" He had his hands up as the group of six heavily armed men worked to pull the weapons off his body.

The man who'd been assigned to him took his second pistol and grunted something to one of the others in German. Or a language like it. He studied them carefully. They didn't move like a group that had worked together for years. The two dealing with Jax seemed to be having an argument.

The man who'd just patted Tucker down glanced Robert's way. "It's none of your business."

Peter or Solo would have known if Levi was working with German intelligence, so logic told him these men were mercenaries. The previous times they'd gone up against Levi, he'd either been surrounded by a military special ops team or had Agency backup. Why was he working with mercenaries? The good news was they could handle mercenaries.

"I hope everyone understands that we're dealing with a group of paid contractors and not US or German military," Robert said.

Jax nodded. "Yes, I got that."

"I did, too." Owen's low growl sounded like a promise.

A large man was rifling through his bag. "We used to be German military. Don't think we're amateurs."

"I wouldn't dream of it." It was good to have confirmation.

Tucker merely nodded his way. They all understood they didn't have to be careful. They would be very reluctant to go hard at US soldiers who were simply doing their job. Those soldiers weren't briefed on which part of the Agency they were working for. A Special Forces team didn't receive pamphlets educating them on what an asshole their boss was. They did their job, and Robert wasn't about to kill them over it.

But a mercenary was just in it for the money, which meant his men could fight with everything they had.

"You will take the package to the boss." The head of this particular group pointed a gun at Tucker.

"I'm going with him." He glanced at Owen. "I will bring her back. I promise. I won't let anything happen to her."

Owen's jaw was tight, and the look on his face let Robert know he would find a way to get clear of his captors. Still, he nodded. "See that you do. And watch your back. I don't like this at all."

He knew exactly what Owen was worried about. Why bother to force them to march down to the lab when Levi could easily have been waiting right outside the doors with his hired army? Why all this drama when all Levi needed to do was reach out and take the bag in Tucker's hands?

Because he was planning something. He wanted something beyond the files, or he had a plan in case he didn't get them.

He looked at Tucker and nodded again and then started for the elevator. There wasn't anything to do. Rebecca was down there and they had to walk into the trap or they could lose her.

Ariel wouldn't be happy with him if he got shot again. She'd been there the first time Levi had shot him.

Don't you die on me. Don't you dare die on me.

Those were the words he'd come to consciousness to in that field in Canada when Levi had first taken Rebecca and Owen into custody and shot him. Ariel had managed to get him out of the car, stabilized him, and then she'd broken down. His angel had been crying when he'd finally managed to fight his way back. And he'd heard the quiet words she said. They'd been like a prayer from her lips.

I love you.

He'd just remembered. She had said the words to him. God, he wasn't going to let today be the last time between them. No. He would get back to her and make her understand why he'd done what he'd done. He would hang around until she forgave him.

If he survived.

He followed the three men escorting he and Tucker. Tucker had slung the bag over his left shoulder, leaving his dominant hand ready if he needed to use it. He glanced Robert's way as if to say *you know we could still take them*.

He and Tucker had always had this shorthand. From the day they'd met, somehow he'd been closer to Tucker than the rest. Theo had been his closest friend and Tucker had Jax, but there had always been this weird connection between the two of them.

He wouldn't have been able to allow Tucker to do this alone. It was a damn good thing Levi Green had realized that. But then Levi might not have known that Jax was coming, and he certainly hadn't wanted to deal with Owen, so Robert had been his only choice.

"Why you?" The elevator was moving toward the fourth floor.

"Why me?" Tucker's eyes were on the display above the doors, marking each floor they moved past. "Why would he want me to bring the bag?"

"He specifically asked for you. Why would he do that? Why not let me handle the whole thing?"

"You should concentrate on getting out of this alive," one of the mercenaries said.

Tucker glanced Robert's way. "He wants something from me."

"Don't you be a fucking martyr," Robert ordered.

The doors opened and the man behind him pushed Robert forward. He stumbled and found his footing. Up ahead he saw a wall made entirely of glass. This part of the building was sleek and ultra-modern. There was a reception desk to his side, but it was empty. The whole place was eerily quiet, and up ahead he could see Levi Green standing in the middle of the lab. He wore what Robert liked to think of as his asshole working outfit. All black, with a bulletproof vest over his chest and a ballcap on his head. It told Robert he was taking this scene seriously and Robert should too.

The mercenary at the front of their group swiped a card over the reader and the glass doors opened with an audible swoosh. The lab was white, almost too bright given how dark the night beyond was. Not that he could tell. The shades were drawn, giving him the impression of being inside an egg. Everything here was white, from the walls to the long desks to the laptops. To his left there was another set of doors that seemed to lead deeper into the lab.

McDonald's labs had been like this. White and always scrubbed clean, though there would be moments when blood would drop to the cold floor, stark red against all that purity.

He couldn't let that be Tucker's blood this time.

"I meant what I said." He muttered the words under his breath as his heart rate ticked up and the adrenaline started to flow. "Don't you dare walk into that room with even the slightest thought of not coming back out."

"I'm going to do what I have to do," Tucker said with grim resolve. "I'll trade myself for Rebecca if that's what he wants."

"Why would he want that?" Rebecca was the prize here. Rebecca was the one who could look through the research and put things together for Levi. Tucker's medical skills were buried deep, and they came out at the oddest of times. When he was under stress, Tucker could do some amazing things, but Robert wasn't sure he could study research and come up with the same things Rebecca could.

So why Tucker? For that matter, why the two of them?

Whatever happened he would have the answers very soon.

* * * *

Ariel strode toward the lift, leaving the sleeping guard behind. She had no way of knowing how long the man had been out, but she knew who to blame. She and Ezra and Solo had only made it as far as the parking garage of the building, but she already knew she was in the right place. "They're here."

Ezra followed her inside. "Let's hope they've managed to take them all out the way they did that one. He's still alive at least. I'm sick of dealing with dead bodies."

"Hey, at least Emily was pretty easy to carry." Kim was the only one who seemed comfortable with their mission. "I had to bury a six-foot, seven-inch Russian operative once. He didn't fit in the trunk at all. Shop class came in handy that day."

The doors closed but didn't move. Ariel reached out to push the button that would keep the lift in place while they decided what to do.

Ezra's eyes slid his ex-wife's way, and Ariel didn't miss the way his lips curled up before he schooled his expression again. "We know the safe they're looking for is on floor twenty-two. I say we go up to twenty and use the stairs the rest of the way."

Ariel's heart nearly stopped when the panel overhead shifted.

She immediately brought her weapon up, ready to shoot whoever had been hitching a ride on this lift. Kim and Ezra had gone into similar positions.

"Hey, guys, how about you don't shoot." A familiar voice floated down. "I'm just your friendly neighborhood Taggart."

Theo Taggart lowered himself down and dropped into the lift.

Ariel relaxed. "How the hell did you make it here so fast? I assume Rob called you in."

Theo was dressed for an op. He'd pushed back the black balaclava that would have covered his face and allowed him to disappear in the shadows. "I was already in Germany. I came over to do some research into Emily Seeger's background. I had just checked into the hotel when Rob called. I'm his secret weapon. But I might be so secret I'm ineffective. We don't have comms, so I'm not exactly sure where the guys are."

"Hey, I'm Solo. It's a name and a state of being," Kim said with a flirty smile.

Theo reached out a hand to shake hers. "Theo, though my nickname is Taken."

"And his wife likes to shoot people," Ezra pointed out with a grumpy look on his face.

"Then I'm sure we could be friends." Kim let go of the handsome Taggart's hand. "Sorry. I'm trying to get back in the dating game. It's just a little practice."

Ezra turned to his ex. “Seriously, we’re on a mission and you’re trolling for a date?”

She shrugged. “We’re always on a mission. It’s not like I can really get on Tinder.”

“You’re impossible.” Ezra gave Theo his full attention. “What do you know about this cluster fuck of an op?”

“I know it’s not going the way Rob hoped,” Theo replied.

“Levi’s here.” Her stomach took a deep dive.

Theo nodded. “He is, but there’s something going on. I infiltrated the building a few hours ago. I’ve been in the ventilation system trying to get a lay of the land, so to speak. I found an excellent perch above the security offices where I watched the cameras. Levi came in with a team of twelve men I’m fairly certain he picked up at Mercenaries ’r Us. I would warn Rob, but like I said, they had to go in without communications. They pulled this together very quickly.”

“Levi’s not working with a black ops team?” Ezra asked.

“No, and that’s the funny thing,” Theo replied. “Because I have some friends who told me there’s actually a team in town.”

“If there is a black ops team in Munich that would be classified,” Kim said.

Ezra’s eyes narrowed as he focused in on his ex-wife. “What do you know about it?”

“I don’t, but I would like to know who is leaking classified information.” Kim was no longer looking at Theo like he was a potential way to poke at Ezra. She was now taking the man very seriously.

“I’ll never tell,” Theo promised. “But I will say I’m worried that there’s a team in town but Levi chose to work with a bunch of contractors.”

“Levi is having trouble with his bosses because the methods he’s using are attracting too much attention,” Kim explained. “I would bet he doesn’t want a team with him because the team tends to be debriefed at some point. They’ll answer questions he would rather avoid. Which makes me wonder what he’s doing in the first place. How advanced is this safe?”

Theo shrugged. “I could have done the job myself if I’d had a little C-4. Rob knows I’m here. Jax is here, too.”

"Of course he is," Ezra said with a little growl.

Theo ignored him. "Jax is with the others, but I didn't get to them before they went in to blow the safe. I'm afraid Levi is going to take them all into custody. I know where Levi is and where he's holding Rebecca. It's a lab on the fourth floor, but it's better protected than the rest of the building. The ventilation system is completely different and I don't fit. None of us will. If we're going in, we have to use the door, and those are heavily guarded."

"We wouldn't be having this problem if Robert had done what he said he was going to do," Ezra groused.

"You know why he did it." Ariel was still angry with him, but she understood who Robert was deep down. He would always have wound up here because he couldn't make the smart play when it came to his friends. He would do anything for them. It was one of the reasons she loved him.

"We need to get someone on the inside," Theo said. "It can't be me. They would shoot first and ask questions never. I think we send in Ari. Levi will underestimate her."

"I doubt that after our last meeting." As much as she wanted to be the one to go in, she knew it couldn't be her. "Besides, you send me in and Robert's objectives change. Honestly, my objectives would be in question, too. I would put him first. Saving his life is my only mission here."

Kim stepped up. "I'll go. I'll let them take me in. Do you know what kinds of restraints they're carrying?"

"No, I'll go. I'll be more of a distraction," Ezra offered.

Kim moved in front of him and her expression had taken on a gravity Ariel rarely saw there. "He will kill you, babe. He'll shoot you dead, and I can't live with that. He won't hurt me. He'll keep me alive."

"Kim's right." Ariel couldn't let Ezra go in. He wasn't thinking straight, and she understood why. "Levi's proven time and time again that he won't kill Kim."

"I can deal with him," Kim said, practically pleading.

Ezra's face went cold. "Of course you can. All right, then. We make our way to the floor below where Robert is working. If Levi is going to come after them, he'll pick them up right outside the office.

He won't let them get on the elevator again without an escort."

"I'll walk into the situation, let them take me. They're counting on maybe three guys," Kim mused.

Ariel took up her line of thought. "They weren't counting on Jax, and they probably still don't know about Theo. Taking you into custody takes men off the rest of them. It gives us a much better shot. Theo, do we know how many Levi has with him in the lab?"

"He's got six with him in the lab," Theo replied. "The other six have been on the move, but I would bet now that Robert is in the building, they're waiting for him. I wouldn't be surprised if they're already in custody. I don't know if he'll want them all in the lab or not. I wouldn't if I was Levi."

"We won't know until we try." Ariel took a deep breath. "Kim, are you sure?"

She nodded. "I'll go up to twenty-two. We drop you off at twenty-one. If Levi is keeping them there, you three free them. I'm going to bet my life that they'll take me down to the lab. You free whoever is left."

"Then we'll storm that damn lab the first chance we get." Ezra pushed the button to release the lift. He touched the buttons for the twenty-first and twenty-second floors. "Let's get our guys."

Her guy. She prayed she got to him in time.

Chapter Eighteen

The door to the lab opened and Robert walked through despite every instinct in his body telling him to run. There was something going on that he didn't understand, something at play that hadn't surfaced yet.

"Gentlemen, it's good to see you, though the circumstances aren't optimal." Levi Green smiled as though inviting them to join his barbecue. "We should get together and have drinks someday when we're not at each other's throats. Wouldn't that be nice?"

"Where's Rebecca?" He wasn't playing games with this monologuing motherfucker. Levi seemed to love to talk about his evil plans for hours before they got down to business. It was one of his worst flaws, and that was saying something since the man was pretty much akin to Satan in Robert's book.

"No small talk, huh?" Levi had two men near him. They were muscular men dressed in the same manner as the rest of the mercenaries. The others were scattered around the room. "That's not very civilized, but then I did shoot you, so I suppose there's some justification. Let's see what you brought me."

He snapped his fingers and one of the men came forward holding his hand out.

Tucker kept the bag in his grasp. "Why should I turn this over to you when we haven't even seen Dr. Walsh yet?"

"Well, it could be because I have a bunch of men with guns and you don't have any," Levi mused and then sighed, a long-suffering sound. "Look, I put this together in a hasty fashion. It's why I'm surrounded by a paid army. I couldn't get a team here in time, though given the nature of the transaction, it's better this way. If this doesn't go well at least these guys won't be reporting everything to their commanding officers, who can then be questioned by my bosses."

"You're losing control." Solo had told them she thought Levi was getting desperate. Here was the proof she'd told them the truth.

"Not the golden boy anymore?" Tucker asked, still holding the bag despite the fact that the guy with the gun was staring him down.

"It can be very hard to stay on top at my position. I'm not one of the big bosses." Levi stepped closer to Robert. "You should know all about this, Sarge. You have some power, but you're always still at someone's mercy, and they often have none."

That was Levi, always dropping hints that he knew more than he was saying. He knew he should ignore it, but impulse forced him to ask the question. "Did you look up my records?"

A secretive smile played along Levi's lips. "I didn't have to. I've known who you were all along. You played a much bigger part in the reason I'm involved in McDonald's case than you can imagine. I know it wasn't kind to lie to you or to keep what I know secret, but it was necessary. Honestly, I thought the reasons you were important were gone, but it's been pointed out to me recently that anything that is lost can be found again."

"What is that supposed to mean?" He was sick of feeling like he wasn't in on the joke.

"Come with me," Levi said with a welcoming smile. Like he was a long-lost cousin inviting him home. "Come back to DC and work with me. A whole world will open up for you. You won't need to try to remember. I can lay your life out for you and you won't have to wonder anymore."

Sure he would. "I'm not buying into your lies."

"You bought into Emily's," Levi replied. "She told you many, and I'm not merely talking about when you were married. I bet she lost her shit when she walked in and realized you were still alive. She couldn't have expected that. I wish I could have seen it. She had to work hard to cover up what she'd done, and one of the ways she did it was to lie about the present. I can fix that for you. I can hand you back your life. Your mother isn't dead, Robert. Neither is your brother. Dante told me Emily fed you a bunch of lies about how you weren't on speaking terms with them. She didn't want you to remember."

Could he be telling the truth? "Yes, she had an agenda and so do you. Did you work with her?"

"You are not listening to me. I didn't work with McDonald, so I didn't work with your wife either," Levi explained. "I came in after you were taken. I rather came in because you were taken, but that's a long story. It's one I would love to tell you. We can talk about it over a beer in DC."

"I'll pass. If I've got family out there, I'll find them on my own. I'm not going to owe you anything." He had to worry about the family he had. He had to worry specifically about Tucker. Levi was playing Mephistopheles again, and Robert would bet Tucker would be the one tempted next.

Levi was on the ropes and he needed to bring in something big. Having one of them cooperate would go a long way to securing his place again.

"And I happen to know that your brother tried to move heaven and earth when you died because he knew something was wrong. He didn't believe that military report," Levi said, his voice thick with sympathy. "I admired him very much. It was sad what happened to him."

"What happened to my brother?" The question came out of his mouth before he could think to stop it.

"Come with me and find out," Levi replied simply.

His brother was still alive but something bad had happened? Did his brother need him?

"You won't find him or your mother because *I* hid them. Do you understand? That wasn't McDonald. I did this, and when I make a person disappear, no one finds them. If you want to know what happened to your family, you have to come with me."

Levi's words were getting to him. His family. He'd felt them in his heart, in his dreams. "What did you do to them?"

"Everything your brother did, he chose to do. You can't pin this on me. I'm the good guy here." Levi took a step back as though he realized he wasn't going to win this one. "I protected your mother. Ask Owen what can happen when McDonald uses a family member for leverage."

Anger simmered in his gut. "You're using her right now. You want to play the good guy? Tell me where she is. No quid pro quo. Just do the right thing."

Levi's eyes rolled. "You should be on your knees thanking me, but I get it. I have a thankless job. I'll send your mother your regards if I see her again." He turned to Tucker. "All right then. I made my play. Tucker, give over the bag."

"Not until I see Rebecca." Tucker had a tight hold on their only leverage. "I'll give you the bag once Rob's out of the building and all the men and Dr. Walsh are safe."

"You are under the mistaken impression that this is a negotiation." Levi nodded and three of his men circled Tucker.

He saw the moment Tucker decided to fight. His body went tense and there was a look in his eyes that always hit before Tucker lost his shit. If they were in a fair fight, he would welcome it, but he couldn't trust that Levi wouldn't decide to take Tucker's legs out. Literally.

"Hey, I don't think this is going to work." Robert used a calm tone, trying to get Tucker to chill. "Give it up. We always knew it would likely come to this."

Tucker stood in the middle of the larger men and stared them all down.

"Come on, Levi. Give us something. We've done your dirty work again. At least let us see Dr. Walsh is here and alive." He had to get Tucker to back down or this could go very poorly.

"Dante, bring her out." Levi looked to the side and nodded again. The door to the back of the lab swooshed open and Dante strode out, a meaty hand on Rebecca's arm.

"Levi, I am begging you not to do this," she was saying as she scrambled to keep up.

"I thought I told you to gag her." Levi tsked his lackey. "Good help is so hard to find. Rebecca, we have talked about this endlessly.

You know I'm a reasonable man. If Tucker merely turns over what I need, everyone is free to go. We'll only have a problem if the files containing evidence of all the high-level people who worked with McDonald aren't in that bag. I'm worried it's not there because some asshole already stole it."

"You don't know what it will do." Rebecca struggled against Dante's hold, but she was so small compared to him.

"What is she talking about?" Robert didn't understand what Rebecca was talking about.

Levi had closed the space between himself and the doctor. He loomed over her. "Do you want me to use my other method right now? I'm quite desperate. I'll do it. It doesn't matter that Big Tag will come after me. There are sharks out there with even bigger teeth than his, and they are circling. Do you want to push me?"

Rebecca went still and tears coursed down her cheeks. "I'm begging you."

"And I will try very hard to accommodate you," Levi promised. "As a matter of fact, why don't you leave with Robert now and I'll handle the rest of our transaction with Tucker."

"Yes," Tucker said quickly. His whole body was tense as if he was holding something in. His skin had paled. He was obviously trying to keep his shit together. "Rob, get her out of here. This is a bad place. Get her to Owen and leave the building."

What the hell was Levi planning to do? He couldn't leave Tucker here alone.

"No," Rebecca said. "I need to be here."

Levi turned, the normally placid expression on his face going hard. "Give up the bag, Tucker, or I swear I'm going to lose my patience, and you won't like it when I lose my patience. I'm not sure which one I'll do first, but one of your friends is about to take a bullet. I'll keep shooting until you comply."

Tucker passed the bag to the man in front of him. "There. There's your freaking intel."

The man took the bag and immediately moved to a laptop set up on one of the long tables. He started going through the drives.

"Let Rebecca go now." Tucker's voice was tight. "Rob can take her to Owen and they'll leave the building."

"I don't think Dr. Walsh is ready to go yet," Levi said.

"Tucker, you need to get out of here," Rebecca began before Dante slid his hand around her throat.

Robert started toward him. "Hey, let her go."

He was immediately hauled back by two of Levi's guards. They gripped his arms tight.

Tucker was held by the other two.

"I told you they would be difficult," Dante said. "They won't listen to reason. It would be better to put Robert down now and do what you're going to do."

"If I can get out of this without Big Tag coming down on my ass, I will." Levi moved to the man who was working on the laptop. He picked through the bag and pulled out the three drives they'd found. "You should worry, Dante, because Big Tag is going to be looking for you. He'll bring along his whole Scooby gang. You won't like what John Bishop can do to you. Or Kay. I don't particularly want to meet up with Kay again. I think she took our last interaction too personally."

The last time Levi and Kayla Summers had met up, she'd been waterboarded at his command. Still, Robert thought there were far worse enemies Levi hadn't mentioned. "I think you should worry more about Ezra."

Levi chuckled. "I don't worry about Ezra at all. I killed him once. He got lucky and happened to be wearing a vest. I can kill Ezra in my sleep. He knows who the better man is. The only reason I don't is Solo has an inexplicable affection for the man. She's going to come around. One of these days she'll see him for who he is, and then everything will fall into place. Or she'll realize I'm the better bet. If I can finish this job properly, I'll be a king at the Agency. She'll be my queen."

"You're psychotic." He'd been around Ari too long. He knew a lot of terminology. "You've got a narcissistic personality disorder with delusions if you think that woman is hiding her love for you."

"A narcissist only thinks of himself. I assure you, I've done everything I've done for my country and for her." Levi's eyes had gone cold. "I love her in a way Ezra never could. His love was a fragile thing. The first time she screwed up, he dumped her. I assure you, my love can survive the apocalypse. I mean, what's a little assassination attempt among friends, right, Solo?"

The door came open and Solo was being led in, her hands in zip ties in front of her. Her long blonde hair had come out of the ponytail she usually wore and there was blood on her cheek.

Levi stalked toward her and stared for a moment before bringing his hand up to brush the blood off her cheek. He inspected her carefully. "You should be very happy that blood wasn't hers. I gave specific instructions about how to handle her if she should manage to show up." He'd never taken his eyes off her. "Hello, Solo."

"I swear, Levi, if you don't cut me out of these right fucking now we're going to have a problem," Solo snarled his way.

He merely winked at her and looked oddly satisfied. "We always have problems and we always work them out. Now where are your friends, because I struggle with the idea that you walked in here alone. These men are not the cream of the crop. If they caught you, it's because you allowed them to catch you."

"I don't know what you're talking about." Solo looked Levi straight in the eyes. "I came here for the data and you know it. I came for the same thing you want. I wanted it so I could turn it over to my boss and send you and your bosses straight to jail."

"Why do you try me so?" He ran a hand over her hair. "We could work together."

"Maybe it's that tiny penis you're packing," Solo replied with an arrogant smirk. "Is that why I can't quite remember sleeping with you? I needed a lot of liquor to get through that night."

Levi's hand came up and he slapped Solo right across the face, his big palm open. The sound cracked through the lab and Solo's head snapped to the side.

Robert tried to launch himself across the room, but those hands held him fast.

Solo spit blood and her eyes came back, flashing fire Levi's way. "There you are, you son of a bitch. That's the Levi Green I know. You mistake obsession for true love. You know what Beck has never done to me in all his anger? Hurt me physically."

"You require a reminder every now and then, Solo. I'm sorry. I lost my temper because I know you've been spending time with him.

It doesn't do well to spark my jealousy," Levi said, going right back to cool and collected. "I'll make it up to you."

"You'll keep your fucking hands off her." He might not trust Solo fully, but he wasn't about to let her be abused. He wouldn't let anyone be abused.

God, it was why he'd gone into the Army. He could remember it as bright as day. He'd stood in front of his mother and told her he was going to protect his country and make her proud.

"Stay with me." Tucker's voice broke through the fog. "Don't leave me, Rob."

Except for a moment he'd heard the name Russ instead of Rob.

He shook it off. It was another life. He needed to stay in *this* life. "I'm here. I'm not going to leave you."

"You're going to do what I tell you to do." Levi came to stand in front of him. "Unless you want to change your mind. There's a place for you in my office."

"I want what you promised me. We gave you what we could. Now let us go. You don't want Big Tag after you." A knot formed in his gut because every instinct he had told him this was going to go bad. He'd known it could, but now he realized the moment was here. This wasn't a handoff. Levi could have easily blown that safe on his own. He wanted something more.

"Like I said, I don't, but I'm in a position where I no longer have a choice." He turned back to the man looking through the files. The mercenary simply shook his head, causing Levi's jaw to tighten. "Nothing?"

The man shrugged. "There's plenty here, but not what you're looking for. He's got blackmail material, but it has nothing to do with McDonald."

Levi nodded, a sharp movement. "Take it all anyway. Let's get ready to move out. I don't like the fact that Solo let herself be taken. It means she's planning something, and we're out of time. Bring me Mr. Tucker."

"No," Rebecca shouted.

Dante tightened his arms around her like a python getting ready to squeeze the life out of his victim.

The two men with hands on Tucker started to move him toward

Levi, who was opening a briefcase.

Robert started to struggle. He wasn't sure what was in that case, but it would be bad. Levi would use whatever was in there on Tucker. "What are you doing?"

Tucker looked back, fear in his eyes. "I've been here before. God, Rob, I've been here."

He couldn't stand that look on Tucker's face. "Green, take me instead. I'll go with you."

He would find a way to get out later, but he couldn't let them take Tucker. Tucker was his responsibility.

There wasn't an ounce of compassion on Levi's face as he pulled out a hypodermic needle. "That plan doesn't work for me. I don't actually need you, Robert. I was trying to be a nice guy."

"What the fuck is that?" Solo asked, her eyes wide.

"It's the cure." Rebecca managed to get the words out around the hand on her throat. Tears coursed down her cheeks. "But we don't know what it's really going to do. It could kill him. I'm begging you not to do this."

"I'm sorry but the truth of the matter is I don't need Tucker at all." Levi's voice sent a chill through the room. "I do need Dr. Razor."

Tucker started to fight, trying to pull away from his captors, but they drug him closer and closer to the needle.

Robert kicked out to the side, making contact with the first asshole's knee and cutting his legs out from under him. He gained his balance and struck the other man trying to hold him with a swift uppercut to his chin. He heard a low growl and the crunching of bones, but he had no sympathy. That asshole had something he needed.

"Don't let him get a gun, damn it," Levi shouted.

Something hard hit his back and he suddenly was held down by two hundred pounds of mercenary. He rolled to the side, trying to get that gun in his hand. He managed to force the fucker off him and pulled the pistol free from the unconscious guy's belt. He glanced up in time to see Solo thrust her zip tied hands high in the air only to bring them down hard. She pulled her hands apart. The ties broke and she was grace in motion. Solo brought her arm up and back, making contact with the man behind her.

"Fall back." Levi shouted the command.

The doors to the lab burst open and he wasn't alone anymore. His brothers were here. Owen and Jax strode in, guns out. They were followed by Theo and Ezra.

And Ariel. She was there, his angel with a semiautomatic. She didn't even hesitate. She immediately fired, taking out the man coming for him. One minute the guy was raising a weapon to fire a shot that would have taken off Robert's head, and the next he was slumping to the ground.

The lab was in complete chaos. Glass shattered from the bullets flying. Ariel reached his side, ducking down because they had a little cover from one of the desks.

"Are you all right?" Ari asked.

"I'm fine." He tipped the desk over to give them more cover. The sound of lab equipment crashing warred with the gunfire. "God, Ariel, I didn't want to put you in danger, but I can't tell you how happy I am to have you here."

There was no one else on earth he would want watching his back, helping him save Tucker.

She was on her knees, but she managed to take his face in her hands. "Rob, I love you. I need you to hear that."

He couldn't help but smile. He'd given her a hard time about not saying it, but he'd known what she was doing. "I know, baby. Now give me some cover. Levi is trying to shoot Tucker up with god only knows what in an insane attempt to bring back Reasor."

"Oh, my god." Ariel nodded his way. "You have to get him away from here. I'm better at a distance. I'll cover you."

"If you can get a shot, take it," he said before brushing his lips over hers. "I love you."

The room went quiet as quickly as it had been thrown into chaos.

"Let him go, Levi." Ezra's voice boomed through the quiet room. "We've got you. There's no way out."

Robert looked over the table and realized they were in a standoff. Tucker was in Levi's grasp, a needle in his neck. Levi hadn't pushed the plunger yet.

Dante was using Rebecca like a shield. Two of the mercenaries were left standing. It looked like Owen had taken a bullet to his left arm, but he was still there, his gun aimed in Dante's direction, but from there he couldn't get a clear line of sight. Rebecca was in the way.

Ariel might be able to do it. They were in the perfect position for a woman with spectacular aim to take a shot.

He didn't want to put this on her. He knew he should be the one to take Dante out. She'd wanted out of this life, but Ariel was Rebecca's best option.

"Drop the weapon, Owen, or I'll be more than happy to put a bullet through your bitch's brain," Dante growled. "Do you know how much I hate you all? It would be my pleasure to kill her."

He watched as Rebecca mouthed the words to her lover. *I love you.* She was ready, was going to give Owen the power in that moment. The power to save her.

But he knew damn well Owen wouldn't take the chance.

Owen dropped the weapon. "Just let her go. You can do whatever you want to me, but let Rebecca go."

"Excellent." Levi seemed perfectly calm despite the fact that he was surrounded. "Now the rest of you can do the same or you'll lose more than the lovely Dr. Walsh. I'm not actually sure what's in this needle. I only know that Dr. McDonald thought it was a cure in case she ever needed to access one of her soldier's past memories. At least that's what her notes said. She'd never actually tried it. So back off or I'll use this on him. Solo, you know you can't kill me."

"I can let Beck kill you," Solo said, but she lowered her weapon.

"I don't think that was within the parameters of your mission," Levi replied with a chuckle that held not an ounce of humor. "She's playing all of you, you know."

Or Levi was lying. Robert looked down at Ariel. They couldn't see her, might have missed her coming in with the rest of them. She nodded up at him as though she understood.

"Robert, I meant what I said. Lay down that gun," Levi commanded.

"I'm okay, Rob." Tucker's words came out shaky.

"Stay still, brother. Don't move." He had to get Tucker out of this. The problem was they were only going to get one shot and they needed to take out two people.

"Rob, I'm okay," Tucker said, more solid now. "Do what you have to do. I'm okay. I'm going to be okay."

Tucker was telling him to take out Dante, to make the choice to sacrifice him if they had to. He was choosing Rebecca's life and Owen's happiness over his own.

Ezra hadn't put down his gun yet and neither had Theo. Jax was too far back, but if the fighting started again, he would move in.

He caught Tucker's gaze, saw the resolve there. Tucker was ready for anything that might happen. He was at peace with it.

He wouldn't be able to live with himself if Rebecca died.

"I'm not joking, Robert," Levi warned. "I'm going to do this if you don't put that fucking gun down. All of you."

He would do it anyway. Levi had always meant to do this. He'd always meant to shove that needle in Tucker's neck to try to unleash the beast inside him. It's what he'd been building toward the whole time.

Rob glanced down and gave Ariel the signal.

Ariel rose. Time seemed to slow for him, but he knew it couldn't have been more than a second or two. He watched as she rose and without a single hesitation took the shot.

A hole appeared in the middle of Dante's forehead and his big body dropped.

Owen was on Rebecca in a heartbeat, throwing his body over hers and getting her out of the line of fire because the last two mercenaries were still fighting.

Robert took his own, firing at the last of Levi's men.

He turned the gun on Levi, but Tucker was in the way. They were too close in height to get a solid line of fire.

"Well, that didn't go the way I wanted it to." Levi sighed. "At least I'll still get something out of it. Time to wake up, Razor."

Robert yelled as Levi pushed the plunger and Tucker's eyes rolled to the back of his head.

Robert took aim because Levi wasn't living through this.

Solo stepped in front of the gun. "I'm so sorry, Robert. I can't let you do that." She touched her ear. "Boys, it's time. Take him into custody. Dr. Walsh, I think you should check on Tucker."

"Kim, what's going on?" Ariel's hand brushed his as she came to stand beside him.

"What do you think is going on?" Ezra's eyes burned as he took in his ex-wife. "She used us and now she's going to save her boyfriend and take the data. I should have known this would happen."

A group of men in all black moved into the room like the black ops team they were. These weren't mercenaries. This was pure American military, and they obviously answered to Solo.

"I feel okay." Tucker was still on his feet. His hands were shaking, but he was able to move away from Levi, who was surrounded by Solo's men. "A little dizzy, but I'm okay."

Robert rushed to Tucker. Ariel was right behind him. Tucker had gone pale, but he seemed solid. He wouldn't be satisfied until they'd figured out what the hell Levi had shoved into his system.

"Let me take a look at him." Rebecca's hands were shaking, but she moved to examine Tucker.

"Beck, I'm so sorry it happened this way, but I need Levi alive," Solo said, her voice low. There was a look of naked pain on her face when Ezra took a step back from her. "I'm following orders."

"Yes, she's only following orders." Levi was in handcuffs but he was still breathing, so Robert couldn't call it a win. He was also flanked by several soldiers, as if they'd been ordered to ensure the man survived. "Looks like I'm walking away with the girl again, Ezra. Your girl."

"You can have her." Ezra turned his back.

"Beck, please. I'm following the letter of my orders. Can't you see that? I should take Tucker, too, but I'm not going to. I'm going to leave that part out of my briefing. Come with me." Solo sounded vulnerable. "You can be right there when I interrogate him. We need to figure out what he knows. I can make this right. I can get you back in the Agency. Come with me."

"The funny thing is I was going to ask you to have coffee with me when all this was done." Ezra shook his head, a rueful gesture. "You got me. You always did. At least you showed your true colors before I got back in deep."

"Beck, you have to know I'm doing this for you," Solo said.

"Are we under arrest?" Ezra asked.

"No." Solo shook her head. "Absolutely not, and we're going to clean the whole place up. We're taking care of everything so you can get your people out. I promise this is going to work in your favor in the end." Her cell phone rang and her face fell. "I have to take this. Please wait for me. We can talk. We need to debrief."

"We have nothing at all to talk about." Every word from Ezra's mouth dripped with ice. "And I can't wait. I have to get my team back to London before Damon realizes Jax is gone. Good-bye Solo."

Solo took a deep breath and answered her cell. "Good evening, Mr. President."

She walked off to talk to her boss.

He couldn't think about it right now. He had to focus on Tucker. "How is he doing?"

Ariel was right behind him, her hand on his shoulder. "We should get him to a hospital."

Tucker shook his head. "No. I want to go home. I'll be fine. You can't take me to a hospital. You know why."

Tucker tried to stand, but his eyes rolled back and Robert had to catch him.

Tucker's body began to seize and Rebecca shouted out.

He looked down at his brother and prayed he would survive.

Chapter Nineteen

"How is he today?" Ariel wrapped her arms around Robert, hugging him from behind. She breathed him in, loving everything about this man.

This was how they'd started every morning for the last three weeks. She would wake up warm and safe in Robert's arms, but he would slip away while she was getting ready and she would find him here.

"He's stable." Robert's hands covered hers and he held her there. "No change."

Tucker lay on a hospital bed, hooked up to an IV. They'd transformed one of the living spaces to a room where they could take care of Tucker. He'd gone into a coma that day in Germany and hadn't woken since. Luckily they'd been in a lab with medical equipment. Rebecca had worked with the medic on the black ops team to stabilize Tucker and keep him out of the hospital system. He was perfectly healthy according to Rebecca, with the singular exception of the fact that he wouldn't wake up. The drug seemed to have only affected his brain, and specifically the parts dealing with memory. None of them understood why he was in a coma, but Rebecca remained certain he would come out of it.

Tucker had missed their wedding. It had been a small affair, held right here in The Garden. They'd married alongside Rebecca and Owen. None of them had wanted to plan a big wedding after what had happened. They hadn't wanted to take the time. They'd realized tomorrow wasn't a guarantee and hadn't wanted to wait a second longer to be tied to the ones they loved.

She'd always thought she would have a big wedding, but now she knew the marriage was the most important thing.

Her husband was the most important thing.

"He's looking good today." Rebecca strode into the room, glancing down at the clipboard in her hands. Yesterday had been testing day. Rebecca was completely focused on her patient. Between her and Stephanie Carter, Tucker had all the medical care he needed.

"He looks the same," Robert replied. He shifted to gently pull Ariel to his side, his arm sliding around her shoulders. "He always looks the same."

Any time they were in a room together, he had a hand on her. He would tangle their fingers or drag her onto his lap. Her husband was hungry for affection, and she was more than happy to give it to him. It was good to be connected.

"Maybe on the outside." Rebecca gave them a sunny smile. "But his latest tests give me great hope. I still don't completely understand what the drug did, but he's healing. I think it's only a matter of time before he wakes up."

"But who will he be when he wakes up?" Robert asked the question that had been haunting them all since that day. "Will he be Tucker or someone else?"

Rebecca lost her smile. "He'll be himself. I have to believe that. We all have to."

Because the idea that they could find themselves losing Tucker and being left with the man known as Razor was unthinkable.

Ariel reached down to touch Tucker's hand. He was warm and looked like he was sleeping. He looked so young lying there. It was hard to believe it had been weeks since she'd seen him smile or listened to him tell a terrible joke. "He'll be Tucker and we'll deal with whatever comes next."

Robert needed to understand that she would do anything to help the men.

“We should get down to the conference room,” Robert said. He leaned over and put a hand on Tucker’s head. “I’ll be back this afternoon, brother.”

She often found him in here. He would sit and read out loud or put a game on the telly and talk to Tucker while he watched. All the lads took turns sitting with Tucker.

“I’ll stay with him,” Rebecca offered. “I don’t need another conference meeting. Owen will talk about it endlessly. I liked it better when we weren’t at war.”

They’d always been at war. It was simply out in the open now. And the man they were at war with was nowhere to be found. Kim had done everything she’d said she would. She’d handled the cleanup at Kronberg. She’d given them the cover they’d needed to get Tucker stabilized and back to England.

And then she’d disappeared with her prize and hadn’t been heard from again until the night before. They’d all gotten the message that they would be meeting with Kimberly Solomon this morning, but she wasn’t sure what they would be talking about.

God, she hoped they weren’t at war with Kim. Ezra still wouldn’t mention her name without cursing.

“Thank you,” Robert said as he took Ariel’s hand and started to lead them out.

“Are you all right?” She knew she asked the question far too often.

He led her to the hallway that would take them to the lift. “I’m as good as I can be, and you’re the reason why.” He brought her hand up and kissed it even as he kept walking. “I love you. I know I say it a lot.”

“I like to hear it.” She squeezed his hand. “I love you, too. Are you ready for this? You haven’t seen her since that day.”

“I have questions for her,” Rob admitted. “But I’m not going to lose my cool if that’s what you’re asking. We might want to watch Ezra though. I’m surprised they’re letting her come in. I thought for sure she would be on the shit list.”

Big Tag had shown up the night before, his youngest brother in tow. It made her think he’d known about this meeting longer than he was willing to admit. Had Kim been negotiating with Tag? Trying to work her way back in? All she knew was they were meeting with Kim, and Big Tag was going to make sure Ezra didn't do something he shouldn't.

"I have to believe she has something important to share with us." She didn't like to think about how Kim would have gotten them answers. Levi was gone, taken somewhere Kim wouldn't have to worry about Geneva Convention restrictions.

"Here's hoping she's uncovered something that will help us with Tucker. Or maybe she's found out something about Sasha," Robert said, sounding more optimistic than before. They were trying to figure out where Sasha had come from. They had a promise to keep to him. He stopped at the wall and looked down onto The Garden. At this time of day it looked like a gorgeous oasis amidst the sleek modern lines of the rest of the building. "You know I used to stand right here and wait for you to walk in."

She'd always known. She would walk in and try not to look up because she'd known her gorgeous protector would be looming above her.

She grinned. "You still do."

"I always will." He kissed her forehead. "Wherever you go, I'll always be waiting for you to come home to me."

She sighed and leaned into him, loving how peaceful the club looked at this time of day. By tonight it would be a decadent wonderland, but she loved it like this, too.

She had to hope Kim had managed to get some information about Robert's family. The Garden was their home, but he had another one out there and she no longer feared it. No matter what happened, they would face it all together.

The door that led in from the lobby opened and Big Tag strode through, Kim walking behind him. She couldn't hear what they were saying, but it didn't matter because she was suddenly staring at the third person who'd walked through the door.

She had rich brown hair that brushed the middle of her back. Petite and slender, she looked young and slightly afraid.

"Is that who I think it is?" Robert asked.

"Veronica Croft."

Kim had brought them the one person in the world who could answer their questions about Tucker, the one person in the world who might be able to save him.

* * * *

Veronica Croft took in the space before her. It was stunning. Solo had tried to explain to her that the place they were going wasn't a normal office, but she hadn't understood. The Garden was magical.

Unfortunately, she was a woman who no longer believed in magic. She forced herself to stand tall. "I'd like to see him before we have the meeting."

Ian Taggart was completely intimidating, and that was saying something since she'd been intimidated by some of the best.

Did you honestly believe he was running away with you? He likes to play with pretty girls like you. That's all you were, Roni. You were a toy to him, and now he's done with you. I'm done with you, too.

She shivered despite the warmth of the day. Sometimes she could still hear Hope McDonald's voice telling her how stupid she'd been. It had been those words that had sent her into hiding because Steven Reasor might have been an asshole who'd used her, but she'd believed him when he'd told her McDonald was dangerous.

It might have been the only truth he'd told her.

"You know he's in a coma, right?" Taggart asked. "He can't talk to you."

It was the only reason she'd been willing to come out of hiding. If she'd found out Steven was alive and out there waiting, she had no idea what she would have done.

"I explained the situation to her," the woman who called herself Solo said. "I didn't lie or anything."

"Yeah, well, you've been known to withhold information," Taggart shot back. "You'll forgive me if I verify every single thing that comes out of your mouth, Solo."

Roni wasn't sure exactly what was going on. The big guy had been polite to her and cold as hell to Solo. She'd kind of thought they worked together, but now she was wondering if Solo had given her a rosy version of the situation.

God, she hoped she wasn't making a mistake. This was a dangerous place to be. For years she'd hidden. Even after McDonald had died.

Even after Steven had died.

She was still trying to wrap her brain around the fact that Steven Reasor was alive and apparently didn't remember who he was. Solo had told her a bunch of stuff she didn't exactly understand about his situation, but she got the gist. He was alive.

And he was in a coma.

"I understand his health situation," she replied. "But I need to see him with my own eyes."

She needed to be sure they weren't mistaken. She wasn't completely sure what she wanted to find in that bed. If it wasn't him, she could go back to hiding.

If it was…well, then her whole world would have changed.

Taggart nodded. "All right. He's upstairs. I'll take you there. You'll see he's getting the best care we can possibly give him. I think one of our doctors is up there now."

"Excellent. I have some questions." *Like will he wake up and decide I'm a risk to him? Will he ever remember that he made love to me like I was the most important person in the world? Will he remember that he left me alone?*

Taggart stopped in front of the elevator. "Ms. Croft, I need to explain something to you."

Now she would get the "I'm a badass spy and you're a nobody and you're going to tell me everything I need to know" speech. She knew the type. She'd been hiding from them for years. "Go ahead."

"You are safe here." Taggart's expression had softened. "I'm not the Agency and I won't allow Solo to steal you away. All I'm looking for is some answers to help my men. You are free to come and go as you please, but if you need protection from something, we are here for you. I don't know what Solo told you about us, but I promise no one is going to fuck with you here. We've got a room for you. If you need sanctuary, you have it."

Tears pierced her eyes. "I haven't felt safe in years, Mr. Taggart."

"Then let's change that today." Taggart turned again, heading for the elevator. "After you see Tucker, I'll take you up to the conference room. You'll meet my partner Damon Knight and some of the men who Tucker is close to."

"If I was going to steal her away, would I have brought her here in the first place?" Solo asked with a long-suffering sigh. "I thought of all the people in the world you would understand."

Taggart frowned. "I left the Agency so I wouldn't have to pull that shit you pulled in Munich. Don't expect me to understand. Also, Ezra's turned into a whiny man baby and it's all your fault. He used to be stoic. Like a man should be, and now he wants to talk about his feelings. You did that to him."

The elevator doors opened and Solo stepped on after Taggart, the two of them still arguing about someone named Ezra. Or Beck. She wasn't sure. They all had too many names to keep up with.

She followed, feeling better than she had before. Maybe she could get what she needed from this. Closure.

And answers.

Answers for herself.

Answers for their daughter.

Tucker, Veronica, and the whole McKay-Taggart crew will return in *Long Lost*, now available.

Author's Note

I'm often asked by generous readers how they can help get the word out about a book they enjoyed. There are so many ways to help an author you like. Leave a review. If your e-reader allows you to lend a book to a friend, please share it. Go to Goodreads and connect with others. Recommend the books you love because stories are meant to be shared. Thank you so much for reading this book and for supporting all the authors you love!

Long Lost

Masters and Mercenaries: The Forgotten, Book 4
By Lexi Blake
Now available.

A stolen past

The only thing Tucker remembers of his past is pain. Used in a doctor's evil experiments, his memories and identity were erased, and his freedom taken. He believed his nightmare was over when he was liberated by the men and women of McKay-Taggart, until he heard the name Steven Reasor. The idea that he could have been involved in the terrible experiments that cost his "brothers" everything crushed him. A desperate attempt to force him to remember the truth almost cost him his life. Now his world is in chaos and his only path to finally uncover the truth and atone for his sins leads to Veronica Croft.

A painful present

Veronica "Roni" Croft knew Dr. Steven Reasor was bad for her, but she also saw a side of the man that no one else knew. Even as she began to believe their employer was hiding something sinister, she was drawn to him like a moth to a flame. Their affair was passionate and intense, but also fraught with danger. When he disappeared under mysterious circumstances, she took her first chance to run and never looked back. She has stayed hidden ever since, running from forces she knows are too powerful to overcome. But now the man she believed was dead, the man she mourned, has returned and needs her help.

A dangerous future

As Tucker and Roni unravel the secrets of his past, a dark force rises and threatens to destroy them. Their only chance for survival will require them to join forces with the Lost Boys' worst enemy. Only together can they finally unlock Tucker's past. But as Tucker's memories begin to come back, will it free them both or tear them apart forever?

Back in Bliss

Nights in Bliss, Colorado 9
By Lexi Blake writing as Sophie Oak
Now available.

Re-released in a second edition with new content.

Logan Green is back in Bliss, but only for a few weeks to help out at the sheriff's office. Everything changes when Seth Stark strolls into town with Georgia Dawson on his arm.

Seth's arrival is anything but a happy accident. He always dreamed of a big house on the river and a wife he could share with his best friend, Logan. After building a software empire, his only goal has been to make that dream come true. He just needed the perfect woman.

Georgia is still haunted by the dark, troubled man who saved her life. She can't get Logan out of her head. Her boss brought her to Bliss to help him decorate his new summer home, but when Logan Green walks through the door she discovers Seth has something different in mind.

Seth has a plan for their mutual happily ever after, but he never dreamed that coming home would put all their lives in danger.

San Francisco Longing

San Francisco Trilogy
By Lila DuBois
Now Available!

She never meant to lie to him, let alone submit to him.

When Christiana discovered the secret BDSM club she threw caution to the wind and snuck in, hoping only to watch the things she'd been fantasizing about.

Until James.

Dominant and charming, he's everything she never knew she needed.

And he wants her.

Three amazing nights together, but then the party's over. He thinks he'll see her again. Christiana knows this is the end.

But how can she say goodbye to the man who claimed her, body and soul?

* * * *

She'd weighed her fear of rejection and pain—quite literal pain because she was sure he would punish her—against her fear of regret. Regret for what she'd done to him. Regret for not mustering her courage and telling him the truth about who she was and who she wasn't. She didn't want to look back on her life and be anguished at her own cowardice. If she'd known what would happen, she wouldn't have lied. Wouldn't have pretended to be someone she wasn't.

It had started out as an adventure. She'd been a stranger in a strange land, an anthropologist studying a foreign culture.

She was still a stranger to him, and to his world. She was a quiet, quirky engineer while he was a rich, powerful, and worldly prince.

A literal prince.

Her body was still bruised and aching from the beating last night. What would he say if he knew in her desperation to get over him she'd tried to find another Dom? It had been a mistake, leaving her body and soul battered and bruised.

He'd come for her. He'd found her. That meant he knew who she was.

"I don't fully understand why you lied. Why you pretended to be a member of the Orchid Club." James Nolen's elegantly accented voice was carefully neutral.

"I told you, I felt like—"

"Alice through the looking glass," he cut in. "But it's more than that, isn't it? You recognized the St. Andrew's Cross."

She couldn't deny it. "Yes, I did."

"That means you're interested in BDSM. Knowledgeable." He stepped closer. "You wanted to see Masters and submissives play."

Her breath was coming faster and she felt flushed. "Yes."

"Because it's something that fascinates you. Is submission what you fantasize about at night?"

"I was just going to look, just that first night," she whispered. "I wasn't going to do anything."

"But you did. With me." His dark gaze bore into her. "You submitted to me."

Christiana shivered at the need, the aching desire, his simple words aroused within her.

She wanted him. Needed him. Especially after the mistakes she'd made last night.

"I'm so sorry, James."

I want you. I need you.

Forgive me

About Lexi Blake

Lexi Blake is the author of contemporary and urban fantasy romance. She started publishing in 2011 and has gone on to sell over two million copies of her books. Her books have appeared thirty-three times on the *USA Today*, *New York Times*, and *Wall Street Journal* bestseller lists. She lives in North Texas with her husband, kids, and two rescue dogs.

Connect with Lexi online:

Facebook: Lexi Blake
Twitter: authorlexiblake
Website: www.LexiBlake.net

Sign up for Lexi's free newsletter.

Printed in the USA
CPSIA information can be obtained
at www.ICGtesting.com
LVHW071312170923
758435LV00002B/167